# Legacy
## of the
### Light

# Legacy
## of the
# Light

*A Novel*

# R. M. Lienau

SUNSTONE
PRESS

SANTA FE

# Acknowledgements

My thanks to the Rio Arriba County Sheriff's Office, the New Mexico State Police, the Santa Fé City Police Department, and especially Betty of Southwest Capital Bank, for their kind and generous help in answering my questions related to the writing of this book.

—R.M. Lienau

Sunstone books may be purchased for educational, business, or sales promotional use. For information please write: Special Markets Department, Sunstone Press, P.O. Box 2321, Santa Fe, New Mexico 87504-2321.
Cover illustration › Leslie Lienau
Book design › Vicki Ahl
Body typeface › Vani
Printed on acid-free paper
∞
eBook 978-1-61139-362-0

Library of Congress Cataloging-in-Publication Data

Lienau, R. M. (Richard M.)
Legacy of the light : a novel / by Richard Lienau.
    pages ; cm
ISBN 978-1-63293-052-1 (softcover : alk. paper)
I. Title.
PS3562.I4533L44 2015
813'.54--dc23
                        2015003194

WWW.SUNSTONEPRESS.COM
SUNSTONE PRESS / POST OFFICE BOX 2321 / SANTA FE, NM 87504-2321 /USA
(505) 988-4418 / ORDERS ONLY (800) 243-5644 / FAX (505) 988-1025

## Author's Note

After *The Truchas Light* was published, I found myself wondering about what might befall the hero of that story, and felt that some who read it might wonder as well. Given that, I was driven to find out. Thus this sequel.

—R.M. Lienau

$\mathcal{S}$ergeant Roger Montaño stood next to Diego Peña as they looked at the medium-sized Japanese car and the rapidly-drying tire tracks next to it. Although close to noon, there was still a chill in the high mountain air of the village of Truchas. They were surrounded at a respectful distance by men, women and children, predominantly members of the town, curious to the extreme, as they murmured to each other and gawked. News of the two dead people, a man and a woman, inside the house the gringos from Albuquerque had been renovating, had spread quickly.

Neighbors who viewed the bodies had informed State Police Sergeant Montaño that the woman was one of the owners of the house, but that they had not seen the dead man before. The buzz amongst the people was that the man was definitely not the husband, one Mr. Jason Thompson. That, in turn, had led to a whispering campaign, fed by shocked speculation, that there had been something going on between Mrs. Thompson and the dead man who lay near her.

Diego Peña, a Rio Arriba County Deputy Sheriff, had been dispatched subsequent to a 911 call by a concerned neighbor. That was after her ten-year-old son had run to her to report that the front door to the Thompson house was open and that his curiosity had driven him to wander inside, only to find two bodies in the living room. Peña, given the nature of the discovery, had in turn notified the State Police. Sergeant Montaño had called in a State Police forensic team and an ambulance to stand by to remove the bodies. One other significant event had taken place. Because of the discovery of two forms of identification on the dead man, one from a little-known news organization, Reuters, the other from the Federal Bureau of Investigation, a call was placed to the Albuquerque office of that organization. Within three minutes after the call to the FBI, a dispatcher there had cross-connected the report with a computer alert, which spit out a printed version and sent an automated call to the case agents attendant with limited paperwork. It was then that Special Agent Marcus Lucero had made Peter Grayson, lead Special Agent on the Rio Grande Laboratories Geronimo Queen case, aware of the deaths in Truchas. That, in turn, caused Grayson to contact the State Police to ask them to put a hold on activities at the crime scene up north until they could be present, since a federal agent was apparently involved.

It was mid-afternoon when Grayson and Lucero arrived at the Thompson house in Truchas. Both men stepped out of their car as on-lookers moved back, awe-stricken at the activities that had seized the attention of the old mountain village. Sergeant Montaño, followed by Deputy Peña, moved to greet the two federal government law men.

Grayson held out his hand to the black-uniformed Montaño. "Grayson. FBI Albuquerque." He pulled out his ID folder deftly and nodded to Lucero at the same time. "Special Agent Lucero."

Lucero shook hands with Montaño wordlessly.

Montaño introduced both agents to Deputy Peña.

Grayson held out both palms. "So, let's see what we have."

As the four law officers moved toward the house, a second State Police car rolled up and parked near a second County Sheriff's vehicle. Another Sheriff's deputy stood at the front door, blocking curious on-lookers. Inside, EMT personnel were in the process of making observations of the bodies. They had been warned not to disturb anything on or about the deceased. The deputy who guarded the door stepped aside with a crisp nod of his head, and the four men entered.

Montaño and Peña stood back while the two FBI agents moved slowly toward the sofa, then around it, one on either end. The two EMTs, one a woman, stepped back deferentially to allow Grayson and Lucero in for a close look. Both men peered down at the morbid scene at their feet, then at each other.

Grayson went to Montaño who stood nearby patiently. "Photos?"

Montaño shook his head. "Not yet. They're on the way."

Grayson looked at his watch. "It's well past noon. Why the delay?" He looked at the sergeant again.

Montaño shook his head. "Sorry. They're comin' outa' Santa Fé. I expect 'em soon. I checked a while back. They were on another call." He cocked his head.

Grayson paced away. "Okay. I'd like shots of everything." He turned. "I know this is your gig, and I—we—respect that, but given the ID on the male—"

"I understand. I spoke with the chief. We'll share photos and forensics with you."

"I don't expect this to become federal, but—" Grayson was silent a beat, then, "We can assist."

Montaño shook his head. "Not a problem. Full cooperation." He paused, then furrowed his brow. "Who's the guy?"

Grayson raised his eyebrows. "Can't really say. And that's not because I know and won't say. It's because we need to find out." He waited two beats, then, "Pretty unusual to find a federal agent here—"

Montaño nodded with emphasis. He scratched his cheek. "We noticed the weapons. Looks odd. One gun with a silencer, the other something different. Not a standard firearm."

Grayson nodded. "Yeah." He looked over at the pistol that lay near the desk behind the sofa. "Can you get permission to let us take possession of the weapons so we can do forensics on them?"

"I'll call in."

Montaño turned to leave when Lucero asked, "What do you make of the muddy footprints?"

Grayson and Montaño both looked at the brick floor. A trail of drying partial shoe prints ran from the front door to the bodies, then back in two different tracks. Grayson moved around the end of the sofa and stopped. He peered at the trail. Montaño stepped aside and also looked.

"From last night?" Grayson asked. "Dried out some."

"Yeah." Montaño nodded. "We'll have forensics analyze 'em."

"Looks like a man's print. In and out. More than once." Lucero pointed, then looked at the other two law officers.

"Mm," Grayson murmured.

With that, Montaño left the house.

Fifteen minutes later, the State Police photographer arrived, and took photos of all that Grayson asked of her.

Jason Thompson had staggered outside under the rising moon, not because of his chronic heart and hypertension issues, but from the shock he had suffered as he watched his wife, Sarah, and Victor Nantes, gun each other down. He had walked several yards over the wet ground, fresh after the thunderstorm that had rattled through no more than an hour before. He had stopped, turned, and re-entered the house after making sure no one observed him. He had picked Sarah's purse up gingerly and felt around for the keys to the Mercedes. Outside once more, as he had stood near the car, he thought of another problem, and went back inside. There, he had carefully rifled through Nantes's pockets and extracted cash, then returned the dead man's wallet. He also went through Sarah's purse for what currency was there, then removed a handkerchief from his pants pocket and wiped Sarah's purse, Nantes's wallet and everything else he thought he might have touched throughout the small adobe house.

It was later, as he drove slowly down the mountain, that he felt he should not have taken the car. On the other hand, he had wondered how he would have been able to get away without being detected. He could have taken Nante's car, but without knowing its status, he favored the Mercedes. If he had eschewed a vehicle and walked along the road at any hour, he would have been spotted, possibly resulting in difficult questions. Aside from those considerations, the way was long and treacherous. He had no good choice.

Weary beyond anything he had felt before, and very late, he had checked into a motel in Española under a fictitious name with the cash from the two deceased people he left behind in Truchas. The following morning, he found a small, locally-run café where he had coffee and toast.

He swallowed a heart pill with orange juice. He found a lonely, graffiti-decorated outside pay phone, dropped coins, and keyed the number of the house. When his son, Justin, answered, he listened briefly, then hung up.

Partially refreshed after a restless night and in the car again, he sat for several minutes and pondered his next move. He clicked the radio on and tuned across the FM, then the AM band for news. He heard nothing about the deaths in Truchas. He started the car, and headed south. He determined to stay well within the law, given the fact that he carried no identification, let alone a driver's license. He also feared the car might soon be on a list of stolen vehicles.

When Jason entered the Albuquerque city limits close to midday, he veered in an easterly direction off the Interstate and onto the so-called "Heights" street grid. He drove to a mall in the northeast section and parked. Hungry, he found a fast-food outlet and ate a fish sandwich accompanied by an iced soda. His sweet tooth in charge, he purchased a candy bar, then strolled around the mall, looking at everything and seeing nothing as his mind reeled.

He spotted a "multi-plex" movie theater, purchased a ticket for a movie he felt sure he would find boring and irritating, and entered. He exited at around dusk, hungry and thirsty again, so he found a chain restaurant and ate as much of a full meal as he could tolerate with a glass of draft beer. He then returned to the movie theater to watch another film, during which he drifted off to sleep. Awakened at the end of the movie, he waited until the other patrons had cleared the auditorium, then left.

He felt better, and returned to his car. As he walked through the mall, he spotted a man he knew. His heart rate up, he turned away and stood close to a shop window where he studied the merchandise until the man passed, then hurried to the Mercedes. In the driver's seat, he dry-swallowed a pill and waited until his heart rate fell before starting the engine. It occurred to him that the car might be recognized, and he worried that it might even now be on a bulletin as stolen. It was Sarah who had used it typically, so to someone who knew her and the car, might wonder, given his reported demise. He tried to shake off his irrational thoughts without success.

He drove to the neighborhood where he, Sarah, and for a time before they moved away, their three children, had lived. He parked four blocks away on a side street that ran at a ninety-degree angle to the street the house fronted. It was well after ten o'clock. At the end of every block, a street lamp illuminated a rectilinear swath of bluish light.

He surveyed the neighborhood for more than two minutes, and watched for movement of any kind. The lights of a car appeared, whipped by on the other street, then disappeared. He got out, closed the door carefully, and locked the car. He then walked to the next street over, that which ran parallel to the house street, and made his way along it. When he reached the corner of the side street that connected to the street the house was on, he stopped, looked around, then walked slowly to where he was able to see the house. He stood under the shadow of a tree, away from the street lamp.

Two light sources shown from the house; one from the living area on the first floor, as well as from a second story bedroom window he recognized as a spare. In the glow from a street light and some of the yellowish light from the house, he saw two cars parked alongside the curb nearest the house, and one across the street. Two of the cars he was sure were police cruisers. One he thought was occupied by at least one officer.

Jason stood for nearly five minutes. Then, two people emerged from the house through the front door and walked to one of the cars parked nearest the house, got in and drove away. They appeared to be uniformed police. He saw what he reckoned was movement inside the living room that caused shadows and shifting light. He waited another minute, turned slowly and walked back to the Mercedes, his head down in deep thought. A sadness swept over him and he fought off tears.

In the Thompson living room, Peter Grayson sat on the edge of a chair across from young Justin Thompson who was on the sofa. Lucero, also seated, was across the room on another chair. Justin sat forward as well, both his arms on his knees, his head down, staring at the floor. All three men wore deeply serious expressions.

Young Thompson's voice was low. He spoke with slow deliberation. "Who was this guy?" He looked up long enough to see Grayson's face. "And my mom?!" His voice cracked, and his face was tear-streaked.

Grayson shook his head, his lips pursed. His voice was also very low. He spoke slowly. "Justin, we only know that he was posing as an FBI agent. More, we can't say." He paused. "We really don't know much more than that. As to your mother, we have little information. I'm sorry." He paused as he held out both palms in frustration. "The investigation is incomplete, but we'll let you—and your family—know just as soon as we have solid information."

The room went silent as Justin nodded slowly. He rose from the sofa and moved, zombie-like, to a front window. His voice, nearly a whisper, was barely audible to Grayson and Lucero. "Why—why would anyone—?"

Grayson shook his head and shot a glance at Lucero. "We have no idea. No clue. I'm sorry."

"And my mom! This is crazy!" His voice high-pitched, he threw his hands up, then dropped them against his sides. He paused. "I have to call my sister. My brother." His voice again cracked with emotion.

"Let us know about funeral arrangements, Justin." Grayson looked at young Thompson from under his eyebrows.

Justin merely nodded.

The FBI agents each handed Justin their cards, voiced their condolences again, told him they were available if needed, and said they would let him know anything new about the case of his mother's death and her role in the tragedy. They left quietly.

The Thompson son called first his sister, Flo, then his brother, Charles. Asked by Charles about the Mercedes, Justin admitted he had been so distraught that he had forgotten to ask about the car.

Grayson and Lucero returned to their car at the curb. Grayson gave the high sign to the police officers seated in the patrol car across the street as he got in. The officer at the wheel raised his foam coffee cup in salute, but made no move to leave.

They sat in the dark for several minutes. Both stared out through the windshield as Lucero idly tapped the steering wheel with his finger.

Grayson said, "We got us a brand-new ball game." He sighed. "A brand-new ball game." His voice a mere whisper, trailed off.

"What the hell's going on?" Lucero asked. He waited a beat, then, "Is the kid okay?"

Grayson looked at his partner. "The kid? Justin? Thompson? Okay?"

"Yeah." Lucero shrugged.

"You think—" Grayson frowned.

"Just asking. We can't leave any stones un-turned."

"What? You think the boy went up to Truchas with a cold-war type dart pistol and shot Nantes after Nantes killed his mother?! Something like that?!"

"Hey, Pete, I'm just throwing it out there is all." He looked away.

"Gotcha, Marc. But wild. Tangential." He hesitated. "You had that state cop institute a BOLO on the car. Mercedes, right?" He peered at Lucero.

Lucero nodded. "Right. Locals said it was a Mercedes. They knew the color. Something like blue-grey, but no one remembered the plate."

"Okay. I doubt if they know, but maybe the kid can find that information."

"State Police can dig it out 'o the DMV."

"Right. Need to find it." Grayson paused as he looked at Lucero. "What's the name of that cop up there?"

"State or Sheriff?"

"State. His take was that the car must have been stolen around the time of the shootings. If the EMTs are close on time of the deaths."

"If that's correct, based on the way the tracks look, the car was taken about that time. Close to midnight. Who the hell was around to go in after the keys and take off at that time of night?"

"Apparently none of the locals knew anything about it." Grayson shook his head and squinted into the night. "Hell, was there a third party involved?"

Lucero stared at Grayson and cocked his head in a question. "Muddy footprints. So, again, what the hell *is* goin' on?" He rubbed the back of his neck.

"You got me." He paused, stuck his hand into his jacket pocket, retrieved a package of lemon drops, offered one to his partner, who refused it, then popped one into his mouth. He sucked on the sweet, then, "Who was this guy? Why was he up north? I see why Sarah Thompson, the ice queen, was, but this guy—what was his name? Nantes? Makes no sense." He looked at his partner.

Lucero returned Grayson's look. "Thompson was cremated, right?"

Grayson looked at Lucero from the corner of his eye, his head turned half-way front, and nodded. "Yeah . . ." The word was inflected as though a question.

"This Nantes guy took charge of the field operation—the clean-up down south, right? Where did he come from?"

Grayson crunched the remainder of the lemon drop into bits, swallowed them, and stared out into the night. "Washington? Did Buckley bring him in? Should be in the file."

"He had to have a team. Appropriations. Back-up. How'd he pull it off? And the weapon."

Grayson shot a glance at Lucero. "We'll see what the lab comes up with. Trace the recovery authority. That woman with a dart gun." He paused. "It's late. I need to hit the sack."

Four blocks away, Jason Thompson got into the Mercedes, sat quietly for a minute, then brought the German-made engine to life.

# 2

*A*s he drove away, Jason looked at the fuel gauge. It read roughly one-quarter tank. He then thought of the money in his pocket and the distance he had to travel. He turned the corner, headed along the main street, then toward Central Avenue, where he was sure to find an all-night station. He filled the tank after handing the lone attendant cash, then headed for the Interstate and got onto the south-bound lane. He drove to Los Lunas, found a motel and checked in. In the morning, after visiting a fast-food drive-through for a take-away breakfast and coffee, he drove south to Socorro.

In the town, he drove west toward the mountains along Bullock Road, then to Canyon Drive. He stopped a mile along the nearly deserted extension, Canyon Road, waited 30 seconds, then turned around and drove back toward the town. He found a strip mall, pulled into a parking place, then craned his neck until he spotted a pay phone outside a drug store.

The phone rang three times.

"Hello?" It was his son, Justin Thompson. "Hello?"

Jason held the receiver to his ear for another three seconds, then pushed the hook down. He looked down at his feet, then around through the plastic bubble that constituted the booth. He went to the car and got in. He drove the same route he had earlier, but farther along Canyon Road until he came to an isolated spot that gave him a view of the road back and of the city. He turned the car in that direction, drove the car onto the shoulder, then cracked the front windows open an inch, moved the seat back as far as he could, removed his glasses and shut his eyes. He wished he had his watch.

After dozing for what he figured to be 15 minutes, he was awakened by the sound of an approaching vehicle. He sat up, saw a pickup truck coming from his rear, brushed at his hair, open his door and stepped out. He stood near the car, peered off toward the nearest land mass with his hand shading his eyes as though studying the terrain, and waved at the driver of the truck as it passed. The man at the wheel awarded him a terse wave in return with a mere momentary glance. Unable to sleep, he sat in the car and pondered his next move. After a minute, he started the car, shut the windows and drove back into the town. At the outskirts, he selected a side street with few houses, mostly older and somewhat run-down. He drove to the end of the dead-end street whose asphalt terminated in a weed-choked field. He parked the car carefully against the crumbling curb, set the break, shut the engine down, wiped the steering wheel and controls clean with his handkerchief, stepped out and locked the vehicle. As he walked away casually, but in such a way that an observer might think he had a firm destination in mind, he wondered what he would do with the keys. He slowed, looked down at the bunch of little metal pieces in his hand, then, unable to decide, thrust them into his pants pocket.

He resumed his walking rate for more than ten blocks until he found a main street. There, he looked in both directions. To the north, he thought he saw a motel sign. Another three blocks, and with his feet hot and hurting, he was gratified to discover that he was correct. He checked in, went to his room, and flopped onto the bed, fatigued.

Jason stayed in his room the entire night, alternating between dozing and watching television. He went out once to the hall niche snack machine. He purchased cheese- and peanut butter crackers and a soda. In the morning, he went to the lobby for coffee, juice and a dry, tasteless pastry. When he found a pay phone and called the house, there was no answer.

He checked out, walked to the bus station and bought a ticket for Albuquerque. There, he found a city bus that took him to within three blocks of the house. It was late afternoon. Although tired and with a blister on his right heel, he walked to a nearby shopping center for food and drink and a pocket book novel. He also bought a small pasteboard box of adhesive bandages. From there, he went to a park two blocks from the house, sat on a bench, and after ministering to his wounded foot, pretended to read the bad romance novel he had picked at random. Every few seconds, he raised his eyes above the book and glanced about. The rare individual pedestrian he saw held no interest in him, and the vehicles that passed contained no threat.

As dusk fell, he ate the crackers and peeled open a candy bar he had bought at the shopping center, and finished the bottle of water. When the street lights popped on automatically, he rose, stiff, from the bench, threw the detritus from the food and the paper-back into a trash bin, and began a slow walk toward the house. With the first aid on his foot, although muscle sore, he felt no more searing pain.

At the corner, he saw that the house was dark. He moved cautiously toward it, watching for anyone in all directions. He stood for more than five minutes as he listened and studied the house, the streets and the neighborhood. There was one empty civilian sedan parked across from the house, and two on the street than ran perpendicular to it. Two cars and an RV were in driveways along the street. He recalled three of the vehicles. House lights were on in half the houses, but he saw no movement in any direction.

He walked to the driveway, then close to the garage. He stopped in the deep shadow, looked and listened. From there, he made his way with stealth up the stairs to the studio above the garage. He raised the porcelain Mexican hat for the key to the studio. The door was locked, but he keyed himself in and closed the door without a sound. Low, diffused light shown in from the street, which allowed him to move through familiar surroundings with relative ease.

He made his way carefully to the small bathroom, closed the door, flicked on the single overhead lamp, then moved to the wash basin. He cupped his hands under the cold water tap, filled his hands, and slurped water into his dry mouth, then over his perspiration-dampened face. With his eyes closed, he felt for, then dried, his hands and face on a towel that hung from a wall peg.

From there, he went to the photo dark room. He closed the door and snapped the room light on. He found the film box he wanted. Inside that was a metal film canister which held a ring with two keys. He found a small cloth towel, wiped the box and canister clean, turned the light off, then left the room, but brought the towel with him. After his eyes were accustomed to the dark, he made his way back to the porch, where he locked the door and replaced the studio key under the sombrero after wiping them with the towel. He cleaned the hat as well. He waited again as he searched the empty street, then moved carefully down the stairs and to the back door of the house, where he let himself in with the house key from the Mercedes ring. He was glad he had not listened to the part of him that wanted to toss the keys into a field.

Again, he waited. Stillness.

As he paused, his heart rate rose suddenly as he thought of something relative to the car key. Why had he locked the Mercedes? It was an instinctive act, but what would the authorities; the police and the FBI, think? How would they react to that fact? He resolved to think about it later. Now, at this moment, it was too late.

He took a deep breath, tried to calm himself, then moved carefully into the dark, cool house.

In the darkness, he went through the kitchen, into the dining and living rooms, and up the stairs as he avoided the one tread that squeaked. He waited at the top. Silence. He went to the master bedroom, whose door was open, and into the bathroom where he used the toilet without turning on the light. He returned to the bedroom, then, still without light, riffled through Sarah's jewelry box, removed the items there, then pulled open a top drawer in her dresser, and left it open. He went to the clothes closet, pulled several articles of clothing down, then pulled down a small box from the shelf above, dropped it to the floor, and removed the .32 caliber semi-automatic pistol and a box of ammunition that fell from it. He allowed two cartridges to remain on the carpet. He went to his dresser and pulled out the two top drawers, removed some socks and underwear, and dropped them to the floor.

Back on the first floor, he stopped, looked around, then picked up a pillow from the sofa, went to the back door, opened it and stepped outside, looked around for a possible observer, put the pillow against the glass pane nearest the latch assembly, and punched it until it broke with little noise. He closed the door, made sure the broken glass was in the proper place near the opening on the floor, and returned to the living room. There, in the deep shadows, he found a vase that rested on a side table, placed it on the floor, then used the pillow to quiet the sound of the crockery as it broke under his foot. He brushed the pillow clean of glass shards with the towel, then put the pillow back on the sofa where he found it, and left without locking the door.

From there, with the small gun, ammunition box and jewelry in separate pants pockets, he went to the garage. He keyed himself in the side door, then felt around for a flashlight on the work bench. With the light held low such that it would not shine through cracks in the side or overhead doors, he knelt down below the work bench and opened one of the cabinet doors. He pulled out a wooden box of small parts and tools, set it on the concrete floor, then shown the light against the wall behind where it had been. He slid a panel to the right to reveal a black leather pouch the size of a large, hard-cover dictionary secreted in the wall between studs. This he removed, set on the floor, then closed the panel, replaced the parts box, and closed the cabinet door.

He stood and wiped the cabinet knob. With the flashlight lying on the work bench, he moved the jewelry, firearm and ammunition to the pouch and zipped it closed. He extinguished the flashlight and returned it to the bench. He waited for a moment, thoughtful, grabbed the flashlight again, played the light over the bench, then picked up a large-shank screwdriver. He move to the overhead door, looked it over with the light, placed the screwdriver shaft behind the galvanized sheet steel bolt receiver at the bottom, and pushed. The receiver bent, freeing the keeper bolt. He moved to the opposite side and performed the same operation there. He dropped the screwdriver onto the floor after wiping it, then cleaned the flashlight, went to the old Ford pickup, opened the driver's side door, and threw it, along with the leather pouch, onto the seat.

He stood for three seconds, then went to the side door, then outside, and with his right elbow, broke out the glass pane closest to the latch, such that the shards fell into the garage.

Inside again, he felt under the driver's side fender, retrieved a key from a hidden magnetic box, then opened the overhead garage door slowly and manually, to prevent the ceiling light from activating. It created almost no sound. He peered outside, walked to the end of the driveway and looked up and down the empty street. Back inside the garage, he opened the driver's door to the Ford, released the hand break, put the vehicle in neutral, then pushed it from the front until it rolled. As it began to clear the garage, he jumped into the driver's seat, then rode the dead vehicle until it was clear of the garage, and applied the emergency hand brake. He got out, closed the overhead door carefully, and pushed the pickup to the end of the drive, where it rolled part-way into the street because of the driveway slope. There, panting from the extreme exercise, he started the engine, backed into the street, cranked the wheel to the right, and drove away slowly. At the end of the street, he turned the headlights on.

When he had driven several blocks along a main street, he came to an empty bank parking lot, where he pulled in and parked. He studied his bare-ly-lit surroundings briefly. Other than light traffic on the street, he was alone. He opened the pouch and removed the contents other than the pistol and the jewels. With the overhead cab light on, he pawed through them. He found two driver's licenses, two passports, and an envelope with cash and traveler's checks in the names listed on the documents. Included was an empty leather wallet and eight credit cards, also in names other than his. There were MasterCard, Visa, American Express and two bank debit cards. He removed all but two of the cards, and moved some of the cash and a driver's license to the wallet. The last items were a wrist watch, a bank safety deposit box key and a small, black bound book.

He took four seconds to riffle through the pages of the book, then put the watch onto his left wrist, while the rest were returned to the pouch. That went into the glove compartment, which he locked with a separate key on the ring with the ignition key. The wallet he slipped into his back pocket. He stopped as he recalled the key ring from the Mercedes. This he retrieved from his pants pocket and put into the glove compartment.

He studied the empty parking lot for a moment, extinguished the over-head light, started the engine, clicked the seat belt across his chest, and drove back onto the thoroughfare.

# 3

$\mathcal{S}$hortly past 9 AM, Grayson and Lucero walked along the narrow hall between their cubicles in the Albuquerque FBI headquarters. Both held ceramic cups of coffee from the refreshment room. They both nodded and smiled at a woman who passed in the opposite direction carrying a file folder.

"State fuzz said they found the car?" Grayson spoke without looking at his partner.

"Yeah. Montaño. Guy we met up there. Asked what we wanted to do. They're hauling it up here to impound."

Grayson glanced at Lucero. "Where was it?"

"Socorro. On a side street. Doors locked. No damage. Nothing in the car. Trunk clean."

"Really?" Grayson frowned.

"Alert local cop answered a disturbance call. Run-down part of town. Spotted the vehicle answering the description and plate. Nobody on the street knew anything about it. Another 24 hours and it woulda' been stripped."

"When's it due?"

Lucero consulted his wrist watch. "Three or four hours. 'Bout one o'clock."

"So, we'll get our guys and go have a look-see."

"I'll give 'em a call."

They stopped in front of Grayson's cubicle.

Grayson sipped at his coffee again and looked at Lucero from under his eyebrows. "What'll we find, Marc?"

"Not a thing." Lucero compressed his lips. "Taking odds?"

"No way." Grayson smiled and turned to enter his space.

Vera Tyler tried to remember the last time she had run with joy. She realized it must have been as a little girl before the truth of her difficult life burst upon her. Behind her, Jason Thompson followed in his re-built pickup truck at five miles per hour.

She pried open the old swinging doors to the combination barn and garage, and Jason eased the truck into the deep shade. He shut the engine down, then stepped out. He was confronted by a mixture of odors he immediately found beyond pleasant. There was dust, fresh and dried hay, old wood, earth and oil, all mixed with a trace of verdant pine. The last wafted up from the dirt under the newly-arrived vehicle. He felt instant pleasure and a sense of freedom, much as he recalled as a young boy.

Vera appeared to him as a black outline against the brilliant, sun-washed background as she stood in the open doorway waiting for him. As he approached, she started to close the nearest door. He stopped her and took her hand.

"Hello," he said. His voice was low, and carried a touch of sadness.

She shook her bent head with a cross between a smile and a frown. "What—?"

He put his hand to her neck, leaned over and kissed her cheek. She gulped, threw her arms around him and kissed him on his mouth. He returned it with reserved fervor. They pulled away and looked at each other with genuine smiles. Her eyes were wet.

She shook her head as they held hands. "Jason—what? I don't understand. What happened?! That man—he told me—"

Jason nodded, looked away, then back. "Could we go in and have that steak you mentioned? I'm starving. I'll tell you everything. Okay?"

She nodded, then shook her head as well. "Of course." She pulled him along with her hand in his. "I'm so glad to see you. I was devastated." She shook her head again in disbelief, such that her hair flew.

Jason closed the screen door as they entered the house. Vera turned to look at him, then, with tears in her eyes, she put her arms around him and laid her head against his chest. He looked past her, brushed her hair with his hand and smiled. He compressed his lips to restrain himself from following her into her mood.

"I love you," she whispered.

He hesitated, confused and unsure of his feelings after all that had befallen him, then, "I love you, too."

She released him, backed away and marched to the kitchen. "Okay," she said with her back to him. "Time to get busy. 'Nough of the nonsense. I need some wood for this here stove. It's through that door." She pointed, then opened a cabinet door and rattled a pan down.

Jason wore a firm grin as he walked through the kitchen to the outside door. "Ye-es, ma'am!"

She fixed steak, potatoes and a vegetable. They both drank milk.

With little remaining on her plate, she pushed back. She looked at him with clear eyes. "Okay, my dear, dead man. Tell me."

Jason nodded, looked down at his clean plate, away for a moment, then directly at her. Close to an hour later, having exhausted his tale, he sat back with a long sigh.

"I just wouldn't have believed it, Jason, had it not come from you. But—"

"But?"

"Your kids. They'll find the truck—your pickup—gone. What'll they think?"

Jason shrugged. "What will everyone think? The police. The FBI. As I told you, I left evidence—"

"That someone had broken in?"

He nodded. "Yes. I drove most of the way here at night. They may not have discovered it missing yet. That won't happen without one of the kids being there." He paused, stood, paced away, then turned. He looked at the old, plank floor. "They'll look for Sarah's car. The Mercedes."

"You left it in Socorro?" She looked up at him as he paced slowly.

"Yes. They won't find anything, but they'll wonder why it was taken and abandoned."

Vera looked down at her hands in her lap.

"I goofed."

"Goofed? How?"

"Locked the car. The Mercedes. Should have left it open."

"Oh. You think that was wrong? To do?"

He shook his head and looked down. "I don't know. I—it doesn't matter."

He made a face, then, "Vera, I want to go to Las Cruces. In your truck."

"Las Cruces?"

"Yes." He moved to his chair and sat. "I need some things. I have money. Enough. Something like this had been planned for. You don't have to do this, you know, but I need to operate—work—from here. It's ideal. Is that okay with you?"

She tilted her head and her face clouded. "Then you'll leave?"

"Vera, listen. Carefully." He leaned forward as he stretched his arm across the table. His voice was low and sincere. "I'm here because of you. Because of us." He waited a beat. "I love you, lady. I do. But I can't—my nature—I can't not do this. Solve this problem. My kids. My daughter. My boys. My life. Do you understand?"

She brightened. "I want to. Yes, I do." She cocked her head in concern.

He rose, came around to her, bent down and kissed her, then stroked her face and her hair. He straightened and looked out the window over the archaic sink. "I want you to meet my kids. I want them to meet you." He turned to face her. "But I tell you this in all sincerity. Regardless of what they feel, however they deal with the truth, it will not change my feelings for you. Please believe me."

She got up, went to him, and they hugged.

"I need to get my things from the truck." He whispered.

She looked into his face. "If the truck were spotted here—?"

He shook his head. "I would come clean, as it were." He paused. "Is that a distinct possibility? Do you get visited—?"

"No." She shook her head. "Sometimes Sheriff Tenorio comes by to check on me, but it's not often. I can tell when he's comin'. He won't be trouble."

"We need a story."

"Story?"

Jason walked toward the outside door. "Who I am and why I'm here."

She nodded.

"I'm a bit old to be a hand." He looked at her ruefully.

She thought for a moment. "You're my husband's cousin. Retired or some such. You write or somethin'. Need the quiet. Maybe—maybe you got some ailment. Need the rest and the air."

He turned to look at her. "Yes. Good." He looked away. "I can use one of my aliases. In case he gets curious."

"Yes."

"Where am I from?"

"From? Oh, yes. Well, Tyler was from Texas, but you coulda' moved away. You don't have the sound of it." She grinned.

"Yes. Okay. Good." He smiled. "Okay; I'll be right back."

"I'll clean up here." She began to clear the dishes away.


The combined State Police-FBI forensic team consisted of two women and four men. All wore medical gloves and special jackets blazoned with their agency affiliation. They had much of the Mercedes pulled apart, save unbolting or unscrewing parts. Carpets out, trunk open; spare tire removed. Hood up, engine exposed. One man shot photos of everything from many angles. After an hour, the car was raised on an hydraulic lift, and the team ran through its routine with the undercarriage.

Peter Grayson and Marcus Lucero watched. Lucero held a plastic cup with cold coffee laced with cream. Grayson paced away a few feet, then turned. He looked at Lucero from under his eyebrows, his head lowered. He shook his head in slow deliberation. Lucero raised his eyebrows, nodded and sipped his beverage.

A State Police Lieutenant stood nearby.

Grayson walked over to the cop. "It was found in Socorro?"

The uniformed officer turned his head. "Yeah. Side street. Problem area. Local cop spotted it. We went in and interviewed some of the locals. Nada."

"So, nobody saw anyone?"

"If they did, they're not coughing it up."

"Right . . ." Grayson paused. "No trouble with the warrant? For the locksmith and all that?"

"No. We can stay on it. Unless you guys wanna' go in."

Grayson took in a deep breath and released it. "I don't know. Trying to put two and two together and not coming up with four. Even if someone saw something."

"Yeah." The policeman nodded.

"Hm, yes," Grayson mused. "Could be worthwhile." He paused as he stroked his chin. "No fingerprints?"

The policeman turned. He shook his head. "None so far. None on the important parts. Steering wheel, door handles, gear shift."

Grayson looked at Lucero, then at the cop. "Theories?"

"Theories?" The State Policeman responded.

"As to why clean. No prints on those parts."

The cop shrugged. "Didn't want to leave a trace."

"Someone thoughtful. A thinker. Careful."

The cop nodded. "Yeah. Looks that way."

Grayson looked at Marcus Lucero. He raised his chin and cast his eyes upward, then looked at his partner with the corners of his eyes. "This is very strange." He stretched the word "very" out.

Lucero nodded, his mouth compressed. He looked at the New Mexico cop. "Check for DNA?"

The cop was silent for a moment, then, "No. Where would we pick that up?" He shrugged again.

"Steering wheel? Perspiration smear?" Lucero cocked his head.

The trooper raised his eyebrows, lowered his head and scratched his ear. "Mm, possible. I don't know. No prints . . . "

Grayson, energized, looked at the policeman as well. "Let's try."

"Okay." The cop looked at both of the federal agents and nodded with a frown. "See what I can do."

Jason returned from his truck and stood at the entrance from the living room to the kitchen. He carried the leather pouch and his jacket. Tired, and drifting away after a full midday meal, he appealed to Vera to forgive him for wanting to nap.

Vera wiped her damp hands, walked up to him, smiled and kissed him on his cheek, then took his hand and led him to her bedroom. "You rest," she said.

Jason looked around, then focused on the bed. "You sure?"

She shook her head, then nodded. "I'm sure."

*4*

*T*he restaurant in the mall at the corner of Richmond High-way and Southgate Drive in Groveton, Virginia, was a typical up-scale chain establishment. It featured a sea of dark wood and red vinyl booths arranged around a two-level floor, whose walls were covered with odd memorabilia, such as photographs of deceased celebrities, old metal advertising signs and the like. The young service staff, likewise, was dressed and trained to be somehow indic-ative of the uncertain motif.

It was late morning as Peter Grayson, Special Agent from the Albuquer-que office of the Federal Bureau of Investigation, sat in an isolated corner booth, alone, with a glass of water and a set of utensils wrapped in a napkin in front of him. Hatless and wearing a dark brown windbreaker, he rested both his hands on the table surface. His head moved only minimally as he eyed most of the eatery. Every few seconds he glanced at his watch.

He was seated for eleven minutes when another man approached his table. He was slightly overweight, just under six feet, with greying, thinning hair. He wore a dark suit and conservative tie. A casual observer would have pegged his age at about fifty.

He slid onto the padded red vinyl bench seat across from Grayson. He looked around the room, filling with the daily business lunch crowd, then fixed his eyes on Grayson. "Peter Grayson. Long time no see." His smile was rye. His eyes sparkled.

"Jerry. Good to see you. Thanks for coming. Yes; long time." Grayson compressed his lips in a matter-of-fact manner.

They shook hands perfunctorily across the table without rising.

A young woman wearing a tightly-laced bodice and short, clingy dark skirt came to the table. "Hi, guys. What can I get you?" She looked at both men in turn with a broad, come-hither smile.

Grayson looked from her to Jerry Madsen. "Jerry?"

"Ah, what the heck. A Sam Adams draft and one o' them great French dips." He looked up at the girl and raised his eyebrows accompanied by a grin.

She made a note, then looked at Grayson. "Sir?"

"Make it simple. The same."

"Be right back with your drinks." She turned and strode away.

"So, Peter. You look well," Madsen declared.

"As do you, Jerry."

Madsen glanced around. "What's goin' on, Pete?" He bent his head in a question. "Why the hush-hush location?"

Grayson took in and released a breath, and fished a two inch by two inch photograph from his inside jacket pocket. He turned it over and wrote on the back of it with his ballpoint pen, then shoved it across the table to Madsen. "Familiar?"

Madsen peered at Grayson, then picked the photo up and looked at it. He turned it over, read the back, then considered the picture again, frowned, studied the ceiling in reflection, then looked at his table partner. "Victor Nantes? No. Doesn't strike a chord." He jutted his chin out with a frown. "Who is he?"

"More to the point, who *was* he," Grayson answered.

"Deceased, I take it." Madsen looked at the picture again, laid it on the table and shoved it in Grayson's direction.

Grayson made no move to pick the photograph up. He leaned back with his hands in his lap. "Quite dead," he said. "Suffered a rather nasty spasmodic death due to the effects of a couple of poison darts. Possibly of old KGB origin. You guys might be able to confirm that."

Madsen squirmed and raised his eyebrows. "Interesting. Where and when? And why?"

"The where, a little town in northern New Mexico called Truchas. When, a few days ago. Why? One of the reasons I'm here."

"You think he belonged to us? Working inside?"

"He wasn't one of ours. Pretended to be. Carried a Reuters card."

"Well, there you are. Have you checked? And why here? Why not Langley?"

Grayson lowered his head with a cross between a frown and a smile.

Madsen looked away, then back. "Yeah, yeah. Okay. But what makes you think he's company?"

The waitress came back, set two amber-filled mugs on the table over bar napkins, then bustled away.

Grayson continued, "He carried a good Agency ID. He did stuff only a pro could pull off. Had company all over it. We're at a loss." He looked around, then lowered his voice. "If he is—was—CIA, I sure don't want to bring it up at Langley. If he was, who else? Inside? Outside?"

Madsen nodded and downed a slug of his beer. "I'll have a look. You said dart? KGB?"

Grayson shrugged after partaking of his drink. "We heard they used tricks like that. If I get it to you, can you have a peek?"

"He had it on 'im?"

"That's what's weird, Jerry. No. A woman. The woman who killed him. She had it." He took a long draft of his beer. "She killed him with it." He looked at Madsen over the rim of his mug as he drank.

Madsen leaned forward. He whispered, "What?!" He looked out into the room, then back.

Grayson nodded emphatically as he set his mug down.

"Who—what woman?! Who was she?! Russian? Iranian?!" Madsen slid his perspiring beer mug to one side.

Grayson shook his head with deliberation. "Nope. American." He paused. "I gotta tell you, Jerry, we got ourselves a dilly. A real dilly."

Madsen, his focus on Peter Grayson, retrieved his mug and swallowed three more ounces of cold beer. He wiped his mouth. "So, tell me." He checked the room again.

During Grayson's account of the Geronimo Queen investigation, the waitress arrived with their sandwiches. Grayson, busy speaking, ate sporadically, while Madsen finished his off with dispatch, then signaled for a second draft beer. Finished with his recounting, Grayson then ate in relative silence.

Madsen leaned hard against the edge of the table and peered hard at the FBI agent. "Let me get this straight. You don't know any more about this woman—this Sarah. Thompson, is it?"

"Right. Nada. Nothing. We're working on it." He chewed.

Madsen sat back. "Jesus." He pondered. "And the husband. Thompson. Dead?"

"That's what we know, Jerry. But here's the thing. If this guy Nantes was company-connected, who? With the resources he mustered—"

Madsen tossed up his palms as he sat back. "I hear you." He blew out a deep breath.

"Can you help?" Grayson used his napkin on his mouth.

"With what? Both? Gun and the guy?"

Grayson nodded and pushed the photograph back in Madsen's direction. "Hang onto this, but for Christ's sake, keep it close. But see if he can be ID'd."

Madsen picked the little photo up and slipped it into his shirt pocket. "I will." He nodded. "The armament—what about your guys?"

Grayson shook his head in quick, short movements. "We checked. Outa' their realm. Looks too exotic. We're domestic. Figured you guys had more experience with that sort of ordnance."

Madsen's eyes widened and he shrugged. "Yeah, okay. Reasonable." He thought for a moment. "I'll poke around."

"We'll send it to you. Personally. Okay?" He pointed.

"Yeah."

"Timing?"

"Mm. On the gun, can't say. On the phony guy, maybe quicker. Gonna be around?"

"I need to get back. Flight tonight."

"Okay. How do we communicate?"

"On anything sensitive, Kappa-drop encryption. Through the Kanucks."

"Hm. That's been awhile. Okay." He hesitated, stood up and reached for his wallet.

Grayson held up his hand. "It's on me. Least I could do." He smiled.

Madsen nodded. "Yeah, 'ole buddy. I accept. I'll get back to ya'. Safe trip."

Jason suggested Vera drive her own vehicle rather than accepting her invitation for him to do so, but he insisted on buying gas. His reasoning was that anyone who knew her would not question her behind the wheel. Another reason he kept to himself, was that he wanted to wind down and needed to think.

They stopped for lunch at the Akela Trading Post half-way to Las Cruces. They sat at a small table near a window. Later, on the road, they both agreed that the food exceeded their expectations.

Vera watched Jason as carefully as she dared, given that she didn't want to stare. She spoke quietly. "Is everything alright? Are you okay? You look out the window a lot."

He looked at her with embarrassment, then down at his empty plate. "Sorry. It's been rough."

"Of course." She wanted to reach for his hand, but held back. "Do you miss her?"

He turned his head aside, then back. "I don't know, Vera. I'm still in shock. Maybe it's because I was involved in a deception for so long. Maybe—"

"But you didn't do anything wrong, Jason." Her voice pleaded.

He sighed, looked down, then up. "But I didn't let the Labs know. I couldn't. What I was involved in was kept secret from them, too. It wasn't easy. I had to manipulate them so I could manipulate Mel. I think I know why now. That came from Nantes. Not at first." He paused. "What I can't figure is how long it was that Nantes strung me along. I don't know if Mel knew Nantes was actually his conduit. Or for how long."

She nodded and looked around at the sprinkling of patrons eating or strolling around looking at cheap Indian and Mexican curios.

"What I want to know—" He stopped, looked around, then leaned forward and continued in a lowered voice, "is who Nantes' control was. Is." He was silent, then, "Whoever it is, they had the means to help him pull off what he did. The plane clean-up. Faking my death—"

"God, Jason—"

He nodded emphatically. "I know. They had to 've fooled the feds." His voice trailed off.

"Sarah, she—"

He shook his head and looked out the window again. "The kids." He sighed and stood. "Let's go. Okay?"

"Of course."

On the highway again, headed east, he spoke above the road noise. "I don't think there was anyone else at the Labs. I can't be sure, but I don't think so. But Nantes' control has got to be out there. They're sure to know I'm not dead."

She took her eyes off the road long enough to glance at him. "How will you do that? I mean, find out?"

"I don't know. I need to think." He glanced at her, then nodded at the passing scenery.

"I didn't—"

He interrupted her. "When we get to Las Cruces, I want to check into a motel away from the Interstate. Keep our eyes open for anything that might indicate they're looking for me."

"But you're supposed to be dead." She frowned.

"If they dig up Cuzco's ashes, they might be able to figure out it wasn't me." He paused. "If they find—*when* they find—trace—Nantes, they could doubt everything." He looked at her. "The whole thing could come apart, Vera."

"My god, Jason!"

He touched her again. "Please don't worry. We'll be fine. You'll be fine."

"I know."

Jason mumbled to his passenger side window.

"What?" She asked.

He looked at her. "Sorry." He paused. "I got to thinking." He held up his finger. "So—Nantes must have told his control I was alive. If that's so, then they'll want to find me."

Vera frowned at him. "You said, but Why? What for?"

Jason pondered, then, "Good question. I don't know." His voice trailed off.

# 5

*T*ao Wang was half asleep as the mid-morning flight he was on was in the final approach to Kansas City. The announcement of the pending touch-down and arrival by the female flight attendant awakened him, and he sat up and peered out the tiny window at the city as it rushed by beneath the aircraft. For a moment, he didn't know where he was as he looked at the person next to him, but that condition soon righted itself. His mood tightened with thoughts of his mission.

He had traveled "light," thus the only baggage he had to worry about was a dark blue cloth overnight bag he dragged down from the overhead bin. Ten minutes later, after wading through a sea of fellow travelers, he went from the lobby to the curb taxi rank where he entered a cab.

What he did not notice as he made his way through the throng was the man who stood near the entrance. He was white Indo-European, of average height, and wore a neutral color sports jacket with coordinated pants and street shoes. He stood reading a magazine through dark glasses. In reality, he was looking over the top edge of the pages at the people moving toward the exit. As Wang passed him, he casually folded the magazine closed, rolled it and walked away, toward the interior of the lobby, then out through another exit.

In the cab, as the car moved away, the driver asked his passenger where he wished to go. Wang referred to a piece of paper he pulled from his shirt pocket, and advised the man behind the wheel.

The motel was an older place, more than fifty years in existence, reno-vated more than once, and situated off the main streets in a section of town not known for quality of life. Wang checked in and made his way to a second-story room along a narrow, cracked concrete balcony with a steel guard rail in sore need of paint. As he inserted the key into the lock, he hesitated, turned around and surveyed the street beyond the old, eroded tarmac parking lot. He saw a window-shielded neon sign proclaiming a coffee shop across the two-lane street. He entered the room, locked the door, then peered out the single, dingy window, scanned the empty lot and the street that fronted it again. He saw three vehicles in the motel lot. He closed the curtains, turned on the single lamp next to the bed, then powered on the old television set.

If he had stood at the window another thirty seconds, he might have noticed the ten year old Chevrolet passenger car that pulled up slowly alongside the curb across the street and stop. Seated at the wheel was the man in the sports jacket and dark glasses who had watched him at the airport.

The man in the Chevrolet shut the ignition off, then removed the plastic lid from a paper cup and settled in with the coffee it contained. After taking his first sip, he turned the ignition key to the first position, clicked the radio on, then tuned it to a station with classical music. His view of the motel and its parking lot was complete. He partook of the coffee again, peeked at his watch, moved his head back against the head rest and closed his eyes.

Shortly after dark, when the watcher in the Chevrolet took the first bite from a sandwich, he noticed the Chinese man leave his room, then watched him come down the outside stairway, cross the parking lot, now populated with seven vehicles, jay-walk across the street and enter the coffee shop. He had removed his dark glasses, but was not concerned that he would be recognized.

Wang did not look his way.

Five minutes later, another car, a Nissan pickup truck, pulled up behind the Chevy sedan and parked. The man behind the wheel shut the engine off, then sat back. The man in the Chevy dusted bread crumbs from his hands as he looked into the rearview mirror. His hands clean, he held up his finger and pointed at the coffee shop. The man in the car behind him nodded, then the man in the Chevrolet started the engine, put the transmission into gear, checked his outside mirror, and drove away.

When, forty-three minutes later, Wang exited the coffee shop and crossed to his motel room, the new watcher kept his eye on him. He then opened up a Thermos bottle and drank from it. After closing the bottle, he keyed a number into a cell phone, waited, spoke three words, and shut it down. At dawn, the watcher picked up his cell phone and made a call. He listened, spoke several words, then closed the phone. With that, he started the engine and drove away.

Wang, bored, dozed on and off, read a few passages of a book he had brought on his trip, watched some television, ate a light meal at the coffee shop, and slept well most of the night. In the morning, he again crossed to the eatery for breakfast. This time, although not of any importance to him, he casually noticed that the first car, then the pickup, he had seen the night before, were no longer parked alongside the curb. As quickly as he made that mental note, he dismissed it. With the sun nine o'clock high and the sky clear, he decided to take a brief walk, and turned to take the sidewalk on the motel side. After a block, concerned over the run-down blight he encountered along with several disreputable looking men he saw, he headed back to his motel room. He used the bathroom, then went to the window and pulled the curtain aside. He looked at nothing while he surveyed everything, but failed to note the return of the Chevy and the man with the dark glasses.

After a second dusk-time sortie to the diner, during which his watcher took note, and in his room, Wang's cell phone chirped. He answered it with a "Hello," listened, then without another word, but an unnecessary nod of his head, rang off. He put his jacket on, took his overnight bag, locked the room door, then went to the motel office and set the pre-paid room key on the reception counter. From there, he went to the curb, where a taxi showed up after a three minute wait.

He found that the driver had instructions as to where he was to go. That was a large, grassy, treed park across the city, near the northern outskirts. The driver told Wang he had been paid, but thanks anyway.

The taxi pulled away, and Wang stood in the semi-darkness, twenty feet from a street light emanating a filmy cone of bluish light, with his overnight bag dangling from his hand. He looked around, then moved tentatively toward the innards of the shadowy greensward. As he did, he entered an area shrouded by bushes and shaded by tall, mature trees, and darker yet. He found the bench he was told would be there, looked about again, then sat on the edge of the wooden slats, nervous. He set the bag down on the stone pavement next to his leg on his right. He peered left and right, tried to see the time on his watch, sighed, and attempted to sit back. It was then that he heard footsteps approach from the dark side of the park.

The man was taller than average, dressed in a dark windbreaker over dark jeans and like-colored Western boots. He wore a dark baseball cap with no legend or symbol. Because his hair style was not cropped, dark brown hair flew out from around the edge of the cap on the sides and back. He stopped in front of the bench, looked both ways, then spoke. "Poor Boy? Wang?"

"Yes."

"Tanner. Not my real name. You understand."

"Yes. I understand." Wang nodded. He started to rise, then regained his seat when Tanner moved to sit as well.

The man checked the surroundings again as he gained his seat on Wang's left. "Listen, I'm sorry about the venue, but we couldn't—" He spoke in a tone only loud enough for Tao Wang to make out his words.

"Yes, yes," Wang nodded in the dark.

"Tao, were you followed?" Tanner spoke only loud enough for Wang to hear him.

Wang shook his head.

"You're sure." It was a questioned framed as a statement. Tanner looked carefully at Wang over his eyebrows, then peered into the dark in the opposite direction.

"Yes, I am most sure. I am told that a source has died." His voice was above a whisper.

"You are correct, but that is not a problem."

"Will I be receiving the information as before?"

Tanner hesitated. "Of course." He raised his head to look around again, then looked beyond Wang, across and behind his shoulders. "What's that?!"

Wang turned, surprised and agitated, to follow Tanner's gaze.

Tanner reached across his own chest with his right hand and pulled a suppressed semi-automatic pistol from the shoulder holster under his left arm. With Wang turned to his right, Tanner pressed the weapon against the Chinese man's left rib cage and pulled the trigger twice. Wang lurched to his right, grunted, flailed, his arms out, turned and fell to the asphalt pavement at his feet. Tanner then pointed the gun at Wang's head and shot him again from a distance of three feet. He then holstered the gun as he looked around, pulled a pair of tight-fitting plastic gloves from his rear pants pocket, reached into his shirt pocket and retrieved a small plastic envelope containing a white powder. He knelt down and stuffed it into Wang's trouser pocket.

Tanner stood back for a few seconds, then walked into the dark of the park from whence he had come. He stopped, returned to the bench, grabbed the dead man's overnight bag, then set out again.

His real name was Stanley Webber, a fact unknown to the recently deceased Tao Wang.

At the opposite edge of the park, as he came to the edge of light created by a street lamp, he casually looked down at his jacket, shirt and pants. He was relieved to note that there was no blood apparent on any of the apparel. He pulled his windbreaker jacket closed, then started the zipper from the bottom and brought it three inches up so that it would not open accidentally and reveal the stark, black weapon under his left arm.

He searched the area again, then walked along a dark side street to a car parked next to the curb. He keyed himself in, then drove away. Ten minutes later, we was on a dirt road that led to the Missouri River. He drove slowly along the rutted, weed- and brush-choked path until he could go no farther, then stopped and extinguished the headlamps. He waited two minutes until his vision became accustomed to the dark, then reached up and switched the dome light to the "off" position. He opened his door, climbed out, and walked slowly and carefully toward the river's edge in the half-light. There, he pulled a handkerchief from his pocket and wiped the pistol and the suppressor clean. He then removed the suppressor from the pistol, and threw each into the water in different directions. He removed the holster and pitched it into the water as well. The handkerchief he dropped to the ground. He kicked away dirt from around the cloth, then pushed it into the depression and covered it completely with the excavated soil. He started to remove the baseball cap, then thought better of it. Back in the car, he turned it around without lights, then made his way carefully to the main road, where he turned the headlamps on and re-traced his route to the airport.

He returned the car to the rental agency, walked empty-handed to the nearly abandoned airport departure lobby and to the Southwest Airlines ticket counter. As he spoke to the ticket agent, he adjusted his dark, unmarked baseball cap lower over his eyes, and looked idly around the immense room. He thanked the black female agent with a mumbled word and a nod of his head, then, after visiting the men's room, found a row of semi-padded chairs where he could stretch out and doze to wait for his 6 AM flight.

When Webber was within a half-mile of his house in suburban Alexandria, with his eyes fixed carefully on the residential street, he leaned over, opened the glove compartment and fished his cell phone out. He powered it on, then entered an auto-dial number on the keypad. In six seconds, he heard a reply.

"Hi. Yeah, hey, sorry. The battery on this damned thing died. Forgot to charge it. Yeah, forgot to charge the damned thing. Hey, no, the dinner went well. Yeah, yeah. He's good. Okay. Right. Sorry. Right. Listen, I didn't sleep well last night. Got a hitch in my git-along. I'll be in late. Tell the chief. Later."

He closed the little phone, slipped it into his shirt pocket, slowed at a corner, and entered another street. It was then that he realized he could barely keep his eyes open, and for a moment, almost dozed off, causing him to lose control of the car. The vehicle swerved a few feet off-track, then his heart rate jumped as he thought of something. He pulled over to the curb, set the transmission into Park, then began to hyperventilate. He removed his glasses and scrubbed his face with his hand.

"Damn it!" He declared under his breath. "God damn it!" He slammed the steering wheel with both palms.

A women in sweats, out for her morning run, watched him as he reacted. She thought of stopping to check on him, then decided against the notion; that she might regret the kindness.

At the Avis Rental Car lot at the Kansas City airport, the girl cleaning the car Webber had used discovered a dark blue overnight bag on the floor in front of the passenger seat. It was among several items forgotten and left in cars turned into the rental company's Lost and Found Department that day. She put it on a shelf in the secured room set aside for that function, then moved on to other chores and promptly forgot about it.

# 6

*T*he houses on both sides of the run-down street mirrored the condition of the neglected, cracked, pot-hole riven asphalt way that divided them. One of the houses, centered between two others, was boarded up. It sported a red condemnation sign on the ratty front door. An ancient, nondescript pickup truck, its paint long ago burned away by the severe New Mexico sun, rested on concrete blocks along one side. All four half-rusted, half- greasy brake drums shown openly, since the wheels and tires went missing long ago.

Marcus Lucero, in the passenger seat of the government car with its white license plate that announced its affiliation, stared at the place on his right as Peter Grayson, at the wheel, pulled alongside the crumbling concrete curb and braked to a stop. "God, look at that place," He said. "Wonder who owns it."

Grayson looked in the same direction, then craned his head around to observe the other houses. "Rest of 'em don't look much better."

"Yeah," Lucero said. He gazed up and down the street as well.

The other houses were nearly all in a state of disrepair with peeling paint, cracked or missing window panes and sad porches. Two of the places also had inoperable vehicles, but with wheels and tires, and those mostly balding. An old car, a stake body truck and a pickup occupied driveways at three of the places. One other car was parked on the street in the wrong direction across from the two government agents.

Grayson spoke. "According to the State Police, the car—the Mercedes— was found right about over there." He pointed. "End of the street. Close to the field."

"Right." Lucero nodded.

"So, let's have a go at this. I doubt if we'll find anything." Grayson pulled the key from the ignition, opened his door and stepped out.

Lucero followed suit, then stood next to the car on the passenger side. He looked at his partner across the top of the car.

Grayson glanced at him. "Let's start with the place next to where the car was." He gestured.

They approached the house that sat back some fifty feet from the cracking, broken-up sidewalk. The residence was narrow, not more than thirty feet wide, and extended into a weed-and debris-choked back yard another fifty feet. Lucero stood back as Grayson rapped on the door. After a second try, the door opened and a lady that Grayson reckoned was crowding eighty, stood in the shadow of the interior. She wore a robe well past its prime, and bent forward as though she suffered from arthritis.

"Yes?" she said. Her voice cracked.

Grayson flashed his ID, and Lucero dug his out at the same time.

"Afternoon, Ma'am. Agent Lucero and I are with the FBI." He gestured toward his partner without looking in his direction. "I'm agent Grayson. We'd like to ask you a couple of questions." He returned his ID folder to an inner pocket.

"Who?" Mouth half open, she squinted at Grayson and glanced at Lucero. She had ignored Grayson's identification as well as Lucero's effort.

Grayson shot a glance at Lucero behind him, his face reflecting pain, then looked at the woman again. "Federal Bureau of Investigation, Ma'am. F-B-I." He stretched out the mnemonic.

"Who?!"

Grayson took a deep breath. "Ma'am, did you see a car parked there? The other day? A couple of days ago?" He turned to point, then faced her again.

"I don't have no car. Can't drive. Pore eyesight." She licked her lips and stared at Grayson, then Lucero in turn. "I shake." She nodded for emphasis, then tugged at the loose garment she wore.

Grayson lowered his head, then raised it. He smiled. "Thank you, Ma'am. Thank you. You take care, now." With that, he turned and moved toward the street. He glanced at Lucero.

Lucero studied the ground as he walked away as well.

The old woman shouted after them, "My boy took the car! Last year! I think it was last year!" She looked around, then at the sky, then retreated into the house and her inner thoughts.

The two federal agents found four more people home and willing to answer questions, three of whom, including a middle-aged man in a wheelchair, had not seen anyone they thought might have come from a mysterious car abandoned along the decrepit street. One of these recalled the car, but had relegated it to lost memory soon after. One of them, an older man, required Lucero's efforts, since he spoke only Spanish.

At the last house on the block, a woman wearing curlers, a bathrobe and slippers, came to the door. She was accompanied by a chubby eight-year old girl. She had seen the car upon recollection, but thought little of it, save that it looked expensive. When asked if she had seen anyone who might have been in the car, she said no.

"I seen him," the girl said.

Lucero knelt down and looked at the girl closely. "What is your name?"

The girl backed up and instinctively grabbed her mother's robe. She put her finger to her lips and looked down as though ashamed.

"My name's Marcus." He smiled. "May I know yours?"

The girl shook her head in the gesture of "no."

Lucero adjusted himself in the uncomfortable position. He cocked his head to one side. He lowered his voice. "Do you think I want to hurt you?"

The girl shook her head again.

"Good," Lucero said, "that's good, because I am not going to hurt you. We are nice men and your mom is right here."

The girl nodded, looked up at her mother, then back at Lucero.

"I told you my name." He pointed vaguely at Grayson. "His name is peter. May I know your name?"

She nodded again, her finger still touching her lips. "Marcie." Her whisper was barely audible.

"What a nice name. Marcie. Hear that, Peter? Her name is Marcie." He paused. "I have a daughter. A little girl, much like you. Her name is Valery."

Marcie nodded, dropped her hand from her mouth, but continued to clutch her mother's robe.

"Marcie," Lucero began, "did you see a man?"

Marcie nodded, wide-eyed.

"Marcie, that's very good. Now, Marcie, we think the man you saw is a friend of ours. A friend of Peter's and me. And we'd like to find him. Would you like to help?"

She nodded again.

"Wonderful. Hear that, Peter? Marcie is such a smart young lady, and she's going to help us." He glanced up at Grayson.

Grayson smiled and nodded at Marcie, his eyebrows up.

Marcie's mother remained mute as she watched the transaction between her daughter and Lucero.

"Now, Marcie," Lucero said, "do you remember what our friend, the man you saw, looked like? Was he tall, was he fat, was he dark? You know. Things like that."

"He was slow."

"Slow? He was slow? What do you mean by that, Marcie?"

"He didn't walk fast."

"I see." Lucero paused and licked his lips. "He was slow. Marcie, did he have a hat? Was he wearing a hat?"

She shook her head with wide emphasis.

"I see." Lucero adjusted his cramped knees. "Uh, was he wearing a shirt? Did he have a jacket? Long pants?"

She shook her head from side to side. "No."

"No?"

"No. He didn't have a jacket." She shook her head with great sincerity.

"I see. Well, Marcie, did he wear long pants?" Lucero glanced at Marcie's mother, then Grayson, before returning his attention to Marcie.

The girl's mother stared down at her daughter.

"Yes."

"Marcie, was his skin like ours? Like you and me, your mother. And Peter?"

She nodded, then took in a deep, young breath, and blurted, "He had mud."

"Mud? He had mud?" Lucero cocked his head to one side and squinted.

"Yes, he had mud." Marcie stared at her interrogator with wide eyes.

"Mud. I see. Where was the mud, Marcie? Where was it on him?"

"His shoes. His shoes had mud." She looked up at her mother with a question.

"Was it a lot of mud, Marcie? On his shoes?"

She took in another breath and blurted her words. "It fell off."

"What fell off, Marcie? The mud? The mud fell off?"

She nodded as she stared at agent Lucero, eyes still wide.

"Marcie, how do you know the mud fell off?"

"I saw it! He scraped it." She tightened the grip on her mother's robe and backed up a pace. She brightened, took in a deep breath, then pointed across the tired street. "He scraped it over there!"

Lucero stood and felt the ache in his knees with both hands. "Over there?"

"Yes. I saw it."

"Very good, Marcie. Very, very good."

Her mother piped up. "She's a good watcher."

Grayson said, "Observant."

"Yeah," the woman said.

The odor of cigarette smoke wafted from her robe.

"Marcie," Lucero continued, "did you see a lot of mud?" He knelt again.

She shook her head and drew in a deep breath. "A little. On his shoe."

"I see, Marcie. Just a little on his shoe."

"Mm-hm." She nodded and looked up at her mother again.

Lucero assumed a squat again to be close to the girl. "Marcie, do you remember the color of the man's hair?"

"Yes."

"What color was it?"

"Sorta' white. Like my grandpa."

"White. Very, good, Marcie. Now, Marcie, do you remember how tall—how big—he was?"

Marcie retreated again. "I don't know." She looked away, then down.

The ache in both of Lucero's legs forced him to return to the erect position. "Marcie, you have been very helpful. Agent Grayson and I want to thank you. And as part of being such a good junior FBI agent, we are going to reward you for your services. First, Agent Grayson and I are going to pay you for your time. Then, Marcie, you will receive, in the mail, a special award for you to keep. Forever. How does that sound?"

"I don't know." Marcie beamed an embarrassed smile.

Grayson and Lucero both peeled off five dollar bills for the little girl, and Grayson jotted their mailing address in his notebook.

As the two federal agents walked to their car, Grayson said, "You drive. I want to ponder this with less distraction." He pitched the keys to Lucero.

"An older man with mud on a shoe," Grayson muttered. He looked at nothing through the windshield.

With Lucero at the wheel, the government car turned the corner onto the secondary street, east-bound.

Lucero threw his partner a silent glance, then concentrated on his driving. His face exhibited concentration. "Should we have collected the mud?"

Grayson thought for a moment. "Not much there. And I think we know where it came from."

"Yeah. Right."

It was then that Grayson's cell phone chirped. His gaze distant in thought, he subconsciously retrieved it from his jacket pocket, opened it and listened. "Grayson." He was silent, then, with the device held against his ear, he reached with his other hand for his small notebook and a pen. "Repeat." Grayson scribbled. "Okay. Got it. Yeah. Yeah. We're headed back. Later." He folded the little phone and returned it to its resting place. "Interesting."

Lucero braked for a stop sign, looked both ways, then accelerated away. "What'cha got?"

"Maybe you remember early on in the GQ case that collateral report that crossed my desk gleaned from CIA about a Chinese business type up in BC? Vancouver?"

"Remind me." Lucero glanced at the rearview mirror, then changed lanes.

"Headquarters had a tip from the company about him. Suspected of passing goodies from someone in the states. Being watched by the boys in red—RCMP." Grayson watched a man unload a crate of vegetables from a pickup, then returned his attention to the road ahead. "Locals found him in a Kansas City park."

"Oh?"

"Very much deceased."

"I see. Tell me more." Lucero guided the sedan right, then up the ramp and onto the Interstate.

"Three bullet holes. .22 caliber. Sub-sonic slugs. One to the forehead. Little baggie of white stuff. Tested positive."

"Frame?"

"You tell me, agent Lucero. You tell me."

# 7

*J*ason and Vera went to a Las Cruces mall, where he bought clothes and shoes, dark glasses, and two head covers; one a white Western straw hat, the other a plaid ivy cap. Then he purchased a laptop computer, a laser printer and a ream of standard white paper.

That night, they stayed in a mid-range motel, ate in a chain restaurant, watched the news, then a movie on the room TV. They saw no reporting on the incident in Truchas. Jason told Vera he felt it odd there was nothing about the two deaths, but that the state and federal governments may have put a lid on the story for security reasons.

He awoke in the middle of the night in a mild, dream-induced panic with thoughts that they knew he was alive, and figured they could flush him out by muzzling the Truchas story. After a time, and using reason, he realized they had nothing, and the news silence was for other purposes, and he drifted back into slumber. It bothered him none the less.

The following day, they drove to El Paso and visited a used car lot, where Jason arranged a cash purchase of a recent model pickup truck. Vera, curious, asked him why he didn't buy a vehicle in New Mexico. He explained he wanted out-of-state plates. He asked her to precede him to the ranch; that he would follow after dark. She was disappointed, but kept her thoughts private.

It was mid-afternoon, after he had settled for a used Toyota pickup, black, that they were back in Las Cruces. They pulled onto a side street, Vera leading. Jason got out of his new acquisition and walked over to Vera's trusty old truck.

"I'll hang around here for awhile, Vera, grab a bite, and be back after dark. Okay? Best you go back alone. I'll follow after dark."

"I worry, Jason. Will you be alright? You look a bit outa' sorts."

"Please don't worry. I'm fine." He kissed her gently on the mouth. "Careful going back." He paused. "You don't mind taking that stuff with you?"

"Nope." She grinned.

He started to turn, then moved back. "Think I'll take the computer. Mess around with it."

"Okay." She reached around for it, and handed him the box.

He awarded her a minimal wave as she drove away, then looked around to see if anyone was watching. There was no one.

He drove the truck slowly along the street, turned a corner, spotted a strip mall, then a pay phone. He parked near the entrance, then walked to the phone and called the Albuquerque house. There was no answer. He dredged up his memory of lab phone numbers, then called Manning's office at the Labs.

Manning picked up. "Manning. Manning here. Hello? Hello?"

Jason pushed the hook down carefully, then stood for several seconds before moving away. From there, he sought, and found, a coffee shop that offered "free wi-fi." Seated at a corner table with coffee, a pastry and the laptop computer open, he studied the booklet that came with the small system. His new soft-cloth Ivy cap remained on his head.

A young man, whom Jason reckoned to be in his early twenties, sat nearby, intent on a laptop computer.

"Excuse me," Jason said. He faced the young man.

The man turned, did a double-take, then returned his gaze to his machine.

"Excuse me," Jason repeated. "Do you have a minute?"

The man looked at him. "Me? Yeah."

"I need some help here. Do you mind?"

"Sure, man. Whatta' ya need?" He rose and stepped over to Jason's table.

"Trying to figure out how to connect to the Internet."

"Oh. Easy." The man dragged a chair over and sat.

Jason offered his hand. "Jason. I appreciate this."

"Hey. No problem. Fred." He smiled, took Jason's hand languidly, looked at the laptop, then at Jason and back. "So, what we got here? Okay—"

Fred spent more than an hour setting Jason's laptop up. Jason bought both more coffee and pastries, and his young, newly-minted, impromptu friend also set up three different Email accounts. He also showed the old, traditional scientist the different "search engines" and how to use them.

Eventually, Fred sprang from his chair after a glance at his watch. "Crap! I gotta'a get outa' here! She'll kill me!" He looked down at a surprised Jason. "Sorry, man."

Jason got up and extended his hand. "Absolutely not, Fred. You've been a great help. I really appreciate it. Now get out of here, and go see whomever she is!" He awarded the young man a wide grin.

Fred shook his hand briefly, turned, gathered his laptop, and raced from the building.

Jason watched him through the big piece of glass that constituted the sidewalk-facing portion of the shop as he ran toward his tryst. He sat, stared at the laptop screen for a moment, then looked outside to gauge the time before checking his watch. It was late afternoon.

Tentatively, he began searching the Internet for the FBI site. Frustrated there, he looked for the name Peter Grayson. He found a number of men with that name, but none were listed as agents of the Federal Bureau of Investigation living in New Mexico. Upon reflection, he realized that would make sense.

He stood, stretched, then went to the counter, ordered and received, a medium "latte" coffee. Offered more pastry, he declined, then returned to the table that had been his work station for more than three hours.

With a sense of dread for which he was unable to account, he sat, sipped the new, hot concoction, then tapped the laptop keyboard to bring up an Internet browser program. Within a few seconds, ads and news stories began to roll up. Each story remained on the screen for a few seconds, then disappeared in favor of another. Stories flashed across the media, then moved on, followed by yet another, attended by photos in most cases. It was after a three-second delay that Jason realized that one of the words in text that popped up was "Truchas." Frantic, he tried to retrieve the story as more came and went. After more than five minutes, and allowing his drink to cool, with experimentation, he found the story and stopped it from evaporating. On the edge of his chair, he read,

"*AP—Santa Fe, NM. The New Mexico State Police report that the bodies of two people, a man and a woman, have been found in a house in the remote mountain village of Truchas, thirty-five miles north of the Capitol. Names of the deceased and cause of death have not been released pending notification of next of kin. No cause for the tragedy has been determined, and authorities are puzzled by the evidence. Speculation is that there may have been a murder-suicide pact.*

*In a related matter, authorities say that a car may have been stolen from the scene, and they seek information on the person or persons who may have taken the car. They believe a man, possibly in his mid- to late sixties, white, or Anglo, and of average build, may be involved. To date, there are no leads, and no more information is available.*

*To add to the bizarre nature of the case, the family of one of the victims claims that their Albuquerque house was broken into, and that personal items and a vehicle are missing."*

Jason stared at the screen for some time, then picked up the cold drink and sampled it. He looked down into the paper cup, made a face, and set it aside. He looked around the room at the few remaining patrons, then shut the computer off, closed it, got up and left, leaving the detritus behind on the small table.

On the sidewalk, he halted, surveyed the mall, spotted a grocery store, and made for the newspaper rack. He picked up copies of *The El Paso Times*, *The Santa Fe New Mexican* and the *Albuquerque Journal,* then went to his truck.

He threw the newspapers onto the passenger seat, then reached into his shirt pocket, retrieved a pill, swallowed it dry, and took in and let out several long breaths to calm himself. His heart still racing, he picked up the first paper.

*The El Paso Times* and the *Journal* had stories about the deaths, but not the missing car. The *Times* treatment was on page three, while the *Journal* story was on page two. The *New Mexican* carried the coverage on page one, below the fold. It was a re-hash of the Internet story, which included the part about the mysterious "older man" associated with the missing vehicle. None of the articles mentioned the break-in.

Jason put the papers aside and stared out the window. Grayson and his partner were not fools. They would soon, if they had not already, realize that Nantes was a fraud, and that when put together with the disappearance of the Mercedes and his close description, they would add the facts and come up with a potentially disturbing conclusion. And, given the manner in which Nantes was able to "con" everyone until the fateful night, his collaborators would triangulate the evidence as well, and not in his favor. He was in danger, and more to the point in his view, Vera Tyler was in danger.

He started the engine, rolled out of the parking lot and looked for a fast food outlet where he could find something to eat on his trip back to the ranch.

# 8

*A*gents Grayson and Lucero stood inside the living room of the Thompson house in Albuquerque with APD officers Standish and Levin. They were in a small semi-circle in front of Florence and her brother, Justin, both of whom sat on the sofa facing them.

Grayson had his hand to his lowered chin, his mood contemplative. He glanced at officer Levin. ".32 caliber shells? On the floor?"

Levin looked at him. He nodded. "Yeah. Three. Gun missing." He looked down at Justin. "Right? The pistol is gone?"

Justin nodded in the positive. "Yes, it's gone. I mean, I can't find it." He leaned forward, both arms on his knees. He waved his hands in frustration. "But I hardly ever saw it. My dad kept it hidden."

Officer Standish pointed vaguely at the broken vase on the floor. "Stumbled around in the dark." He looked at the two siblings in turn, then the FBI agents.

"So it would seem," Grayson offered. "Justin," he continued, "the pistol was kept where? In a closet in you parents' bedroom?"

Justin rolled his eyes up, searching his memory. "I think so. Yes. On a shelf." He stared at the agent.

Grayson looked at Levin. "The master bedroom was messed up? Ransacked?"

Levin cocked his head. "To an extent. Whoever was in here was in a hurry. Stuff got tossed."

Flo rose from the sofa and walked slowly to the front windows. Without turning her head, she spoke. "I owe you an apology."

Grayson turned in her direction and shot a glance at his partner, Lucero. "I'm sorry, Flo; I didn't hear you."

She faced him and raised her voice. "I owe you an apology. Both of you."

Grayson sighed and shook his head. "No need, Flo. No need."

Lucero nodded. "Same here. I appreciate it. It's been rough for your family."

She walked back toward the sofa where her brother sat, then stopped. "Who would break in here? Take dad's gun. And his truck?"

Lucero moved toward her a step. "Do you know of anyone—in the family or not—who knew of the truck and would have taken it?"

Flo shook her head slowly, as did Justin.

"Are you looking for it?" Flo asked. She looked at the two policemen.

Levin spoke. "There's a BOLO out."

"BOLO?" She frowned.

"Be on the lookout," Standish put in.

"My dad had friends. At work. They knew. They had a sort of a club. Old cars and trucks." Justin looked at each of the men, then his sister.

"That's right," Flo said. "But none of them—"

Officer Levin asked, "Can you put together a list? The car club?"

Both Thompson siblings shook their heads as they looked at each other, then at the policeman.

Levin made a face and looked at Grayson with a shrug.

Grayson paced away, his head down in thought. "I agree. Far fetched. Someone else."

The two police officers moved toward the front door.

Levin turned. "We'll be movin' along. You let us know if anything turns up, or you can think of anything else." He looked from Flo to Justin, then at the federal agents in turn. "Grayson. Lucero." He tipped two fingers to his forehead.

"Thanks, guys," Grayson said. "We'll be in touch." He moved to a chair placed at an angle to the sofa and sat. "Do either of you know any of your parents' friends? Your mother's? It would be good if we had a list." He looked from Justin to Flo, who regained her seat on the sofa.

Both shook their heads.

Flo spoke. "Peter—agent Grayson—I left almost twenty years ago. Justin left—how long, now, Justin?" She looked at her brother.

Justin cocked his head, then shook it slowly. Ten—no, eleven—years ago. I don't know anybody. Any of their friends." He looked up.

"I have no idea," Flo said.

Lucero, who had moved to the front windows, returned to the center of the room. He looked from sibling to sibling. "Do either of you know if your mom or dad kept a journal? Notebook? Maybe a call list?"

Flo looked down, then up. "Mom may have."

"Could you look?" Lucero asked.

Flo stood. "Sure. I'll have a look in mom's drawers." She turned to her brother. "Justin, why don't you look around the kitchen, then in dad's stuff?"

"Okay," he said, and got up.

As the Thompson siblings left the room, Lucero went to Grayson. He leaned over, close to Grayson's head. "We scoured the studio during the case. Nothing, right?"

Grayson looked up, then away. "Right. Nada." He paused. "Except for that clay thing. They were careful."

"What about the garage?" Lucero asked.

"No warrant."

"Yeah, right."

"I wonder if they'd let us look?" Grayson mused.

"Maybe," Lucero said.

The tone both men used was subdued and heavy with frustration.

Justin came back into the room. "I found this calendar notebook." He flipped it open and peered at a page. "Some dates in here. My mom's watercolor club. Couple 'a things about dinners." He handed the book to Lucero, who remained standing.

"Thanks," Lucero said.

Justin sat down as his sister came down from the bedroom story. She carried a small, black book.

Justin jumped up. "I forgot about dad's stuff." He turned and mounted the stairs.

Flo handed the book to Grayson, who had risen from his chair.

"Thank you, Flo," he said.

She went to the sofa. "I don't know what's in there, but I trust it will be treated with discretion."

"It will. I'm going to give you a receipt," Grayson said.

"Could we have your permission to take a look in the garage?" Lucero asked.

Flo took a second, then responded, "Yes—yes. I see no reason why not."

"You or Justin will have to accompany us," Grayson said.

"Oh? Flo furrowed her brow.

"We have no warrant," Lucero said. "It must be with your consent and presence."

"Of course. I'll go with you."

"I can't find anything." This from Justin as he returned from his search.

Grayson looked at him. "Okay, Justin. Thanks."

"We're going to the garage, Justin," Flo said.

Justin nodded and Grayson, Lucero and Flo moved for the outer kitchen door.

Flo keyed the trio into the garage through the door with the broken glass pane, then Grayson and Lucero began a cursory look around the big empty space. The men separated and strolled along the walls and looked at everything in general and nothing in particular. Flo stood near the door, watching, her arms folded across her chest. When Lucero passed by Jason's workbench with the tool rack on the wall above it, he stopped and fingered some of the items on the bench. Then he looked down under the bench surface and opened the cabinet doors beneath. As he closed the last door, he said to no one in particular, "Guess there's no way of knowing where Mr. Thompson kept the key to his pickup."

"I certainly can't tell you, Mr. Lucero," Flo said. There was no malice in her voice.

"I understand," Lucero said.

Both federal agents thanked Flo and Justin. They reminded them that they would stay in touch and advise them of anything new in all three pending cases. They also asked that if either of them had anything of value to offer to please call. They both presented them with their cards, and Grayson gave Flo a receipt for her mother's journal, which he guaranteed would be returned shortly.

In the car, Lucero asked Grayson how he would handle the journal. Grayson assured him that the book would be subjected to every "eyeball" and laboratory scrutiny in the Bureau's arsenal. Lucero allowed as how he'd like to take a closer look at the garage without being observed by the owners. Grayson concurred.

"Warrant?" Lucero asked.

Grayson looked out his window on the passenger side. "Maybe. We'd need probable cause."

"Black bag?" Lucero watched the road ahead.

"Could be."

Lucero was quiet.

Grayson looked at him. "And we can't find the Sanchez woman."

"We'll find her."

"Might be nothing, but suspicious, given those contacts she had with the Thompson woman."

"Yep."

"We need to find her."

Lucero nodded and spoke in a low tone. "As I said. We'll find her."

Grayson sniffed and looked away. "Did the package go out?"

"Jan handed it off to the courier yesterday." Lucero shot Grayson a glance. "Think your guy can ID it?"

Grayson shrugged. "Time will tell."

"Nantes. Your company guy didn't know 'im?"

Grayson shook his head. "No. He said he'd poke around. He has a copy of the picture on the driver's license."

"And no more next of kin for Sarah Thompson besides her kids," Lucero said.

Grayson scratched a spot on his forehead. "Orphaned. According to her bio and her kids. Maybe; maybe not."

"Who's your guy at CIA?"

"Madsen. Jerry Madsen." Grayson was terse.

"Reliable?"

Grayson shot Lucero a look. "Yes, Marcus." He looked away. "I know what you're thinking. Nantes. I've known Jerry a long time. Old time bureau type. He's okay." He shifted in his seat with the irritation he felt. "Which reminds me; have we gotten off that thing we promised the little girl down south?"

Lucero shot him a glance. "You mean Marcie in Socorro?"

"Yes."

"May surprise you, but yes. I had Jan send off one of the kid's award certificates. She can frame it."

"You know what the odds are of that."

"10-4, boss."

Grayson shot his companion a frown then looked away in silence.

Jason pulled into the ranch garage at a few minutes past ten. He shut the engine down and the headlamps off, then, in the dark, felt his way to take the laptop and lay it in the bed of his new truck while he went to his old, re-built one. With the dome light on, he keyed open the glove compartment, zipped open the leather pouch, and felt for the notebook. This he stuffed into a rear pants pocket, returned the pouch to the dashboard box and locked it.

As he walked into the house, the light in the bedroom came on and Vera straggled into the living room. She wore a shapeless cotton gown that reached to her ankles. "You're here." She smiled sleepily, both her hands to the sides of her head.

"Yes, home again, home again." He grinned. He set the laptop onto a chair seat and went to her.

They hugged and kissed in the shadow created by the meager light emanating from the bedroom. The top of her head reached his eyes.

"Did you eat?" She backed away to look at him. "I have something for you. Cold supper. Sandwich?"

He demurred. "I grabbed something on the way. Thanks."

"Yeah. Some o' that awful food from a burger whatcha-ma-callit." She threw her hand out in a dismissive wave and made a face.

"You're right."

"How'd it go? Anything?" She sobered.

He pulled away and walked back to the chair with the computer. "Yes. Articles in the papers and on the Internet." He picked the machine up.

Vera stroked her hair in a nervous gesture. "Did—did they say anything 'bout you?"

Jason thought for a moment. He frowned. "Not exactly. Reference to an older man who might have a connection with the missing car." He looked directly at her, then away, as he gathered his thoughts.

Vera, silent, shook her head. "What does that mean? Do you think?"

He raised his eyebrows. "I don't know. They—the authorities—think I'm dead. It doesn't prove anything." He paused. "Although . . . "

"Yes?"

He sighed. "Hey, lady. Let's get some sleep. You were asleep, and I require it. I'm bushed." He turned. "I'll be right in. Gonna put this in my new office!" He smiled at her as he held up the little computer.

She returned his expression. "Alright now, you! You be quick!" She turned and retreated to the bedroom.

Jason went to the other bedroom which he had commandeered as his office and flicked the solitary lamp on. He put the laptop on the table that substituted for a desk, then looked around for a place to hide the book he took from his pants pocket. He stopped and stared at the old door frame. He moved toward it slowly, then ran his fingers up the right side. The old, dried, four-inch wide decorative slat ran from the floor to the cross piece. In two places, at eye level, the plaster had broken off, leaving a two-inch gap under the frame. Jason inserted the little book into the crack. It fit. He removed it to test its availability, then re-inserted it. He turned, surveyed the room for two seconds, shut the light off, and went to join Vera.

*9*

*S*tanley Webber awoke at around one-thirty in the afternoon. For a few seconds after he opened his eyes, he was startled, because he didn't know where he was, which kicked his heart rate into high. Then he realized he was in his own bed in his own house in Alexandria. He turned to his right to see if Angelina were there, but she wasn't, and he recalled that she and their two pre-teen children had gone to South Carolina to visit her parents.

He sat up, and slightly dizzy, sat on the edge of the bed for ten seconds to allow his body to recover its bearings. He stood, and felt a slight pain in the small of his back, then took three steps to inspect his image in the floor-length mirror on the closet door. What he saw was an average-size man with dark, but greying hair, wearing a wrinkled, under arm sweat-stained white tee-shirt and like-colored boxer shorts.

As he stood in the shower with the warm water rushing over him, shaving, he recounted the events of the night before. The thought of the pistol jerking in his hand caused him to twitch involuntarily, and he nicked his chin with his razor.

Dressed in a dark sports jacket and coordinated pants with his security badge evident on his jacket lapel, Webber passed through the security check and into the wide main corridor of the Central Intelligence Agency. He strode quickly along the way, then marched into a side hall to his right. Within two steps, he nearly collided with a man and a woman who came from the opposite direction. They side-stepped each other with smiles and unnecessary apologies and moved on.

"Hey, Stan." Jerry Madsen came toward Webber, nodded at him, then walked on.

"Jerry," Webber replied. He cocked his head and kept up his pace.

Madsen halted, turned and raised his voice. "Stan! Hey, Stan! Hold up."

Webber stopped and turned to face Madsen as the other man approached him.

"Yeah, Jerry. What can I do you for?"

Madsen came close to Webber, lowered his head and shifted a folder he carried from one hand to the other. He looked about and spoke in a low tone. "Stan, listen. I hear you're connected with arms research, ID and config. True?"

Webber was silent for a second, then, "Yeah; yeah, I am." He furrowed his brow.

"Listen, if I bring something to you, you think you could have a look and tell me the whys and wherefores?"

Webber shook his head in puzzlement. "What—what is it, Jerry?"

"I don't have it yet, but will soon. Hand weapon. I need an analysis. On the Q T. Can you do it?"

"Inside or outside channels?"

"Uh, maybe on the outside. Not sure yet." He leaned forward, screwed up his face as though in pain, looked around again, then faced Webber. "Like you to take a peek first. Off site. Then we'll go from there. Okay?" He righted himself.

"Time frame?"

"Soon. Day or two. You at the same number?"

Webber nodded.

"Okay. I'll get back." Madsen held up his finger in assurance, turned and rushed away.

Webber stood still for several seconds, then turned slowly and continued. He studied the floor as he moved.

He used his badge with the encoded magnetic stripe on the back side to unlock the door to his office. Government- Spartan in appearance and function, it measured, as did all offices along the long hall, twelve feet by twelve feet, with a standard 8-foot ceiling. A computer screen and keyboard sat on the desk, along with the standard appurtenances required of a federal functionary. The desk was clean. No papers or open volumes, and the security file cabinet was closed, locked and signed as such, with the dial "zero" in red, straight up.

Webber sat behind the desk, the blinds over the window behind him shuttered. He pulled in close, then reached out to the button-rich phone, picked up the handset, and touched a key. After a five second wait, he heard an answer. "Yes, good afternoon. I'd like to order some flowers. Yes . . . "

He offered the name of the recipient, address and credit card information, said thank you and hung up. He sat back, stared at the desk top, then took in and let out a deep breath. His expression was one of deep concern. He looked at his watch, engaged the phone again, and spoke.

"Yeah, Hal. In. Yeah, feeling better. Rough night. Musta' been the salsa." He grinned into the mouthpiece. "Yeah, I'll go over that report and get you an analysis. No. Late. Angelina and the brood are at her mother's. Yeah. South Carolina. I know, I know. Right. In the morning for sure. Got it. K."

He rang off, wiped his mouth with his hand, rose from his chair, went to the secured file cabinet and twisted the combination lock dial.

The time was 14 minutes past nine that evening when Webber folded the cover over the file he had updated, dropped it into a Pendaflex hanging file slot in the secure file cabinet, closed the drawer and spun the combination lock dial. The time on the security check station clock read 9:24 when he showed his badge and walked toward the main lobby outside door.

As he approached his residence, he slowed, then craned his neck about, scouring the front of his house, the sidewalk, and the neighborhood in general. He accelerated, circled the block, then guided his car up the driveway and into the garage past the remotely-controlled door. Inside, he killed ignition, touched the button on the remote transmitter, and the door behind the car closed.

He entered a code into the security panel next to the house door, waited for the green LED to glow, then keyed himself into the house and allowed the door to close and latch. The first room he entered was small. It contained Winter boots, coats, hats, gloves, two snow shovels and other snow, water, dirt and mud clean-up tools. Cabinets high up sheltered more arcane devices and products used on occasion. From there, he entered the kitchen, where he hung the car keys on a hook over a scribble-covered dry-erase board, then opened the refrigerator and peered in. He grabbed a bottle of beer, set it on the counter, then opened two of the food storage drawers. He found two pieces of fried chicken; a wing and a breast. With both in hand, he tore a piece of paper towel off the roll under a cabinet and lay it on the counter next to the beer. He put the chicken breast on the paper, then gnawed on the wing before opening the beer and gulping a mouthful.

With his late night hunger and thirst under control, he headed for the front door. There, he found three pieces of mail on the floor under the slot in the door for that purpose. With mildly chicken-greasy fingers, he picked the envelopes up, looked them over, then set them on a side table. The remainder of the chicken wrapped in paper towel and the half bottle of beer were cradled against his chest as he opened the door to the stairs that led to the basement. He flicked on the light to illuminate the steps, then made his way down after closing the door. At the bottom, he opened another door that led into a small room on his right. He operated the switch next to the door on the inside, and a lamp on a desk across the small space popped on.

He put the remnants of the viands and bottle on the desk, sat and finished both. He wiped his hands on the towel after throwing the bones, which had bits of left-over, grey meat clinging to them, into a trash container, then brought the computer on the desk top to life.

He surfed to a special web site, used a unique name and password set, then wrote, "Lovelady needs assistance in hinterland now. More to come."

He thought about the message for several seconds, then, with the mouse, pointed to and clicked on the "Send" command. The message was fired off with high-numeric encryption.

He turned the computer off, took the bottle, killed the light, and mounted the stairs to the main floor of the house. After securing everything there, he went to the bedroom he shared with Angelina. As he disrobed, we went to the window that faced the street and looked out. The half-light from the street lamp revealed that the way was devoid of vehicles and people, but he saw a light-haired cat move surreptitiously from the sidewalk onto the lawn.

Two thousand miles to the west, Jason Thompson, awoke with his right arm numb and his nasal passages uncooperative. He turned, listened for Vera's slow, rhythmic breathing, then crept from the bed with care. He tip-toed from the room, grateful that the old floor boards did not move against each other to create sound. Barefoot and in nothing more than his underwear, he walked out onto the hard pan and into the nearly pitch-black night. He removed a small pebble that lodged between his right big toe and the next one, then shook off what he imagined was an ant on a late-night mission for its busy earth-bound clan.

He looked up at the slowly rotating stars, then at the faint outline of the mesa ridge where the Piper Cherokee had crashed, then later burned. He thought of his children, Sarah, Mel Vaslovic, Nantes, then the people with whom he had worked for so long at Rio Grande Labs. His stomach turned at the thought of what he must do. Who, beside the federal government would be looking for him, dead or alive? What did they want—any and all of them? What was the end game? Who was he, after all?

He turned toward the house, glanced in the direction of the two pickup trucks secreted in the barn-cum-garage, then picked his way back to the porch, into the house, and to the bed where the newly-found woman and friend in his life lay gently in slumber.

# 10

*J*erry Madsen pecked his wife, Jane, on the cheek and left his house in Reston, then traveled the short distance to Dulles International Airport. After parking his car in the garage general area, he made his way to the Midway Air Package Pickup Office. He showed his ID and signed for the five pound package from Albuquerque.

After he left the airport grounds, he pulled over to the side of the highway and keyed a number into his cell phone, put the device up to his ear, and listened. "Stan. Jerry. Madsen. Yeah. Early. Sorry. Listen, I have that item. Right, right. Pick a place. Just between the two of us for now. Yeah, yeah. Later."

He sat for a moment, looked at his watch, checked his rearview mirrors, then pulled out into traffic. He had started to call Grayson, but realized that it was two hours earlier in New Mexico.

His cell phone chirped. He opened it and held it to his ear. "Madsen. Yeah, Stan. Okay. Got it. Half hour. Right."

Webber arrived first at the Tyson's Corner Galleria, and guided Madsen to his car by phone. He had parked as close to the entrance of the huge parking lot as he could, faced out. Madsen found a spot three slots away. When Madsen saw him pull in, he waited several seconds, then emerged, left his car unlocked and walked to Madsen's vehicle. As instinct and training dictated, he surveyed the area in an unobtrusive manner. When he arrived at Madsen's car, he opened the front passenger door and slipped in.

"Jerry," he said. He did not offer his hand, nor did he look at his mobile host.

"Stan. Thanks for coming." His inflection rose, as though voicing a question, when saying his guest's name.

"We aim to please." He offered Madsen a wry smile as he cocked his head in the direction of the man next to him. "You got the item?"

"I do, indeed." Madsen reached under his seat and withdrew a thin, brown paper-wrapped cardboard box. It was covered with labels and bar-code stickers. He handed it to Webber.

As Webber took the package, he looked out of the car windows.

"We're okay," Madsen said. His voice low and unassuming.

Webber nodded and looked down. "Yeah; I know. Force of habit."

"Yep. Serves us well. Most of the time." Madsen smiled.

"So. What's inside?" Webber shot Madsen a glance. "I guess this's not a good place to open it."

"Right. Not a good place." He sighed. "Pistol. Doesn't fire bullets. Fires darts. Nasty ones."

Webber looked at Madsen, his head bent, his eyebrows raised. "Really?

"Really."

"Hm. Fascinating." He caressed the surface of the package with the palm of his hand.

"You got that right." Madsen nodded.

"I guess you're not in a position to tell me from whence it came?"

"Eh, not now." Madsen turned his head to glance around at what he could see of the lot.

"Company?"

Madsen shook his head. "No." He hesitated. "Don't think so. Out there in the weeds. Most likely."

"Even more intriguing."

"Think you can help?"

"So, do you know the track, or is it third party top secret?"

"Eh, kinda' sorta' where it was discovered. Under wraps for now. Not the origin. That's what I need to know. What I can say is there might be some embarrassing implications for some folks." He lowered his head and looked at Webber from under his eyebrows.

"Us folks?" Webber pointed at his own chest.

"Possible." Madsen waved his hands in a dismissive manner.

"Wait a minute, Jerry. I need more than that." He shook his head with a sour look and lowered his voice. "You know more than you're saying."

Madsen hesitated and looked out his window, then back at Webber. "You're right. I do know more. But I'm sworn, man!" He lowered his voice to a whisper.

"Well, all I gotta' say is, it's gotta be something big." He paused, then lowered his voice. "Thing is, Jerry, ole' man, I don't need to get in the middle of something that could mess me up."

"I get that. I get that." Madsen nodded emphatically. "But you won't. Hey, just have a look at this piece and let me know. Hell, look at it, photograph it. Encrypt the files, then hand it back. Poke around. Whatever." He raise his eyebrows and threw his hands out. "Okay?"

Webber sighed deeply. "Yeah. Okay."

"Can you help? I repeat." Madsen looked at him with sincerity.

"I'll try. What's your drop-dead?"

"A-sap."

Webber paused. "Okay. I'll get on it."

"Thanks."

"I'll call you."

Madsen nodded wordlessly.

"Hey, good to see ya." Webber opened his door and stepped out.

Madsen peered at Webber and started the engine. Webber strode away, the package held tightly in his right hand at his side.

In his basement office, Webber placed the package Madsen had given him carefully on his tool bench, then pulled on a pair of thin, white cotton gloves. With a sharp knife, he cut open the brown outer wrapping paper and fed it into the shredder next to his desk. With studied care, he cut the tape that bound the flat cardboard box, and opened it. Inside, he found the hand weapon also wrapped, this in clear plastic, sealed with tape. He cut through the covering, placed that in a trash bin, then picked up the pistol.

He peered at it closely as he turned it over several times at different angles. He moved to his desk, sat in the roll-around arm chair, and flicked on a high-intensity light that flooded the desk surface. He inspected the flat sides of the chamber portion, then opened the desk drawer and pulled out a magnifying glass. He saw that the markings had been filed down such that they were unintelligible to the naked eye, even with the glass.

He laid the heavy, blue-steel object down carefully, then stared ahead at the wall, pondering.

After locking the weapon in his hidden office safe, he trudged up to the bedroom he and his absent wife shared. As he removed his tie with slow, deliberate movements, he stood at the street side window. The street and sidewalk were quiet. He leaned forward and peered first left, then right to observe the front of the house as far as he could. He then closed the blinds and turned away.


"Jerry? Stan."

Jerry Madsen swivelled to one side in his desk chair as he held the telephone headset to his ear. "Yeah—yeah. What's up, Stan?"

"Hey, you into baseball?"

"Uh, yeah . . ." Madsen leaned forward, picked up a pen and began to doodle on the calendar pad that covered much of his desk's surface. His mouth dropped open as he waited for Webber's next remark.

"Gotta a couple a' extra tickets I can't use. Thought you might like 'em."

"Eh, why, sure, Stan . . ." Madsen frowned and looked at the ceiling as he kept the pen moving.

"Let's do lunch, and I'll turn 'em over. It's for tonight."

"Yeah, yeah. Sure."

"Meet ya' in the lot. Eleven-thirty okay? We'll take my car."

"Okay. Right. Eleven-thirty."


Madsen got into the passenger seat of Webber's car, and they pulled out onto the CIA Roadway past the guard shacks and onto Route 123, Dolly Madison Boulevard. From there, they headed to McLean.

Webber glanced at Madsen. "Fast food okay? I'd like to avoid a sit-down. What I have to say won't take long, but better we're not seen."

"Not a problem," Madsen answered.

"Not that there's a chance it'd make any difference, but caution's the by-word." He turned the wheel and the car entered a secondary street.

"Right. Right." Madsen nodded. "I'm all ears."

Webber drove through an ordering and pick-up lane, and both men ordered hamburgers, fries and cold drinks. Webber parked the car in the business lot.

As Webber opened his victuals in his lap, he spoke. "You need to know what I found—which isn't much, Jerry."

Madsen, his mouth full, said, "What you got?"

Webber took a bite, chewed and swallowed. "Not much. And I need help."

Madsen shot him a glance. "Yeah? What sort of help?"

"As you might expect, there are no identifying marks. On the gun. They've been ground off. Expertly." He took another bite, brushed some crumbs off of his pant leg, finished, then said, "I can't determine the origin."

Madsen murmured, "Mm."

"Yeah."

"Now what?" Madsen looked at him.

"Tell me."

Madsen frowned. "Tell you what?"

"Tell me. What's the story? Where'd the piece come from?" Webber's voice carried a trace of low-tone menace.

"Shit." Madsen wadded up the stiff paper his burger had been wrapped in and dropped it to the floor of the car.

Webber shook his head. "I gotta know more. Plus, if we need to know names and numbers, then I gotta have access to an x-ray." He pursed his lips.

"X-ray?"

"X-ray. Shows the impressions in the steel. Even with 'em removed. We could read the markings. The kind of X-ray they use to check welds. Pipes."

Madsen looked out his window, then down. "You guys got x-ray, no?" He bit into his sandwich.

Webber moved his head in a way that demonstrated his frustration, and the tone of his answer revealed it. "Yes, Jerry, but with something—something like a piece—especially a piece like this, there's all kinds of headaches." He held his hamburger up to his mouth and took a huge bite.

Madsen shook his head. "Yeah. What kind of headaches?" He spoke past the food in his mouth.

Webber turned to face madsen. With the sandwich in his left hand, he held up his freed right hand and began to fold his fingers back one by one. "You gotta' sign it in, photograph it, declare its ownership and origin, then—"

"Okay. Okay. I get it." Madsen sighed. He looked away, then back. "I get it." He spoke softly.

"Where'd the piece come from, Jerry?" Webber stared straight ahead.

"I've sworn not to say. To secrecy."

"Goddamn it, Jerry, I'm gonna divorce myself from this gig unless you get straight with me! That's it."

Madsen sighed again. He turned his heavy body toward Webber as he finished chewing and swallowing. "Okay. But goddamn it, you keep this to yourself, Stan. Clear?" He wagged his finger.

Webber nodded. "Clear. I don't need trouble, and this sounds like trouble."

"Maybe. Not sure. But here's what I know, and it's not much . . ."

Madsen revealed what he knew from his FBI source. When he mentioned the name of the dead man whose death was caused by the dart pistol, Webber's eyes rolled around in his head. He stared straight ahead. "Who'd you say? What's the guy's name?"

"Nantes. Why?"

"Uh, peculiar. That's all." He made a negative gesture with his head.

Madsen was quiet, then, with his eyes narrowed, said, "You heard of this guy?"

Webber shook his head in shirt, rapid movements. "No. No. Of course not. As I said—"

"Hey, Stan, if you know something—"

"I don't, Jerry!" He raise his voice as he shot a severe glance at his companion. "I don't, goddamn it!" He paused and lowered his voice. "I mean, why would I? This whole thing—" He balled up the paper which had protected the hamburger, and flipped it over his shoulder onto the rear seat.

"Alright. Okay. Take it easy. We're all intense. No big deal."

"Right. Right. No biggie."

"So, where do we go from here? I need to get this thing ID'd."

Webber, calmer, blew out a long breath. "I'll figure it out. Can't say now, but I'll figure it out." He nodded. "I'll find an X-ray."

Madsen chewed on the last morsel of his hamburger and dusted his hands between his legs. "Good. I have confidence you will."

Stanley Webber dropped Jerry Madsen off at CIA headquarters, then drove out of the compound and back onto Route 123. His mood was somber as he drove under the speed limit, causing more than one other driver to exercise the horn on their vehicle. Jerry Madsen had suggested a possible x-ray source exclusive of the "company," but his thoughts were directed at the story Madsen had told. Especially the name of the dead man.

One hand on the wheel, he grabbed his cell and called his office to let them know he would be absent the remainder of the day. An angry motorist blared his horn as Webber drifted into the wrong lane.

In his basement office, the door secured, he fired up his computer and sent an encrypted message.

Madsen walked into his office, shut the door and sat behind his desk. Next, he invoked a special web site, keyed in the appropriate identifiers, and sent a prime number-encrypted message to Grayson over the Kappa network.

In the Albuquerque office of the FBI, Agent Peter Grayson sat and pondered a gallery of photographs tacked to a tack-wall in his cubicle when a chirp from his computer indicated the receipt of incoming mail.

## 11

*J*ason shared breakfast with Vera, helped to feed the animals, then retreated to his ad-hoc office. With Vera tending the garden, he retrieved the small book he had secreted in the door frame, took it to the desk, sat, and opened it. He briefly looked through the open door to ensure that he was not observed, then began to pore over the contents. With a ball-point pen, he made several notes in a pocket pad, then returned the book to the crack in the wall.

Over a bowl of pork stew at lunch, Jason spoke, his head down. He looked at Vera across from him from under his eyebrows. "I need to go."

Vera nodded, pinched her lips together, then looked up. "For good?"

He smiled and shook his head. "No, Vera, dear. I'll be back." He paused, took a sip of water, then continued, "I need to get to work."

She cocked her head. "Yes?"

He sighed as he toyed with the remainder of the stew with his spoon. "Someone besides Nantes knew I was here. Someone besides Nantes knew I had survived the crash and fire."

"And?"

"As I told you, I'm a loose end." He rose, went to the window over the sink and looked out. He saw one of the horses grazing past the pasture fence. He lowered his voice. "They don't know what or how much I know." He turned and studied the floor. "And I know little. There had to be a connection between Nantes and Mel. Mel and Sarah. There had to be something—" He went silent and paced away toward the opening to the living room. He shook his head. "God!"

Vera got up and moved toward him, then stopped.

He spun around to face into the kitchen and looked down at the old planks which constituted the floor. "I've got to unravel this. Not just for me. You could be in danger. My kids."

"Will you tell the FBI?"

He looked up at her, his face pinched. "No. Not now." He pondered. "Eventually."

She shook her head. "Can't they help?"

He moved toward her with his arms splayed out. "Vera, I don't know who to trust. I think Grayson is okay, but is there someone else? At the labs? The FBI?" He moved across the room and threw his arms up, then down. "I know, I know. It sounds crazy." He stopped, went silent, then continued. "I honestly don't know what I'm doing, or exactly how to do it, but I must." He looked at her pleadingly. "I hope you understand."

"I do, Jason." She waited, then, "How long will you be gone?" Her voice had lowered to a whisper.

He paused, then, "I don't know." He faced her. "I worry about you."

"Me?" She moved toward him.

"They know—someone knows—knows where this place is." He held up his hand with the first and second fingers pointed out. "Two things. If they come back—and I don't know if it would be more than one—if I'm not here." He paused. "If I'm not here, they might look around, then move on. But if I am here . . . " He stopped, looked blankly at nothing, then, "If I'm here, it could get dicey." He looked at her. "That could involve you. You're vulnerable. But if I'm not around . . ."

"They would leave me alone?"

He nodded. His expression was grim.

"I don't know how much time I have."

She nodded. "I know." She moved closer. "I'm sorry. So sorry."

"Thanks. I'll be okay. I just want you to be okay."

They hugged, then Jason pulled away, driven by his anxiety.

"What will you do? How will you find out? Where—" She held out her arms.

He moved farther away. "I have some ideas. I have to go back. To Albuquerque. I think I know—"

"Isn't that dangerous? Someone might see you." Her voice carried a plea.

"It is. Possibly. I have no choice. That's where it began and ended."

"Will you stay in touch with me?"

He took in a deep breath. "I want to, but—"

"I know. Stupid of me." She looked away as her voice trailed off.

"We'll work on it. You'd have to leave the ranch. To get messages."

She nodded.

He moved to the chair he had used during lunch and sat. He scratched his cheek. "The people at the store. The station and store. Where we went first when I was here?" He looked up at her.

She moved to the other chair. "Yes?"

"You know them?"

"Yes. Yes. Alice and Jorge. Known 'em a long time."

"You trust them." It was a question spoken as a statement.

She nodded and smiled. "Yes. I do."

He thought for a moment. "I could call and leave messages for you."

She nodded agreement, thoughtful in the process.

He looked away, pondering. "We need a code. Something so that only you know what the message says."

She looked at him, wide-eyed, with a concerned frown.

"I'll work on something. Needs to be simple. Something we can understand quickly."

She whispered, "Yes."

"Hm." He looked at her. "I'll give you a book to give them. They can write the messages down." He was silent again. "But who will be leaving messages? And why? They'll get suspicious."

She nodded gravely.

"Need to work this out fast. There's not a lot of time." He stood.

"Yes . . ."

"No! No. Better idea. I don't like the station." He jabbed his finger at nothing.

Vera cocked her head. "Why?"

"No. Listen. We use cell phones."

"What? I don't think they'll work—"

He paced away in thought. "I know. But I think there's service along the highway." He looked at her with determination. "You'd have to drive to the highway anyway. Then you call me. Not the other way around."

"Oh . . ."

"Right. And no one need know. No subterfuge."

She nodded with a wan smile.

"But we would have to be circumspect in what was said. No real names. No real places, and so on. You know, they can listen to what's been said."

"My god." She paused. "Who?!"

"If they—the FBI—or whoever. If they found the numbers. The chances of that happening are remote. But—"

"Yes."

He took in a deep breath, exhaled and looked at her. "You need a gun."

"I have a gun."

"A pistol. You need a pistol. Do you have one?"

She shook her head. "No."

"We need to go to Cruces. Real quick. You'll have to apply to buy the pistol. I can't. I have the money."

"Why do I need a pistol?" She frowned.

He nodded emphatically. "Because, Vera, my dear lady, you need something you can keep close. Even when you come to call me. I can't predict, but I am nearly certain that we—you—will get a visit. I don't know who, when or how, or how many. I want to be here, but I'm not—" He paused. "I want you safe. I know it's a lot . . ."

She nodded, stood, and walked toward the outer door.

"I'm sorry," he said. His voice was close to a whisper.

Turned away, she shook her head. "It's okay."

He barely heard her words.


They drove to Las Cruces in Vera's pickup. She purchased a 9mm Beretta Nano semi-automatic pistol with holster and a box of ammunition. Jason instructed her on what to say and do while he remained outside and out of sight.

The transaction took up the better part of an hour, principally because of the background check. They then visited an electronics store, where she arranged for two cell phones on the "family plan." In each case, Jason provided her with cash.

On their return, they stopped for food and fuel.

The following morning, Jason went through a brief training regimen with both the armament and the little communication devices. He told her she should follow him to the main highway upon his exit, where they could make a live test of the phones.

Concerned over who might see him leave, Jason, followed by Vera in her vehicle, left the ranch at dusk. It was dark when they reached the highway. They parked both trucks in a space with a wide, flat shoulder, and Jason got into Vera's truck. They were able to get a decent signal, and to link up.

Jason pulled Vera in close. They hugged and kissed, and she began to cry.

"I'm really worried, Jason," she whispered through tears. "You've been through so much. And I've waited so long for you. Someone like you. Please come back. I don't want to lose you."

Jason bowed his head. "Vera, sweet lady, I love you, too. I'm coming back. When I do, it will be for all time, and we'll be free of this." He kissed her again.

They sat for another five minutes in silence, then with admonitions to call him as often as she could, and a reminder of their codes, he drove away into the night.

Vera, for her part, resolve stiffened, cranked the engine to life, and headed back to the ranch and her animals.

# 12

Jason flopped at a motel in Las Cruces. In the morning, he bought copies of the local and other New Mexico papers and scanned them over a cup of coffee and an English muffin. He found nothing new in their pages. He re-fueled the pickup and headed north on Interstate 25. He tuned across the AM and FM bands for what bits of news he could hear, but encountered only re-hashed, puerile nonsense from so-called right-wing "pundits." The remainder consisted of music that assailed his ears.

That night, he parked in a residential section two blocks from the Thompson house. He unlocked the glove compartment, took out the .32 caliber pistol and a small, high-intensity flashlight, re-locked the box, donned his ivy cap, and stepped out. He pulled on a nylon windbreaker jacket, then looked about as he stuffed the semi-auto pistol between the small of his back and his belt and ensured that the jacket hid the weapon. He locked the truck, then walked away, using the sidewalk.

Lights in the living room and in a room upstairs were on. He detected no motion on either floor. He watched for another minute, then moved for the driveway and the rear gate. With slow stealth, careful in the dark and shadows created by incidental light, he took the stairs to the studio over the garage. The key was under the pottery sombrero. He had feared it might have been removed, then recalled that he, Sarah, and most likely Mel, were the only ones who would have known of it.

With careful deliberation, he let himself into the big room. He closed the door, allowed it to latch in the locked position, then stood still until his eyes adjusted. He removed the gun, laid it on a chair seat next to the door, then, with the flashlight from his pants pocket, he began to search the room, with care not to let direct or reflected light escape the sole window in the north wall.

Ranged along that side was a series of floor-borne, as well as ceiling-high, cabinets, all with sliding-panel doors. He went to the ones on the floor, knelt down, and slid the first door open carefully so as not to create any sound. With the light, he inspected the interior. He found two boxes of clay, several carving tools, a small pile of clothes, and two small, finished, but broken, pieces. He knocked on the wall behind these artifacts and looked closely at the edges of the wall. He then pushed on the wall surface and tried to cause it to slide in either direction, to no avail. He took the boxes of clay out one at a time and opened them. They were sealed in clear plastic to protect them from drying. He looked them over closely, then closed and returned them. He also made a close inspection of the broken samples, inside and out.

He went through this procedure with each cabinet, top and bottom, then turned and stood in the dark, thinking.

He crossed the short distance in the deep shadows to Sarah's workbench and throwing wheel. He ran his fingers over the flat, rough surface and picked up dried, powdery clay in the process, then moved the wheel idly. Behind him, light from a passing vehicle briefly lit the room up in select places, then died away. As it did, his eye was drawn to the high shelf on his left where the flash of light had hit. In that moment, he saw that the surface supported three objects; two squat pots and a tall vase. He knew them to be products of his late wife, Sarah. He vaguely recalled her making them years earlier.

With care and without the flashlight, he moved to the wall with the shelf. To his left, through the window, he noticed one of the lights coming from the residence extinguish. He waited, listening, but heard nothing. He wondered who was in the house. One of his sons? His daughter? All of them? He reasoned it would not be someone with nefarious intent under the circumstances.

He took in and released an anxious breath, then reached up and carefully removed each of the pottery pieces and put them on the drainboard to his right. With slow precision, he moved each of the works to the darkroom. This time, he used the flashlight, its beam directed to the floor, which allowed enough offset light to move safely. He placed each of the three pieces on the work surface, then closed the door and snapped the interior light on. With the flashlight held at a steep angle, he studied each of the hand-made containers carefully, over their outer surfaces, inside, as well as their bases.

With a ball-point pen that lay on the work area, he carefully tapped the sides and bottoms of the pots, then the vase. Each of the pots demonstrated virtually identical sounds. Dull and flat. The sides of the vase resounded with a slightly higher pitch all the way around. When he turned it over and tapped the bottom, it sounded odd, as though the material were thinner than those of the pots. He tried them all again, then set them in a row and stared at them.

He opened one of the shallow drawers under the work surface and rummaged for a 12-inch wooden ruler. This he lowered into the vase until it touched the bottom. He registered the depth, then did the same with the pots. By deduction, he realized that the bottom of the vase was at least a half inch thicker than those of the pots. He re-checked his figures, then put the ruler down and looked at the pots and vase again.

He picked the vase up, turned it upside down, and peered at the bottom closely. With a magnifying glass from another drawer, he focused in on the bottom and the edges close to the outer periphery. He sat, lay the vase on the surface with the bottom facing him, and gently rubbed the surface of the fired clay with his finger. Some of it came away as powder. Beneath was a tiny crack. He wiped further, and found that the crack, in varying widths, followed the circumference of the vase.

He looked at his find for another minute, then pushed against the flat bottom with his thumb. With increased pressure, it gave, then broke across the diameter, and the crisp, half-moon shards dropped onto the bench. He tipped the base up a few degrees off the table, and a small, bright metal key fell out. Surprised, he halted for several seconds, then, without inspecting it, he thrust it into his pants pocket.

He carefully brushed the bits, pieces and dust from the vase into a small, empty film box, then cleaned the bench with a damp paper towel, which he wadded up and stuffed into his pants pocket. He took the three pieces of pottery back to their resting place, looked around once more, took the shard box, flashlight, pistol and left. As he stood for a moment on the landing after quietly latching the door, he saw movement in the kitchen below and to the right, where the light had popped on. He was unable to see clearly, but he believed the shadows he saw belonged to his daughter, Flo. He started to choke with emotion, but stanched the feeling.

He remained motionless until the kitchen went dark two minutes later, then returned the latch key to its hiding place under the Mexican hat, and made his way down the stairs and to the driveway with caution. He moved quickly back to his truck, where he re-installed the pistol in the glove box and locked it. The flashlight he put on the passenger seat; the box and used paper towel he placed on the floor in front of the passenger seat. He then drove toward the city center and found a remote parking place at a mall. He checked his surroundings, then removed the key from his pocket and examined it. It was small; not designed for a door latch assembly. He reckoned it belonged to something much smaller, perhaps a bank safety deposit box, an idea that continued to plague him. It was stamped with a set of two letters whose purpose he was unable to discern.

He turned the flashlight off, and with the key squeezed in his hand, he stared ahead for several seconds, then looked around, thinking. Frustrated, he returned the key to his pants pocket and killed the light. He started to close the box, then, as an afterthought, took out the cell phone and powered it on. There were no messages. If Vera had tried to call, she did the right thing, and hung up before the invitation to leave a voice mail. It was at that moment he regretted not setting up a call time schedule, something he vowed to do. He turned the phone off, put it back, and locked the glove box.

He then drove to a motel in Bernalillo.


In the morning, Jason went to a nearby McDonald's fast-food emporium, purchased coffee, orange juice and a breakfast sandwich, all of which he took back to his room. With the viands ranged about him on the window-side table, he picked up the key and studied it, as though by that action, it would reveal its purpose. He palmed it, squeezed his frustrated hand around it, rose and stood at the window, then turned and looked across the room. He looked at his watch. It was a quarter past nine.

He went to the table, downed the last of the cold coffee, ignored the remainder of the muffin sandwich, and along with the key and his wallet, headed out. He wore the Western hat he had purchased in southern New Mexico along with a pair of dark glasses over his eyes.

In Albuquerque, his first stop was at the bank where he and his deceased wife, Sarah, had banked for many years, First National. He asked to see the person responsible for handling safety deposit boxes. He showed her the small key whose shank had rectilinear cuts along the shaft. The letters "LC" were stamped into the thumb portion; nothing more.

The woman looked the key over, then handed it back to Jason. "It looks like a deposit box key. I don't recognize the brand. It's not ours." She wore an apologetic aspect. "But—"

"But?"

"The shank. The part that works the lock. It's shorter than a normal deposit box key. If that's what it is."

"I see," Jason said. "I suppose it would be difficult for you to know—to direct me—to the bank—or a bank—that uses this brand? If it is?"

She turned to her desk-top computer. "Let me see if I can track down the company that made it. That might help narrow it."

She tapped a few keys while Jason watched from behind the flat monitor.

"Hm," she hummed. "Interesting." She glanced at his face, then at the screen. "It appears the key is from a company in Canada. Lebreton Clef." She looked at him with steady eyes.

"Clef?"

"Key. French for key."

He stared back, then nodded mildly. "Of course; interesting." He paused. "Is it possible keys from a Canadian company would be used in an American bank?"

"I have no reason to doubt it. There are many offshore banks. Swiss, German, Canadian, British banks. Here. In the states. No reason to believe they wouldn't bring their own technology—methods, people—with them." She tilted her head to one side.

"Yes, yes. Of course. That makes sense." He nodded and smiled.

She awarded him another professional smile. "May I ask you a question?"

"Sure," he said as he leaned to one side to pocket the key.

"If—if you have that key, why do you not know where it's from?" She moved her head again with the question.

Jason cleared his throat, shifted in his chair and made a minor adjustment to the wide-brimmed Western hat he had not removed. "You see, my wife is—she is recently deceased. I found it in her things, but unfortunately, I haven't been able to find any record of where she kept the box." He effected a rueful smile.

She frowned. "Oh, I'm so sorry. Well, Mr. Thomas, I must be frank. Unless you can provide adequate proof of ownership, such as a death certificate, her identification and ownership of the box, or a probate order, that would be difficult. It's true of all banks." She tapped the calendar pad that covered her desk with her finger. "But you might be looking for a foreign bank."

Jason nodded. "Hm. Yes. I was afraid of that. But it makes sense." He smiled and paused. "Well, thank you for your help. Saves me a lot of time and running around." He rose. "I'll just have to find that record, won't I?"

She got out of her chair. "'Fraid so." She held out her hand and they shook. "Good luck with that."

Jason went to his pickup, got in, put his hat on the passenger seat and stared out the windshield. He then fished the little key out of his pocket and looked at it for several seconds before reaching down to start the engine.

It was late afternoon when he had drifted off to sleep, fully-clothed on the surface of the motel room bed, when the cell phone that lay on the side table sounded. Startled awake, he didn't realize what the sound meant for two seconds. When he did , he rolled over quickly, picked up the little instrument and flipped it open. "Hello?" His voice croaked.

"Jason? Hello. I called yesterday . . ."

"I'm sorry. I don't remember—"

"It's okay. Are you alright? I was worried."

"Yes. Fine. No names, please. I—"

"Ooh, sorry. Where are you?"

"Motel. Uh. Up north."

"Oh, okay. Have you found anything? Any luck?"

"Yes. But. Well, you know, best we not talk about it. Okay?"

"Oh, sure. Of course. I understand. Okay. Well . . ."

"How's the family? You know."

"Oh, just fine. Fine."

"Okay, well, I better go. You take care."

"Yes, yes. You, too. You, too. Okay. Bye."

"Tomorrow, okay?"

"Yes. Okay. Bye."

"Wait!"

"Yes?"

"Dusk. At dusk. After sundown. Okay?"

"Dusk?"

"Yes. When you call."

"Oh—of course. Yes; okay."

"Good. Bye, then."

"Bye."

Jason lay back down on his back, threw his arm over his eyes, and tried to return to sleep. He dozed for awhile, then, unable to sleep with his mind racing, sat up and looked around the depressing room.

After struggling down another fast-food hamburger, he pointed the truck south along old highway 85 through Bernalillo, then Alameda, until he came to a convenient street to rise from the flood plain of the Rio Grande to the piedmont of the Sandias, the so-called "Heights." He drove to the same spot where he had parked before, and brought the vehicle to a halt nearby.

He assumed the house was occupied, because he spied bright internal lights, and further assumed that his daughter, Flo, was still in residence. He stood in the shadows, near a tree, his ivy cap on in place of the Western. He looked at his watch in the faint light, and made the time as nine thirty-six. He returned to the pickup, got in, set the seat back as far as it would go, pulled the cap down over his eyes, and closed them.

He awoke, startled by a passing loud exhaust, and looked at his watch at eleven-twenty. He took in and released a series of deep breaths, sat up, brought the seat upright, adjusted his cap, and looked around at the dark street.

He subconsciously looked at his watch again, retrieved the penlight and keys, eschewed the firearm, and got out.

The house was dark. To ensure that status, he circled the edifice outside the property boundary on the sidewalk, peered at the windows of both floors, then remained in the shadows another three minutes. He reasoned that Flo, if indeed it were she in the house, would be in her old bedroom, not in the master bedroom, where he and Sarah slept.

He went carefully through the rear gate, and approached the house slowly. He watched and waited with every step. He had removed the latch key from his key ring earlier to prevent any key-to-key noise. This he inserted carefully into the lock mechanism, turned it slowly, and then, with the bolt out of the keeper plate, opened the door. He heard one small squeak from a hinge that required lubrication, but none other. Immediately inside, he closed the door quietly while he peered through the glass in the top half, then knelt down and removed his shoes. He righted himself and stood for several seconds in the dark, then moved incrementally across the kitchen floor by half-sliding, half-walking until he reached the open portion of the house. There he stopped, looked around in the dark, then moved cautiously for the stairs to the bedroom floor. As he reached the bottom step, he recalled that two of the treads creaked when stepped upon, but was uncertain which, so as he mounted the stairs, he placed his stocking-covered feet as close to the rails as possible, trusting that the response would be firm and quiet. He was correct. At the top landing, he stopped again to peer into the gloom and listen. He was rewarded with nothing.

He moved, close to the wall, across the carpeted hallway to the master bedroom. The door was closed. It was open the last time he was there, and supposed that Flo had decided that she wanted to close off painful memories. At that moment, he hoped she had not decided to clear the room. He opened the door and stepped in. The hinges made no sound. He closed the door, grateful that it had been closed, giving him more freedom to do what he had come to do, should his daughter arise and pass by.

He took the penlight from his shirt pocket, clicked it on and began to play its narrow beam about the room. He pointed it at his watch. Seven minutes after midnight. He wondered what his daughter's habits were now that she was a married woman in her late forties. Would she be up early? Did she get up in the middle of the night? Would she become sentimental and come into the room? Other tortured ideas flashed through his mind. He wondered if he should reveal himself. No, he thought. Far too early and far too dangerous; yet he wasn't sure why. He dismissed these thoughts which only served to quicken his heartbeat. He reached for a pill in the small envelope in his pants pocket and gulped it down dry.

He pointed the light at the big bed, the dressing bench at its foot, the dresser, then the closet, then the small escritoire where Sarah liked to sit in her ladder-back wicker chair and write letters and cards. He clicked the light off as he tried to imagine where his intelligent, smart wife would have hidden things—papers, documents—she could access quickly should the need arise.

He moved to the closet and shown the light over the clothes, his and hers, that remained on the hanger bar, then the shelf above. There, a row of old boxes for shoes and other odds and ends rested. The floor held more shoes, a small traveling case, and a soft sport bag with his tennis togs and a racket.

He thought about the underside of the king-size bed and rejected the notion. He played the light over the dresser. A false bottom? How would she have managed that without him knowing? So as to cover that aspect, he went to the chest of drawers and pulled open first the top drawer on her side, then the three below. In each, he tapped the thin wooden bottoms and looked briefly at the edges for any tell-tale signs of a mis-match. There were none he could fathom. He pulled out one of the large drawers and inspected the back wall of the furniture, then returned it. He pulled the bureau out and shown the light over the back side. Nothing out of place.

He went to the bench and sat. He thought of the compartment below the seat, stood and opened it. He discovered random sewing paraphernalia. A sewing box, a card of needles, several spools of colored thread, and a book, a treatise on crewel work. There was nothing under the bench. He sat on it again.

He looked, in the half-dark, at the writing desk. Where had they obtained it? As he sat in the dark, he tried to put the pieces of his memory together. Then he recalled receiving the piece when Flo, their eldest, was about the age of seven. Sarah had received a letter from her bank trust officer. Something about a relative in Canada leaving the desk to her. He found it strange at the time, but quickly forgot about it. Sarah's early life had been, to say the least, tragic, and called for a need to leave it in the past.

He got up and walked slowly to the desk. He stopped, looked toward the door to the hall, listened, then turned his attention back to the ornate wooden object. He pulled the ladder-back chair away, then, with the penlight on, he drew the shallow drawer under the pull-out desk surface out slowly. The light played on nothing extraordinary. Erasers, pencils, ballpoint pens, a small tablet, paper clips, a stapler, some push-pins and a half-used roll of postage stamps. The outer and upper surfaces of the desk proved no more revealing. That included a row of open boxes ranged along the top of the desk above the writing surface. A high-intensity lamp rested on the top shelf attended by two porcelain figurines from Germany.

He pulled the desk away from the wall and played the light over the rear surface. It appeared normal, in that it featured a thin, wooden panel with vertical straps of dark wood screwed into it for additional strength and support. He backed away and clicked the light off. He thought for a moment, then looked again with the penlight. Yes. When he looked closer, he noticed that the straps were screwed in on the top ends, but not on the bottom, against the horizontal rail there. He pulled the desk out from the wall farther and knelt down. He played the little beam all over the rear surface and along the top side. The panel was inserted into a top horizontal cross-piece. The bottom was likewise inserted into, and behind, the bottom rail structure. He clamped the flashlight in his teeth, put both hands on the vertical panel support rails, and lifted. The panel moved up to the point where he was able to clear the bottom rail and angle it out and away from the main structure. He removed the entire panel without noise, laid it against the wall, and shown the light on the interior. Where the rear of the shallow wooden miscellaneous drawer would be, he found a grey metal panel of the same width and depth. In the center of that was a small round lock with a slot for a key.

With care, he managed to grasp the sides of what proved to be a steel box, and slide it out. He angled it out and laid it on the carpeted floor. He kneeled down, stopped to control his breathing, then took the little key from his pocket and inserted it into the lock. It slipped all the way in. He turned the key, and the lock responded. He started to lift the lid, then stopped, locked the box and removed the key. That, he hastily returned to his pocket.

He remained still for a moment, got up, returned the wooden panel to the rear of the escritoire, placed the legs in the carpet impressions they had made, looked the desk over, then picked the box up. He stood in the dark for the next two minutes going over what he had seen and done in the room, then went to the door to stop and listen, the steel box under his arm.

With increased attention to stealth, given what he now had in hand, Jason made his way down to the rear kitchen door and out, where he put his shoes on. He walked for a block, half-way to his vehicle, where he stopped in the shadows. He bent over, shaking and gasping for breath. He nervously fished out one of his heart pills and pushed it into his mouth, then found a short garden wall to sit on. At that moment a man and a woman, walking a dog, came up to him. The dog sniffed and wagged its tail.

"Are you alright, sir?" the man asked.

Jason looked up, his breathing still rapid. "Ye—yes, yes, I am. Thank you." He pulled the metal box close to his leg.

"Are you sure?" the woman asked. "Do you need a doctor—an ambulance?"

The panting dog tugged at the leash the man was holding.

"No, no, I'm sure; thank you very much. I'm fine. On my way to my—my truck. Visiting a friend." He pointed. "Truck's that way. 'Bout a block. Really." He shook his head, then nodded.

The man pulled on the dog's leash to coax the animal away from his inspection of the man on the wall. "If you're sure. We could always—"

Jason raised his hand in protest. "I am. I am sure. Thank you for caring. Very nice. Just stopped to rest a moment. I am truly fine." He realized he was not truly fine, but was loath to admit it.

"Well, okay, sir. Come one, Ruff," the man said, and moved off.

The woman had walked three yards away, where she turned to watch and listen.

Jason waited until the Samaritan pair had disappeared around the corner onto the next street, then pushed his cap back to wipe his brow, rose, picked up the box, and moved quickly for the truck. Nervous, he waited another minute once inside the vehicle before he started the engine and pulled away from the curb. A rush of paranoia swamped him, and he tried to shake it off. He was alone, yet because he had made what might prove to be a huge discovery, he feared someone was looking over his shoulder. The FBI—and who else—would give anything—perhaps kill—for what he now had? If he were correct . . .

At the motel, he brought everything from the truck along with the steel container to his room. That included the .32 caliber handgun.

There, after ensuring the door was double-locked and the curtains drawn, he set the box on the table. With the Canadian LC key, he unlocked and opened it. Without touching anything, he spied four passports, a driver's license, a small semi-automatic pistol, a box of cartridges, a long, narrow brown envelope, four stacks of neatly-bound one hundred dollar bills, and a small, black, hand-size, hard-cover notebook. The last item was a small, narrow cardboard box imprinted with the picture and logo of a $CO_2$ cartridge. A box for 5, one was missing.

Slowly and with care, he removed the contents and spread them out on the table. In the bottom was another key, which he was sure must be to a bank safety deposit box. It had two rows of characters stamped into the rectilinear handle; one with numerals "00039," the second with a "T" followed by a space and the numbers "9684." He counted the money, a stack about a third of an inch thick, bound with a rubber band. There was ten thousand dollars in hundred dollar denominations, all old bills. He felt there would be more in a bank somewhere.

Each of the passports had Sarah's photograph, with progressive age changes to match their issuance, which covered a period of forty years; four 10-year sets. He looked at them closely in the light of the table lamp, and detected no apparent flaws. If they were forged, they were well-executed. The date of birth on the documents was the same on each, that of which he had been aware. The name difference was the same. It was not Sarah Smithers Thompson. The name on each was identical, that of one Raisa Didiane Picot, one with which he had no familiarity. Of the four passports, only one was current with two years to run out of ten; the others expired. All were Canadian.

He found an old driver's license from Connecticut, in the name of Picot. He froze to consider how she might explain a passport with one name, and a driver's license with a different name were she to use the one she had from New Mexico. Of course, she might not need a license, one under Thompson, at a border crossing or airport. Unless . . .

He set the passports and license aside and released a sigh, scrubbed his face hard with his palms, then picked up the little 3-inch by four-inch book and opened it. He estimated there to be no more than 20 pages, most of which were blank. Beginning with the second page, inscribed in a hand he didn't recognize as that of his deceased wife, were a series of numbers and letters, in blocks of four. The next two pages were much the same, but with variations in number and letter sequences. These, he felt, had been inscribed by his wife. Following that was another encrypted series, in lines, similar to sentences. Nothing made sense; no complete phrases or sentences, per se. He flipped through the remaining pages. They were blank. He peered at the back of the book. It was imprinted with a name and logo in French.

He picked up the pistol and turned it over to look at the marque and serial number. It was a black Czech CZ-36 .25 caliber slide-operated, semi-automatic handgun. He was not surprised to find there was no serial number. Its erasure appeared carefully professional. He pulled the slide back and peered into the chamber. It was clear. He popped the magazine out. It was loaded with standard round-nose cartridges. He pushed down on the spring-loaded receiver plate. It gave. The magazine was missing one round. He brought the muzzle up to his nose and sniffed. He smelled the faint odor of gun oil with a background of gun powder. He held the gun up to the light, closed one eye and peered down the rifled barrel. He saw tiny bits of black particles.

He froze as he thought of how he had found Mel Vaslovic and of the results of the murder investigation.

He laid the pistol down, pushed the items around, then opened the book again. He found nothing that might suggest a reference to a bank. He reasoned that was contained somewhere within the encrypted data in the book.

He picked up the long brown envelope. It featured a broad flap, whose seal was broken with a precise cut along the hinge. Before he opened it, he noticed that it felt lumpy, as though it contained something other than paper. He looked inside, then held it at an angle to pour the contents onto the table. Three objects rattled out onto the plasticized table surface. Each was a tiny cylinder with a diameter that appeared close to that of a .22 caliber bullet. He picked one up and examined it. About half an inch long, at one end was a cavity. Inside that, its point flush with the outer brass casing, was a bantam needle. The other end was closed, without a flange, such as that on a rim-fire bullet; nor was there a center insert where a firing pin would set off a charge. He realized that was the reason he heard only the metallic click and whoosh of Nante's suppressed pistol accompanied by two similar sounds as Sarah fired at the man with what he thought had been a firearm; deadly, sickening sounds that occurred that night in the living room of the house in Truchas.

It was shortly after two in the morning when he realized how mentally and physically fatigued he was. He sat for another half minute, then rose slowly, turned toward the neatly made bed, pulled off his shoes, flopped down onto his back, threw his arm over his eyes, and promptly drifted off.

He had failed to turn the table lamp off.

Twenty minutes later, as he entered his first REM sleep, he jolted awake and sat up on his elbows in the partially-lit room. He blinked his eyes and stared straight ahead. Where had Sarah gotten the dart pistol? Why the ammunition in the box, yet the key secreted in the vase?

After a minute without a clear answer, he flopped back, his breathing deep and rapid.

Sleep was slow in coming.

# 13

*T*he early afternoon sun cast a shadow of the mesa ridge to the west at a steep angle as Vera Tyler trundled a bale of fragrant, fresh, green hay from the feed shed to the pasture fence line on an old wooden barrow with a squeaky iron wheel. The younger of the two horses, the pinto, knew what her approach meant, and he made his way to the barbed wire line that confined him and his older mate, the roan, who continued to nibble at sparse grass yards away, seemingly unaware.

She heard the car before she saw it out of the corner of her eye, despite the fact that it was a relatively quiet four-door sedan, not a truck of some description. She didn't turn, rather continued to the fence line and her chore. She sensed what was about to happen; perhaps not who was in the vehicle, but why whoever they were had come. She cursed herself mentally for not following Jason's prescription in regards to the Italian firearm.

The neutral grey Chevrolet came along slowly, then halted a few yards from her. She glanced in the direction of the car as she continued to throw rectilinear chunks of sweet straw over the wire. By this time, the older horse had decided to join in on the meal, and moved with slow deliberation toward the feast, nodding its great head in anticipation. Then she dusted her gloved hands, removed them and laid them on the empty trundle bed, adjusted her hat, and turned to look at the white license plate without moving. It read, "U.S. Government" in the upper left corner. She ignored the remainder lower and to the right. She developed a mental picture of the Beretta that lay beside her bed.

Peter Grayson emerged from the passenger side, and Marcus Lucero got out as well. Both closed their respective doors, and Lucero stood next to the car while Grayson came around the front of the vehicle and moved toward Vera.

He held his ID card out at arm's length and up high. "Mrs. Tyler? Vera Tyler? Peter Grayson, FBI."

Vera hesitated a moment. "That's me." Another pause as she watched Grayson put his ID away. "What can I do ya' for?"

Grayson moved closer, then stopped. "May we have a word?"

Vera pulled her floppy straw hat down an inch more over her forehead. "A word? Before we have one word or more, mister, you're gonna hafta' pull that identification out again so I can see it. I couldn't read it from where you landed."

Grayson, stunned, shot Lucero a glance, then reached inside his jacket pocket. "Of course. I'm sorry. I'm so used to—"

"Hand it here."

"Well, I'm not—"

"If you can't hand it to me, then hold it close. I'm not stupid, but I don't see too good these days."

Grayson responded to the firmness in her voice. He drew in a deep breath, then let it out as he came within three feet of Vera and held his plastic-covered ID out at arm's length.

Vera peered at it. "Okay, now him." She gestured with her chin.

Lucero moved immediately to stand next to his partner. He held his ID out.

She looked at both men in turn. "They better be real. I know the sheriff—"

"I assure you, Mrs. Tyler, we are who we say we are." Grayson's voice was conciliatory as he pocketed his ID. He instinctively rotated his body toward the government car as he spoke, then faced her again.

"Okay. What do you want?" She turned, grabbed the handles of the barrow, and started pushing it toward the barn. The old, pitted steel axle engaged in a high-pitched conversation with the unlubricated tube that served as a bearing for the ancient, rusty, spoked wheel.

The two agents looked at each other, curious at the woman's apparent disregard for their presence. They both followed.

Vera trundled the wooden flat-bed wheelbarrow with the front stop-barrier to the edge of the porch, where she turned to look at the two men. "So?" She asked. She stepped onto the porch, sat in one of the two wooden chairs, removed her floppy straw hat and set it on the floor next to her.

"We have a few questions, ma'am." Grayson continued toward her, then stopped.

"I 'spose it's got to do with that plane and those men. So ask away." She crossed her arms across her chest. "Let's get to it. I ain't through with my chores. Animals don't care 'cept to eat, drink 'n sleep."

Both men stood at the edge of the porch. Lucero smiled at her declaration and looked down.

Grayson glanced at Lucero, then turned his attention to Vera. "You helped a man who apparently crashed a plane. Is that true?"

She looked up. "Take a load off. I can get another chair from inside." She thumbed at the interior of the house.

"Thank you." Grayson stepped up onto the porch and sat in the other chair, then retrieved his ubiquitous notebook. He adjusted the chair to face her.

Lucero shook his head. "I'm okay." He leaned against a porch support post.

Grayson glanced at his partner, drew in a breath, exhaled, and returned his gaze to Vera. "Do you recall the man's name, Mrs. Tyler?"

Vera rubbed her forehead. "Jason something?" She squinted at the fenced field as though for guidance.

"He came from the plane that was here, is that correct?"

"That's right. Up there." She pointed at the mesa ridge.

"It was at night?"

"Yep. Came stumblin' across that field." She pointed. "Made it down in the dark. Thought he was a drug-runner." She pursed her lips.

"I see. Was he hurt?" He wrote.

She nodded emphatically. "He was that." She paused. "Collapsed on that chair in there." She gestured toward the innards of the house with a head motion. "All scratched up."

Lucero pushed away from the porch post and strolled toward the fence line where the horses were finishing their treat and nodding their heads as though asking for more. He stopped and looked up at the traces of black that remained from the fire.

Grayson watched Lucero, then continued. "So you helped him . . . And another man showed up?"

"Two others."

"Two men. Do you remember their names? Can you described them?"

"I do." She hesitated, looked away, then back. "Not the names. Nope."

"Okay." Grayson wrote again.

Vera spent several minutes describing the man who took Jason at gunpoint up the escarpment, then the second man who exchanged firearms with her and gave chase. She described the fire that consumed the airplane, and how the second man brought one man down, leaving the other apparently dead.

"Which man died, Mrs. Tyler?"

Although a lie, she peered at the FBI agent with firm resolve. "He tole' me it was the one what flew here."

"Jason Thompson."

"If you say so. Yes, I guess so." She raised her chin as she held Grayson's gaze.

He looked down at his notebook, scribbled, then looked away, formulating his next question. He looked at her again. "So, you went for help, but when you came back, he was gone. The second man was gone."

"He left a note."

Grayson took several seconds to absorb this information, then, "A note. Do you still have the note?"

She shook her head. "Nope. I threw it."

Grayson nodded. "Do you recall what it said?"

She shrugged and raised her eyebrows. "Well, not much. That he took the live one."

"I see. Nothing else?"

"Mm, he sorta' signed it."

"Signed it?"

"Yep. The letter 'N'."

Grayson nodded silently as he jotted the information.

Vera grabbed her hat from the floor, donned it, got out of her chair and walked to the edge of the porch. She looked up at the ridge where the plane had been. "They come—came—later for the other man."

Grayson rose and followed her to the porch edge. "When?"

"Noise woke me. Couldn't see too well in the dark, but it looked like a white truck or van or somethin' like that."

"How many came for the body?"

She looked down at the ground at her feet. "I didn't see 'em. Musta' been more than one."

"Hm. And the plane?"

"Two days. Flatbed. Some men brought the wreck down."

"Did you talk to them? Were they NTSB?"

"En-tee-ess-bee?" She squinted at Grayson.

"National Transportation Safety Board. They investigate accidents. Planes. Trucks."

She shook her head. "I don't know. I didn't see anything like that. No, sir. They went about their business and was gone."

Lucero returned from his sojourn to the fence. He stood apart and kicked at the dirt.

Vera pointed. "You look carefully, you can see the burned spot."

"Yes," Grayson responded.

"It exploded."

"Of course." He paused. "Mrs. Tyler, did Mr. Thompson say anything to you, uh, explain what he was doing here, where he was going?"

Vera scratched the back of her head and looked down. "Nary a word. Couldn't get much outa' him. He was hurt. Slept a lot." She looked at Lucero, then back at Grayson.

"Slept? Did he intend to stay? Weren't you concerned?"

"I was. At first. Sure. When he got sane, he said he had to leave."

"Where did—did he say where? Where he would go?"

She shook her head slowly. "Nope. Then the man came. One with the pistol. Never did find out."

Grayson stroked his chin and looked at Lucero.

"Sorry he died. Seemed nice." Her voice, flat, was barely audible.

"You weren't frightened? Really?" Grayson frowned.

"At first." Her voice raised in pitch. "When he came stumblin' outa' the dark. Seein' that plane come down." She waved at nothing and paused. "But he was older. No gun. Didn't threaten me." She paced away onto the hard pan and looked up toward the escarpment. "Needed help. I helped 'im."

"Of course. What else could you do." It was a statement.

Lucero came closer. "Mrs. Tyler, the man who came later. The second man. Did he show you ID?"

Vera turned to look at Grayson's partner. "Yeah, he did that."

"Did you get a good look at it?"

"Same's yours. I didn't look as close, but it seemed the same."

"He claimed to be FBI?"

She nodded. "Yep."

"How did the fire start?"

"Heck, they was shootin' at each other!" She paused and looked at both men with incredulity. "I traded guns with the FBI guy. Let him have my .30-.30. The other one had a pistol. I think it was a bullet from my rifle. I don't really know!" She shook her head, sighed and made a gesture as though she were dealing with insanity.

Grayson frowned at her. "Traded guns?!"

She looked at him, eyes wide. "The one who took Jason—Mr. Thompson— he had a gun!"

Lucero and Grayson traded concerned glances.

"He was tryin' to get the other to stop. To come back down."

"Why did they go up there?" Grayson asked.

"Beats me." Vera shrugged. "I couldn't figure it out. Glad it's over." She started away.

Grayson called after her. "Mrs. Tyler—"

Without turning, she waved a dismissive goodbye as she strode away. "Got animals to feed and chores. 'Less you got somethin' more to say, I gotta get back to work."

The two federal agents traded glances and shrugs. They both called out their thanks, then turned toward their vehicle. Vera, for her part, began to shake off her nervousness at the lies she had told.

Lucero stopped, pondered, then spun around and looked toward Vera who was half-way between the house and the first outbuilding with the ancient barrow. He raised his voice. "Mrs. Tyler!"

Vera stopped, turned and looked at Lucero with a frown. She dropped the simple vehicle and raised her arms half-way in a questioning gesture.

Lucero took another step toward her. "Mrs. Tyler, have you talked to Jason Thompson lately?"

It took Grayson two full seconds to react to Lucero's question. He lunged at his partner's back, grabbed his left arm and swung him around. "What the goddamn hell, Marc?!"

Vera stared at the two agents with her jaw dropped. Her reaction was slow, then, "Get the hell off my property!" She took two steps toward them and stopped. "I'm goin' to the sheriff! You ain't heard the last of this!"

Grayson pulled Lucero up close, such that his face was almost nose-to-nose. He lowered his voice to a growl. "God damn it, Marcus, what the fuck do you think you're doing, man!? You can't blurt something like that out! You're going to get a departmental reprimand at the least, get your ass fired at the most!" He paused and looked away. He spat the word "Jesus!" under his breath. With that, he started for the car. "Let's get the hell out of here before you say something else stupid!"

While Vera stared at them from a distance, fuming, the two federal agents moved quickly for their car.

Grayson got into the passenger seat, while Lucero resumed his role as driver. He backed up, made a quick turn, and pushed the accelerator pedal hard enough to cause the rear wheels to dig into the dirt and throw up a cloud of dust.

They drove a hundred yards beyond a bend in the road where they could not see the ranch buildings when Grayson spoke. "Pull over and stop!"

Lucero did so.

"Shut the engine off." Grayson looked out his window, then down at the floor of the car. His voice was low, slow and gruff. "What was that all about, Marcus? What?!"

Lucero stared straight ahead for several seconds, then, "It was a test, Peter."

Grayson looked hard at Lucero. "A test?! A goddamn test?! You were accusing the woman of lying! You're intimating that Thompson is not dead and that she knows how to contact him?! What the hell, man?!"

Lucero took his time. He nodded, then shook, his head. "I was wrong. In my approach. But—but—" He raised his finger and tilted his head.

"But what, man?! What you've done could strip us of our authority to investigate this case!"

Lucero was silent again, then spoke quietly. "Peter, I want you to consider some things. Where is the NTSB? Was the crash even reported? Hell, where's the wreckage? Where was Thompson's body? They held a funeral for an urn with someone's ashes. No forensics. The Thompson woman kills an imposter FBI agent with a cold-war style dart gun in a far-away mountain village. He can't be traced. So far. Think about it." He nodded again.

Grayson pondered, then, "These are all facts, Marcus; facts, I admit. It's true, there's something going on here we have yet to uncover, but accusing that woman of something—what I would call outrageous—*is* outrageous!" He slapped the upper part of the dashboard.

"Want me to go back? Apologize?" Lucero looked at Grayson from under his eyebrows.

"Give me a break, Marc. It's too late. The damage has been done. What would you say to her?" He paused and lowered his voice. "Say Thompson is not dead. That he's around somewhere. That the whole thing was faked so he could disappear. That doesn't mean he'd come back here. If he's alive, he's no dummy, and he'd think twice before coming here. Makes no sense."

"Maybe. Maybe not."

"Yeah, okay, but we're not going back."

Lucero was quiet, then, "What if I say, 'sorry, ma'am, I was out of line. We just have some suspicions, and we—I—was out of line. Hope you can understand' and all that."

Grayson shook his head. "Marc, we'd have to show our hand. We'd have to tell her why we think Thompson may be alive."

"And? Why? No. I disagree. Where would that lead? Who's she gonna tell? No one—unless—"

"Unless Thompson's alive."

"Exactly."

"And if he is alive and she's in contact with him, do we want him to know?"

"Maybe so," Lucero said.

Both men were silent.

Lucero broke the silence. "If so, and guilty, it'd drive him deeper underground. If not, and we approached it as being on his side, etcetera, it might flush him out."

"Hm."

"Wish we could get a search warrant."

"To find what? Some underwear and socks he left behind?"

Lucero shrugged.

"Not an option. Not an option. Let's go." Grayson's mouth was firm.

When they reached the highway, Grayson flipped his cell phone open, pressed a single button and put the device to his ear. "Jan; Grayson. We just left the interview. Yes. The Tyler woman. Jan, have you had anything from the NTSB?" He waited. "No?" Again a pause. "Okay. Get hold of them and find out if they have anything on the crash down here. You have the coordinates?" He listened. "Good. We're on our way back. Call one way or the other. Soon as you have an answer. Okay?" After another few seconds, he closed the cell and dropped it to his lap. He spoke without looking at Lucero. "We shall see."

"Keep tabs?" Lucero kept his eyes on the road as he spoke.

"Tabs? What, surveillance?" Grayson frowned at his partner.

Lucero nodded.

Grayson shrugged. "How? Down here? On that ranch out in the middle of nowhere? Who? How would we pull that off?" He was quiet, then, "Marcus, I believe you to be one of the best damned agents in this man's FBI. Yeah, and woman's." He paused. "But what I don't get, man, is why you are so focused on the late Jason Thompson. I really don't."

"I appreciate the kudos, Pete. Maybe I'm going too far. Hey, hear me out." Lucero stopped to gather this thoughts. "Thompson disappears, makes it down here in an airplane whose ownership and registration we don't know, crashes it, is apparently killed in a shoot-out between people we have yet to identify, and re-appears as ashes. So far, so good?" He glanced at Grayson, who stared at the pavement rolling up underneath the car. "Then—then, out of the blue, Sarah, his wife, and this guy who claimed to be agency, show up dead. Where? In an old house in a back-water town." He was silent.

"I'm listening."

"Put all that together with the suspicions we had—have—that his story at the labs was full of holes. He takes off—or vanishes somehow—making his case worse. We ain't got spit." He paused again. "And this woman." He shook his head. "This woman. What's her story?"

Grayson nodded and looked down. "We'll ask for a stringer to look into her story. Maybe somebody saw her somewhere." Grayson pointed at Lucero. "But don't get your hopes up. I doubt if we find squat."

"The girl."

"The girl?"

"In Socorro."

"What about her?"

Lucero nodded, a secret smile across his face. "She saw him."

"Maybe. Maybe not."

"She saw him." Lucero's voice was a near whisper as he nodded in his certainty.

"You know, Marc, there's another aspect—another possibility to this."

"Okay."

"If, and I say if, Thompson was legit, that he was part of something we've not uncovered; if that were the case, and he's still around, he'd be scared. He'd be in hiding. He'd have the protection of being a non-person, but without friends."

Lucero looked at Grayson for three seconds with his head dipped, such that he appeared to Grayson with the aspect of a teacher giving a lecture to an errant student. "The break-ins at the Thompson house." He returned his attention to driving.

Grayson thought as he scratched his forehead, his eyebrows up. "Yup. Right. Why?"

"Why, indeed. Too coincidental for me to buy," Lucero said.

"Thing is, Marc, the Director has us on a short leash. He and staff want to know what we expect to find, and with budget restraints—"

"I know. I know." There was frustration in his response.

"However, I agree with you to the extent that there's a lot unexplained that could lead to other problems."

"If nothing else, this Nantes guy. And the Thompson woman. Shit!"

"I'll work up a detailed report. With your help."

Lucero motioned his agreement, and the two men fell silent.

"Akela Trading Post coming up. I could eat," Grayson said.

"So could I," Lucero replied.

Vera, rattled but in control, looked at her watch, then at her surroundings in an attempt to gain a sense of reality. She had a four and a half hour wait before she could drive to the highway to call Jason.

## 14

*T*he time was a few seconds past 2330, or 11:30 PM, when Stanley Webber arrived at the entrance to the farm.

The house sat back amongst a grove of indigenous deciduous trees mixed with a few evergreens, a pine common to southern Pennsylvania, approximately a half mile off the public road, Parks Drive. That, in turn, was half-way between Marion and Guilford, a mile east of Interstate 81, and a few miles north of the Pennsylvania-Maryland state line.

The road in, gravel-covered dirt, featured two curves in the forested verge between the house and Parks Drive, thus preventing casual observers from enjoying a view of the house and the two outbuildings associated with it from the Parks Drive vantage point.

The house, nearly a hundred years old, was a two-story shiplap, whose paint was peeling here and there, but otherwise in good condition. It featured a porch along the length of the front, with a bench swing and a white wooden railing in good repair. The porch light was not on, but the interior of the house was aglow.

The buzzer and a small red lamp next to it on a panel adjacent to the front door activated, alerting a woman who had been watching television to rise from her overstuffed chair and go to one of the windows that faced the porch.

She called out, "Jack! Someone's coming. Jack!"

A man appeared in the doorway that lead from the living room to the kitchen. "I hear you." He went to the only light source in the room, a reading lamp next to the chair the woman had occupied and shut it off, and the room went dark except for the lambency from the television.

The woman continued to peer through the window.

"Anything?" he asked.

"Not yet. No—there."

In the distance she spied a pair of unmoving headlamps that flashed off, then on, then off, twice.

She reached for the switch that controlled the porch light and toggled it on, then off in the same sequence.

The man went to a side table, pulled the drawer open and removed a nine millimeter semi-automatic pistol. He popped the magazine out, checked it for bullets, re-inserted it, then pulled the slide back and let it spring forward, forcing a round into the chamber. He pointed the weapon at the ceiling, let the hammer down gently, released the safety and inserted it between his belt line and the small of his back. He then joined the woman at the window.

Webber had stopped his car at the second bend, from where he was able to see the house, and where he sent the signal with the headlamps. After he saw the recognition sign, he drove on and parked near the porch. When he stepped from the car, he closed the door quietly, then stood and looked about for several seconds before he approached the porch. At the front entrance, which featured an outer screen door, he rapped twice slowly, then three times in rapid succession. It was then that the inner door opened.

The woman held the door open as Webber walked in. She looked at him wordlessly and without any outward recognition, then went past him onto the porch. A fully automatic AR-15 assault rifle with a laser sight whose power was off, dangled from her right hand. In her left was a large flashlight. She stopped immediately before the steps.

Webber turned to watch her. "Ruth," he said.

Without turning, she said, "Stan," barely loud enough for him to hear, then moved down onto the ground, where she began to search the area with the powerful hand-held light.

The man came up to Webber and held out his hand, which Webber took. "Stan." His aspect was flat, unemotional.

"Jack." Webber turned his head toward the front door. "I didn't see anything." He turned back and went toward the big chair where Ruth had sat, that which faced the TV. "And no, I wasn't tailed." He sat without being invited to do so.

Jack moved to a nearby sofa and sat as he laid his pistol on a side table, an action which Webber openly ignored but registered nonetheless.

"She likes to roam around in the dark," He said.

"And what would she do if she found someone?" Webber compressed his lips.

"She knows better than to fire. She'd hoof it back here and alert me. I know, it's a lot 'o gun. It's got a suppressor."

Webber scrubbed his face hard with both hands, then dropped them to his lap. "Is she reliable?"

"Reliable?" Jack screwed up his face at the question.

"Let me put it this way, can she be trusted?"

"Trusted in what way?" Jack controlled his annoyance at the question.

"Whatever is needed." There was weariness in his answer.

Jack got up from the sofa and went to one of the two windows that looked out onto the porch. "Why are you going there, Stan? What's going on? Shit, you know her history with us. She was great in New Mexico."

Webber ignored Jack's plea and changed the subject. "You got my flash mail?"

Jack turned. "Yes. Two, in fact. And the flower order."

"Poor Boy is no longer."

Jack stopped in the middle of the room. He hesitated. "What? What's going on?"

Webber sighed, got up and trudged across the room as well to peer into the exterior dark. "Where is she? I don't see her light."

Jack went to the other window. "Around the bend. Not unusual."

"Okay. Hope she doesn't do that in daylight."

"She's a pro, Stan." He paused. "Poor Boy, Stan; what's going on?"

Webber returned to his chair. "He's gone. He had a regrettable accident."

Jack peered at Webber. "Were you involved in the accident?"

Webber looked at the ceiling. "I had reliable information that the gentleman was on the FBI and red coat watch lists. Possibly MI6." He paused. "Plus, I got wind he was planning a trip to China. Possibly for good. Loose cannon. Too risky."

Jack sat down on the sofa. "Want something to eat? Drink?"

"No. I'm good. Grabbed something on the way up."

"So, what now?"

"No, hey, I could use a beer. Got any beer?"

Jack stood and made for the kitchen. "Local brew. That okay?"

"Sure. Local brew is good." He paused. "We lay low for the time being. It's one of the reasons I ask about the woman. Ruth, right?" He raised his voice to be heard from the other room.

"Yes, Ruth. She's okay, Stan." He spoke louder as well.

"Means no throughput for now. Drop in income. But there's more to this."

Jack came back into the living room and handed Stan a brown bottle. "I didn't catch that."

"I said, it means less income. Dried up source."

"Yeah. So you indicated."

Webber drank, then answered, "Yes." He smacked his lips and wiped his mouth with his sleeve. "Not bad. Thanks." He raised the bottle in salute.

Jack lowered his head in glum reaction to the news.

"However," Stan said.

Jack raised his head to look at the other man.

"Despair not, my friend. I may have another contact. On the outside."

"Yeah? How so?"

It was then that the front door opened and the woman, Ruth, entered. She looked briefly at both men, turned and leaned the long automatic weapon against the door frame, stood the flashlight upright on a side table, then strode for the kitchen.

She was no more than five feet-two, with brown hair that fell a few inches short of her shoulders. A trim figure held up a pair of beltless blue jeans under a tucked-in neutral color blouse. Her feet were buried in slim, black Western-style boots. Webber considered her pretty, but with a severe cast to her demeanor.

"Hello, Ruth," Webber said.

"Hello yourself, Stan the man." From inside the kitchen, she asked, loud enough for both men to hear, "Any more 'o that brewski?"

Jack shook his head in amusement. "Yes, Ruth, dear, in the fuckin' frig! Where else?!" He executed an irritable swipe at his hair.

"Thank you, dear!" came back from the kitchen, laced with sarcasm.

Jack and Webber traded amused glances.

Ruth returned to the living room, the sound of her footwear on the old wooden floor preceding her. She draped a bottle of beer from her hand, then raised it to her lips and sipped as she walked to a chair across the room and sat. "We got trouble, right, Stan, otherwise you wouldn't be here. Am I right?"

Webber looked away momentarily, then at the woman. "Yes and no, Ruth. Something Jack, here, and I have been discussing, and which you would know about if you hadn't been outside risking our position."

Ruth took a long pull on her beer, then dropped the bottle close to the floor. "And fuck you, too, Stan! I do my job!" She looked away with obvious disdain.

Webber raised his eyebrows and smiled. "I truly love you, Ruth. You are a real stalwart."

She shook her head in an expression of contemp. "Jeez, Stan, what the hell does that mean!? Hell, you don't even know me, and you're making judgements!"

Jack started to speak. "It means—"

"I know what it means, Jack, you idiot." She looked away in disdain.

Jack shook his head, looked away, then at Stanley Webber. "So, where were we?"

Webber drew in his breath, then exhaled. "Poor Boy's partner or boss. I don't know which. Vancouver."

"Yeah?"

Ruth's voice was a near growl. "What's with Poor Boy? I have a right to know."

Webber looked at her. "You do. He's no longer with us."

"He's no longer with anyone," Jack said.

Ruth sipped her beer again. "Do the Chinese believe in heaven?" She smirked.

Webber got up, walked to a side window and peered out into the dark. "I do love you, Ruth. I know; I don't know you, but I still love you."

"So—" She said.

"So, I don't know who among our slant-eyed friends think there's life after death, and because I knew little of his personal life, I wouldn't care to hazard a guess in his case."

"Are you vulnerable?" She asked. "Are *we* vulnerable?"

Webber turned. "Vulnerable? Why the question?"

"Because, Stan the man, I assume you're the responsible party. That's why."

"Interesting," Webber said.

"Why didn't you ask *me*?" She asked.

Webber cocked his head at her. "Very interesting. Why not, indeed. Well, Ruth, it didn't occur to me, frankly. I figured it was my job. Plus, I figured it was best not to involve too many others. And, I had the time and opportunity. No offense, mind you." He lowered his head at her.

She sucked on the last of her beer and put the bottle down carefully on the un-carpeted floor. A ring of wet developed where moisture from the bottle eked down its flanks. "None taken."

"Good."

"So," she asked, "what's next?"

Webber moved back to the overstuffed chair and sat. He looked at his empty bottle, then up.

"Another?" Jack asked.

"No. Thanks. I'm good. Need to sleep soon, though." He ran his fingers through his hair.

"There's room," Ruth said. She had become conciliatory.

Webber nodded. "Thanks. I want to know a couple of things first."

"Shoot," Jack said.

"What did you do with the wreckage and how did you take care of the body?"

"Mexico."

"Mexico?" Webber asked.

"Mexico," Jack said. "We found a junk dealer from Agua Prieta. Across the border from Douglas. He took the wreckage. The body we got to an undertaker in Prieta. The guy knew his way through Douglas. Right through back alleys and back doors of American stores. Easy. Hell, the immigration guys have no idea. No idea." He sat back and looked at both people in the room. "If they do, they're on the take."

Webber nodded his head. "Good. Excellent. What'd it set us back?"

"Twenty-five large."

Webber nodded again. "Good. Cheap."

Ruth flashed her eyes between Webber and Jack.

Jack pointed at Ruth. "Stalwart, Stan. She did good. Real good."

Ruth sat back, relaxed and triumphal. She thumped the arm of the chair with her finger to an internal beat.

Webber pointed at both of the people across the room in turn. "The two of you? No help?"

"We had help, but Ruthie pulled her weight."

"Who? Who helped?" Webber asked. There was angst in his voice.

Jack stirred. "The junk guy. Mexican."

"Is he safe? Not good, involving outsiders."

"This guy's an outside outsider, Stan. He's got problems of his own, so he skates along the fringes. He's good."

"Where'd you find 'im?"

"Some folks over Arizona way. I have my connections."

"It better not be traceable." Webber's eyes were slanted at Jack.

Jack shook his head. "It's not. Lot 'o green scratch changed hands."

"Okay." Webber compressed his lips.

Jack leaned forward and peered at Webber. "Who was he?"

"Who was who?" Webber asked.

"The dead man," Ruth cut in.

Webber threw his hands out in a gesture of futility. "I don't know." He emphasized the word 'I'.

"So the target got away. He survives?"

"According to Nantes. Yes." Webber looked at both across the room.

"Who was *he*?" Ruth asked.

Webber sat back and shook his head, frustrated. "Same. I don't know. Double blind, Ruthie. I don't know." His answer conveyed irritation.

"But he may be alive?" Jack asked.

Webber drew in a breath and let it out. He nodded emphatically. "Yes, it appears."

"So he could be a loose cannon. Not on our side," Ruth said.

"He could."

"Allied with the feds? In their pocket?" Jack asked.

Webber shook his head. "I don't know." His nerves frayed, he got up and moved slowly across the room as he spoke. "Nantes was vague—too vague—and we didn't get it all. What I do know is that the source—Nantes' agent—made it out. Then—and here's the weird part—Nantes is killed with a Cold War type dart pistol. Probably Soviet."

Ruth bent forward in her chair. "What?!"

Webber looked at her and lowered his head. "You heard me." His voice was soft.

"Who?! Who killed him with a dart, for Christ's sake?! The guy?!"

Webber nodded his head deeply. "According to my company source, the wife of the source. Nantes' guy. The guy who may be alive." He looked at Jack and Ruth in turn, then spun away.

"That's wild. Crazy!" Ruth blurted. "What happened to her?"

"FBI source told my guy that Nantes killed her. Same time, apparently." He shrugged.

"Jesus," Ruth whispered.

"How do you know about the dart gun?" Jack asked.

"I have it."

"What?!" Ruth exclaimed. "You have—!"

Webber looked at the ceiling as he rubbed his chin. "Part of what I do. FBI brought it to my source. He brought it to me."

"Shit," Ruth said under her breath.

"Have you ID'd it?" Jack asked. He leaned forward with intensity.

Webber shook his head in a short, jerking motion. "No. Markings 'er all gone." He paused. "Need to find an X-ray."

"X-ray? Why?" Ruth asked.

"It can uncover the filed-down marks. Serial numbers. Maker's marks." Webber waved his hand.

"You guys have that, no? The CIA?" Jack asked.

"Yes. And I also have to sign it in and out. Total scrutiny. No way." He created a circle in the air with his finger.

"Who the hell *was* Nantes, anyway?" Ruth asked.

"Victor Nantes. All I knew him as. Alias. Real name? I don't know."

"Company, right?" Jack asked.

"I assume. I met him once. Once. Never saw his face." Webber held his palm out as he returned to his seat. "He knew all the plays."

Jack leaned forward. "Never saw him?! How the hell does that work?!"

Webber looked at the floor, then at Jack. "He was in disguise."

"Disguise?" Ruth asked.

Webber nodded. "Wore a wide-brim fedora, false beard or something, dark glasses, the whole bit."

"How the hell'd you meet? How'd he find you?" Ruth asked.

Webber's mind drifted off . . .

*He found the slatted-wood bench. It was a foot away from a concrete path that curved through a treed park in Washington, D.C. People strolled by in the still, warm early afternoon sun. A youngster, disobeying the posted restrictions, caromed by on a skateboard and nearly ran an elderly woman down. A middle-aged couple, dressed for the part, jogged by in the opposite direction. A man dressed as though it were Winter shuffled by, throwing peanuts onto the pathway for the pigeons that befouled it. The man stopped, muttered to himself, then turned to retrace his steps. He walked a few feet past the bench, stopped again, then turned, came back to the bench and sat. He belched as he did.*

*The man held out the greasy sack with the nuts, threw a few out, then offered it to Webber. "Nuts?" His voice was muffled behind his turned-up collar, over his scraggly beard and beneath the dark glasses that hid his eyes.*

*Webber replied, "Thanks, no. I have a peanut allergy. Stuffs up my nose."*

*After a long pause, the bum said, "Okay." He pulled the sack away.*

*The two men on the bench watched as three more people went by singly without turning their heads.*

*The bum said, his voice now effectively normal, but barely high enough for Webber to understand, "Take care. Trust me, I know how to deal with uncooperative folks. Nod if you understand." He had not turned his head toward his bench partner.*

*Webber nodded.*

*The bum pulled a folded-up newspaper from somewhere inside his decrepit outfit and laid it on the bench, rose slowly and wandered away, muttering, as he threw more peanuts onto the path.*

"Stan?" Ruth looked at him. "Where'd you go?" She asked.

"Oh. Sorry. Mind fart. Thinking about something else. "Uh, as to your question, rather not say. Too risky to play this game in-house and pal around. No offense." He paused as he looked at both the man and the woman n turn. "It was an outdoor meeting. You know, classical movie shit. Park bench, people walking by. Pigeons wandering around under foot. The whole bit." Webber rubbed his face with the recollection and the fact that he had no intention of revealing all that he knew. "Hell, he never looked at me. Kept his face away, watching people and nasty pigeons through very dark shades." He chuckled. "He even brought bird feed!"

Ruth smiled blankly, and Jack let out a short laugh.

Ruth screwed up her face. "But—how did he know—"

"Ah, yes, children," Webber said. He raised both his arms then slammed them down on the armrests with fanfare. "Ah, yes." He looked away, at the ceiling, the floor, then at both of the others in turn. "Well, you see, it's like this. I didn't know him—still don't—but he knew me. He knew two things about me. One, I was an insider in the company. Two, he knew my history. Knew I had a legal problem—had *had* a legal problem—that, if known by my government employers, could have caused me to be fired and lose my clearance. I don't know how he knew, but he did. He also knew I could serve his interests. Watch the store, as it were, plus some other assistance. Other goodies." He paused with a sniff, rose and strolled to a dark window and looked out. "It's been lucrative, and he made me his heir." He turned and strolled back to his seat. "So, I can't complain. That's it. There ain't no more."

During his wandering spiel, Ruth followed him intently with her eyes. Jack studied the back of his hands and his nails as though disinterested.

Jack asked, "Did Nantes get anything? Anything to you? For Poor Boy?"

"If he did, he died before he could pass it," Webber said. "I was copied on everything—so far as I know. Checked it against company ops and stings." He reflected for a moment. "Shit, that's the main reason he used me." He shook his head dramatically. "No, he took it with him. Or it's hidden somewhere, probably never to be found." He sighed as he waved his arms.

"Where's the money?" Ruth asked. She had calmed.

"Offshore. No worries; you're both in line. You'll get it. Fact is, I brought you some." Webber pointed at each, was quiet, then, "Is this place safe?"

Jack was nonchalant. "Yeah, it's safe." He thumbed over his shoulder. "Sixty acres back here. Mostly in orchard. Do some truck gardening. Ruth's good at that." He smiled at her, then let the expression fade.

"Enough to look legit?" Webber asked.

"Nobody's said anything or poked around so far. We're not the only farm around here that works that way." Jack tilted his head and looked at Webber askance. "We're community."

"Hey, I trust you." Webber waved his hand.

"What now?" Ruth asked.

"I got a meeting," Webber said.

"Who and where?" Ruth asked.

"Uh-uh. Best you not know anything more. Your protection. That's all I can say."

"You think Nantes left an empty trail?" Jack asked. "How do we get more saleable goods?"

Webber raised his eyebrows. "I'm looking into that. There might be another someone else at Rio Grande Labs. I have to pick up the emergency packet Nantes left."

Jack stared at the floor. "Nantes dead. The body. Traceable?"

Webber shrugged. "Photo. They'll probably track 'im back through the company. Get his real name."

"Good or bad?" Ruth asked.

Webber drew in and released a long breath. "I don't see how they could trace him to me or us. All communication was external and secure."

"Yeah, well—I'm not happy about the wife and the darts," Ruth said.

"Who was she working for?" Jack asked.

Webber shook his head. "Guess is as good as mine."

"Feds?" Ruth asked.

Webber pondered, then, "And the FBI brings me a dart pistol? Not so much, Ruth."

She sat back. "Yeah. Right. Stupid question."

"Unless it was a ruse," Jack said.

Webber was silent again, then he said, "Sharp, Jack, but why? Means they'd think the company's involved. Eh, no."

"As long as we don't know, Stan, it's a threat from left field," Ruth said.

"I agree. I'm on the case." Webber nodded at the two of them. He looked at his watch. "I need a couple of hours. Need to be on the road before first light."

"Car?" Jack asked.

"Rental. Maryland plates." He paced for several steps. "Speaking of circumstances, I'm going to the car to get the envelopes. Be right back."

Jack and Ruth watched Webber leave, then they looked at each other.

"Think he'll bring back more than envelopes, Jack?" Ruth had her hand to her chin as she peered at him.

"Possible." He reached for the semi-automatic he had lain on the side table, cocked the hammer, checked the safety, then slid it under his leg.

Two minutes later, Webber entered from the porch. He had two brown envelopes in one hand; the other was free. He went to Ruth first and gave her one of the packets, then to Jack for the same action. Then he sat in the big chair. "You thought I was going to get rid of you?" He looked from Jack to Ruth and back.

Ruth's jaw went slack, and Jack twitched.

"What?! How the—?!" Jack exclaimed.

Webber gestured toward the side table where Jack had placed his gun earlier. "The pistol. Did you decide to put it away in my absence, or is it hidden under you?"

"Jesus, Stan," Jack whispered.

"I understand. I'd be wary, too." He watched his finger play along the fabric of his chair. "But here's the thing. I trust you both. I need you both. So, we're joined at the hip. For the time being." He awarded each a mild smile. "Now, do you both have an exit plan? Do you have your walking papers handy? Money?"

Both nodded; both speechless.

Ruth spoke first. "Do we need 'em? Now?"

Webber shook his head. "We're safe. I give Victor Nantes this; he followed protocol. Frankly, I shouldn't be here. You know that. But there's no connection. We follow the rules. You follow the rules. So long as we all follow the rules—we're safe. I needed to be here. Under the circumstances."

Another long silence ensued.

Jack broke it. "Stan, whose plane was it, and who the hell flew it?"

Webber shook his head with emphasis. "No idea, Jack. No idea. Yes, I do have an idea. Probably the cut-out. The source. If so, how did he get it and why? Search me. If Nantes knew, he didn't say."

"Should we go back? Keep an eye on the place?"

"How, Jack? We'd be the proverbial sore thumb. You were there, I wasn't. Wide open spaces, spot someone a mile away, suspicious old broad. You kidding?"

Jack nodded, chastened.

"Hey, I know. We should. We probably should. But how? Hire on as a hand?"

Jack merely nodded, and Ruth threw both her hands out in futility.

"Did either of you see Nantes in New Mexico? Or anywhere else?" Webber looked at both in turn.

Ruth shook her head.

Jack said, "No," as he moved his head in the negative. "We got a message, urgent message, and we headed out. He had us set up in Deming, then let us do our thing. Followed the encrypted instructions. Used the slush fund. Came in from different directions, left the same way. Came back here alternately." He gestured at the old, bare tongue-and-groove floor with a wave of his hand.

"Good. Good," Webber said. "And we don't know last names. We keep it that way."

The three of them nodded at each other, then all rose and left the room.

A few minutes past five the following morning, Ruth shook Webber awake. She set a cup of coffee down on the small table next to the single cot he had slept on. After slurping some of the hot liquid, and a visit to the bathroom, he accepted a doughnut wrapped in a napkin, thanked Ruth, and was in his rental car and gone.

Ruth returned to her bed while Jack slept in another room.

## 15

*T*he time was dusk as Vera Tyler sat in her pickup truck parked on a wide spot along the paved state highway verge. Although she reasoned that no one was watching her, she was nervous nonetheless. There were no buildings within her purview, and the last vehicle she saw, a passenger car, passed in the opposite direction six minutes earlier. But the appearance of the two men from the Federal Bureau of Investigation had thrown her off balance. That they appeared was bad enough, but when one of them intimated that Jason Thompson was alive and in contact with her, it had left her bereft in her thoughts. She bit her lip, then looked at her wrist watch.

Jason answered on the third ring. "Hello?"

"Hello. It's me."

"Hello. Are you okay?"

"No."

There was a short period of silence. Vera thought she could hear him breathe.

"I see. Uh, what seems to be the trouble?"

Vera hesitated, then, "I had visitors." She checked the feeling that she would break down.

"I see. Visitors." It was a question framed as a statement.

"Yes. Two."

"The cousins?"

"Yes. Cousins."

"The cousins—they—?"

"They know about granma."

"They know?"

"They don't know, but they think they do."

"Can you be more specific? What is it they think they know?"

Vera paused, trying to come up with the right think to say. "They think she's alive."

"I see—"

"Yes. They think the old lady may be alive."

"I see. Okay."

"I am—I am—"

"Of course. I understand. Uh, did the cousins say—tell you—they would return?"

"No."

"Let me—did they do more than speak with you? Look around? Search? For granma's things?"

"No."

"Good. Good."

An oil tanker appeared on the highway, moving at the speed limit. It rushed by, the sound from it drowning out Jason's words. Its bright headlamps nearly blinded her as it approached.

"What was that?" He asked.

"Truck. On the highway."

"Okay."

"What should I do?" She was close to tears, but contained herself.

"Do you expect another visit? From the cousins?"

"No. I don't know."

There was a pause. "Act normally. Normal routine. But—"

"But?"

"But watch. Be vigilant. Uh, anything unusual, make a note. Write it down. You know how cousin George can be."

"Okay."

"If you do, put it in a safe place. You know."

"Yes. Yes."

"How is it—?"

"Headway. I'm making headway."

"Good. Good."

"I will be—I'll be gone. Traveling. You understand."

"Yes."

"Take care. You know how I feel."

"Yes. I feel the same."

"Yes. Soon. Bye for now."

"Bye. Bye." Her voice cracked.

She sat for several minutes with tears on her face, but resisted sobbing. Then she started the truck, checked her mirrors and drove away in the dark.

Jason sat on the edge of the cheap motel roll-around desk chair and stared at the floor. He held the cell phone loosely, such that it started to slip from his hand. That event awakened him, and he firmed his grip on it and set it down on the narrow desk surface after powering it down.

In the morning, after coffee, juice and a shower, he pored over the papers in the metal box Sarah had secreted in the old escritoire. There was nothing that connected to the key he had found; a key he surmised must fit a bank deposit box.

He picked the key up and turned it over in his hand more than once. He fished around for the key that had opened the box that was before him, and compared it with the other. There were distinct differences. One, that which opened the secret box, featured the two-letter manufacturer's ID stamped into the presumably French Canadian-made key; the other, a differently-shaped key had what appeared to be a box number, and below that another stamped numerical code. It looked much like safety deposit keys he had seen; similar to the box he had used years before. The most distinct difference was that the shank was longer than that of the secret box key.

He set the key down and picked up the small book with the pages of as yet unintelligible inscriptions. He thought of the "god's eye" he had hung in his office. It was comprised of bands of colored yarn, in a diamond shape, sequenced to represent a security door code; that based upon the resistor manufacturer's color code for numerical resistor values. Likewise, there would have to be a key to Sarah's postings in the book. In the arcane world of spies and security agencies, there were a number of different ways to encrypt and decrypt codes. What had she used? Was it hers, or was it given to her? Would she have used it to communicate with her control? Did she have a control?

He stood and walked across the room to the single window. He pulled the curtain aside and looked out. The morning sun was at about thirty degrees, and had since washed its light over the Western face of the Sandia massive. He saw the mixture of industrial buildings and yards between the motel and the Interstate. Beyond was the piedmont which led to the sharp escarpment of the mountain named by Spanish invaders for a watermelon. Cars and trucks coursed north and south along the four lanes of the highway. To his left he noticed the row of fast food emporiums and service stations convenient to the inter-city traffic. Vehicles of all make and model moved along the access road and in and out of the businesses. He thought of how similar this old, Spanish-established place had become to the rest of the nation.

He mulled on that notion, then it dawned on him that Sarah, given the long periods of time that must have existed between accesses to the data in the book, probably used a simple way of encrypting her writing, in the same way he had used the so-called "RMA Code" in the god's eye. That led him to think she must have used what some code makers called a "one-time pad," a single reference source based on something such as a published book. If that were the case, what would his deceased wife have used as a source? Might it have been a root for someone else as well? That would not matter, since she would have to have that same reference material.

He turned and walked to the blank wall across the room to within a few inches of its surface, and stared at it as though it would reveal something. He walked back to the cheap little desk and opened the small book from Sarah's box. There were a half-dozen pages of penned numbers. The first page appeared to have been written in some random fashion, but the following pages were disciplined, in that there were rows and columns of numbers. Each set of numbers was laid out in a pattern of distinct groups. The first part, on the left, was comprised of from one to three numbers, followed by a space, then a four group series of numbers in sets of one or two each, with separating spaces as well.

Jason turned each page carefully, looking for anything else. Beyond the pages with the number series, there was nothing. Blank. He sat back and spent several moments thinking.

It was close to midnight when he arrived at his old residence, the place where he and his wife, and until grown and on their own, their three children had lived. The house was dark; both outside lights, that on the front porch and the one that lit the rear entrance through the kitchen were off. There was no car in the driveway, but the garage door was closed, and it was possible that one of the children, Flo, Justin or Charles were in the house, and their car was inside the garage.

As he had before, he stood a long time in the shadows, more than five minutes, listening and observing. His head gear was his new ivy cap, and he wore the darkest clothes he could muster. He went through the back gate with stealth and to the outside door to the garage. Afraid to risk using his penlight to look through the glass of the window in the door, even the frame with the broken glass, he cupped his hands over his face to block out as much of the faint ambient light he could, then pressed his face against a pane and peered in. The garage appeared empty. He stood back, relieved, then made his way to the sidewalk, then around to the front of the house. The street on that side was empty. He reckoned the house was devoid of family. The street was clear of police cruisers or other suspicious vehicles.

He returned to the rear of the residence and again waited in the dark. Could this be a trap? He thought of Vera's frantic report. Did they suspect he was alive, would return to the house, lay in wait in hopes he would show up? In his view, it made no sense, but he would have to maintain caution.

His trepidation rose as he approached the rear door and keyed himself in. As he did so, thoughts of why the lock was the same flitted through his mind, once again leading him to paranoia. But there was dark silence inside.

With the penlight on and off as he moved, careful not to point it at a window, he made his way to the first-floor book shelf he and his wife had filled and maintained over the years. He shown the light briefly over the five shelves that ranged from the floor to close to the ceiling in three parts. He pondered, then headed up the stairs to the master bedroom. Oddly, he thought, the door was closed as it was the last time. He hesitated, then turned the knob carefully, his mind full of dark thoughts of a possible snare. He pushed the door open wide, but remained in place for another count of five. Nothing. He peered in.

Faint light filtered into the room from the street, such that he was able to barely make out shapes in the room.

Tense, but more relaxed than he had been over the past hour, he moved carefully to the escritoire. He played the light over the top surface. The decorative pieces he had moved and replaced when he had pulled it out from the wall were where he had left them. He then moved to the big bed he had shared with Sarah. After stanching a feeling of remorse, he played the light over both bedside tables. He then went to the small table next to Sarah's side of the bed and pulled the drawer open. There, along with a hair brush, a padded-cover address book and some random costume jewelry, was a book.

He picked it up and looked it over. The title was *The Woman in The Garden*. He went to the dressing bench at the end of the bed, sat, and with the penlight in one hand and book in his lap, he opened it. Inside was the name of the author, one Anfisa Fyodorov. Below that was the following: *Translated from the Russian to French by Abram Galerkin and from the French version to English by Helen Yarborough.* Then, *Published by Courier Press, Montreal, 1936.*

He flipped through some of the pages. The last was numbered 257. He opened it to the approximate middle and read a passage. *She hungered for the passion she had felt as a young woman, that for the man who had swept her from her delicate feet.* The rest of the paragraph was in the same vein; a middle-aged woman's pining over the feelings of a lost youth.

He closed the book as he recalled Sarah laughing at such passages; that she had liked the story overall, but that she did not identify with the main character. He remembered her acquiring it at about the same time as the escritoire had arrived. From a Canadian relative. But why keep it next to her bed? Why not place it on a shelf with the other tomes they had acquired over the years? With the book in one hand, he rubbed his forehead hard.

Jason exited the house, careful to leave everything, save the book he carried, as he had found it. He traversed a different route to his truck which he had parked two blocks away and in a different direction. Although well after midnight, he was anxious to avoid the man and woman with "Ruff the Dog," as he had the last time. Safely in his vehicle, he popped a pill despite the fact that he was as calm as he had been for the entire day. He sat again, waiting, he realized, for nothing. If someone, or more than one person, were looking for him, or worse, tracking him, he detected no evidence of that.

Back in the motel room, and although tired and sleepy, he decided to test his theory. He removed the little black book from the metal box he had placed under the bed, then sat at the small desk with the single lamp on. He opened the notebook to the second page, that which was the first page with the more disciplined, sequenced notations. He read the first number of the first sequence, and turned to the page in the novel with that number. With the second number, he traced down the page to the line that number represented with his finger. The third number led him to the word on that line, which he then wrote onto a separate piece of paper. The fourth and final number represented a letter within the word. That, in and of itself, meant nothing. But after tracing out ten words and letters using the black book and the novel, he had a sentence that made sense. He was correct.

Though fatigued and bleary-eyed, he decoded the entire first page before he stood, snapped the light off, trudged to the bed and flopped down on it, fully-clothed. After three minutes of a partial dream state, he rose, pulled off his shoes and pants, threw back the covers, rolled onto the bed, pulled a pillow up under his head and fell asleep.

Parking was not easy to find near the Bernalillo County Court House. Jason was forced to hoof it for three blocks after putting what he hoped would be enough change in the meter to cover his stay. He found that there were half a dozen clerk windows, with all but one staffed. He made a rapid count of the number of people seated who waited for their number to be called. He took one of the tiny strips of paper from the machine that dispensed them, and took a seat next to a middle-aged woman whose bottom flowed over the edges of her chair seat. He counted nineteen minutes before his number was called.

The young Hispanic woman behind the protective glass was very pleasant. "Yes, sir, what can I do for you?"

"Uh, let me get my ID out here—there." He handed her his true driver's licence. "I'd like to get a copy of my father's probate papers."

She awarded him a adept smile. "ID not necessary sir. Your father's name?"

"Oh." He re-pocketed his wallet. "Thompson. Ira."

"What year was his estate probated?"

He gave the clerk the information she needed, and in turn, she provided him with a pristine copy of the probate papers.

Ensconced again in his motel room in Bernalillo and at the small desk, he invoked the word processor. With the papers at his side, he proceeded to copy, word for word, font for font, the entire document, save for the places where names and dates were different. When he was finished, three problems remained. One, he must print the results, and because he had left the associated printer at Vera's place, it required that he take the data somewhere to have it reproduced. Second, he must forge the judge's signature, and that of the clerk. Third, the most difficult, he must replicate the clerk's receipt stamp.

Before he picked up a milk shake at a fast-food place in Albuquerque, he visited a computer store, where he purchased a so-called "thumb drive;" a portable memory device. In his truck, with the shake safely on the floor and the laptop next to him on the passenger seat, he plugged the little memory stick into the computer and transferred the concocted document into the portable memory device. As the action took place, he scanned the lot where he had parked. No more than three people walked within a car length of his pickup, and none had an interest in him. From there, after finishing the drink, he drove to the nearest Kinko's, where an attendant showed him how to print the file resident in the stick. He made two copies, paid for the service, took the papers and the memory drive, and left.

While he waited for the prints, he had scoured the local directory for a hobby store, and made a note of one not far from where he was. There, after he left with the printouts, he spent half an hour as he looked over the rubber stamps available, most of which were designed for children. He selected three, a stamp pad with black ink, and an Exacto knife with extra blades.

He purchased a fast-food excuse for dinner, then returned to the motel. Settled in at the desk, he spent the evening hunched over his task. Much of that time involved cutting away certain parts of the rubber stamps.

At close to the appointed time, he spoke with Vera for three minutes, then continued to work. Finished close to midnight, he looked his handiwork over once more, and satisfied, went to bed.

The following morning, he made in-room coffee, showered, grabbed a cold, stiff, sugar-coated pastry in the pitiful excuse for a dining room in the motel lobby, and went to his pickup. With his usual caution, he looked about without being obvious. He detected nothing unusual. With him, he had the doctored papers. His innards churned as he thought of the possible negative outcome he faced.

As he entered the highway leading to the Interstate, he began his routine of watching for a possible tail. Once on the four-lane divided highway north, he was comfortable with the assurance that there was no one with an interest following.

The drive to the village of Pecos took him a little more than an hour, and he arrived twenty minutes before the bank opened. He parked in the otherwise empty parking lot and waited. In an attempt to stay calm, he flicked the dashboard radio on and listened to a music station that came in partially despoiled with static. He reckoned the condition was caused by interference from the high, rugged terrain between his position and the mountain-top transmitter to the southwest.

He noticed as one, then two, cars drove into the lot and parked in the section striped for employees. Then a third car appeared and parked there as well.

When the time on his watch read nine o'clock, he exited the truck, locked it, and headed for the main door of the bank. It was locked, but a few seconds later, a young lady with a ready smile unlocked the door and he entered.

The small lobby was empty, but the two teller windows were staffed. He walked up to one of them.

"Can I help you, sir?" It was the girl who had unlocked the door.

"Yes, uh, I need to get into a safety deposit box." He produced the key and laid it on the narrow counter.

"Do you have your ID and pass card?"

"No, you see, this is my late wife's box, and—"

"Well. We'll need—"

"I have the probate papers here." He pulled them nervously from his jacked pocket, unfolded them and handed them to the girl.

"Oh, of course." She glanced at them, then said, "One moment, sir. I'll be right back. Why don't you have a seat?" She gestured at the set of two chairs that graced the other side of the lobby.

Jason turned and went to the chairs, where he lowered himself into one of them stiffly. He stared at the floor, then forced himself to look around at the decorative prints that graced the walls, fearful of what might transpire next.

He saw the girl and an older woman converse inside an office with a large window that faced the lobby. He noticed the older woman glance at him during her examination of the forged documents.

A minute and a half passed before the girl came up to him as he remained in the chair. "Would you come into the manager's office, please, sir?"

His heart leaped as he rose from the chair, fearful that he was about to encounter a problem. He was relieved when the older woman greeted him pleasantly and asked him to sign a card showing that he was about to open a box. He was then led to the vault by the younger woman who, using her bank key, helped him open the door to box 39 and retrieve it. She indicated a small anteroom with a table and chair, where he was invited to sit with the box.

"Take your time, sir." She smiled, left and closed the door.

With trepidation, Jason lifted the cover to the grey steel box. Inside were several items. Largest of them was a black, six by nine hard-cover note book. On top of that were two passports and a two-inch thick stack of large currency bills. Between the book and the edge of the box was a small piece of gold jewelry, and beneath the book was a brown envelope, bulging against its contents.

He gathered the items, which cleared the box, then went back to the teller window.

"I want to close out the box."

"Of course, sir." The girl awarded him a wan smile as he handed her his key. "Uh, do you have the other key?"

He looked at her, perplexed, and shook his head. "No—no, I don't. I didn't find one. You see. I—"

She nodded. "It's alright. I understand. No problem." She smiled.

"Thanks," he said. He turned and walked away.

In the truck, he laid the contents of the box on the passenger seat, then opened the bound book. He recognized Sarah's handwriting.

He read, *"My Dearest Jason, what I am about to say, to write, will most likely shock and dismay you, but I beg you to understand and forgive me . . ."*

He read two pages, then dropped the open book onto his lap and lowered his head until his chin touched his heaving chest. After a few seconds, he raised his head and stared through the windshield as tears made their way slowly down his cheeks.

A woman who arrived in a small car and parked next to him, got out and closed her door, then looked at him through his passenger-side window. She realized he was weeping, and embarrassed, turned her head and hurried away.

# 16

*T*he big, heavy, shiny wooden conference table was capable of seating fourteen people. Six on each of the long sides and one at each end. It was oval shaped, a concession to the idea of conferees afforded the ability to see each other. Six more chairs were placed against the walls on either side of the room. The sole door to the room was heavy as well, with no observation window. It featured a code lock on the hall side. The room was sound-proofed and swept periodically for bugs.

Peter Grayson and Marcus Lucero sat on one of the long sides, a chair separating them. Three files, two manila, one red, not all of the same thickness, lay in front of them, within reach. Across from them was another man, Samuel Buckley, Senior Special Agent of the Albuquerque Office of the Federal Bureau of Investigation.

Grayson's hands were folded on the table. Lucero's were on his lap.

Buckley sat back, a foot away from the table, his elbows on the arm rests, the fingers of his hands laced across his chest. The expression he wore was one of contemplation, concern and disbelief. "You think this guy, this Thompson, may be alive?" He moved his head purposefully to face each of the special agents across the table from him as though challenging his subordinates.

Grayson lowered his head, paused to look at the files that lay in front of him, then glanced at Lucero before setting his eyes on Buckley again. "We don't know, Sam. We—"

Buckley straightened and grabbed the chair's arm rests. "You know what the director is gonna say if I present this nonsense?" He pointed his finger at Grayson, then Lucero. "He's not going to say anything. He's gonna' explode!" He looked at the ceiling and shook his head.

"I—"

"Okay, okay, Peter, go over it again. Convince me that we should commit more resources to this fucking fiasco!" Buckley returned to his relaxed position.

Grayson nodded his head, his lips pursed. "Right. Somehow—somehow, this guy Nantes—we think an alias—found out the Thompson guy was at a ranch in the southern part of the state. One—"

Lucero opened a file, moved it toward Grayson and pointed.

Grayson read, "Tyler. Vera. Her place. Lives alone. Widowed. From what we can figure, Thompson may have flown there—"

Buckley interrupted, "Flown there?!" He leaned forward and squinted.

Grayson shook his head broadly, raised his eyebrows and held out both of his open palms. "From what we can figure. At any rate, this Nantes guy apparently tracked Thompson to the ranch, but—and here's what gets weird—another man, unknown to us to date—shows up at the same time, and, according to the woman, there's a shoot-out, and Thompson is killed. We don't know if it was from the fire when the plane exploded or gunshot—or both."

"Jesus," Buckley muttered. He looked away.

"Then," Grayson continued, "this Nantes, who ID'd himself to the Tyler woman as one of us, brings in his own janitorial service." He paused as he fingered a file, glanced away to gather his thoughts, then back at his boss. "The other man disappears along with the wreckage, Thompson's ashes are eulogized here at the Episcopal Cathedral, and we think it's over. Then the two bodies in Truchas. One of which was Thompson's widow; the other this Nantes guy. NTSB on the plane? Nothing."

Buckley nodded during the ensuing silence and studied the carpeted floor between his feet.

Grayson stood and walked to one end of the table, then turned. He looked at nothing. "Then, we have a car go missing. From the crime scene. Up north. A Mercedes belonging to the deceased Thompson woman. It shows up in Socorro, and a young girl there remembers seeing an older man who could match Thompson's description." He turned to look at Buckley, then Lucero, who had his head down in contemplation.

Buckley kept his eyes on Grayson.

"So, what was Nantes doing there? With Sarah Thompson? Why are they both dead? Why was one of the weapons a Cold War piece? Apparently wielded by the woman?" Grayson threw his hands out in a gesture of frustration.

"Nantes?" Buckley asked.

Grayson returned to his seat. He sat and sighed. "I talked to my guy inside the company. He had never heard of a Nantes—but that doesn't mean he wasn't there, given the way they operate. But inside the states? Not kosher. CIA methods? You better believe it. Methinks that gentleman was as dirty as they come." He stared at Lucero for several seconds, then looked away. "But dirty how?" He tilted his head. "Why was he with the Thompson lady, and who the hell was she?" Silence, then, "We think Nantes was the head janitor down south, but who were the janitors? And the third guy? Sarah Thompson? The man in Socorro?" He held up his hands, then placed them on the table, where he fidgeted with his fingers.

Buckley sat silent as he nodded his head. "Write it up. Details. Precise time-line. I'll hand-deliver it. Looks as though the—Geronimo Queen, was it? Is a bigger case than we thought." He paused, then rose and straightened his clothing. "I'll get the funds. Stay on it until I say 'no.'" He glanced at both men and left the room.

Grayson and Lucero sat quietly for a minute.

Lucero spoke first. "You know that mesa, that ridge, to the west of the Tyler place?" He didn't look at his partner.

"Yeah."

"We could plant ourselves—or something—up there to keep an eye out."

"We could."

"We could."

"What do we expect to find? To see?" Grayson worked a crick out of his neck.

"I don't know, Pete. Something. Maybe."

"Maybe."

"Have there been eyes on the house? The Thompson place?"

Grayson drew in a deep breath and released it. "You mean APD? Not that I know of."

"Seems to me if the old guy is still around, he might show up there."

"Mm."

"Kinda odd that someone went in. The house. The truck. Stolen? Nowhere to be found? Eh."

"Yep." Grayson thought, then, "So if he's around, where is he? What's he up to?"

Lucero stood and went to one of the plaques on the plain wall. He spoke as he appeared to read the legend on it. "If we knew when the plane flew and from where . . ."

"Planes that didn't return. Their owners. Good thinking."

"We need a warrant to search the ranch." He turned and looked at Grayson.

"FAA? Flight plans?"

"Back to the labs? Somebody might know if Thompson was a pilot."

"Lunch?"

"Lunch."

Stanley Webber had returned the rental car and retrieved his own by mid-afternoon. As he got onto the highway back to Reston, he keyed a number on his cell phone.

"Yeah, Hi. Listen, I'll be in later to tidy up some stuff, but I need to run an errand. Yeah, thanks."

Forty-five minutes later, he directed his car into the parking lot of a set of buildings that housed a variety of doctor's and dentist's offices. He parked close to the outer road, exited without locking the car, then strode to the porch-covered building that housed the "Dental Associates of Reston."

In the lobby, he was surrounded by a mixture of seated people waiting to be called. He went to the receptionist's window.

"Can I help you, sir?" She was a middle-aged woman.

"Ah, yes. Uh, I'd like to speak with Dr. Berman."

"Well, he's with a patient. Do you need an appointment?"

Webber smiled, looked around the room, then back. "No. Personal matter."

"I see." She looked at her computer screen, then back. "He's busy until four." She looked up.

"Uh, okay." He looked at his watch. "Look, I'll be back. Could you tell him I want to see him? Here?" He raised his eyebrows and pointed.

"Of course, sir." She picked up a ballpoint pen. "May I say who?"

"Yes. Yes. Webber. Stanley."

She wrote, then looked at him. "I'll deliver the message. And you'll be back?"

"Yes. Thanks."

When Webber returned to the dental office at ten minutes to four, there were two patients in the lobby. He went to the reception window.

"Hi," he said.

She turned to face him. "Oh—you're back. I gave him your message. He should be through soon. He had an emergency. A patient. Please have a seat."

At five after four, the hall door to the lobby opened, and a slight man with thinning brown hair and wearing glasses over a white, waist-length jacket appeared. He went up to Webber as he stood.

"Stanley, how are you? Tess gave me your message. What can I do for you?" He glanced at the two other people in the room.

"Ollie, thanks for seeing me. Uh, could we talk in your office?"

"Sure, sure. C'mon in." He gestured.

The two men entered Berman's office. Berman sat behind his desk, while Webber took a chair in front of it.

"Okay," Berman began with a smile tempered by curiosity. "What can I do for you? What do you need? Got a problem with the pearly whites?" He grinned.

Webber conjured up a phony smile. "Ah, no, Ollie. Not at all. Something—"

"Hey, how's the family? Everything there okay?"

"Yes, yes, Ollie. Everybody's fine. Just fine. No, I need a favor." He nodded with sincerity.

"Okay . . ." Berman drew out the "o" in "okay."

"Ollie, you know—probably know—if not known, guessed—that I work for the government."

"Yes, yes. Sure." He tilted his head to one side and brought the fingers of both his hands up to his chin in a pose of sincerity.

"I—here's the thing. I work in a field that requires a lot of, shall we say, secrecy. Know what I mean?"

"Hey, I get that. No problem, Stan. No problem." He paused. "My lips are sealed." He grinned and chuckled.

Webber took a silent moment while he glanced at the floor. He faked embarrassment. "Right, right. That's good. So, Ollie, given that, sometimes I have to do things, get involved in things that require a whole lot of—shall we say—side-stepping. Know what I mean?"

"I do. I do. Yes. Sure. Side-stepping."

He did not, something Webber knew, but to which he didn't react.

"Okay, Ollie. Bottom line. I need an X-ray."

Berman was silent for several seconds. "An X-ray." His voice had moved to a lower register, and he furrowed his brow.

"Yes. X-ray."

"For—bad tooth? I don't—"

"Here's the thing, Ollie. Where I work, we have X-ray. But I can't use it." He stared at Berman with a look of pure innocence.

"You can't?" Berman shook his head in one short, jerking motion.

"No. I can't. You see, if I did, it could compromise something very sensitive. National security." He waited as he studied Ollie Berman's reaction.

"So, this is not for a tooth?"

"No. Not a tooth. Something else."

Berman squirmed in his chair. "How—how would I be involved. I mean, would I—?"

Webber leaned forward on the edge of his seat in a gesture of sincerity. "No, no, Ollie." He shook his head. "No. You would not be in any sort of trouble. Any sort of problem. Hey, there's money involved. I'm prepared to pay."

Berman gave Webber a side-long glance. "Stanley, is this—?"

"What?! Illegal?! Hell, no, man! Of course not!" He calmed. "I work for the federal government, Ollie." He paused and lowered his voice. "Look, there are times when there are, you know, investigations. That's what this is. The problem

I—we—have, is this investigation may involve people inside. The government. And we can't let it get around. Hey, simple as that." He sat back. "Simple as that. What do you say?"

"What is it you want to X-ray?"

"You want protection? You want immunity? You want to be far away from this? Right? Then you don't need to know. I'm talking two, maybe three pictures. That's it. In and out. Off hours. I'm gone. None the wiser. An envelope on a table and you haven't seen me or know me."

"Sheez, Stan." Berman lowered his head and wiped his brow.

"Question for you, Ollie."

Berman raised his head to gaze at his visitor with a look of misery.

"Five minute training. I use the X-ray. Yours is a bit different, but it'll work. Leave out three films. Two or three in the morning. Leave the door where I can get in. I watch my back—and yours. You get extra vacation money and we're square."

The defeated Berman nodded his head. He sat back, closed his eyes, then looked at his watch. "Be back here at ten. Tonight. Only time I can do it. Marge's got something at her goddamn club. I'll have to help you. I'd rather."

"I'll be here. Family's out of town. Perfect. You're a jewel." Webber stood.

"I hope so." Berman's voice expressed sad resignation.

Webber reached across the desk to shake Berman's hand. Berman hesitated, then responded meekly.


Jason Thompson sat in the motel room bedside chair, watching television news when his cell phone chirped.

"Hello," he said.

"Hi."

"How are you?"

"Okay. You?"

"I'm alright." He waited, then, "Something that needs to be done. Soon."

"Yes?"

"There's a road—is there a road—that goes up the side, you know, behind?"

"Uh, yes. Yes."

"How far?"

"'Bout a mile. Maybe more. Wh—?"

"Everything, everything needs to go up there. Get my meaning?"

"I think so . . ."

"Vehicle, everything. Soon. Out of sight. The cousins. You know."

"Oh, my . . ."

"It's okay. Precaution."

"Sure. Sure."

"Okay? Means hoofing it back."

"Yes. That's okay. In the morning. Okay."

"Good. Sorry."

"I—I understand. Has to be."

"Yes. Has to be."

"I feel—"

"Me, too. You know how I feel."

"Yes. Okay. Bye."

"Bye, bye."


Webber sat behind the wheel of his car in a dark corner of the nearly empty night-time parking lot. Across the expanse of tarmac and intervening concrete barriers and walkways, cones of bluish light created filmy, visible circles in the otherwise ten o'clock night. He held his watch up to what little illumination there was. Berman was late.

It was then that he saw the twin lights of a car enter the lot and drive up to a paint-marked slot two places away from the doctor's establishment. Webber waited until he saw the dentist get out, stand and look around briefly, then shut and lock his car door and make his way around the back of the building. Webber was annoyed as he saw Berman, shoulders hunched, turn his head to look around every fourth step until he disappeared around a corner, as though guilty of some crime he was about to commit. Webber then took the small, weighty package that rested on the floorboard in front of the passenger seat, exited his car, surveyed the empty lot once more, then made briskly for the corner where Berman had disappeared. He did not look around as he moved.

He caught up with Dr. Berman as the man keyed himself into the rear door of his office complex.

Berman turned as he heard Webber approach. "You're here."

"Yes. As are you, Ollie. Let's do this thing."

Inside, Berman checked to ensure the outside door was again secure. As he turned and walked past Webber, who waited, he glanced down at the package his visitor held. "That it? The thing?"

"Yes."

Berman moved at a quick, nervous pace along the hall to his office suite, one of four in the complex, and unlocked the door. Inside, he switched on the panels of ceiling fluorescent lamps, then moved on as they flickered to life.

"It's in here," he said. He opened a door half-way down the narrow hall that led to his main examining room. There, he turned on the lights, spent three seconds looking around, then turned to face Webber. "I better help you with this."

"You can't just give me a leg up?" Webber frowned at him.

Berman shook his head once. "Please, Stan, this makes me nervous. I want to make sure everything goes okay—nothing left behind. No trace. Please." His voice was pleading.

Webber looked past him for a moment, then looked him in the eye. "Listen, Ollie, and listen good. This is national security stuff. Sensitive stuff. What I have in my hand shouldn't be here. Hell, it shouldn't be in the state—in this town. In my hands. You get that?"

Berman nodded his head with a pained look.

Webber shook his head as he hesitated. He put his hand on Berman's shoulder. "Look, man, what I'm doing here is not illegal. You know how it goes. There're things going on within the agencies that are, what? Under the radar, so to speak. This is one of them. I've been tasked with this for another agency. Not mine. It can't see the light of day where I work. Okay?" He paused as he dropped his hand from the nervous dentist's shoulder. "Now, you're going to be compensated. Well compensated. I've got it with me. We do this, we part company, my people get an answer to a question, and none's the wiser. Okay?" He looked hard at Berman, who nodded meekly. "Now, can we get started?"

"Yeah. Yeah."

"Good. Good man."

Berman went through the steps required to set up his X-ray equipment, then turned to Webber. "Okay. Ready. What do we have?"

Webber pulled the brown wrapping paper away from the thin, rectilinear box, opened it and removed the dart pistol.

Berman watched him. "Jesus Christ, Stanley! What the hell?!"

With the pistol in his hand, Webber turned to face Berman. "What's your problem?! Calm the goddamn hell down, man! What did you expect me to bring in here?! A fucking toy?!"

"But—"

"But what?!"

"Why—what is it?!"

Webber set the pistol down, then put both his hands on Berman's shoulders. "Look at me and listen." He paused. "That gun is a fucking dart pistol. It's probably Russian origin. It was used to kill an agent of the United States government. Its markings, the serial numbers and ID have been removed. Filed away. If we do our job right, that X-ray there—" He stopped and pointed, then returned his hand to Berman's shoulder. "That X-ray there will divulge the markings. And then, Ollie, I—and others—will be able to do our jobs and track the goddamn gun down to its origin. We might just be able to find out the who and why of things. Now do you get it?"

Berman, his face a mask of misery, nodded pathetically.

"Okay." Webber dropped his hands and took a step back.

The miserable Dr. Berman walked past Webber, stopped, turned and gestured at the pistol. Webber picked it up and followed Berman into the X-ray cubicle. Berman set up the first plate, and they both stood outside while Berman fired the machine up. They re-set the position of the gun twice more, took the shots, then moved the plates to the dark room.

Berman snapped the processed films into the wall-mounted, back-lighted inspection platens as Webber stepped in close.

Webber peered closely at the black-and-white images. "Ha! Do you read Cyrillic, Doc?" He continued to look at the pictures.

"Cyrillic?" Berman's voice was weak.

Webber turned and backed away. He folded his arms across his chest as he continued to stare at the films in glee. "Russian, Ollie old man. Russian. Cyrillic characters. Most likely Russian."

Berman shook his head in a gesture of despair. "God. What am I involved in?"

Webber frowned at him, his arms still across his chest. "Involved? Shit. You've done it, old man! Done it. We can read the markings! You're a hero!" His voice was a register higher in his excitement. He smiled.

"I don't know, Stanley. Makes me nervous." He paced away to stare at the wall. "What's going on?" His voice was barely audible.

Webber dropped his arms to his sides and shook his head. He lowered his voice a decibel and an octave. "Jee-zuz, Ollie. You're making this out to be something it's not." He took two steps and stopped. "I am an agent of the government, Ollie. I'm doing my job. We had a problem. This weapon came in from left field. The truth? We—I, and others—believe there's someone or something going on within the agency. Something that could jeopardize certain operations." He stopped, turned a circle and faced Berman. "This had to be deep cover. Clandestine. I don't know where it will lead, Ollie. Maybe there's nothing to it. Maybe it's not inside. But—and here's the thing. You look at that weapon. That's not your everyday killing machine, Ollie. That's left field. Outside. Get it?"

Berman nodded in silence.

"Are we good, Ollie? Are we good?" Webber stared at the back of Berman's head.

"Yeah, yeah," he whispered. "Yeah. Good."

"Okay, man, let's boogie." Webber's voice was couched.

When the two men reached the outside door, Webber stopped Berman with his hand on his sleeve. "Leave first. But Ollie, walk with some confidence to your car, man. Not fast. Normally. Don't look back, and don't look around. Look as though you're in charge. Look at your watch, take your cell out and make a call, or pretend to make a call. I'll follow after you're gone. Okay?"

"God! You think someone's watching?!" Berman's voice was whiney.

Webber dipped his head in frustration. He lowered his voice to its lowest register. "No, Ollie, god damn it. No one's watching! But this is peripheral, man. When something like this comes down, we take extra precautions. Okay?"

"Yes, yes. Okay."

"Alright, Ollie; drive normally. Don't race away. Take care, okay? And thanks."

"Yes. Yes." Berman remained in place and peered at Webber expectantly in the shadows.

"Oh, right. Forgot." Webber reached inside his jacket pocket and withdrew a white number ten envelope. He handed it to the dentist. "You'll be pleased. Untraceable." He winked and made a clicking sound with his mouth.

"Thanks, Stanley." Berman nodded with a wan smile, hesitated a moment, then turned and walked away. He obeyed Webber's mandate to behave normally for a man walking across an empty parking lot at close to midnight.

Webber watched from the dark corner as Berman went to his car and drove away. His face set in a frown, he then skirted the lot well within the shadows to his car, the large brown envelope with the X-ray films inside, dangling from his hand along with the shallow box that contained the dart pistol. He stood for a moment, surveyed the area, got in, put the re-packaged gun and the packet of films on the passenger side floor and drove away.

No one had observed either man when they arrived or departed.

# 17

*V*era rolled out of bed before the sun had crested over the eastern escarpment behind the house. She sat on the edge of the bed for half a minute, gathering her thoughts and tightening her muscles. She then plodded into the kitchen to brew a pot of coffee after relieving herself , splashing warm water over her face and controlling her hair with a comb.

After downing a cup of cream-doped coffee with dispatch, she grabbed her thick, sheep-lined sleeveless work jacket, banged out of the front door as she pulled it on, and headed for the horse barn. She found a sturdy wooden crate amongst a stack of the same, and went back to the house. There, she put every-thing she could find that belonged to Jason into the slatted box. That included clothes, papers and the new printer. Unaware of the tiny book secreted between the wall and the doorframe in the room he had commandeered for his office, that remained. After clearing the room, she restored the sparse furniture to its arrangement before his arrival.

She carried the box to the barn-cum-garage and loaded it into the pas-senger side of Jason's old, restored Ford Pickup. As she crossed the open space between the house and the dark hiding place, she scanned the escarpment ridges to the west and the east, and took a cursory look behind at the road in. She realized that if someone were hiding up high, the likelihood of her seeing them was negligible, but she was also comfortable with her knowledge of the landscape and felt she might spot something out of place. A moment after doing so, she considered that if there were someone watching, that what she was about at the moment would serve more to expose her actions than not. She reasoned that it was a risk she had to take.

With her work gloves on, she went to the horse barn and selected a rope hackamore, then went outside and whistled to the roan as she moved toward the pasture gate. The animal made for her at a walk, and five minutes later, as the first beams of light from the sun washed down over the ranch, the horse was saddled and waiting patiently for her to back the Ford out into the yard. She then attached fifteen feet of nylon rope to the horse's bridle and the other end to the driver's side corner of the pickup bed. She soothed and talked to the roan, then got into the truck and started out at a rate of five miles per hour. The horse followed dutifully behind.

The old ranch/forest road up onto the plain to the north was no more than an upbound dual trace caused long ago over a long period, together with sparse evidence of animal presence in the guise principally of hoof prints and occasional spoor. It was ingrown with weeds and grama grass. Piñon and cedar branches reached out to confound all that passed. Some served to scratch at the sides of the pristine vehicle with loud screeching, causing Vera to grit her teeth and curse beneath an audible level. She knew Jason would be distressed, but the situation called for whatever had to be accomplished at the moment, including minor damage. Behind the slow-moving truck, the patient and obedient roan came apace, with the rope dangling in a low arc between the animal and the vehicle. She kept an eye on the brute through the driver's side mirror.

As the forlorn roadway arced over onto more level ground, the prevalence of ponderosa, cedar, piñon and occasional blue juniper rose significantly. Vera brought the old vehicle to a halt and looked around as the engine idled with a smooth purr. She recalled an ancient cedar post fence with three or four strands of barbed wire that stretched east and west along the northern boundary of the ranch property, but she had not seen it in years. She reckoned that the old, minimal road must run at least to that line.

She looked behind, then shut the ignition off, opened the door and stepped out. The roan waited patiently, but stamped a foreleg and nodded its great head as it watched her. With the truck door ajar, she walked carefully away and into a high arbor of ponderosa branches. She looked up to study the canopy. The sky was, for the most part, obliterated over an area she thought to be approximately two hundred square feet, more than adequate for the truck.

Vera walked back to the overgrown clearing that ran the length of the old road and to the pickup. She untied the link rope, then went to the roan and spoke to the animal as she removed the rope from the halter, coiled it and looped it around the saddle pommel. She threw the horse's reins loosely over a low tree branch, and returned to the pickup. She then drove it into the shaded open spot under the tree bower, stopped, killed the ignition, removed the key and locked the doors after exiting. With her gloves still on, she threw tree branches and other foliage over as much of the truck as she could. Finished, she stood away and looked at the results.

Satisfied with the camouflage, she went to the horse, freed the reins, picked up a long, thin pine branch with most of its needles intact, and swung into the saddle. She began riding slowly back toward the valley, the barns and the house, and leaned over to smooth the ground where she found obvious tire tracks from the Ford as she moved along the old trace. She continued the practice all the way to the covered space where the re-built Ford had been parked, then encouraged the roan to turn back to the base of the ancient road, where she threw the pine wand away. Then she made sure the area was well marked with hoof marks before releasing the horse from its duty to enjoy the freedom of the pasture.

In the barn, she found a niche few outsiders would recognize as a hiding place for a set of keys.

At the same time that Vera sat down to more coffee and a simple breakfast, seven and a half miles to the southwest, a black Chevrolet SUV turned off the main, paved, two-lane highway, through an opening in a barbed wire fence, onto a dirt road leading north. Attached to it at the rear with a ball hitch, was a six by sixteen-foot flatbed trailer. On the trailer was an over-sized, four-wheel, four-seat all-terrain vehicle, or "ATV," in military camouflage colors. A man was at the wheel of the SUV. Alongside him in the front passenger seat was a woman. Seated behind them were two men. The driver was dressed casually, part of which was a dark blue wind-breaker. The three passengers were all in military-style camouflage with boots, leggings and field hats. They all wore semi-automatic side arms. Behind the rear seats was a jumble of technical gear in black, high-impact plastic cases accompanied by camping gear and tent.

Fifteen minutes later, the vehicles halted at the point where the road petered out near a forbidding rock formation. With little conversation, the group exited the SUV and busied themselves unloading the ATV from the trailer and the gear from the big vehicle. The equipment from the SUV was transferred to the rear storage area of the ATV and lashed down with bungee cords. One of these was a special case in the shape of a rifle. With little fanfare, the empty trailer was backed and turned. The three people in camouflage exchanged cursory waves with the SUV driver as they mounted the ATV, and the SUV pulled away, the trailer dutifully behind.

One of the men sat in the driver's position on the little vehicle, started the engine, and maneuvered it onto what comprised a trail up and away from the big rocks. In less than a minute, an observer in the area where they had off-loaded would not have been able to see the trio, but they would have heard its muffled exhaust for another 15 seconds.

Stanley Webber and Jerry Madsen sat across from each other in a cramped booth; that in a long, narrow diner which evoked memories of that sort of establishment made from discarded rail cars. The place was in semi-dark, though it was nine-thirty on a sunny morning, and that because the sole source of light was the grease-filmy plate glass front that faced the street. Each man had a cup of coffee and a plate in front of him. Madsen's plate was covered with an egg dish, bacon and potatoes, while Webber's was a lonely sugar-painted doughnut.

Webber sat on the side of the narrow, plastic-covered table that faced the front. Every few seconds, he leaned to his left to eye the door and anyone arriving or leaving. He sipped his dark brew.

Madsen stirred the mess on his plate, took a large bite, chewed and swallowed. He lifted his cup to his lips, drank, and set it down. He looked at Webber, who worked slowly on the pastry with a fork. "Russian."

Webber nodded. "Keep you voice down."

Madsen looked around, shrugged, and dug into his fare again. "Okay." He raised his eyebrows. "No one's gonna hear us, and if they do—"

Webber shook his head, drew in a breath and sighed. "That may be, Jerry, but just that attitude that can get folks in trouble. Killed."

Madsen worked his bulk into a gesture of agreement. "Yeah. You're right." He took another bite. After clearing his mouth, he asked, "Russian characters you say?"

"Cyrillic. Who else?" Webber attended to his coffee.

Madsen sat back, sated. "Translation?"

"Serial. Date. No manufacturer I could ascertain."

Madsen nodded. "Not that it matters. Merely confirms suspicions. Probably KGB internal manufacture."

"You'll get back to our friends with this?"

"Yep. Soon's I can."

Webber re-positioned himself in his seat. He glanced around the room, then leaned in against the table edge. "Jerry, what do you know about what the FBI knows? About this weapon?" He tapped the surface of the table. "Where'd they get it? Who had it?"

"It was like pulling teeth, but my source told me there was some sort of shoot-out. Hell, I told you this." He had lowered his voice.

Webber frowned. "Yeah, yeah, I know, but you said they think there's something rotten in Denmark. Inside the company."

"Possibly." Madsen slurped his coffee.

"And the guy? The guy the woman shot. Killed?"

"Hey, Stan, this needs to stay close." Madsen shook his head and pointed his finger at his table partner.

"You told me a name."

"I did? Really. I don't remember." He made a face.

"Yeah, Jerry. Something like 'Nancy.' French, I think." Webber's voice was whisper-conspiratorial. He knew what the name was, but feigned ignorance.

Madsen leaned forward. "Yeah, okay. I remember. Nantes. Nantes is the name. I haven't heard anything else." He kept the fact that he was in possession of a photograph Grayson had handed him.

Webber nodded, then shook his head. "Yeah, right. Never have—"

"So, where'd you find an X-ray?"

Webber effected a playful grin. "Ah, well, Jerry, turn-about, tit for tat and all that jazz. Rather not say. I will say I found a civilian source." He stared at Madsen.

"Sure. That's fine. Okay. But, now we know. Ruskie."

"Looks that way. Want it back?"

"Yeah, I need to get it back to my guy."

"It's in the car." He jerked his chin up instinctively, pointing.


When Agent Grayson received the special Email signal, he invoked the Kappa Network. He decrypted the message, then returned a short encrypted response. He shut down the site, then left to find Lucero. He met him in the hall, and the two men stopped.

Grayson looked along the hall in both directions, then at his partner. "Russian."

Lucero cocked his head and frowned.

"The pistol." Grayson maintained a low voice. "Dart. The dart pistol. Russian. Cyrillic characters show the date and serial."

Lucero nodded. "Good. What now?"

"It's on its way back."

"So, it's what we thought. The gun."

"Yep." Grayson ran his fingers through his hair and looked down. "Question is, how do we trace it?"

"Do they know how old it is?"

"Guy who did the forensics thinks it's more than twenty."

"Yeah, yeah."

Grayson blew his breath out. "We gotta trace that woman."

"Thompson's wife?"

'Fraid so. Some travel comin' up."

"Mm."

Grayson started away, then came back. "Did our guys get set up down south?"

"They're in position." Lucero nodded.

"Too early for anything."

"If there *is* anything."

Grayson lowered his head, compressed his lips, and looked at Lucero from under his eyebrows. He nodded, then turned and walked away.

Vera chose another place to park along the highway shortly before the sun set. She looked at her watch, then took the little phone from the glove compartment and keyed the number.

"Hello?" She heard Jason's voice.

"Hello."

"Are you well?"

"Yes. Are you?"

"Yes."

"Took a trip," Vera said.

"Yes?"

"When?"

"This mornin'."

"Good trip?" Jason asked.

"Yes, it was. I found some nice shade."

"Shade—ah, good. Good."

"Tree shade."

"Of course."

"And you."

"Me? Things are good. Getting things done. You know."

"Sure."

"Well, good to hear from you. Soon."

"Yes, soon."

Later, after Vera checked on the welfare of her animals, she entered the house, went to the kitchen, poured half a glass of milk, and took it to the bedroom. She drank some of it, then disrobed and lay down.

She fell asleep quickly, but awoke amid a disturbing dream at shortly after three. She felt as though she should get up, but was half awake and certain she would feel worse if she were to do so. She reached for the lamp on the bedside table and snapped it on. The glass with the milk contained no more than an inch of the liquid. She thought of finishing it, then decided against the idea of downing it at room temperature. She turned to look at Jason's side of the bed, which was undisturbed. Fatigue swept over her, so she shut the light off and flopped back down on the pillow. Tears came to her as she lay on her back, then she turned on her side and beat the pillow into submission to accommodate her wet cheek.

She awoke later than she usually did, and when she realized the time, sprang from her bed, grabbed her robe and padded first to the bathroom, then the kitchen. With a cup of fresh, hot coffee in her hand, she did what she always did, look through the window over the sink onto the pasture. There were the roan and the pinto, busy moving about the pasture, seeking a more succulent morsel of grass with each step as the early sunlight swept over it. She sipped at the brew, then started to turn away when she caught a flash of light, which disappeared as quickly as it had appeared. She set the cup down on the drainboard, put both her hands on the edge and looked up to what she perceived to be the source. It had been up high, along the mesa ridge. Why would there be light from there? The sun was behind the house, and there was nothing up there but ancient sedimentary rock and arid country verdancy; nothing shiny, reflective. She stood still for more than a minute, then crooked her head to look about, trying to fill in the blanks of her thinking.

With deliberation, she fixed a small breakfast, got dressed and with her traditional clothes and head cover on, went about the morning business of the ranch. She was careful not to look up toward the Western ridge as she moved about outside.

A half hour before noon, her riding boots on, a straw Western hat on her head, she saddled the roan, slid the .30-.30 rifle into the saddle scabbard, and trekked up the old road where she had secreted Jason's re-built Ford pickup truck the day before.

She proceeded up the trail until she was well hidden behind dense forest, then found her way with the aid of the horse's good sense along age-old, proven animal trails to higher country farther to the west. Half an hour passed before she was on the flat of the mesa. From an opening in the trees, she looked down at the ranch buildings and the roadway. It was devoid of human activity, but she spied the pinto in the pasture.

She clicked the roan forward, and continued close to the edge for another hundred yards, then pulled the reins so they moved farther west, away from the edge. She and the horse moved slowly and with as little sound as possible. When she reckoned they were directly west of the place she recalled seeing the flash of light, she guided the horse east, toward the mesa ridge.

After she had ridden a few yards, she brought the horse to a stop with a pull on the reins and a low sound as she patted the animal's neck. She looked about, dis-mounted, then pulled the rifle from the leather scabbard. She stood for a moment, listened and looked around, then walked slowly and carefully toward the ridge after looping the horse reins around a low branch. Three minutes later, she stopped and peered forward.

Ahead was a small, four-wheel vehicle with camouflage colors. Beyond that, she saw a large tent, but no movement. With the rifle held muzzle high at an angle across her chest in both hands, she moved carefully along, avoiding leaves and twigs until she came to the tent. She peered around the edge of the portable structure. There, grouped together close to the ridge, was an odd assortment of paraphernalia. Principal among them was a circular dish, its concave side directed east and down toward the ranch proper. Behind that device was a man seated in a camp chair. He wore something on his head, which she supposed were headphones. Next to him was another man, also seated in a chair. From her right, and behind the men, she saw a woman, dressed as were the men, in camouflage military-style clothing. She carried a cup, and stopped long enough to partake of its contents.

Vera waited for half a minute, then, with no more care for making noise, walked to within ten feet of the trio. With the gun still held across her chest, she levered a round into the chamber. The steel-on-steel -on-brass sound from the rifle caused the woman to swing around in surprise. She said something Vera was unable to make out, although she reckoned it to be out of alarm. Whatever she said caused the man without the headphones to turn, then rise. The man and the woman looked at each other, then the man who had risen tapped the one with the phones on his shoulder, which caused him to look up. He then looked back as the man pointed at Vera. All three took in Vera and the rifle she held pointed vaguely at them.

The man and woman took several tentative steps toward Vera. Both were aghast and wordless as they raised their hands, palms forward.

The man spoke. "Uh, what are you doing here? This is—we—"

"What am *I* doing here?! What are *you* doin' here?!" She waited a beat. "You're on private property, by god, and it looks like up to no good!" She gestured toward their devices with the long gun.

The woman glanced at the man next to her, then at the man who had removed the headset and risen tentatively from his chair. "You don't understand, ma'am, we—"

Vera interrupted with, "What I understand is, Yo're trespassin'!" She gestured with the gun again, then hesitated while the three people she faced, shocked and speechless, stared at each other and her, still with their hands in the surrender mode. "Now you gather your things and get the hell off my property. That's what I understand, and what you better damn well understand!" She continued, "I know why you're here. To spy on me. But it's over. So gather these contraptions, put 'em in this here buggy and skedaddle." She was silent again, then after looking up and around at the foliage, spoke again. "After I get back down, I'm gettin' in my truck and goin' to the nearest phone to call the sheriff and the state police. They are then gonna' look for you, because I'm gonna' charge you with trespassin'. That's what *more* you need to understand!" She raised the rifle so that its muzzle pointed skyward, turned and started to walk away.

The man without the headphones, after a few seconds of hesitation, followed. "Ma'm, we're with the federal government, and we—"

Vera stopped and turned to face him. She held the firearm with both hands, pointed at him. "I know who you are with. The eff-bee-eye, that's who, but you ain't got no right to sit up here on my land and watch me! And that's the simple truth!"

"Ma'am—"

Vera pushed her hat back and squinted. "Don't be 'a-ma'amen' me, mister! I tole you what's gonna' happen! An' if you intend to stop me, you better reach for that firearm you got strapped to you an' we'll settle this here an' now!" She glared at him.

He shook his head and turned away. In a barely audible voice, he said, "Okay. Let's wrap it up." He waved his hand in disgust and defeat.

The woman, who had not budged, asked, "How did you know? How—that we were here?"

Vera waited several seconds, then took a step nearer. "Couple 'a things, my dear. One, I know this place. Two, if you're gonna come here and do somethin' stupid like this, you oughta' be more careful."

"But—"

Vera smiled, tapped the brow of her hat, turned and walked back to the roan, where she slid the rifle into the scabbard and uncoiled the reins. As she pulled herself into the saddle, the nervousness she had suppressed finally came to the fore, and she started to shake, but her face was firm with resolve, and a tiny smile crept across her ruddy face.

She kept her promise. When she got back to the ranch proper and took care of the roan, she put the rifle away, changed her clothes, got into her truck and headed for the gas station and the pay phone.

That evening, some two thousand miles distant from Vera Tyler's ranch and two hours later in the Reston, Virginia media coverage area, the principal "top of the hour" news story concerned a certain Dr. Oliver H. Berman. Video showed the scene as many local, state and federal police agencies, most with their cars with garish red and blue lights flashing, swarmed about the location where the local dentist had been found, slumped over the steering wheel of his car. One television channel featured a "news hen," microphone in hand, hair unkempt across her pretty face lit up by the photographer's lamp, the dark behind her, reporting that she had been able to glean bits of information from a sheriff's deputy. He had, in turn, indicated that drugs and money had been found in the car with the deceased doctor. She learned further that he had died from bullet wounds inflicted to his chest and head with what it was surmised, at first glance, to be a large caliber firearm.

# 18

*J*ason went to Albuquerque and a business called "Quick Print" on Menaul, a few minutes after they opened. He placed an order for the minimum quantity of a business card of his own design. He spent the two-hour wait for the product at a nearby fast-food restaurant, husbanding a cup of chocolate-spiked coffee.

Back at the motel, he packed everything he had with him carefully into a new dark blue canvas overnight bag with handles and zipper closure. He had also acquired a cloth zipper briefcase, dark in color. Into this he put Sarah's notebook and most of the items he discovered in the Pecos bank safety deposit box. He included her identification documents, such as the passports and driver's licenses.

That night, the cell phone buzzed and he answered. "Hello."

"Hello. How are you?"

"I'm okay. You?"

"Fine.

"Any more relatives?"

"Yes."

"Yes?"

"Yes. They didn't stay long. Couldn't abide 'em." She grinned at her remark.

"I see. Same relatives? Cousins?"

"Different ones this time. I chased 'em off. Three."

"I see. Okay. Good. Some relatives can be annoying."

"Indeed they can."

"The rest of the family. How're they?"

"Just fine." She smiled in the dark of her pickup.

"I have a bit of travel."

"You said . . ."

"Yes. Tomorrow. Early."

"Okay. Well, I hope you stay safe an' all."

"I will. Don't worry."

"Well, I do, but I know—"

"It'll be later for me when you call."

"That a problem?"

"No. No. Just mentioned it. Not a problem."

"That's good."

He was silent for five seconds. "Stay well. If the cousins show up again, say little. Nothing about granma. Okay?"

"Yes, of course."

"Well, good night. Talk to you tomorrow."

"Okay."

"Listen—if I don't answer, or I don't answer right away, don't worry."

"Okay. Sure."

"'Night now."

"Night. Bye."

Jason killed the power to the little portable telephone and set it aside.

Vera started to choke up, caught herself, started the truck and drove away.

The time was shortly after eight in the morning when Jason checked out of the motel and carried his belongings in one trip to the Tacoma pickup truck. The bag and hats he set on the passenger seat, the briefcase and laptop under them. The file carrier he shoved under that seat. He opened the overnight bag, removed the thirty-two, and with an envelope stuffed with cash, he placed both in the glove compartment and locked it.

He drove to the nearest major brand service station, filled the fuel tank, then pulled into a slot in front of the so-called "Mini-Mart." Inside, he paid for the fuel with cash, then looked for, and found, both state and national road maps in a rack. Because he recalled problems with accuracy he had discovered with Rand-McNally maps, he chose instead the national map book by DeLorme. With that, he chose a small bottle of milk and coffee in a paper cup. He eschewed more than that, in order to avoid stopping to relieve himself.

In the truck again, he arranged the map to his right, between the two seats, unsealed the milk, drank from the cup of mediocre coffee, then opened the map book to the national pages. He soon realized that the shortest route dictated driving first south to Albuquerque, then east on I-40, then to pick up the series of Interstates that led east. For more than one reason, he decided to go north first, then across northeastern New Mexico and up into Western Kansas on secondary highways. The chances of remaining disappeared, in his view, were greater by staying away from his home base.

He made his way cross-country to the East Coast in three days, staying at, or below, the posted speed limits. Twice, he was slowed by traffic congestion due, in one case, to an accident; in another case, road construction. He was of two minds as he traveled. One, he developed a rare feeling of child-like freedom. The other, the opposite, a certain overcast of doubt and angst, as though he were escaping from something or someone. Oddly, he felt, Vera did not evoke that feeling, so he was unable to discern from whence it came. He finally decided that he was away from, and in a way, escaping from, himself.

He entered the greater Boston area on I-90, took the exchange to I-93, the Southeast Expressway, then the Columbia Road exit, which led to the JFK University of Massachusetts Rail Station. He found plentiful space in the huge, open car park. For no good reason, he parked the Toyota pickup in such away that few would notice the Texas plates, as though anyone would be interested. He looked at his watch. The time read one-thirty in the afternoon.

He picked up his cell phone which was off, because of a fear he knew was irrational, that he might be tracked for some reason by whom, he knew not, and powered it "on." He keyed in the code for Information, listened, then asked for the number for a taxi company.

The taxi delivered him to the Meeting House Bank on Dorchester Street. Dressed in faded blue jeans, a dark blue Western-style shirt under a turquoise bolo tie and his Western straw hat over street shoes, he paid the driver and stepped out. He carried the cloth briefcase. He stood on the sidewalk for several seconds and looked about, attempting to quell his nervousness. He adjusted his hat, then headed for the main entrance. He was struck, at first, by the lack of customers, then realized that it was mid-week, and the foot traffic would be low. He spied three people at teller windows. An old man sat in a chair, apparently waiting for someone. A stout woman stood making out a deposit slip at a convenience counter. No one noticed him as he stopped in the middle of the big room to look around.

A young man carrying a clipboard came up to him. "May I help you sir?"

Startled, Jason turned to him. "Ah, yes. Yes. The trust department?"

"Yes. Would you like to speak with the trust officer?"

"Yes, I would. Please."

"Just have a seat, and she'll be with you shortly. May I have your name?" He poised a ballpoint pen over the sign-in sheet on the clipboard.

"Yes. Kittridge."

The man wrote, then looked up. "Thank you. A short wait, sir. Please have a seat. There's coffee." He gestured, smiled and moved off.

Jason went to the one empty over-stuffed chair and sat. He thought about the coffee, then dismissed the idea. Too late in the day.

He sat for another two minutes, when a man emerged from the Trust Department cubicle. Jason had looked away, but when he detected motion from the corner of his eye, he looked up. His heart jumped as he realized he had seen the man before. He required another three seconds, then it dawned on him. He was one of the FBI agents who had worked with Agent Grayson during the GQ investigation.

Jason ducked his head and looked down and away, glad he had not removed his hat. The man, Agent Lucero, crossed the lobby without noticing Jason, and exited onto the street. Jason's hands shook as he searched for one of his heart pills in his shirt pocket.

The young man with the clipboard approached him, a look of concern obvious. "Are you alright, sir?"

Jason looked up. "Yes—Yes. Sorry. I mean, yes, just a bit of a headache." He tapped the left side of his chest as he swallowed the little white, dry pill. "Ticker."

"Are you sure? I can get you some water."

"No, no. It's okay; really. I'm used to taking these damned things without. Uh, water." He forced a wry smile.

"Well, do you need more time, sir? The trust officer is ready to see you."

"No. I can. I can see him—her—now." He sighed, took control of the briefcase he had held in his lap, and rose. He was unsteady at first as the greeter stepped back and watched him with concern.

"Well, if you're sure, sir, this way." The man walked toward the cubicle opening and gestured.

"Thank you," Jason said.

"Most welcome, sir. If you need anything—" He stood aside.

Jason looked at him and gave him a look of assurance. "I'm fine, really. I'll be fine."

Without another word, the young man nodded and walked away.

A middle-aged woman sat behind a large desk. As Jason entered, she rose, smiled, and put out her hand. "Good afternoon, sir; please have a seat. And tell me how I can be of service."

Jason shook her hand over the corner of the desk. "Yes, thank you." He sat and again placed the briefcase on his lap. He removed his hat and placed it on a corner of the desk, crown down.

She sat as well. "Now, sir, how may I help?"

"Yes. Well, I represent a client. In New Mexico." He stopped, stood the briefcase upright on his lap and zippered it open. "One moment . . ."

"Of course." Her hands were folded on the desk.

He fished for a few seconds and retrieved one of the false business cards he had made in Albuquerque. He handed it across the desk to her.

She looked at it. "Kittridge. J. J?"

"James. Middle name Jackson. Forebear." He smiled and went back into the case. He spent several seconds looking, although he knew exactly where the document was. "Ah. Here. Sorry." He pulled out two sheets of stapled paper and handed them to the woman.

She mumbled a "Thank you" as she watched the paper cross her desk and into her hands. She then spent several seconds perusing both pages before laying them down flat before her. She looked up. "So, what I have here is a declaration, a request for release of documents."

Jason nodded. "Yes."

She laid the papers flat onto the desk, folded back the first page, and looked at the bottom of the second page. "This is the signature of the decedent?"

Jason nodded. "Yes, it is."

"And you—"

"You know, I must apologize, Miss Unger." He held out both hands wide. "I'm retired, but have retained my fiduciary responsibility to the family. At their request, of course. I'm also taking advantage of this trip to visit relatives and friends here on the coast. You know how that goes."

She smiled, looked down, then up. "It's actually, Mrs., Mr. Kittridge. It's okay." She touched the papers. "Although I am curious. This is a bearer request."

"Right. Because of my retirement, the closing of the offices where I was partner, and because the Thompsons were unsure of who would be representing them, they changed the directive. They checked with my partners, and they agreed. But we were also friends for many years."

"Alright. I see no reason why I should not honor it." She paused, then, "The husband?"

"Deceased as well." He nodded.

"I see. Children?"

"Three. All spread out, you know. I'm here on their behalf. Florence, Charles and Justin. Grown and gone. This would have been a burden. In more ways than one." He worked the position of his head and his facial expression to accompany and enforce the lie.

"I understand. Of course." She looked at him for several more seconds, then stood. "Well, give me a moment while I track the file down. We keep trust documents in the vault." She started toward the opening, then stopped. "Are you comfortable here? May I get you something?"

He turned to look up at her. "No, really; I'm okay here. Just fine."

She nodded, then left.

Jason took in and released a long breath in an attempt to calm himself. Given that the small room was walled with glass above the wainscot, he maintained a controlled stiffness out of fear that somehow observers would detect his connivance were he to react physically to his discomfort. Yet he knew he need not have worried.

Mrs. Unger returned after a wait of nearly ten minutes. She went to her desk and sat. "I'm sorry I took so long. The file was misplaced. But I found it!" She looked up with a broad smile.

"Good."

She opened the file. "Let's see . . ." She proceeded to thumb through several pages, then stopped and read. "Hm, okay; it appears the trust funds are to continue to the heirs, and that would be . . ." She read more on the same page, then flicked forward and back. "Yes, of course, here it is . . . Yes, Florence, Charles and Justin." She looked up. "The addresses I have here—"

"Uh, right. Probably not current." He paused. "You know, I'm going to have to get those for you. I'm working off a phone call from Flo, the daughter. She called from California. She's the eldest."

"Hm," She mused. "The attorneys of record are Trenton and García. Santa Fé." She continued to read.

"That's correct. I joined the firm a little more than eleven years ago. The partnership is actually defunct. Age and a death. I was asked to stay on, even in retirement. Special case. I have three others, in fact." He chuckled. "It doesn't interfere with my hobbies."

She looked up, then closed the page she had been reading. "Of course."

He made a calm face in acknowledgment. Internally, he was not as sanguine as his outward appearance lead her to believe.

She tilted her head. "Is there a trust bank out there—in the west—New Mexico or California—we could use as a conduit?"

"I'm sure, but wouldn't that complicate things?" He awarded her a sincere frown.

"Yes, probably. Probably best we get good personal addresses or individual bank names and addresses. Banks best. The trust. Yes." Her professionalism came to the fore.

"Understood. Best. Yes. Well, it appears all is in order. I certainly thank you, Mrs. Unger." He reached for his hat and started to rise. "Oh, yes, one more thing."

He sat again, the hat and cloth briefcase in his lap. "The kids—the children—asked me—actually this request came from Charles—to ask you where the funds originate." He paused. "You know, it *is* a good question. Even I, in the time I've been involved, have not known. Or really thought about it. Didn't think to ask. Odd, indeed." He raised his eyebrows; an expression of innocence.

She looked down as she closed the file. Hm, yes . . . Oh! You need to take the letter back. You may need it."

"Yes; I almost forgot! Thanks." He took the letter, re-opened the briefcase and shoved it inside, then looked up expectantly. She had saved him from having to ask for it.

Mrs. Unger made a face. "I may have a problem, although after all this time, I'm not sure it is one, given that the chief recipient is deceased. It was not to be revealed during her lifetime; that was firm in the instructions. But—now—" She smiled, picked up a pen and a note paper, then wrote on it. She handed it to him. "No telling how cooperative they'll be, but you can give it a try." She sat back.

He read what she had written. "Bank," he said.

"Yes." She nodded.

"Makes sense." He folded the paper and shoved it into his shirt pocket.

He stood, extended his hand, and she did the same.

"Thank you for your help. The heirs—the children—will be pleased. And I'll get you those addresses." He wagged his finger.

"You're most welcome. Yes, please; as soon as you can." She paused. "And enjoy your stay."

When Lucero crossed the lobby of the Meeting House Bank, he didn't notice the older man seated in the comfortable chair in a corner of the great room, although he might have, given the head gear the man wore. He pushed through the big, heavy glass doors and strode onto the sidewalk, where he pulled his cell phone out. He keyed a number.

"Yeah, hey, Jan; Marc. Put me through to Pete, okay? He's there, no?" He waited. "Pete, Marc. Yeah. The kid—Justin—was right. It's this bank where they get their mom's funds. Listen, we got a problem. We're gonna' hafta' get a warrant or subpoena. My ID didn't impress 'em. They won't talk to us unless—yeah .

. . yeah . . . yeah. Okay. Do I standby, or come back? You'll let me know? Bueno. I'll hang loose here. What the hey; there's stuff to see in Boston. And eat and drink. Yeah. Yep. Later."

Jason Thompson made sure the bill of his wide-brim hat was down low over his forehead as he left the bank. A few feet beyond the doors, he stopped to scour the sidewalk and street for the man he had seen in the bank lobby, the FBI agent he had recognized. He was not apparent in either direction, nor did he see him sitting in a nearby car. All of the vehicles parked within his purview were either empty or occupied by people engaged in coming or going. He retrieved his cell phone and keyed the number for the taxi company.

As Mrs. Unger watched Jason's back recede toward the street door of the bank through the glass partitions, she picked up the hand set to the desk telephone. She opened the Sarah Thompson Trust file, flipped to a back page, tapped a long number into the phone keyboard and waited.

"Hello, HSBC Bank, Montreal? Yes? This Mrs. Unger, Meeting House Bank in Boston—well, Dorchester. I'm the trust officer here. Yes. Would you put me through to the trust department? Thank you. I'll hold." She waited a minute, then heard a voice on the other end. "Hello? Yes, Unger. Yes. Trust officer. Yes. Yes. I have a request. I believe you are the originating bank for the following trust . . ." She repeated the information from the documents in front of her. "Yes, I'll hold. I'll wait." With the handset held to her ear, she sat back and roved her eyes around looking at nothing in particular. Three minutes passed when she heard the voice in the phone. "You have it? Very good. My instructions, as you can see, are to notify you should there be a non-family inquiry from an attorney not of record or any law enforcement agency. Correct." She nodded her head as though the person with whom she communicated were in the room. "The FBI and an attorney not of record. Yes. The name? Moment— the name is—yes—the name is . . ." She picked up the little pasteboard business card Jason had presented and read, "Kittridge. Kittridge—" She spelled the name. "Yes, first name James. Attorney. From Santa Fé, New Mexico. Yes. I feel you'll see Kittridge. I gave him your information. The FBI needs a warrant, but you may see the attorney. Yes. Alright—yes—th—thanks. Thank you. Very good. Bye."

She replaced the handset, closed the file folder, rose, and took it from her office.

# *19*

*J*ason paid the driver and went to his truck. He slid the briefcase onto the passenger side floor, then opened the DeLorme map book. He spent several minutes studying his possible route, then left, and got onto northbound Interstate 93.

He found a motel in Manchester, New Hampshire, then a small, local diner, where he ate dinner with a beer. At the appointed hour, he powered the cell phone "on." He was watching the news on TV when the device buzzed.

Their conversation was much the same. Jason attempted to let Vera know of his success at the trust bank without revealing his position, while she let him know there was little to report from her end. They continued to be cautious about expressing affection or anything of consequence that might be misconstrued later by a third party. They said goodnight, and Jason stayed awake another two hours before falling asleep.

The following day, he found Canadian road maps and fueled up before leaving Manchester. He used I-93 to Burlington, then the 89 to the Canadian border at the Highgate Springs Border Station. He showed his Thomas passport and was waved through after explaining that he was entering Canada as a retirement gift to himself to "see the sights." The single odd moment he experienced at the Customs House was when the agent remarked that he didn't sound like a Texan. Jason explained that not all Texans speak with a regional accent. The agent had smiled, looked away, and waved him through.

He drove several miles north on Highway 133, then stopped to study the map. He established a route, then drove on. It was late afternoon when he arrived in Montreal, so he sought and found a motel. After a quick meal at a tavern, he went to the motel. Although he turned the portable phone on, he had explained to Vera in couched terms that she might not be able to make an international call. Either she failed to call, or he was correct, because the phone did not ring that evening. He suspected it was the latter reason.

In the morning, he showered, shaved and dressed in a manner he felt befitting an attorney from New Mexico. That included the bolo tie he had managed to keep from his labs days. Rather than fight city traffic, he opted for a taxi as he had done in Boston, and called for one from his room phone. Part of his reasoning was parking, and further, he didn't need anyone of note curious about the license plate. He gave the driver the Avenue McGill address for the HSBC Bank.

The Trust Officer was a middle-aged, older man named Ansel, whose desk was in an open, half-wall cubicle without glass. When seated at the man's invitation, Jason handed him his fake card and the letter written by his deceased wife, Sarah.

"All seems in order, Mr,—ah, Kittridge." He studied the faux business card, looked up and smiled patronizingly. "But there is a problem."

Jason took a few seconds to absorb his words. He tilted his head. "Problem?"

"Yes. Although you have what appears to be a genuine document from the decedent beneficiary, Mrs. Thompson—and I have no doubt as to its validity—it doesn't supercede the wishes of the donor. It may carry weight in the U.S., but not here in Canada, I'm sad to say." He paused. "I'm in sympathy with your client, uh, ah, the—" He pawed through the file, then, "Yes, the heirs, the children of Sarah and Jason. Let's see. We have Charles, Florence and Justin. Is that correct?"

Jason nodded while he hoped he carried the mantle of a professional.

"Well, then, I see that we have completed—er, well, not—but this is the most I can do, Mr. Kittridge. You can, at least, assure your clients that they will continue to receive funds from the trust. That is clear in the instructions." He sniffed.

Jason nodded again, lowered, then raised his head, and stood. "Well, thank you. They will be disappointed, but I did warn them."

The two men shook hands, Jason turned and left for the exit.

As he did, Ansel looked at a man seated near a post in the great room who had kept surreptitious watch over the proceedings in the cubicle, and nodded minimally. The man, in his early thirties, burly, with a head of heavy dark hair, who wore a black leather jacket, switched his attention to Jason as he moved across the lobby and exited the building. He got up as Jason's back was to him, and followed.

Jason had reached for his cell phone as he exited the building to call for a taxi. When he reached the street, he stopped, realized the call would not go through outside the United States, and put the little phone away. Behind him, the man in the leather jacket slowed, walked a few feet away and stopped. The man put a cell phone to his ear and pretended to speak with someone.

Jason, confused, turned first to his right, then left, as he tried to plan his next move.

The man approached him. "May I help, sir? You seem confused."

Jason looked at him. "I—my cell—doesn't—I need a taxi."

"Of course. Let me." The man then made a call.

Three minutes passed before a taxi pulled up alongside the curb. Jason moved for the rear, passenger-side door and opened it. His briefcase was in his left hand. At that moment, the stranger moved quickly behind him and followed him into the back seat. As he did, he produced a semi-automatic pistol and showed it to the startled Jason. Then he said something to the driver in French, and the taxi moved out into the street. The man whispered to Jason to be quiet, then sheltered the gun with his jacket.

The taxi moved along the street for two blocks, then took a right turn and stopped half-way down the block. The man with the gun paid the driver, then motioned for Jason to follow him out. Jason obeyed in silence, the briefcase held close. With the pistol secreted beneath his jacket, the assailant held Jason's arm and guided him to a four-door sedan parked alongside the curb. A man was at the wheel. He turned to look as Jason was urged into the back seat. The driver started the engine, looked first in the rear view mirror, then the outside mirror, put the transmission into "Drive," and guided the car into the street.

The man next to Jason pocketed the gun, then reached inside his jacket for a bandanna. He held it up for Jason to see. "It is necessary," he said, then proceeded to wrap it around Jason's head to cover his eyes.

Jason touched the area of his shirt over his heart. "Pill."

"Pill? Heart?" The man asked.

Jason nodded and fingered out the little envelope he kept in his shirt pocket. Then, despite the blindfold, he tapped out one pill into his hand, put it into his mouth and swallowed. His hands shook, and he tried to settle himself by grasping the briefcase in his lap with both hands. His head was swimming with questions as he tried to stem the rising panic he felt. He thought about the few words he had heard the man say, and tried to fathom his accent. The French sounded normal; the English not. Was it Slavic in tone? Russian?

He reckoned they had traveled more than a half hour when the car slowed, turned, came to a stop, and the engine was shut down. He figured they had driven over well-traveled highway, then onto less used because of the varying rushing sounds that had come from outside the car. During the entire trip, neither of the men had spoken. At one point, Jason asked where they were taking him, but there was no answer.

With the blindfold still in place, he was guided from the vehicle by the man with the gun. When they had walked some fifty feet or so by his reckoning, the man said, "Step." This was repeated three times before they reached another flat surface. A few seconds later, the sound and ambience changed, and he heard a door close. It was then that the bandanna was removed.

Jason blinked his eyes and looked around. He and the two men who had captured him at gunpoint stood in what appeared to him to be the foyer of a large house. The gun was not in evidence, but Jason spotted a bulge in his captor's jacket side pocket. The driver, whose face he saw for the first time, appeared younger yet; Jason reckoned in his twenties. The younger of the two looked at Jason, down at the floor, then walked toward the inner door.

Jason turned to look at the front door. It was of heavy, dark wood, whose upper half consisted of expensive leaded glass in a floral pattern. Through some of the small, clear, but distorted panes, he noticed a well–groomed graveled drive. On either side of the tiny room were wooden benches. Above were shelves, and alongside one bench an umbrella rested in a well for that purpose. Plate glass mirrors adorned the wall space above the benches.

The man with the firearm gestured toward the open interior door. "Please," he said.

Jason was led into a wide hall. The floor was of polished dark wood, which lead to a stairway at the opposite end, and four doors, two on either side. Three were open.

His guide held out his hand at waist level. "You wait." He then went to the closed door, opened it, disappeared into the room and closed it. A minute later, he reappeared. He stood aside, looked at Jason, gestured, and said, "You go in."

His briefcase still in hand, Jason walked tentatively into the room.

It was large. With a quick eye measurement, he assumed it to be something close to twenty feet by thirty feet, with a high ceiling of dark paneling. Two of the walls were covered with book shelves, all full. Across from the wide door were high, wide multi-light windows. They were complimented by like openings to his left that faced the front of the house. Close to those, arranged in a small rectangle, were two dark-leather sofas separated by a glass-topped coffee table. To his right as he entered was a large, ornate wooden desk, cluttered with books, papers and a green glass-shaded table lamp. Behind that was a high-backed, black leather chair. Spaced about were small statuary and occasional photographs and prints.

"Welcome, Mr.—" The voice came from Jason's right, in the corner that joined two walls of bookshelves.

Jason hesitated, cleared his parched throat, and answered. "Kittridge. James Kittridge."

"Of course." He was an older man, well into his late seventies or early eighties Jason guessed. He shoved a book he had been reading into a slot in one of the shelves. He moved slowly, with a slight limp, toward Jason, and held out his hand. "Andrei. I am Andrei. Again, welcome. Please, let us sit." He gestured toward the sofas. "I would say, spell it differently, but I am a stubborn old man. I stay with the Russian version."

"Thank you." In part because he was unable to understand what was happening, Jason's voice had become hoarse, and croaked as he spoke. He cleared his throat again as he walked toward the meeting square.

The man turned to the gun-toter, who stood, his hands folded across his front, in the doorway. "Kirill, Water. Get water. Please." He gestured with impatience. He looked at Jason. "You have heart problem? Yes?"

Jason looked at his impromptu, unannounced host. The man was half a head shorter than Jason, with a round, ruddy face. He was mostly bald, with fringes of grey hair confined to the sides of his head above his ears. He wore a loose sweater over a plain-color shirt, pants loose against his slight belly, with slip-on shoes protecting his feet. He spoke chopped English with the same sort of accent as his captor.

"Yes. Not serious. I take—how did you—?"

The old man peered up at his guest with a wide grin. "Kirill. You took pill. Yes?" He paused. "Please. Sit. He will bring water. You must be tired and thirsty." He gestured toward the seating arrangement. "If you need doctor—"

Jason sat and put the briefcase on the sofa to his left. "No, no—I'm okay. Fine."

The old man continued to stand. He looked down at Jason from across the low table. "I must apologize. You are Kit—" He then sat slowly, as though arthritic.

"Kittridge. James." Jason opened the briefcase and handed a faux card across the table.

Andrei took the card, looked at it, and laid it on the table. He was silent for a few seconds as he looked at Jason. His visage sobered as he stared at Jason, then he developed a wry smile. "I think not."

Jason blanched and shook his head in a jerking fashion.

"No, I think not." Andrei stood and walked slowly to the windows that faced the front. "I think you are Mr. Jason Thompson, husband of Sarah—or so she calls herself." He pronounced the name as Sah-rah, the "r" more as a soft "d" than "r."

"How—?"

Andrei, his face still toward the outside, said, "How do I know? Simple. I have picture. Of you. A picture of you, Mr. Jason Thompson." He turned and walked back to the facing sofa and sat. He tilted his head and looked at Jason. "And I fear you have come because of some disaster. Some terrible news. No?"

Kirill entered with a cut-glass carafe of water and two tumblers, set them down on the table, turned without looking at either man, and left. He had removed his leather jacket, and the pistol was not in evidence. Andrei made no move to acknowledge the servant. He leaned forward, poured one of the glasses half full and held it out for Jason.

Jason took the water and downed it entirely without stopping for a breath. "Thank you," he said as he set the glass down. He cleared his throat.

"So. Please tell me, Mr. Jason Thompson, why you are in Canada, trying to find out things? With a false name?" He cocked his head with an eyebrow raised.

Jason hunched forward and massaged his face with both hands. He sighed. "You're correct. Sarah is dead." His voice expressed resignation.

Andrei dropped his head and shook it slowly. "Tell me, please." He whispered. His mouth dropped open, held for a moment, then closed and became pinched.

Jason's face showed pain. "I—Wait. Wait. Please, first, who are you, and why am I here?" He held out his hands, then dropped them. He cocked his head with the question.

Andrei watched him and nodded. "Of course. You want to know. So. I will tell you." He drew in his breath and released it. "But first, you must tell me of Raisa's—Sarah's death. This news pains me, and I must know."

Jason started to react to the name the old man had used, then changed to Sarah, then stared at him for a moment. He decided to wait for an explanation, then related what he knew from the time of the labs field accident to the deaths in Truchas. Finished, but with the story incomplete, he said, "Now, please explain. The truth."

Over the course of the next hour and a half, Andrei explained who he was and what his relationship to Sarah, whose real name was Raisa Picot, was. Her parents, both long deceased, had been Canadian citizens. Her father, born in Canada, was of French extraction; her mother from Russia, who became naturalized after marrying her father. He, a history professor, in part at her mother's urging, had become enamored of classical Marxism and disillusioned by Western capitalism. They had raised two children, a boy and a girl. The boy, Raisa's older brother, was killed in the Second World War, fighting for the Soviets. The parents both joined a local Communist cell, and were eventually recruited to spy for the NKVD, Russia's equivalent of the CIA and British MI6, or SIS. They were not very successful, in part because neither had any important relationship to Canadian institutions with valuable information. But they kept the faith and stayed at the ready.

Raisa had been sent to the United States to study, specifically the University of Connecticut. Because she and her parents feared she would be targeted by the FBI, her name became Sarah Smithers. Smithers, because her father's sister had married a man by that name, and they wanted the distance it provided. With the attitude toward the West imbued by her parents, she kept a lookout for a way to help her mother's homeland and all the wistful, wishful thinking fellow-travelers of the world. When she met Jason and his friend Mel Vaslovic, and reported her findings about them, her parents and their control jumped at the chance to place the newly-minted Sarah as a deep-cover mole, and she agreed. A trust and a back story were initiated, and funds from the Soviet Union were flushed through offshore banks, then to a Canadian bank, then one in the United States, and finally to Sarah. She was to stay in contact with her Canadian-Russian controllers through various routes, while overseeing and reporting on the two scientists, her husband and his associate.

But events, international and local, changed the game. The rise and fall of Joseph Stalin, the terrible Gulag system, rampant poverty and police state totalitarianism in so-called "Communist" countries that were nothing more than fascist dictatorships under the name of Communism, capped off with the collapse of the Soviet Union, all served to call for an examination of purpose. And a change in direction.

Former Communist Party officials—even NKVD, then KGB agents—opportunists all, became overnight capitalist moguls. Crime sky-rocketed, while initially, the currency was nearly worthless, because there had been no production of goods the world was willing to purchase, or Russians themselves to use. The disillusionment trickled down to Raisa as well.

Raisa Picot-cum-Sarah Smithers had married Jason Thompson for two reasons. The primary was that she was a good Communist rank and file soldier;

the second, which became prime, was that she fell in love with him, and had children by him. That, combined with the experience of a calm, productive, easy life in the forbidding capitalist U.S., turned her against her former ideas and therefore their control over her. But that had fallen away as well. At the same time, she had retained her so-called "trade craft," some of its tools and some of its human connections.

Kirill, the man who had stuck a gun in Jason's side and forced him to go with him came into the room, sans the weapon, to deliver lunch. It consisted of good, fresh, heavy bread, three blocks of different cheeses, hinds of beef and ham, and a good red wine. Horseradish and mustard were offered as well. That was topped of with a tin of Black Sea caviar. He laid it on the coffee table, after which Andrei insisted that Jason, whom he assumed must be famished, partake. Jason did not disappoint, in great measure because he had become relaxed in the realization that he was not in immediate danger.

"So you, Andrei, you were her control?"

Andrei, his mouth full, chewed while he dusted his hands of bread crumbs, and made closed-mouth noises. He swallowed, then as he cut another piece of white cheese and took a healthy sip of his wine, replied, "Yes, of course." He executed a shrug, then dug into the black fish eggs with a broken cracker.

His nonchalance took Jason off balance. He shook his head as he also cut more bread and laid a piece of yellow cheese on it. "But you are here . . ."

"You are very observant, my friend." He smiled wryly.

"Mm. It makes sense. You should be here, I suppose."

The old man waved his nearly empty wine glass around. "Indeed. Easier to communicate. And far from Directorate." He chuckled, sipped and set his flute glass down.

Jason looked down and away, then back at the old Russian. "What was she to do? What was her—her assignment? I mean, to my knowledge, she never learned anything. I never told her anything of what I did. I hid it from her. From everyone. Except for Mel."

Andrei nodded and added two fingers of wine to his glass. "That is true. Quite true. She was not directed to spy. She was directed to watch. To watch you and to watch Mr. Vaslovic." He raised the glass to his lips, sipped and set it down. "To spy, she would be spying on you, and that would not work. No." He shook his nearly bald head.

Jason made a face. "What good did that do? For Russian Intelligence? The Russian government?"

Andrei sat back against the couch cushions and laced his fingers behind his head. He looked at the ceiling, then at his coerced guest. "Ah, yes. You see, my good man, good husband to Raisa—Sarah—we were aware of Mr. Vaslovic—Mel, as you call him—long ago. But we did not control him. No. We did not receive an iota of information from him. No. We assumed he was controlled by a mole in your government. Who was his conduit. Yes. That is quite true." He unlaced his fingers, leaned forward and helped himself to more wine, then tore off a nibble of sharp cheddar and popped it into his mouth. "We believed this mole was in the Central Intelligence Agency. Indeed." He peered at Jason from under his eyebrows, in wait for a reaction, then sat up straight. "We—I—do not know who this man—person—is."

"I do know," Jason said. His voice was above a whisper.

Andrei stared at him in silence. Jason nodded his head, then drained off more of the wine in his flute.

"You know? You know what? Who we speak of?"

"Yes. The very man who was controlling me."

"How—how do you know this?" Andrei's face went dark.

Jason had not told the whole story. To round it out, he completed the story of the fatal night in Truchas. How Nantes had been exposed by Jason after putting all the pieces together, and how he and Sarah ended it by killing each other." He paused. "That brings up another question. Who were Cuzco and the woman who took me by plane? Do you know?"

Andrei shook his head as he chewed. "I do not know them. Assistance was provided from the network. I believe they were Puerto Rican separatists. Yes." He nodded. "I was not involved."

"I see." Jason pinched up his face, then continued, "I have her journal. It coincides with what you tell me."

Andrei was silent as he looked down, away, then up at Jason. "Journal? She kept a journal? That was against our rules!" He stared blankly at Jason.

Jason shook his head. "She hid it. I found it in a bank safety deposit box. I think she meant it for later. After her death. She didn't have time to leave me or the children the information about its location. Nonetheless, it agrees with what you have told me. Not everything, though. Not at all." He paused "But," he continued, "I still don't understand what Sarah's—Raisa's—role was. How did it help you for her to be there?" He frowned. "If she was not spying?" He held his hands out wide.

"Amazing," Andrei said. "Amazing. We thought at first, early, that she could pass information, but that was not to be. She was frustrated. As were we." He rose from the sofa slowly and put his hand on his hip as though soothing a pain, then walked to the front windows. He looked out. "When the parents died, because of her back story, she could not reveal to you the truth of their deaths. So, she came to Canada, you see, 'to visit'. To be here at their funerals. And to speak with me."

Jason nodded.

"We warned her. Warned her, that she could jeopardize herself, you, everything."

"This place. House, grounds, servant. How—?"

Andrei bobbed his head around in a yes-no way as he remained standing, turned slowly and smiled. "Aha! KGB. Officials with connections. Natural gas, my friend. Natural gas!"

"Natural gas?"

"Russia has much natural gas; big, as they say, Jason, my friend!" His voice was higher by an octave. He swept his arm around in an arc. "That is where this came from! I am now Western capitalist!"

"Okay. Okay. I get it. I understand." Jason's voice had dropped to barely above a whisper. He nodded first, then shook his head.

"Yes. Now you get it!" Andrei stretched the word 'yes' out and punched his forefinger in Jason's direction.

Jason looked up. In a normal voice, he asked. "The money—the trust. Where—?"

"Not from me," Andrei answered. "Oh, no. From offshore bank. Source? Natural gas. And other commodities that I and others of the old regime have stolen from the people of Russia. And her former client states. Yes. Of course." He moved slowly for the other set of windows. "So, my dear Jason, it will serve nothing for the FBI or the Royal Canadian Mounted Police in their beautiful red uniforms to look for me. Even to find me. I have nothing to do with it." He chuckled.

"Andrei, how did you know I was here?"

"Excellent question, Jason Thompson. Excellent. Yes." He turned and started back for the sitting area. "The trust papers have certain—how do they say—stipulations, I believe it is. They order the trust officers to notify our attorney. In Montreal. To notify him should someone ask about the trust. So, you see, even when you were in Boston, we knew you were coming." He sat down again across from Jason. "What we didn't know," he said with a squint, "was who was this James Kittridge. So, our attorney investigated. Investigated this James Kittridge. Ha! He could not be found. Not in Santa Fé. Not in New Mexico. Not anywhere." He nodded his head for several seconds. "So, we decided to have a look at this man who called himself Kittridge. And who do we find? Mr. Jason Thompson pretending to be this James Kittridge."

Jason peered at Andrei from under his eyebrows, helped himself to more red wine, then sat back with a tiny smile.

"I am old, Jason Thompson, but I am not stupid. I knew something was wrong. What you have told me I believe. You were in shock, as they say. Raisa—Sarah—did her job. She kept her secret until the last. Now, you may hate her. But she loved you. She was faithful to you."

Jason sipped his wine, leaned forward and set the glass down. He shook his head. "But she shot and killed Mel, then she shot and killed Nantes. I'm troubled." He peered at the old Russian secret agent. "How am I to deal with that?"

Andrei was silent, then, gently he said, "I don't know. Truly I do not." He paused. "She remained true. To protect you and your children. That is all I can say."

Jason nodded. After several seconds of reflection, he said, "Andrei, when I was in Boston. The bank. One of the FBI agents from Albuquerque, one of the investigators. He was there. He didn't see me, but—"

"They find dead end. They find nothing. All has been erased. I assure you." Andrei waved impatiently. "Okay." He picked up his wine glass and raised it. "To you and to Raisa."

Jason raised his as well and they both drank.

Andrei was silent for a bit, then set his glass down. He looked at Jason with a deeply serious tone. "You are dead, right?"

"I'm supposed to be."

"You said there were others. Others who think you are alive, yes?"

"Yes."

"And so you stay dead to most."

"So far."

"But you are worried."

He nodded. "Yes."

"This is because?"

Jason sighed. "Because I think there's still someone inside. Inside the labs where I worked, and I think the people who worked with Nantes—whoever he really was—know I'm alive and would very much like to make me really dead. Because of what I know. What they think I know."

"Yes, yes. Of course. That must be the case. They must not leave trail." Andrei had reverted to the Russian habit of dropping the article before a noun. He pondered, rubbed his chin forcefully, then spoke. "Listen, Jason, there is little I can do to help, but I can do this. You did not fly here; you drove here, yes?"

"Yes."

"Okay. Kirill will go with you to your vehicle. What kind?"

"Truck. Pickup truck."

"Pickup. I like these. He will go with you, and he will change your license plate to Canada plate to cross border. Now, you keep your American plate. But—go west. Go far west across Canada to other crossing. We find a good one. Remove Canadian plate and put on American plate. Later. In U.S. Okay?"

Jason nodded, pondering this move.

"Do you have gun?"

"Yes."

"What kind?"

"Uh—.32 caliber automatic."

"Yours?"

"Yes. Why?" Jason frowned.

"Where was it? When did you get it?"

"Why, my house. A few days ago."

"Registered?"

"To me, yes. Wh—Oh, I think I understand." He looked down.

"Yes. Traceable. If—"

Jason nodded and raised his hand in understanding.

"You need better."

Jason frowned at Andrei. "I—"

"Listen. If your pistol is traced; if you have to shoot, and can be traced; not good. We give you untraceable gun. Leave yours with Kirill. It will disappear. Okay?"

Jason compressed his lips in newfound understanding. Okay, Andrei. Okay."

"Stay dead for now, my friend. You understand?"

"I understand." He awarded the old Russian agent a wry smile.

Andrei said, "When FBI hears that Kittridge has come to bank to ask questions, they will look for Kittridge. You must not return to U.S. as Kittridge."

"Huh?!"

"No. Not Kittridge. You need new passport. Canadian. We will provide." He raised his finger. "We kill Kittridge." He smiled.

Jason's face betrayed concern.

"When you cross at new station, they will not know you. When you are in U.S., change plates and destroy Canadian passport." He waved his arms. "Simple."

"I see . . ."

"Give me your key."

"What?!"

"The key to your vehicle. And your room. Hotel. Motel." He made an impatient, dismissive gesture.

"Why?"

"Kirill and Joseph will go to bring the truck here. You stay. You rest. They check you out, pay your bill, and bring truck. Your things, We have work to do." He waggled his finger.

Andrei rose and went to the door. Three seconds later, Kirill was at the opening, where he leaned over to listen to the old Russian. After a brief tete-a-tete, Andrei turned to look at Jason, and waved for him to approach.

# 20

"*S*he held them at gunpoint?!" Grayson leaned into Lucero with his face contorted into an expression of incredulity.

Lucero shook his head in a minor fashion. "That's what they said, and that's not all."

Grayson looked away, his mouth half open, then back. "What else, for chrissakes?!"

"They were stopped by the State Police." Lucero shrugged with a face of contrition.

Grayson peered closely at his hapless colleague. "What?!"

Lucero shook his head with a sad face. "The plan back-fired."

"Let's go to the conference room." Grayson turned and moved in that direction.

In the conference room, with the door closed, both men stood and faced each other.

"Marc, what the hell, man! This Tyler woman faced our guys down with a gun?!"

Lucero was silent as he nodded. He stood while Grayson slumped onto one of the chairs that ringed the big table.

"What—what kind of gun? Pistol?" Grayson swept his hand through his hair in irritation.

Lucero shook his head. "Rifle. They think it was something like a .30-.30. Lever-action." He sat down.

"The state cops. How did they get involved?" Grayson allowed his mouth to stay open again in his dismay.

Lucero sat. "She told 'em she was gonna' call the state police and the sheriff. They didn't think she'd do it. They had to wait for a pick-up—you know, to load the ATV and the gear—and when they got to the main highway, there they were." Lucero held up both his hands, then dropped them to his lap.

"Shit," Grayson exclaimed. He leaned forward, thought for a moment, then looked hard at Lucero. "How the hell did she know they were there? They were up on the ridge, right?"

"Right; right. I don't know Pete, and they didn't either. One of our people, Ginny, said she made a remark, like 'you should be more careful,' or something like that."

"More careful," Grayson muttered with a frown. He paused. "She must have spotted their movements or something."

"I agree."

"Shit. Tough ole' broad." Grayson developed a tiny grin at the thought.

"Yep."

"What now? Were our people charged?"

Lucero 's head moved in the negative. "No. Warning. They explained what they were doing, but because they couldn't show a warrant—"

"Right; right." Grayson rotated his chair ninety degrees and stared at the wall. "What does this mean." His question was more a statement.

"What—?"

Grayson interrupted. "I mean to say, what does it say about this woman's actions." He became more reflective as he moved his chair back to face Lucero across the big table. "Does it mean she has something to hide, or it's totally innocent, and she's just protecting her property and her privacy."

Lucero shifted in his chair, still reeling from the facts. "Well, I ask the question again, do we get a warrant?"

"I get you, Marc, but I really can't see a judge agreeing. We can put this to Sam, but what grounds do we have? We've been over this. What's in our statement for cause? That we think Thompson is alive, or if not, that she knows something about thc GQ case? What evidence? Far-fetched circumstantial." He was silent for a few seconds, then, "In all honesty, why do we—you and I—the FBI—care? To gain what?" He looked away and shook his head.

Lucero shifted again. He thought for a moment, then pointed his finger at the ceiling. "Sake of argument. Okay? Thompson is alive. We were snookered.

What we thought we witnessed didn't happen. But, Nantes and company screwed up. Their plan disintegrated. Because of the Thompson woman." He leaned forward intently, lowered his head so that he looked at Grayson from under his eyebrows, and continued. "Tyler knows he's alive, is protecting him, maybe knows his whereabouts. He's in hiding, but—I would guess—actively trying to solve this thing. Clear himself." He was silent to gather his thoughts.

"Yeah, yeah. Go on." Grayson rubbed his chin stubble.

"Say Thompson had no part in the labs breach. Say he was a good guy. A victim. Say he's now out there in the cold, afraid for himself—maybe even his kids—that somebody knows he's still kickin', and wants to eliminate him. And what does he do? What's his next move?

"If he's alive."

"We'd want to know what he knows and what he's doing."

"Exactly."

"So, going back to our tough gal, if she could lead us to him—assuming he's alive—"

"Means we need to get to her, or around her. Near her. Warrant or not."

Grayson said, "But if Thompson is really gone, then . . ."

"Either way, we still have the mess up north. That, all by itself, makes no sense. That we still have on our plate, like it or not."

Grayson leaned against the table edge and tapped the surface with his finger. "I think trying for a warrant will only get us thrown off the case. They'll shelve it."

Marc Lucero sat back; his intensity diminished. "We have two tracks. Nantes—whoever he was—Sarah Thompson, and Tyler if Thompson is still with us."

Grayson nodded, was quiet, then, "Almost forgot. Tell me about Boston. How'd it go?"

"Aside from the seafood and beer?" He grinned.

"Well, as I told you, after I got the subpoena, I learned they had a visitor. Guy named Kittridge."

"Right. And?"

"Attorney out of Santa Fé. For the family. Or so he claimed." Lucero pulled out a notebook and consulted it. He was silent while he read. "That's about it, except they referred him to a bank in Montreal."

"And you went up there." Grayson swiped at imaginary dust.

Lucero cleared his throat after a cough. "I did. Very polite. Very Canadian. I was reminded that I was not in the United States, and they were bound by Canuck law, etcetera, and so on. I was assured that the funds they receive for the trust—which they did admit to—comes from offshore accounts, blah, blah."

"Of course," Grayson said. He cocked his head in annoyance.

Lucero went on, "And, as to any other visitors, they were not only not bound to say, but advised me that the red coats would frown on any further inquiries on my part."

"Of course. Well—"

"So, that's the news from Lake Woebegone. I had to back off."

"This Kittridge guy. Do we know how to find him?" Grayson turned to look at the wall.

"Looking into the gentleman as we speak."

Grayson wheeled back. "Good. Okay."

"Mm. Which reminds me. Anything on the Sanchez woman?"

"Let me check with Jan." Lucero started to rise from his chair, then he regained it. "I'm still up in the air about Tyler. Do we pursue or drop?"

"I don't know, Marc. In my view, a warrant is out for the reasons I've stated. We blew the spying op, but that might not have yielded much anyway. If—and a really big if—there's anything there, it'd call for eyes on the ground."

Lucero nodded. "Are you inclined?"

Grayson shut his eyes and blinked as he sucked in then blew out a long breath. He re-adjusted his position in his chair. "Man, I don't know. Really risky. "You've got a middle-aged woman living alone on a remote ranch—keen-eyed, mind you—suspicious as it is, so who the hell would we inject? A Mexican day-laborer looking for work? A a woman who wants a job as a cook?" He shook his head. "And say we do get someone in there who's accepted, what do they look for? A sock the man may have left behind?"

Lucero nodded in silence.

"One possibility." Grayson got up slowly.

"Yes?"

"We put someone to watch the road in and out."

"And?"

"A tail. If Thompson is alive, and she realizes we're interested—which she has to now—she'll warn him by some means to stay away."

"And she could go to him."

"Precisely."

"Sam'd have to go along."

Both men rose and moved for the door. Lucero stopped. "Anything from your company guy?"

"Nada." He paused. "If we're wrong about this Nantes guy being company—"

Lucero moved closer to the door. "We know he wasn't one of the agency's, right?"

Grayson peered at his partner and shook his head. "True."

"'Tis a mystery," Lucero said. He opened the door, and both men entered the hall.

# 21

*S*tanley Webber arose well before sunrise in his Alexandria house, performed his morning ablutions, dressed, ate a minimal breakfast with coffee and juice, then visited his basement office.

There, he opened the wall safe normally obscured by a framed plaque, and removed a notebook, a small box, and an identification card and driver's license in an assumed name. These he placed on his desk. He flicked on the desk lamp, looked briefly at a page in the book, picked up one of his business cards and wrote a series of numbers on the reverse side copied from the book. This he put into his shirt pocket. He opened the box, removed a key and slipped it into his pants pocket. The IDs he moved to his wallet, and the box and book he returned to the safe, which he locked and covered with the hinged plaque. He turned off the desk lamp, and left the office. From there, he went to his garaged car after ensuring the house was locked and the alarm set, and drove away.

Less than an hour later, he boarded a flight at the Dulles airport under his own name. From there, he dog-legged across the country through Atlanta to Chicago, then Memphis to Denver, thence finally to Seattle under the name of Millard, S. At Sea-Tac, he rented a small, two-door sedan and drove to the town of Ferndale, not far from the Canadian border. It was close to sunset when he entered the medium-sized town.

He stopped the car on a side street, left the engine running, and true to his training, looked about and into the mirrors. He then reached for a small piece of paper in his shirt pocket, unfolded it, and read the marks on it. He laid it on the passenger seat, then, with an occasional glance down at it, drove away. Within fifteen minutes, he was in the parking lot of a strip mall with less than a dozen businesses. One of them, its neon sign bright in the fading light, was "The Jade Flower."

Webber parked the car, shut the engine down, then sat for several minutes, watching. He saw two cars leave with two people each, then another car arrive. A woman emerged and walked into a beauty supply shop. He looked at his watch, then got out, took the keys, but purposely failed to lock the doors, and walked to the end of the strip to a drug store at the end. The bright overhead lights of the interior revealed, at his count, three customers. One of them, a woman with purchases in hand, went to the cash register to pay.

He stood outside for another minute as he surveyed the area, then strolled to the restaurant. As he entered, he was immediately assailed by the smell of Chinese food. A young Asian woman, whom he assumed was Chinese, came up to him carrying a large, fold-out menu. She was dressed in a tight, green, form-fitting silk gown decorated with floral patterns.

She smiled, and nodded her head in a subservient way. "May I seat you, sir?" Her accent was purely U.S. English.

"Uh, yes," Webber answered. He took a quick look around.

The place was long and narrow, with mainly red decorations and arches. A line of white cloth-covered round tables dominated the center, while both sides, hard against the walls, was a series of padded booths.

"A booth?"

"Yes, sir. This way, please." She started off.

He looked back toward the street door, then glanced around at the few patrons. Three of the booths were occupied, while two of the tables were. The booths held two people each, while the tables seated four at one and three at another. He noted that not one of them appeared to register his presence outwardly.

The girl indicated a booth on their right, and she placed the menu on the side that looked toward the back. Webber slipped in on the opposite side, that which faced the street door.

The girl stepped back in mild embarrassment and moved the menu. "Would you like something to drink, sir?"

He looked up, rolled his eyes, then focused on her. "What do you have on tap?"

"Only bottled beer, sir. The list is there." She pointed at the menu.

"Any Chinese beers?"

"Yes, sir. Tsingtao is the best."

"I'll have one of those." He nodded.

She turned and left. As he watched her go, he reached into his sports jacket side pocket, pulled out a three-inch high, gold figurine of the Buddha and set it a few inches away from the edge of the table, centered.

Two minutes later, a waiter arrived with the beer and a frosted glass. He set the glass down, but held the bottle. "Are you ready to order, sir?" He asked.

"Ah, thank you, no. I'm waiting for a friend." He smiled as the waiter poured two fingers worth into the glass, then put the bottle down carefully.

Webber had drunk half his beer when he sensed someone walking to his right, toward the front of the restaurant. It was a man, dressed in a dark suit, who appeared to be looking for someone or something. He turned and looked in Webber's direction, such that Webber recognized him as Asian, probably Chinese. The man spotted the Buddha and moved toward the booth where Webber sat. In that instant, Webber turned to look toward the kitchen and the innards of the restaurant. He then understood that the man had not used the front door, rather the back, or had been waiting toward the rear. At the same time, Webber felt something else. This man who was coming toward him must know the owner, manager, or someone else in the eatery, or had simply barged in through the rear. If that were the case, why?

The man stood at the edge of the booth table and looked down. "Mr. Tanner?"

Webber started to rise.

"Please, not to get up. I am Chen." He held out his hand and executed a tiny bow from his hip.

"Right. Yes; Tanner. Glad to meet you Chen. Sit. Please."

Chen slipped into the booth before Webber's invitation had been voiced. He folded his hands on the table surface and glanced at the statuette. "Interesting," he said. "Smart idea."

"Thanks," Webber said. He was quiet for a moment as both men studied each other's faces and demeanor. "Were you waiting, or did you come in from the rear?" He jerked his head toward the back.

"You are correct. From the rear. I find it wise to use certain precautions at times. I believe this is one of those times."

Webber nodded. "Do—do you know these people? The owners? Manager?" He squinted his eyes unintentionally, then wished he had not.

"The owner of this establishment is a cousin of my wife. She—the owner—is not here, but has instructed the staff to allow me to come in the back. They prepare a delicacy from my home for me." He nodded and emitted a short laugh. "Yes."

Webber wasn't convinced the man who called himself Chen was telling the truth, but the result for him was that he felt better for reasons not clear to him at the moment. Ultimately, he had no choice.

"You are curious, no?"

The question shocked Webber. He reacted with a look of surprise. "Well, frankly, yes. To an extent, I—"

"Please do not worry, Mr. Tanner. No one knows my business. No one. Not even my wife." His mood had become serious, unsmiling.

Webber nodded again, with emphasis. "I'm okay. I'm good, Chen." He looked at the Buddha. "That's for you." He jerked his head toward the gold figurine. "Look inside. Later."

"Of course. I will take it with me." His hands remained on the table. "I will be pleased to open."

Webber nodded as he peered at Chen closely.

"I see you are drinking a Chinese beer. Have you ordered?" Chen asked.

Webber picked up the empty bottle and turned it over in his hand. "Yes. Not bad. And no, I haven't ordered. Thought I'd wait for you."

"Very polite of you."

"Thanks, but I'd like for you to order for me. Okay?"

"Okay." Chen smiled and gestured at the big menu. "May I?"

"Yes, please."

Chen opened the menu and read it for ten seconds, laid it down, looked out into the room, and nodded to the waiter. While Webber remained quiet, Chen ordered for the both of them, added a beer for himself, and asked his table partner if he wished a second libation, which Webber declined.

As the waiter rushed off to fill the order, Chen looked at Webber, alias Tanner. "So, you come from east coast?" He smiled.

"Yes. East coast. Your English is good. My Chinese is bad. Non-existent." Webber returned the smile, as was Chen's expression, it was tentative and strained.

Chen looked down at the clean white tablecloth, then up. "You will agree, Mr. Tanner, that our relationship must be very—shall we say—close. That only you and I meet—if ever again—and that the manner in which we communicate must be likewise."

Webber kept his eyes on Chen. "I could not agree more."

It was at that moment that the waiter returned with Chen's beer, set a glass on the table, poured for him, made a quick bow and hurried away. Neither man looked up or removed his eyes from the other.

Chen said, "These matters, you see—and I am sure you understand—are extremely delicate. I have not met you before now, and you have not met me. If we are both honest men, we understand that we do not represent our governments. Yes?" He had sobered. He looked away to add enough beer into his glass to fill it half-way. "If you are who you say you are, and you come here to 'seal the deal,' as you Americans say, then we are on the right track." He sipped his beer without taking his eyes off of Webber. He set the glass down, picked up his cloth napkin and applied it to his mouth. "Another American expression."

Webber smiled genuinely as he looked down, then up.

"You see, if the FBI were to burst in here, they would find in me an innocent Chinese businessman lodged in Vancouver, Canada, here with a purchase order for certain products." He tapped the area of his suit jacket over an inner pocket.

Webber nodded. "Good. Very good."

"And you, Mr. Tanner?"

"For my part, I must wait—as you must."

"Indeed."

The waiter showed up with an assistant, and they both set several plates and dishes onto the table with practiced and expert flourish, while both men sat back to allow them elbow room. Both servers backed away, bowed their heads and rushed away. Chen assumed the role of host and gestured at the vapor-emitting food.

Webber helped himself by moving spoonfuls of food to his plate. "Thank you. I appreciate you ordering. I get confused with Chinese food. Love it, but confused."

"Of course," Chen replied. "American food is simpler. Easier to understand."

Both stopped their tete-a-tete to eat.

Chen put his chop sticks into his rice bowl and reached inside his jacket. "I have something for you." He had pulled out enough of an envelope for Webber to see what it was.

"No!" Webber's command was spoken barely above a whisper. He shook his head and glanced furtively around the nearly-empty restaurant.

Chen halted his maneuver, froze his hand in place and peered at Webber. "Not here, not now."

"Oh?"

"No." Webber put his eating implements down. "Not until I have something, and not in this way. Ever." He leaned forward, looked quickly to his right, then at Chen. "I have nothing now. There will be a delay. And you will receive instructions on how and where to make your remissions. Okay? Understand?"

Chen jerked his head in a nod. "Yes. But a delay?"

"The source is, shall we say, unavailable."

"Hm. I see. Unavailable. Perhaps deceased."

Webber nodded, picked up his chop sticks and managed a piece of sweet pork into his mouth with them. "You might say that."

Chen sat back. "I have had news that my predecessor is also unavailable."

"Oh?" Webber looked up, his mouth full.

"Is this true?"

Webber also sat back. He wiped his mouth with his napkin. "Is what true? I'm not getting your drift." He worked his face into a mask of innocence.

Chen grinned, lowered his head, then raised it. "Ah, Mr. Tanner, I believe we understand each other. My sources tell me that my predecessor was found in a city in the Midwest, as you call it, deceased. Apparently he was involved in some criminal activity involving drugs."

"Really?" Webber brushed at his chin with his napkin once more, a convenient prop to enforce his faux innocence. "I'm sorry to hear that."

"Yes. It is very sad. His family are grieving."

"I would imagine they are," Webber said. He folded the napkin slowly and carefully, then laid it on the table. He locked eyes with Chen.

Chen was the first to allow his eyes to drift away. He picked up his chop sticks and toyed with his noodles. "He was not a careful man. He allowed himself to become engaged in dangerous pursuits." He looked at Webber. "That is my understanding."

Webber nodded, phony sincerity in his reaction. "I see. Terrible. Dangerous. Yes." He paused. "Of course, I was not privy to him. Not directly, you understand. One might say that—uh—the establishment is under new management, as it were." He wore an insincere smile, then failed to maintain it.

"I, on the other hand," Chen continued, "am more cautious; much more cautious. Older and more cautious."

"A good thing to be cautious," Webber said. I admire cautious people. I like to associate myself with cautious people. I like to work with cautious people. Indeed, I do." He reached out and picked up an egg roll with his fingers and popped it into his mouth.

Chen asked, "Are you wearing a wire, Mr. Tanner?" He cocked his head to one side.

Webber developed a smirk, then a genuine smile. He raised his eyebrows. "No, Chen; are you?"

"Trust is vital, Mr. Tanner. No, I am not."

"Then neither of us is wired, are we?"

"No, Mr. Tanner."

"Do you require proof, Chen—or whatever your name is?" Webber also cocked his head.

Chen dipped his head and smiled. "Not in the least, Mr. Tanner—if that is your true name."

"Touché," Webber said. He smiled again. He reached into his left-hand jacket pocket, pulled out a paper-back novel, and shoved it across the table to the Chinese man. "I thought you might find this book of interest. It coincides with the Buddha messages."

Chen took the book, looked at the cover, and flipped through the pages. "Yes. How thoughtful. I'm sure I will enjoy reading it." He looked at the cover again and read the title. "Heartland Travail. Hm."

"I found it both heartening and sad at the same time."

"I am sure," Chen said. "I am much obliged. And with the little Buddha."

"I'm happy to oblige, especially for a new-found friend."

"I have something for you, my new friend." Chen reached into an outer jacket pocket and removed a book. He handed it to Webber.

Webber took the book. He read, "An American's guide to China, its Customs and Practices." He looked at Chen. "Great. I will carry it with me on my next visit. Very kind."

Chen merely nodded, closed, then opened, his eyes. He then reached into his shirt pocket, took out a small, thin metal container, snapped it open, and retrieved a business card. He handed it to Webber.

"Ah, thanks. Almost forgot." Webber took a similar action and produced a business card for Chen.

Chen looked at the watch on his wrist. "I must go. My home is north of Vancouver."

"Of course." Webber started for his wallet.

Chen held up his hand. "No, no, Mr. Tanner. My pleasure. It is taken care of."

"You're sure? I—"

"Quite sure, my friend. We are, after all, business partners, are we not?"

"You got that right, Chen. Partners in business." Webber resumed his former position on his seat.

Back in his rental car after leaving the ingratiating Chen, Webber felt, on the one hand, rationally, that the meeting had gone well, and that the Chinese man was who he claimed to be, and was trustworthy. On the other hand, his irrational, or "gut" side, maintained creeping doubts. His job in the Central Intelligence Agency was far easier.

A thousand miles away, Vera Tyler, parked alongside the dark highway, tried again, to no avail, to contact Jason Thompson. She held back her tears with her bandanna, started the pickup's engine, and drove slowly away.

# 22

*P*eter Grayson and Marcus Lucero sat at a four-place table in lunch-time crowded Little Anita's restaurant in Old Town Albuquerque. Each had a beer; one imported, one "domestic." Grayson was half-way through a blood-red chicken enchilada, while Lucero munched on a green chile-laced hamburger.

Grayson finished masticating a bite of his food, set his fork on his plate, then cleared his mouthful with beer. "So, the only Sanchez listed on the water-color club roster is a Rose Sanchez?" He wiped his mouth as he looked across the table at Lucero.

Lucero used his napkin to make his hands partially free of the combination of beef fat and condiments from the plump sandwich. "Late sixties, somewhat overweight, and hasn't actually been active for more than two years. Diabetic. Pretty much confined."

"No one had heard of another Sanchez?"

Lucero shook his head. "Nope."

"Mm. Me no likee." Grayson picked up his fork.

"And no sign of an attorney in Santa Fé named Kittridge. Jan's team went back fifty years." Lucero picked his hamburger up with both hands and bit into it.

"Albuquerque? Any place else in New Mexico?" He chewed.

Lucero shook his head and swallowed.

Both men looked at each other, then Grayson scratched a place on his cheek, looked down, away into the seated crowd, then back at his partner. He pursed his lips.

"Who else could it be?" Lucero asked.

"I don't know, Marc."

"Do we follow the Tyler woman?"

"I don't know, Marc. More curious every minute."

Lucero took the last bite of his lunch, popped two French fries into his already full mouth, chewed and swallowed, then washed everything down with the last of his beverage. He wiped his hand vigorously with his napkin, then sat back. "Shall I write it up? Argument for a tail?"

Grayson, also finished, spoke as he stood and reached for his wallet, "I guess we work something up. What the hell, at this point, what do we have to lose? All they can do is say no."

As the two federal agents left the restaurant for their car, Grayson's cell phone chirped. He pulled it out and activated it as he moved. He recognized the number. "Yeah, Jan?" He listened, then slowed as Lucero walked ahead of him for the driver's side door. He stopped to listen. "Okay. He left a number? Hang on." He followed Lucero to the car, laid the little phone on the hood, and pulled out his ubiquitous notebook. "Okay, Jan. Shoot." He listened, then scribbled on a page of the tiny book. "Thanks. Marc and I are headed back. Yeah. I'll call. Thanks."

Grayson got into the car where Lucero awaited him. He held out his phone. "Our friend in Virginia. Need to call 'im."

Lucero grunted, started the engine, navigated the crowded parking lot and onto the street.

Grayson keyed a number into his phone and pressed the button that caused it to dial. He waited. "Jerry. Pete Grayson. Got your message." He listened. "Fishing? Uh, yeah. Yes, sure do. Yeah. Yeah. Hey, sounds good. Friend of yours? Okay. Hey, let me get back to you. Okay, man. Hey, thanks. Later."

Grayson closed the phone, put it away and stared in silence at the street ahead.

Lucero looked at him wordlessly.

"Madsen."

"I gathered." Lucero came to a stop sign looked both ways, then accelerated away.

"Fishing trip."

"I gathered."

Grayson smiled. "You are a good gatherer, Marc."

"Hey, thanks. Fishing for new fish, or has he caught one already?" Lucero kept his focus on his driving.

"I am presupposing. Presupposing." Grayson looked out his side window. "Maybe some positive movement," he muttered.


After leaving the rental car at Sea-Tac and ensuring he had left nothing behind in the rental vehicle, Webber, still traveling under an assumed name other than Tanner, flew to Denver, where he checked into a motel. The following morning, after leaving the motel and a quick breakfast, he took a taxi to the Bank of America branch on 17th Street. He wore a sports jacket and dark glasses.

After presenting his faux ID and the key he had pocketed in his basement, he was led into the safety deposit box room. Left alone to examine the contents, he removed a fat, number ten envelope, a business-size card and a Spanish coin.

Later that day, he boarded a south-bound Amtrak train, disembarked at Lamy, and took the shuttle to Santa Fé. He carried his overnight bag with the contents from the bank box securely inside. He wore a tan windbreaker and a Denver Broncos baseball cap over his dark glasses for the entire trip. He rode a city bus to the La Quinta Inn, where he checked in, then sought out a local eatery.

The following morning, he left the motel, walked three city blocks to a strip mall where he found a wall-mounted pay phone. He pulled out the small card from the Denver bank, then checked his watch. At one minute before ten, he placed coins in the slot, keyed a number and waited. "Hello, is this Switt and Company? No? Sorry, I guess I dialed wrong. I was looking for Joshua Switt, the—right. Can't find it. Thanks for going to the trouble. What number?" He then called out the number that appeared on the phone box. "Yes, sorry to bother." He hung up. Forty-five seconds later the phone rang and he picked up. "Millard," he said into the mouthpiece. He listened for four seconds, said, "Understand," then hung up again. He checked his surroundings, then returned to the motel.

That evening, a half hour after dark, Broncos cap firmly in place, Webber walked to a nearby fast-food outlet and purchased a chicken sandwich, fries, and a soft drink. These he took back to his room, where he stretched back on the bed and watched television. Aside from using the bathroom twice, the only other overt activity he engaged in was to use the room phone to call his Alexandria house. There was no answer, which didn't surprise him, given that his wife and children remained with out-of-state relatives, so he hung up. To have checked for messages would potentially have caused a recorded link between his room phone and the home answering hardware, a condition he wished to avoid.

The following morning, awake before five, which was seven in his eastern time zone, he arose, showered and shaved, then fully dressed, went to the motel lobby. A small group of tourists milled about or sat at the small tables provided for enjoying the morning repast provided by the motel administration.

He asked for, and received, a rubber band from the morning concierge, bought a copy of the daily *Santa Fe New Mexican*, and returned to his room. He folded the envelope he had found in the Denver bank inside the pages of the newspaper, and secured the bundle with the rubber band. He waited in the room until eleven, when he donned the baseball cap, put on his windbreaker and dark glasses, and left the room with the doctored paper. He boarded a bus which delivered him and a gaggle of tourists to a stop a block from the Plaza in the heart of the city. He spent the next half hour walking around the open space and along four of the streets leading into the famous square.

At ten minutes before noon, he stood on the corner of the sidewalk across from the La Fonda hotel, his hands in his jacket pockets, the folded newspaper cradled between his arm and his torso. He watched people as they milled about, cross to and from the *portal* along the south side of the Palace of the Governors, purchase burritos, glazes and fake Indian jewelry from vendors not allowed at the Palace, and sit on the benches arranged along the four paths leading to and from the center. He saw no one, man or woman, whom he considered suspicious. No one who stood or moved slowly, dark glasses in place, moving about, looking while pretending not to look, such as he, himself, was doing.

He peeked at his watch often, then at five minutes before the hour, he sauntered across the busy street to the opposite sidewalk and to the lone pizza-slice vendor. There, he purchased a slice with pepperoni without green chile, a food he didn't understand, and with it in a sack, walked onto the Plaza proper. He went along the angled path to the obelisk commemorating battles fought within the territory, and chose the bench nearest it on that path. He sat against the decorative ironwork armrest, put the bound paper at his clear side, and rather than open the sack, set it on the paving stone at his feet and between them. He then roved his eyes about, watching for anyone who might be watching him.

He did not see the woman across San Francisco Street who had been loitering on the sidewalk under the *portal* with the "Santa Fe Arcade" sign above, who took notice of the him as he sat on the bench in the Plaza grounds. She was four inches more than five feet tall, of average weight, and wore a white, wide-brimmed straw Western style hat, blue denim pants, black leather Western boots and a moderately-sized silver and turquoise buckle across her midriff. She also wore a leather vest, open over a turquoise Western shirt. Large area, very dark, metal-rimmed glasses covered her eyes. Slung over her left shoulder was the leather strap to a large, brown leather bag that rested against her thigh.

As she kept her gaze fixed on the man on the bench some seventy-five feet away, she reached into the bag and pulled out an expensive camera equipped with a telephoto lens. She raised it to her eye, then pressed the trigger. The result was a series of faint, metallic clicks from the device as it recorded a high-resolution picture for each sound. Satisfied, she lowered the camera into the bag, checked her surroundings, and stepped off the curb onto the street. She angled across onto the greensward such that she would not move directly for her objective.

Webber noticed her as she approached the bench from his left, near the obelisk. What he saw was an overall shapely woman with firm breasts, something that triggered deep, positive feelings in him. He watched her surreptitiously until she stopped in front of the bench.

"This seat taken?" She asked as she sat two feet away from Webber on the other side of the newspaper.

"It is now. Welcome," Webber answered. He was shocked at the unexpected turn of events, and realized instantly that he should have made an excuse to refuse, but knew he could not. He looked around as a crease in his forehead appeared, an outward indication that he was trying to think of his next move.

The woman was silent for several seconds, then asked, "What's that be-tween your feet? Lunch or for the pigeons?"

Webber started to look at her, his mind spinning, then checked himself. "Yes, it is. Lunch. Pizza. I can share." He didn't look at the woman, but wanted to in the worst way.

"Not a pizza fan. Makes ya' fat." The woman kept her eyes away from Webber as she looked up at the branches of a nearby tree.

Webber felt she had stressed the "ya" as fakery, wondered why, then tossed the thought away as he continued to peer at members of the meandering crowd. "Are you—did you bring anybody with you?" He didn't look at his bench partner.

"Nope," the woman answered. "Did you?" Likewise, she continued to look away.

Webber took in and released a noiseless breath. "No."

"Do you have it?" the woman asked.

"Do I have what," Webber said. "Listen. I—"

"Games?" the woman asked. She looked down at his fingernails. "Didn't expect a woman, did you?"

"Games? What games?" Webber countered. "No, I didn't. You better be genuine."

There was a pause, then the woman said, "Better be genuine?" She emitted a short breath in the way of a chuckle. "What kind of nonsense is that?! You have thirty seconds left, then I'm gone." There was a touch of menace in her lowered voice.

Webber, his breath held in check, reached into his pants pocket and retrieved the Spanish coin he had found in Denver. He held it out in his palm. "Ever seen one of these?" He stared at the coin as he continued to avoid looking at the stranger.

The woman looked at the coin, rotated her head to look around, then said, "What a coincidence." She reached into her vest pocket, pulled out a coin and held it up with two fingers.

Webber took the coin, then offered his to the woman. Both then spent the next few seconds scouring their surroundings.

"They aren't very valuable, but I like looking at 'em," Webber said.

"Yes. Interesting," the woman answered.

"Well, I've got a date, and my pizza's getting cold. Nice chatting." Webber got up, put the woman's coin in his pants pocket, took the sack and walked away.

"Nice talking to you," the woman called after him. She sat for another few seconds, then picked up the newspaper Webber had left and walked away in the direction from which she had come.

Webber returned to his motel room, checked out, then made his way to the downtown Rail Runner station, where he traveled to Albuquerque. From there, he flew to Dallas, then Atlanta, on to Baltimore, then to Dulles International. He changed his identity once.


Peter Grayson, dressed casually, enplaned from the Albuquerque Sunport to Denver, then to Jackson Hole, Wyoming. He found a shuttle that took him and a dozen other people, men and women, to the Jackson Hole Mountain Resort. There, he checked in and was guided to his room by a young man of Indian heritage.

After the bell boy set Grayson's overnight bag on the bed, he turned to leave.

"Hang on," Grayson said.

The boy stopped, turned and faced the FBI agent. "Yes sir?"

Grayson held out a five dollar bill. "What's your name?"

"James, sir." Unsmiling, he looked into Grayson's face, then down at the currency. "Too much, sir."

Grayson ignored his remark and made no move to take the money back. "You Indian?"

James nodded minimally. "Yeah, I guess. Some call us Native Americans." He cracked a slight smile, looked at the bill, then back at Grayson, sobered.

"What tribe?"

"Lakota, sir."

Grayson walked to the window that looked out onto the pool below and the mountains in the distance. "Any good fishing hereabouts?"

James, confused, answered, "Not close by, sir. Gotta' get outa' town for good fishin'."

Grayson turned. "Where?"

"Mountains, sir. Lake up there." He pointed with his chin.

"Maybe you could help me find it."

James was quiet, then, "Yes sir." He smiled for the first time.

Grayson turned to look out the big sliding glass door. "I have a friend who should be here later today." He glanced at his watch. "Maybe we could meet and you could point the way. What do you think?" He looked at the boy.

"I can do that, sir."

Grayson paused, then, "In school?"

"Working on a degree."

"What in?"

James looked at the floor, embarrassed. "Criminal justice." He looked up.

"Criminal justice. Great." Grayson started to say something about his work, then thought better of it. "How far along?"

"One more year. University of Wyoming." James had relaxed. "Sir, I can't accept this large a tip. The hotel—"

"Yes, you can, James. You're doing a service to a customer." He nodded his head. "So—we'll see you later. Okay?"

"Yes, sir. Thank you, sir."

"Enough with the 'sir,' James. I'm Peter. Look for me." He held out his hand.

James hesitated, then did likewise, and the two shook hands.

The clock on the wall behind the check-in desk of the hotel read eleven minutes past two when Grayson looked up to see Jerry Madsen walk in. Grayson was seated in one of the comfortable chairs ranged about the large, well-appointed lobby. He didn't rise, but merely glanced at Madsen, then away.

Madsen, who trailed a roller-board, stopped in the middle of the big room and looked in Grayson's direction. "Hey!" he shouted. He wore a floppy, wide-brimmed, fisherman's hat, a fisherman's vest covered with pockets, two of which were decorated with fly fish hooks. Strapped to the roller board were two long, fiberglass tubes which contained fishing rods.

Some of the few people who occupied the lobby looked toward the loud

CIA agent, and Grayson looked in his direction as well. General interest waned immediately.

Madsen turned and walked toward Grayson. His burdened roller board trailed him.

"Hey, yourself!" Grayson shouted. He stood up.

"Hey, fancy meeting you here!" Madsen said, loud enough for all to hear.

Grayson held out his hand to meet Madsen's. "What the hell you doing here, Jerry?!"

"Same question for you, you old sock, you! Came to try my hand at fly fishing!"

"Hey, same here, man. Hey, have a seat. Tell me what's goin' on." Grayson nodded to the chair nearest his.

Madsen positioned his roller board with its add-ons next to the big chair to prevent it from falling, then sat. "Long time no see, man. How're things? The family, all that?" He continued to speak loudly enough for everyone in earshot to understand.

"Eh, you know. So-so. Everybody's fine. Work same old, same old. Kids in school. University. Wife pissed off over my work load. You know." Grayson made a face, then grinned and eyed the room.

"Well, hey, that's great, man." Madsen looked around, then leaned in close. "Except for the wife being pissed." He grinned. "Hey, lemme check in and we'll bring us up to date and all that. Maybe a suds?"

"Yeah, yeah," Grayson answered. He looked around, then gestured. "Bar's that-a-way. See you in a bit. I'll be sitting in the dark." He grinned.

"Right-O, man. Hey! Great to see you! Be down soon's I get a room and take a leak." This last phrase he moderated as he glanced around to see if anyone would notice his remark.

Grayson looked around surreptitiously, got up slowly and sauntered over to the small off-lobby book, magazine and miscellaneous store. He looked over the selection of paper-back novels, magazines, and the range of over-priced sweets. He selected a candy bar, paid the girl at the counter in cash, then walked away as he peeled back the wrapper. He stopped, bit into the bar, and looked at each of the people in the lobby. He didn't see James, but did spy another bell hop, this one, also in uniform, was a young woman. An elderly man sat in one of the soft chairs, staring at nothing. Two middle-aged women sat on one of the settees, chatting rapidly at each other. Two boys, whom he reckoned to be around the age of ten, ran through the lobby and out the big glass front door. A woman in her thirties chased after them. He saw no one he recognized or anyone who appeared to take an interest in him. No one hiding behind a newspaper.

He went to the bar, where the lighting was less than half the value in the lobby. He looked about. A man and a woman sat on stools at the bar. One of the high-back booths was occupied by two men in animated conversation. He went to the counter as the tender, a man, spotted him and came over.

"What'll it be, sir?"

"Uh, hey, let's see. How about a local draft. Over in that booth?"

The bar tender smiled and nodded. "Got it, sir. Be right over."

Grayson thanked him and moved for the booth farthest in the back. Another minute passed when the tender showed up with a tall glass of amber liquid, placed a small, white napkin on the table and the beer glass on it.

"Waiting for a friend. Should be here soon."

"Right, sir," the tender said. He turned and walked away.

Jerry Madsen came in a few minutes later. "Hey, where's my pal?!" He stopped in the middle of the narrow aisle between the line of bar stools and the booths against the wall and swung his head around, as he pretended not to know where Grayson sat. "There you are, you old sock!" He pointed, then went to the booth the FBI agent occupied and slid in. He held out his hand to shake as he did.

Grayson got half-way up as he extended his hand. The two made a show of briefly shaking hands.

"You found me!" Grayson made sure his voice was loud enough to carry.

Madsen settled in, looked at Grayson, then out into the half-lit room as Grayson imitated him.

"What're you drinking?" Madsen asked, his voice now a normal level.

"Local draft. Not bad." He leaned out to look in the direction of the long bar.

The tender saw him, and Grayson held up his finger, pointed at his glass, then at his booth-mate. The tender responded with a nod, and went into action to fill the order.

Grayson turned to Madsen. "Okay, Jerry, why the venue and why the act?" His voice was moderated. "What you got?"

"As to the act, it just seemed appropriate. As to this place, it's because what I have to tell you needs to be as far away from Reston, Washington and Albuquerque as possible without leaving the country."

"Really." It was a question framed as a statement.

"Really."

"Am I going to like this, or hate it?" Grayson worked his mouth in a nervous reaction.

"Maybe neither. But it is serious, in my view."

"I assume it has to do with our friend Mr. Nantes."

The tender arrived with the beer order for Madsen, and set it on a napkin. "You gentlemen want anything else? Something to nibble on? We've got some pretty good sandwiches and appetizers." His hands were folded across his midriff as he eyed each of the seated men. "Bar nuts?"

Grayson and Madsen looked at each other.

Grayson piped up, "Not for me. Ruin dinner." He jerked a nod and smiled.

"Same goes for me," Madsen said, "I'm good for now. Thanks."

"Not a problem. Thank you, gents." The tender walked away.

Madsen looked at Grayson, his brow furrowed. "Not a problem? What the hell does that mean? Why would it be?"

Grayson chuckled. "Hear it all the time. Anyway, before we were so rudely interrupted."

Madsen looked into the room again, then back. "I found our guy. Nantes. But his name wasn't Nantes. It was Negron. I suppose to keep the initials the same. First name Alphonse."

Grayson peered at Madsen, his lips compressed.

Madsen raised his glass, sipped, set it down, and began to doodle on the surface of the table with his finger. "He was expatriate, deep cover, Europe and the Soviet Union with a crew he controlled."

Grayson continued to concentrate on Madsen.

"Second generation. Degree in finance from Columbia. But here's where it gets dicey." He took a long draft on his beer, then set it down. "He was close to the Director."

Grayson furrowed his brow and leaned in. "The Director now? The sitting Director?"

Madsen nodded, peered out into the room again, then focused on Grayson.

"So, you think—what—what do you make of this?" Grayson's voice was a near whisper.

Madsen raised his eyebrows. "I don't know, Pete. I don't know. What I do know is that any further investigation—look into—this, could raise some hackles."

"So—I don't get it. He was close, but how close?" Grayson shook his head, then drained an inch of beer from his glass.

Madsen nodded emphatically, looked down, then up. "Family."

Grayson shook his head again in a jerking motion. He squinted. "Family?! What family?!"

Madsen leaned closer. He whispered. "He was his brother-in-law."

"You're shitting me!" Grayson's exclamation was a whisper as well. He shook his head, his mouth open in shock. He rolled his eyes. "How the—how the goddamn hell did you find this out, man?!"

Madsen sat back, tipped his glass up to his mouth, drank and set it down. He took a deep breath and exhaled. "Just so happens I know a lady. This lady works in HR. This lady is a close friend of mine. Okay? No questions." Madsen peered at Grayson under his eyebrows.

Grayson nodded, closed his eyes, shook his head, then looked again and sat back. He breathed heavily, then settled down.

The two men were silent for a minute when a figure stood near the booth. "Sir?"

Grayson looked up, then straightened. "James. Hi. Hello."

"Hello, sir. I have the information you asked for." He glanced at Madsen, then focused on Grayson. He held a map in his hand.

"Well, hey, that's great!" Grayson gestured toward Madsen. "This is my old friend, Jerry. Showed up here outa' nowhere, and wants to fish, too!" He cracked a grin.

James looked down at the flustered CIA agent. "Hello, sir. Pleased to meet you."

"James has agreed to find some good fishing." Grayson smiled as he looked at James, then Madsen.

James held out a large, colorful map. "I marked a coupla' places for good fishin'."

"Hey, thank you, James! Wonderful." Grayson took the map and spread it out in front of him.

James leaned in and pointed to two places. "This is a lake. This is a river. Good fly fishin' here." He straightened. "Trout. Cutthroat, brown, like that."

Grayson and Madsen both nodded.

"Wow, great," Grayson said.

"Ditto," Madsen put in.

Grayson stood, reached for his wallet, pulled out a bill and handed it to James.

The young Lakota man looked at it. "A hundred bucks?!" He looked at Grayson, aghast. "I can't accept this! I didn't do anything. Just got a map!" He glanced at Madsen.

"Yes, you can, Grayson said. "It's worth it to me and Jerry here." He shook his head. "I insist. Well worth it."

James, in a state of shock, stood still, the paper currency still in his extended hand. He looked behind toward the door to the bar, then back. He lowered his hand. "I could get in trouble for this."

"Nah," Madsen said. "Separate deal. Hotel can't interfere." He paused. "Listen, if they do, you come to me—to us—and we'll make sure this happens off site. Okay?"

James shook his head slowly and studied the floor. "Wow. Okay, but—"

Grayson nodded. "Jerry's right, James. Stick that in your pocket. You've earned it. Put it against your education." He sat down.

Madsen said, "Move aside, James. Let me up."

James stepped back, puzzled at Madsen's request.

Madsen then pulled out his wallet, fished around for a one hundred dollar bill and thrust it at James. "This is for being a poor sport, James!" He grinned and slapped the young porter on the back.

"Sir!" James said. He frowned and smiled at the same time. "Please! I can't—"

"Okay, James, I hate to be rude, but my buddy here and I are very busy, so you scat. Okay? Shoo!" Grayson's smirk was wry.

Madsen sat. "Yeah, James, you're annoying us, now git!" He looked up and awarded the young man a broad smile.

"But—"

Both seated men waved their hands at James. He backed away, incredulous, then took another step.

"Hey, thanks for the map and advice," Grayson said. He saluted, then waved James off again.

James stood for a count of three, then turned and walked slowly toward the saloon door as he shook his head. When he reached the opening, he stopped, buried the money in his pants pocket, took a last look into the somber room, then walked away.

Grayson looked at Madsen. "So, back to cases. Two questions. Why here? And what're we gonna' do?"

Madsen took in and released a big breath. "You know how dangerous this could be. I gotta' tell you, I watched my back all the way here. And I *am* gonna' go fishing. Because if I did miss something, it's gotta' look good." He paused, then leaned forward. "Do you have any idea as to the implications? Shit! All the way up to the administration. The president!" He leaned back, waited, then, "As to your second question, I'm not sure, Pete, but I think we need to bury this." He emptied his glass and set it down with a thud.

"If we let it go public, the Director—"

"Exactly."

"Meantime, the family has no idea. Where this guy is and what happened to him."

Madsen nodded. "We need a story."

"I agree. Hold on." Grayson pulled out his cell phone, keyed a number, and waited. He looked at his table companion and held up his hand for silence. "Jan. Pete. I need Marc, pronto. I'll hold."

There was silence at the table as Grayson finished his warming beer.

"Marc, Pete. Yeah. Okay. Listen—listen, Marc. Listen very carefully. Yep. When we're through, get to Buckley and tell him the thing up north has to be buried. Deep. I can't say why now. Just do it. Then get to the state fuzz and tell them the same. You heard me. Yes. Buried. As in no, nothing, nada. A hold on everything. I'll be back soon and tell everybody why. Yes. And when you've done both, get back to me. I may be in transit, but keep trying. Later." He closed the phone, stared off into the distance, then looked at Madsen in silence.

Madsen's nod was almost imperceptible while he pinched his nose hard in frustration. He leaned forward against the table, looked toward the door and pointed with his left hand over his right arm. "What's with the kid? The fishing holes and loot?" His voice was caged.

"Well, maybe it was a dumb-ass thing to do, but I figured I'd make a big deal out of the fishing thing. No one can accuse either of us of not showing an interest." Grayson stood and threw a twenty dollar bill onto the table. "I gotta' get outa' here. Have to stop that show in New Mexico. Nice seeing you, despite the news."

Madsen looked up at the Special agent. "On your way out, ask the bar keep to send another one o' these over." He pointed at his empty tumbler. "I think I'll eat."

# 23

*T*he female Border Patrol Officer was five inches over five feet in height, with a slim, boyish figure. She wore the standard brown uniform with little trim, and a like-colored baseball cap over dark brown hair pulled back taut. A tight, well-made braid fell ten inches down her back beneath her narrow shoulders.

She stood on one of the sheltered concrete walkways that made up part of the Antler, North Dakota, Border Station, where Canadian Highway 83 joined the north-south U.S. Highway with an identical number. She waved a dark blue Volvo sedan with Canadian license plates through to continue into the United States.

The next vehicle in line was a Toyota brand pickup truck, a Tacoma, black in color. A bearded and mustachioed man with thinning, nearly all-grey hair, was at the wheel. She held her hand up, the signal to stop, more out of instinct than necessity, because the truck rolled to a halt under the weather canopy from a speed of three miles per hour without her bidding. She walked slowly around the back of the truck, wrote the license number of the Canadian plate on a clipboard-secured form, then moved toward the driver's window. She eyed the truck bed, empty, but for two ancient, dried pieces of two-by-four lumber and the remnants of a bale of hay.

"Good day, sir," she said as she looked at the man at the wheel. She moved her head a few inches to the left to look inside. She spotted a newspaper that had been opened, folded, and scattered randomly on the passenger seat. She saw a page on the floor as well. Jason's somewhat worn and grubby Western hat rested, upside-down, on the papers on the seat.

"Morning," Jason said.

"Passport, driver's license and registration, please." She was matter-of fact, without a smile.

"Eh? Oh, sure. Just a minute." Jason fished into his inside windbreaker pocket and pulled out his Canadian Passport and handed to her. He then leaned to one side, took out his wallet, removed his Canadian Driver's License and showed it to her.

"Can you please remove it for me, sir?"

"Eh? Sure. Sure." Jason fumbled with the plastic-covered card while she looked at the line of vehicles piling up behind the pickup truck.

He handed her the card.

She looked, placed the driver's license over the passport and read each. "Theroux, Jonas." She looked up. "Winnipeg?"

Jason nodded and hesitated. "A bit outside. North." He pronounced the word 'outside' as 'oot-side.'

"Yessir. Insurance and registration, please." She stuck her tongue out and clamped her teeth against it in irritation as she pressed the two documents to the clipboard with her hand.

"Lemme see," he said. "Think it's in here." He leaned over, opened the glove compartment and rummaged through a stack of assorted papers and envelopes. "Gotta' be here somewhere, eh?"

"Sir," she said, "where are you headed?"

Jason adjusted himself upright and looked at her, his mouth half open. "Huh? Headed? Down to Bismark. Got a cousin there. He's feeling bad. Old. Older than me!" He chuckled as he reached into his shirt pocket for a heart pill, looked at it, then shoved it into his mouth with slow deliberation.

"Are you okay, sir?" The border agent furrowed her brow.

"Yeah, yeah. Bit of a ticker problem." He tapped his chest.

"Well, I hope you're okay, sir. Do you have the registration and insurance papers handy?" She cocked her head to one side and looked in the direction of other vehicles stopped behind the pickup, then back at the old man who stared at her as though in another world.

"Uh, yeah. Lemme look." He leaned over to the glove compartment again and pulled out the messy stack of papers. Three fell onto the floor onto the orphaned newspaper page; the rest he put on the seat with the remainder of the newspaper. "Okay," He mumbled as he flipped from one piece of paper to the next. "I think. Yeah. Here it is. Okay." 'Okay' was pronounced as 'Ookay.' He straightened, handed the registration, a single sheet, and three sheets of stapled paper, the insurance documents, to her through the window.

She held her clipboard out level and laid the two new documents on it. She compared the registration with the information on the passport, then looked at the insurance papers.

Satisfied, she handed the four documents back perfunctorily. "Nice hat." She jerked her chin toward the head cover.

"Eh? Oh." He glanced at the hat, then looked at her. "Yeah. Gotta' take that along. Gift from him. My cousin. He'd be disappointed if I didn't show up with it on. Damn near wrecked it, though." He nodded.

"Well, have a good trip. And please be careful." She stepped back, assumed a military stance, and waved him through.

"Thank you. You too." He looked at her and licked his lips.

Without gathering up the papers on the passenger seat or closing the glove compartment, he took several seconds to put the papers she had studied on top of the mess there, and put the truck into gear. He stared forthrightly through the windshield, both hands firmly on the steering wheel, then moved off slowly, which served to annoy the female border agent even more. She shook her head and slapped the clipboard against her leg, then beckoned the next vehicle forward.

His heart still pounding, but tapering off, Jason pushed on the accelerator pedal to pick up speed as he watched the border station recede in his outside rearview mirror. With the air flow rising in the cab, he pushed the button to raise his door window, then tried to settle back. The thought crossed his mind that he might see flashing red lights behind, but as the miles passed, he realized he had pulled something off that Andrei, Kirill and the others had master-minded with precision and élan.

It was nearly sundown when he came close to the intersection of 12th Street, the continuation of Highway 83, with I-94, in the city of Bismarck, when he saw the sign for a Motel 6 on his left. After maneuvering to the opposite side and the motel parking lot, he checked into a room on the first floor. He was careful to maintain his bogus Canadian persona, complete with the characteristics of speech, as he negotiated for the room with Canadian currency.

In the room, he used the toilet, then inspected his growing beard and mustache in the fading mirror that graced the space above the lavatory. He checked his watch, then removed his cell phone from his overnight bag and clicked it "on." Tired, but hungry and thirsty, he walked out onto the sidewalk and looked in both directions. To his north, he spied Kroll's Restaurant, a half block away on the same side of the street.

He was led to a booth in the eatery, and ordered a beer, water, and a light supper. He started to eat as the cell phone in his pocket rang.

"Hello?"

"Hello! You're there!" It was Vera's excited, but nervous voice.

"Yes, yes; I'm here."

"Ah—my goodness, it's been so long."

Jason heard the joy and relief in her response. "Yes, I'm sorry. I, uh, I think there was something wrong with this thing. You know." He furrowed his brow and closed his eyes for a moment, forcing himself to invent his story in real time.

"Yes. That happens." She chuckled. "Did—uh—did you get your stuff done? You know—"

"Um, yes. I did. Uh-huh. Yep. Saw the folks."

"Well, that's just fine. I—I'm glad."

"Thanks. They sent their regards."

"Uh, how long—"

"I don't know. Shouldn't be too much longer. You know how it goes."

"Sure. I understand."

"Uh, I should be at the store soon. Soon."

"That'd be nice. It would."

"Well, thanks for calling."

"Sure. Well, goodbye now."

"Bye-bye."

Both Vera and Jason ended their conversation with smiles, then both killed the power on their phones. Vera, for her part, started the engine of her pickup truck as she bit her lip and tears of joy welled up. Jason looked up to see a young waitress standing next to his booth table, a beer mug in one hand, a glass of water in the other. He pondered the fact that the food had arrived before the beverages, but said nothing.

Shortly after ten o'clock that night, after watching the news, then a serial program on the room TV, Jason went to the one window that looked out onto the faintly-lighted parking lot and peered through the dingy curtain. The lot was not full, and what vehicles were there were spread out in various marked spaces for customers. Satisfied that the lot was essentially empty, he put on his jacket, took his keys, exited the room and locked the door. He scoured the area again, then went to his truck, which he had parked as far from the office as possible, guaranteeing that it would be completely in the nighttime dark.

He keyed himself into the cab, found the small flashlight he kept in the console, then with his penknife, shone the light on the special fabric panel under the driver's seat that Kirill had placed there, and cut through the stitching. He looked inside, then pulled the Texas license plates out and set them on the seat. He reached inside and felt for the small screwdriver that accompanied it. With both these objects, he stood back, clicked the light off and scanned the lot and beyond again. He was alone.

At the rear of the truck, then at the front, he removed the Canadian plates and replaced them with the plates from Texas. The out-of-country plates he shoved into the special compartment beneath the seat, put the screwdriver in with them, then insured they were well back and secure before he returned the flashlight to its place in the console. He then closed and locked the truck and made his way back to his room.

The following day he followed I-94 west out of Bismarck to a few miles short of Billings, Montana, then south on I-90 to Buffalo, Wyoming, where he joined I-25 southbound. He drove at the speed limit or under all the way, and kept a close eye on all traffic, including vehicles that passed him in the opposite direction. He spent two nights out before entering New Mexico from the north, through Raton Pass and the city named after it. As he approached the off ramp to Rowe and Pecos on I-25, his mind raced about his next move. When at the bank in Pecos, he had noticed the rise of the land east of the river and some of the isolated dwellings on that side, many hidden by thick forest. He slowed and took the ramp, then north through the Pecos National Monument Grounds to the village of Pecos. He pulled into the small parking lot that served the old country store that had been founded by descendants of Lebanese immigrants.

He stopped the truck's engine after pulling close to the old, rickety "coyote" fence that delineated the eastern verge of the property. His truck was flanked by two cars. A child and a young woman exited the store and headed for the car on his side of the truck. He watched as they got in, then moved away.

He emerged, hatless in the strong sun of mid-afternoon, and entered the store. The original floorboards from the early 1920s were dark, unadorned and well-worn, with shiny nailheads exposed here and there. The place was long and narrow, with a high ceiling decorated with stamped sheet metal to hide the original beams above. Long shelving, two against the stone walls, rose to the ceiling with row after row of bread, snacks, candy and canned goods. Toward the rear was a meat counter, and behind it, a walk-in refrigerated meat locker. On both sides of the front door were well-worn sales counters, reminiscent of the 1930s.

Jason went to the shelving with the candy, chose a popular brand bar, and took it to the one counter staffed at that time by a pleasant woman whom he reckoned to be in her late sixties or early seventies.

"Hello," the clerk said. "Find everything?" She smiled.

"Yes, yes, I did. Sweet tooth." He returned her facial greeting. "Uh, do you know where I might find someone with a place to rent? Know anybody?"

She thought for a moment as she took the proffered paper currency and made change. "Just a minute. Let me ask Marie."

She walked around the end of the counter and went toward the rear of the store, where she disappeared for a minute. She returned and said, "I have a number. Local. This lady might have something." She wrote the number on a slip of paper she tore from the receipt machine and handed it to him.

He took the note and looked at it. "Thank you. I'll give her a call." He raised his finger to his forehead in salute.

He made the call from his truck, then waited for the woman to show up. She arrived in ten minutes. An Hispanic woman he reckoned to be in her fifties, she parked her small Japanese car next to his truck, ducked her head to see him, then emerged and approached his driver's side window. She was pretty, with a subtly-lined, intelligent face. He sensed immediately that she found him attractive. Her name was Vickie Martinez.

She rode with him in his pickup to a narrow dirt road on the east side of the river and to a single-wide trailer set into a clearing in the *piñon* and cedar-dominated forest.

She keyed them into the sparsely- but adequately furnished dwelling. After he looked around, they negotiated for the monthly rent, he paid her in cash, and she handed him two sets of keys.

As they returned to her car in the parking lot on the west side of the river, she made a gallant effort to pick his brains. One of the items on her impromptu agenda were Texas license plates on his truck. Prepared, he explained that he lived in Texas, but traveled a fair amount and had business in New Mexico, and would be resident for awhile. He added that he liked the state, and preferred the northern mountains for hiking and fishing.

As they pulled into the lot where her car was, she suggested he might be fatigued from his trip, and that she would welcome him for dinner. This accompanied her remark that she had been a widow for nearly two years. Jason politely declined, but asked if he could take a 'rain check.'

He drove back to his rental place immediately, moved everything loose in the truck into the sparse house, then crashed onto the bed and into a deep, satisfied sleep. After awakening near sundown, he powered his cell phone on, fixed a sandwich from groceries he had purchased in Las Vegas, then went outside to look around, the food in one hand, a can of beer in the other. The nearest dwelling, another "single-wide," was more than five hundred feet away, behind a stand of *piñon* and juniper-cedar. A pickup truck, older than his and of another make, was parked nearby. Other than that, he saw no other houses, people or movement. To the southwest, above the trees, he made out the edge of the so-called Glorieta Mesa. Above, two huge, black birds swung past, complaining to each other with loud shrieks.

He finished the last of the sandwich, raised the half-empty can to his lips, and went inside. He found the special bag the Russians had provided him in Canada, opened it, and removed a large cross-point screwdriver and a flashlight. He also pulled a small tarpaulin from the bag, then went outside and to the truck. He stood for a moment, looked around, and satisfied that no one observed him in the growing dusk, slipped under the truck cab after preceding himself with the tarp.

On his back, protected from the harsh, rocky ground with thick material, he flicked the flashlight on, then played its beam across the bottom of the vehicle. He spotted the six places where Kirill and Joseph, per instructions from Andrei, had placed 10 mm screws to hold a black steel panel, covering the original stamped panel of the manufacturer, in place. He applied the screwdriver, then carefully lowered the sheet steel. It was heavy with the flat box that it hid. It was then that his cell phone rang.

He set the panel aside, not without straining in the awkward position he occupied, and fumbled for the phone he had placed in his shirt pocket. "Hello?"

"Hi." It was Vera's voice.

"Hi. How are you?"

"Okay. You?"

"Okay. Fine."

"You—you sound weird. Are you really okay?"

"Yeah. Yes." He smiled with his eyes closed. "I'm in an awkward position right now. Nothing wrong. Just something I'm doing."

"Oh, okay. Wondered. You know."

"Sure. Sure. Listen, I need to go, but I hope to be at the store soon. As I said."

"Oh, that's be great. Sure would. Great."

"Yes, I agree. Okay?"

"Okay. Well, g'bye now."

"Right. Bye."

He wriggled out from under the Tacoma, dusted himself off, then took the folded tarp, tools and panel-attached box inside the narrow house. There, he set the cleverly-designed container on the floor and opened it. Inside, he found his briefcase, papers and Sarah's journal. In addition, wrapped carefully in a cloth, was a 9mm Beretta semi-automatic pistol, a box of shells and two magazines, loaded. He picked the gun up and looked it over. The serial number had been skillfully removed, and the firearm was in perfect condition. It smelled of cleaner and gun oil. He pulled back the slide and looked into the chamber. It was empty, but he spotted a round in the grip magazine, ready to ride up into the firing position. He locked the slide open, then let the magazine fall from the grip before he allowed the slide to snap forward. He then re-inserted the magazine and lowered the hammer against the firing pin.

A dual feeling wept over him. On the one hand, he felt good about the weapon and the treatment he had received at the hands of the old Russian spy; on the other, he felt a sadness combined with a sense of guilt. Neither emotion he was able to fathom. He looked at the beer can next to him, lifted it to his mouth and downed the remainder.

With dusk close to dark, he went to the truck, unlocked it, removed the Canadian license plates and the screwdriver, and returned to the little house with them.

The following morning, after coffee and juice, he bent the Canadian license plates in four places until they broke into five bent pieces. With the shards and the foreign personal and vehicle identification he had been provided, along with anything else he thought might place him across the northern border, he got into the pickup and drove away. He entered the main road, turned east, and drove deep into the mountains until he found a deserted Forest Service offshoot road. At the end of the well-hidden road, he stopped, shut down the engine, gathered the detritus, and climbed several hundred feet up into the dense forest.

He checked the area, laid the rejects on the ground, and dug into the soft woodland floor as deeply as he could using one of the larger plate shards. He then buried the plate pieces, phony IDs, three receipts, the remainder of his Canadian currency, covered them, and worked the ground until the area over and surrounding the grave appeared untouched. He thought of the faux bottom plate and the box. He decided he would return it to the bottom of the truck and deal with it later.

# 24

*G*rayson, Lucero and Sam Buckley sat at the big conference table in the secure room of the FBI Field Office in downtown Albuquerque. Grayson was positioned half-way along the big wooden slab, while Lucero sat at one end. A coffee cup sat in front of Buckley, who sat on the edge of his chair, slouched against the table, both arms spread out on the surface to form a circle, his hands clasped together. There were no papers or files present.

"You gotta' be shittin', me, Peter. Tell me you're kidding." Buckley shook his head slowly, blinked his eyes, then scrubbed his face with his hand in frustration.

"Wish I were, Sam." Grayson's voice was low. He looked at Lucero, then dipped his head.

"How do we know this is the case?" Marc Lucero asked as he eyed the ceiling. "I mean, for sure?"

Buckley tilted his head to look at Lucero.

Grayson said, "As of now, all we have is Jerry Madsen's word." He paused and sighed. "I don't see how we can go nosing around Reston without causing a real dust-up. This would work all the way up to the White House." He scratched his cheek and looked at nothing. "But I have no reason to doubt Jerry. He had inside info." He pursed his lips, then, "And he was scared. A frightened man." He paused. "He was like a ghost. I've known Jerry a long time. From when he was in the agency. Cincinnati." He paused. "Hell, he put on a good show, but I saw he was on his mettle. I could tell."

"You worked with 'im?" Lucero asked.

"Some big ones. The Donneti case. Biggest for us." He pointed at his chest. "He was a fun guy. Not now. Damned near got shot and brushed it off. Then."

Buckley worked his mouth, wiped his face again, nodded, and said, "I remember that case." He shook his head "No. We keep it here."

"How do we handle the state police? The media?" This from Lucero.

Buckley pulled at his nose, but was silent.

"False ID?" Grayson asked.

"Do we go to the Director?" Lucero queried.

Buckley sat back and brushed imaginary dust off his shirt front. "Well, for now—and maybe for all time—we take a hands off position." He waited two seconds, pushed his chair back, stood, and paced away, then stopped. "I seem to remember that our Director is a golfing pal with their Director. He may have his ear. We can't." He dropped his head to his chin and shook it.

"That could really muddy the waters," Grayson offered. He stared at the carpet at his feet.

"What about Madsen? Does he have a dog in this fight?" Lucero asked.

Grayson frowned at him. "I can't see why, Marc. How would he?"

Lucero shrugged. "Just asking."

"Well, he'd have to be allied with Nantes and whoever else is involved." Grayson shook his head adamantly. "No."

"I agree," Buckley added.

"He meets you in the middle of nowhere. Could be a ruse." Lucero raised his eyebrows and looked at both men. "Lead us off the trail."

Grayson reacted by moving in his chair and swaying. "No, Marc, goddamnit. He'd be exposing himself if he were a part of that thing. Hell, his problem now is he's thinking there's someone else inside. The company. No." He pointed. "And if it's as serious as I think it is –

and he thinks it is—he could really be in harm's way. Hell, and his source!"

"Makes sense," Buckley commented. "Okay!" He leaned over and slapped the table. "Get with the state people and put a lid on. Tell 'em because this is a federal doo-doo, we have to tighten our grip. Make sure no photos get out." He paused. "I think we leave the name Nantes as is—but let's try to keep it out of the media. Pronto. They'll fuck it up."

Lucero looked at Buckley, then Grayson. "Do we stay on the gal down south?"

Buckley looked at Grayson. "What's your take?"

"We have a team on it. Grace and Marty. They should be in position," Grayson said.

"You guys really think this guy Thompson is still around?" Buckley scowled at both special agents.

Grayson sucked his breath in through his teeth and raised his eyebrows. "Stranger than fiction, Sam; but look at the news Jerry Madsen brings us." He waved both his hands in a questioning gesture.

Buckley said, "Yeah, maybe." He pointed his finger, first at Grayson, then Lucero. "Now, listen, goddamnit, don't break any laws. You tell 'em to be cautious. This is bad without a warrant. You guys are flying by the seats of your pants on this! And my ass is on the line as well." He pondered, then said, "This could also drive our target—and unknown targets—deeper underground." He tilted his head and eyed the other two. "If they spot us."

Grayson and Lucero glanced at each other, then their boss.

Buckley rose and picked up his empty coffee cup. He started for the door, then stopped. He turned and looked at Grayson. "Can you stay in touch with Madsen? Is it safe?"

"Yes," Grayson answered. "Encrypted Email. The old Kappa network."

"Mm," Buckley murmured. "Keep it out of the office."

"Right."

"Good. Keep me in the loop." He went to the door. As he opened it, he said, under his breath, but loud enough for the other two agents to hear, "Shit!"

Grayson walked into the hall, followed by Lucero, when Jan approached. She was a petite woman, three inches shorter than Grayson, and plain, but pretty in her intelligence. Grayson and Lucero stopped.

She looked at both men, then focused on Grayson. "Voice message from Dancer."

Grayson changed the angle of his body to look at her more forthrightly. "Yes? Yes?!"

"Yes. Made contact. Eyeball."

"Man or woman?!" Grayson cocked his head, peered at Jan, then Lucero.

Lucero let his mouth drop open.

Grayson repeated himself. "Man or woman?!"

Jan shrugged and raised her eyebrows. "Disguised voice. I couldn't tell." She made a face as she looked at both special agents.

Grayson shook his head. "Wow. Well, okay. How? When?"

"The burner. Couldn't trace it. Didn't say. It was short. While you were with Sam." She nodded in a matter-of-fact way.

"Okay," Grayson said. "We'll get on it. Excellent. Thanks, Jan." He touched her shoulder as she turned to leave. "Wait!"

Jan stopped and turned.

"Have you heard from our southern friends?" Grayson asked.

Jan moved her head in the affirmative. "Checked in. They're in place."

He saluted Jan with his open hand, then looked at Lucero with his lips compressed. "I told you this case was a dilly." He shook his head and looked at the floor before moving off.

When Vera Tyler joined the main, two-lane paved highway that connected to the dirt and gravel ranch road that lead to her place, she only casually noticed the old pickup truck in the gathering dusk, most of its original paint burned away by the harsh New Mexico sun. It was parked several yards away on the opposite verge, the hood up. It was faced in the direction away from hers. She was too excited and relieved by re-connecting with Jason to be as alert as she should have been, and her thoughts drifted aside.

As she guided her truck onto the highway, helped by barely sufficient late-hour light, she was aware of the older man who was looking at something under the raised hood, and the equally senior woman in the cab, then dismissed the scene. Ordinarily, she would have stopped to see if the pair needed help, but she was driven by her mission which was too important, in her view, to bother. If she had looked into her rearview mirror fifteen seconds later as she gained speed, she would have seen the old pickup, miraculously operational, turn and follow.

In the old truck, Grace and Marty, in truth much younger than their appearance would have the causal observer note, said nothing to each other as they watched Vera's truck ahead. Although not on their persons, they each had high-caliber semi-automatic handguns within reach. Beneath the dash was communication gear capable of satellite linkage. Under the hood was a powerful engine, accompanied by up-to-date transmission and running gear.

They settled in behind Vera at her speed, a quarter mile behind.

"Hey! She's slowing! Brake lights!" Grace shouted from the passenger seat.

"Yeah. What the –?!"

Up ahead, Vera slowed, then made a U-turn onto the opposing lane and pulled to a stop on the wide shoulder.

The FBI tail moved by. As it did, neither occupant looked in the direction of the woman rancher's pickup truck.

After they had moved around a bend, and no longer able to see the tail lights of Vera's vehicle, Marty, at the wheel, slowed, then made a fast reversal and pulled over. "Shit! What the hell is she up to?!"

"Think she spotted us?" Grace asked. Her brow was furrowed.

"How could she? Makes no sense." He thought for a moment, then, "Get the camera ready. Try to get something as we pass. Only one chance. Damn it!" He hit the steering wheel with the palm of his hand.

Grace reached behind her seat to the rear floor and picked up a high-speed, high-resolution, night-vision capable camera. "Gotcha."

Marty pulled the truck forward and back onto the highway after waiting for a passing car traveling in the same direction to disappear. Grace readied the camera, and as they passed Vera's pickup, she pushed the trigger that set the picture-taking device into action. It clicked more than a dozen times before they were out of range and she dropped the expensive machine to her lap.

They were around another bend and beyond the ranch road where they had spotted Vera when the truck pulled over and stopped. Marty allowed the big V-8 engine to idle.

"Let's have a look," he said.

Grace picked the camera up, opened the viewing screen and powered it on. She held the camera over the gap between the seats, and they both watched as the series of grey-green, night vision images came into focus.

"Son of a bitch!" Marty whispered.

"Wow," Grace muttered.

"We gotta call this in." Marty put the truck into gear, then moved it back onto the highway. "See if you can get through."

Grace put the camera back onto the rear floor, then pulled out a microphone from the under-dash equipment. She reached down, flipped a switch, then waited five seconds. "Dealer, this is Southbound Two. Repeat. Southbound Two. Over." She listened for a reply, then said, "Dealer, South Two here; South Two. We have pix; repeat we have pix. South Lady, no travel, no contact; repeat, no contact. South lady using mobile phone. Repeat; mobile communication; assume cell." She listened, then, "Correct. Advise next move." She listened. "Copy that; copy that; Southbound out."

She flipped the power off and returned the mike to its hiding place.

"So?" Marty asked. He focused on the headlight-revealed black pavement that rolled up under the old vehicle body.

"They'll get back to us." She cocked her head, then looked out her side window at the passing sage brush.

"Nothing more we can do here now. Back to the motel?" He asked.

"I could use a drink first. Then get this wig and makeup off." She shook her head in disgust.

Vera made nothing of the fact that the pickup with the faux middle-aged couple she had placed in her vacant short-term memory had passed her as she sat parked alongside the highway. Her call to Jason was answered on the third ring. She hear him say, "Hi."

"Hi. How are ya?" She replied.

"I'm okay. You?"

"Oh, okay."

"Anything new?"

"No. You?"

"No. Uh, I'll see you soon."

"Oh? That's good." She had difficulty hiding her joy.

"Right. Fairly soon. Okay?"

"Yes. Okay."

"At the store. Okay?"

"Uh, yes. Yes."

"Three, four days. I'll let you know. Understand?"

"Yes. Yes; okay. Understand."

"Well, we'll talk again soon."

"Yes. Take care, now."

"You, too."

"Bye." Her smile was accompanied by tears as she started the engine.

Grayson had walked through the front door of his house and shut the door when his cell phone buzzed. He fished for it, opened it and said, "Yes. Grayson." He listened, then said, "Hm, okay. Thanks. We'll look into it."

He thought for a moment, pressed a speed-dial key, then put the little device to his ear and waited. "Marc," he said, "Pete. Have Jan check with tech to see if we can break into live cell traffic."

# 25

*T*he dark wood, decorative clock that rested on Stanley Webber's desk read eight minutes after nine when he keyed himself in, set his briefcase down on the visitor chair closest to the door, and removed his windbreaker jacket.

As he pulled the light piece of clothing off, he sniffed the air, and mouthed a silent remark that the room, despite the air conditioning, smelled stuffy and somehow of plastic. The thought ran through his mind that it always seemed that way after an absence of several days. After hanging the jacket on a high peg of the portable hatrack that stood in the corner beyond the chair, he went to his desk, and, before sitting, keyed the internal number for Jerry Madsen. He waited, then one of the line numbers began to blink. He transferred his outbound line to the incoming.

"Hello. Webber." He arched his back and looked at the white, sound-proofed ceiling.

The voice he hear was female, and familiar. "Stan?"

"Yeah, Marsha. Wha—"

"I saw you were trying to get hold of Jerry. He's out."

"Out."

"Yes. He went fishing. Can you believe it? It's been years."

"Ah, okay. Fishing." Webber's mind was reeling. "Fishing. Really. Where, for Chrissakes?"

"He didn't say."

"Ah. He didn't say." He wanted to frame his remark as a question, but decided against the idea. He gathered his thoughts. "Why—Well, heck, we both know 'ole Jerr. He's a crazy 'ole coot."

Marsha chuckled through the phone line. "Yes, I know."

"Hm. Okay. When's he due back?"

"Next week."

"Hm. Hey, Marsha, did his wife go with him?"

"You know, he didn't say, but I got the impression she didn't."

Webber's thoughts swam again. "Uh, okay, well. Hey, you know, I need to get a message to him. Do you have his number? Cell?"

"Yes, but I tried yesterday and couldn't get through. He's probably out in the middle of nowhere. Is it important?"

Webber thought for a moment. "Nah. It'll wait. Hey, thanks, Marsha."

He hung up slowly, then sat, stared at the door opposite his desk for a few seconds, then allowed his gaze to take in the room. He then invoked the computer that occupied a portion of his desk, pulled up a file, then picked up the phone and keyed a number he saw on the screen.

"Janie? Stan. Stan Webber. Hope I didn't wake you."

"No, Stan, I was up. Coffee in hand. You know." He heard a smile.

"Great, Janie, I hate to bother, but I need to talk to Jerry about something, and I understand he's on a fishing trip."

"Yes, yes."

"Uh, Janie, don't you normally go with him?"

"Not always, but I do like those outings. He was in a rush—or seemed to be. It was odd."

"I see. That is odd. I wonder—Well, no matter." He hesitated. "Do you know where he went? Marsha—his secretary—said he didn't say."

"Well, Stan, he asked me to keep it to myself, but I really think he has a meeting. The reason for the hurry."

"Ah, sure. Okay. Uh, do you know who? Where?"

"Well, you know how you guys work. Sometimes. He just rushed off. He asked me not to say. Grabbed his gear and took off."

"Have you spoken with him?"

"Once. He called when he got to the hotel where he's staying."

"Not since?"

"No. I guess he's out there somewhere."

"Do you know the name of the hotel? Maybe I can get hold of him at night."

"Well, Stan—"

"Thing is, Janie, I think his meeting has to do with why I need to contact him." Webber waited.

She was silent for twenty seconds. "Oh, my. I hope I'm not doing the wrong thing. But it is you." She paused, then, "It's the Jackson Hole Mountain Resort."

"That's great, Janie. You're a life saver."

"I hope it's nothing serious."

"No, no. But it could be. You know how it goes with the government."

"Sure. Well, good luck. Stop by sometime."

"I will, Janie. Thanks. Bye."

Webber hung up, then sat quietly for a minute before picking keys on his computer keyboard. He found what he wanted, grabbed the telephone handset and entered the number. "Yes, good morning. I'm looking for a guest you have there. Yes. Madsen, first name Jerry." He waited. "No? You're sure?" He waited again. "Okay. Thanks."

He hung up, then scratched a place on his nose as he stared vacantly at nothing.

In Albuquerque, Grayson and Lucero met at a Dunkin' Donuts shop in the Northeast Heights, two miles from FBI headquarters, where they both bought coffee, then retreated to Grayson's car.

Lucero slurped at the dark, hot liquid in the paper cup, swallowed, then spoke as he looked forward through the windshield. "The only way we can listen in to a cell conversation is through the NSA, with a FISA Court permit. Then, after the fact." He looked to his left at Grayson. "We'll have to stick with eyes on the ground."

Grayson nodded almost imperceptibly. "So be it. We let team south know. No choice."

"Yep. She's talkin' to someone."

Grayson looked left through his door window which was lowered three inches. "True story, Marcus. True story." He sipped his coffee.

The one New Mexico statute Jason Thompson disobeyed as he drove away from his new mountain retreat in East Pecos, was that which mandated the possession of a loaded firearm in a vehicle using public roads. It was to be openly exposed, a law that ran counter to those in most states. But he was nervous about doing so, and had slid the 9mm semi-automatic pistol, wrapped in a cloth, under the driver's seat, butt forward, instead. He doubted if he would be stopped and challenged, let alone have a reason to reach for the weapon.

On the passenger seat to his right was his Western hat and nothing else. In the glove compartment were the registration and insurance papers for the Texas-registered truck he now controlled. On his hirsute face he wore a pair of dark glasses. His shirt, newly acquired, was of blue denim. On his feet were black Western boots.

Always aware, though he was sanguine in the belief that no one knew him or cared who he was, especially in this remote place, he watched all vehicles and the few ambulatory people he saw as he made his way west on New Mexico Highway 50, then to the Interstate, I-25 South.

Rather than struggling to find a radio station with the least offensive fare, he spent his time moving at the speed limit, reviewing all that he knew, and much of what bothered him about his situation.

His feelings about Sarah concerned him the most. He had been whip-sawed by the revelation that she had been, down through the years, a mole for a foreign government, then had murdered a man and had him, her own husband, kidnaped in a desperate tactic to save him from possible prosecution for espionage. All that was counter-balanced by the fact that in their line of work, their dedication to a life outside of the mainstream, that the day might come when events would overcome them and force them to do things that were beyond the pale. Yet, all that was softened further, in some strange way, by his encounter with the old Russian spy-cum-turncoat. He realized he would require the remainder of his life to deal with all that and more. As he thought about his years at the Labs, nagging thoughts, questions, arose that until recent times, he had let drift away, given the relative normalcy of his work and home life and that of playing watch-dog and control over Mel Vaslovic, the real foreign agent.

But now, in retrospect, thoughts long buried began to surface; about what and who he couldn't, in daylight, tell. There had been dreams, dreams of people and events that repeated, and now, of late, they were recurring. There were people in the dreams whom he knew, yet could not identify. Some were in opposition; some seemed protective and knowing, as though they could peer into his subconscious and point, at what, he knew not.

He held his hunger in check until he reached Socorro, where he exited the Interstate and stopped at a Subway along the main street that ran through the town for a sandwich and drink. He sat in his truck to down the filling meal, again as he watched everyone who came and went.

On the highway, it was close to sundown when he activated his cell phone and set it on the passenger seat. After dark, and still south-bound on I-25, the phone rang. He picked it up and opened it.

"Hello."

"Hello. How are you?"

"Okay. You?"

"Okay."

"I can't talk long, but I thought I'd recommend a good lunch place."

"Yes?"

"Yes. You remember the place? The store?"

"Yes, yes I do."

"Great. Good food. Good lunch."

"Yes. Of course."

"Good. Okay. Need to go."

"Okay. Bye."

"Bye. Take care." And he was gone.

Webber filed a fake incident travel report before leaving after sundown. Equipped with another set of false identification papers, rather than flying from Dulles, he drove to Washington's Reagan International. There, he boarded a flight for Chicago, then on to Denver, where he rented a car and drove to Jackson Hole and the resort hotel where Jerry Madsen was purported to be temporarily housed.

He stood at the front desk for two minutes before the clerk turned to him. "Yes, sir. Sorry about the delay."

"No problem. Yes. I'm looking for a friend of mine registered here. Madsen."

The clerk said, "Yes, sir. Let me see . . ." Nearly a minute passed before the clerk looked up from studying the computer screen. "I'm sorry sir, we don't have anyone by that name registered. Perhaps—"

Webber responded after pondering, "Well, he said he'd be here. He's delayed. That's what it is." He generated his best phony smile.

"You're welcome to wait, sir." The clerk gestured toward the generous lobby.

"Thanks. I appreciate that. I'll wait. "I'm sure he'll show up." He slapped the desk top with his hand and strolled away.

Webber had left his single, hastily-acquired, overnight bag in the rental car. As he stood off to one side and observed the people come and go, he pondered the idea of checking in, then in an effort to be inconspicuous, picked up a complimentary brochure from a rack, went to a corner chair, sat, and pretended to read as he considered his next move.

He looked at his watch. He reasoned that if Jerry Madsen were still at the hotel, but actually fishing during the day, he would eventually come through the lobby. The idea of waiting for something that might not happen caused Webber to be nervous, and wish he had not taken this measure; yet he reckoned he had no other choice.

It was at that moment that James, wearing his house uniform, approached. He stopped short of Webber's chair. "May I help you sir?"

Webber, startled, looked up wordlessly.

"I noticed you lookin' around. You a guest?" James smiled, his hands clasped across his belt line.

Webber lowered the pamphlet, shifted in his chair, and answered, "Ah, uh, no. No, I'm not. I'm actually waiting for—looking for—a friend." He cursed himself silently for seeming to lose his cool, maintaining it being something he regarded as one of his greatest talents.

"I see, sir. Have you checked at the front desk?"

Webber, now in instinctive defense mode, set the folded paper aside. "Yes. Yes. I did. Uh—I thought he'd be here about this time." He looked at his watch unnecessarily.

"He's a guest?"

"I'm told he is." He gestured toward the front desk. "He said he'd be here." He raised his eyebrows, eyes wide, in a shrug, then checked his time piece again..

"Can you describe him, sir. Perhaps I've seen him." James remained in place.

Webber went through the drill of describing Madsen as James listened intently.

"If he were here, sir, do you think he might have met with someone else?"

Webber thought carefully for a moment. "Yes. Probably. A mutual friend."

"Would he have come with personal fishing gear?"

Webber nodded. "Most likely. He's quite an angler, you know." He grinned.

James nodded. "I think I know who you're looking for. If it's who I think it is, he's out on one of the streams I recommended."

Webber brightened. "That would make sense!" He adjusted his position in his chair in response to the news.

"Yes, sir. If it's the same man, he did meet with your friend." James looked around, conscious of his job.

"Of course," Webber said. He peered hard at the name tag over James' breast. "James, is it?"

James instinctively glanced down in the direction of the tag. "Yes, sir. James."

"So, James, do you recall our friend meeting with, with—?"

James pointed in the direction of the lounge. "In there, sir. The lounge."

"Sure, sure. Makes sense. Right." Webber stalled for time, hoping James would tell him more.

"Kind of embarrassing." James glanced around the big room again.

"Embarrassing? How's that, James?"

"Well, sir, when I gave 'em advice on where to fish, they both gave me money. A lot." He nodded and smiled.

"Well, that figures. They're both pretty generous."

"His friend was generous twice."

"Oh?"

"Yeah. When I took him to his room, we got to talkin' and he gave me a huge tip. I really shouldn't say that."

"Your secret's safe with me, James." Webber awarded him a smiling frown.

"Yes, sir. Thanks."

"So, James, do you know if our friend—mutual friend—is still here?"

"He's not sir. He checked out real quick after their talk. In the lounge."

"Hm. Too bad. I wanted to see him myself." He felt his probe was bearing fruit. "Mm, you say he checked out real quick. Do you know why, by any chance?"

James moved away for a few seconds, looked toward the otherwise empty front desk, then returned his attention to his questioner. "No, sir, I don't. They were talkin' about fishin', so far as I know. They were in the back booth. In there." He swung his body and pointed toward the lounge. "Drinkin' beer. I left. They both gave me too much money for my fishin' advice. A few minutes later, I saw the other man leave in a hurry. Not too long after, he was gone with his luggage." He shrugged.

Webber pinched his nose. "And he was—the other man—he was here just one night. Did you say that?"

"Um, I don't remember, but yeah. One night. Nice guy. The fellow you're lookin' for came the day after. If we're talkin' about the same one." He paused. That one came all ready to fish. Lotsa' gear."

"Did the other man, the one who came first—did he have fishing gear?"

"Mm, no, sir, not that I know of. Guess he was gonna' buy some or rent some." He turned to look around again, mindful of his position. He looked at Webber again. "Funny. He never asked." James made a face to express his curiosity.

"James, have you seen the man I described today?"

"If it's the same guy, he left this morning with his rods and other equipment." He nodded.

"James, do you have any idea when he might return?"

"Mm, hard to say, sir, but I'd say after dark. A bit after dark." He watched as a man, a woman and a small child entered through the main exterior door. He stepped back. "Sorry, sir, but I gotta' run." He pointed.

"I understand. Great help, James. I'll keep an eye out for my friend." He nodded deeply with a wink and his thumb up.

Fearful he would miss Madsen should he come back to the hotel while he, Webber, was absent from the lobby, based on his belief that Madsen was registered under a false name, he confined himself to whatever he could find in the way of victuals from the magazine and trinket stall off the lobby. He avoided liquids, and calculated that if he were to spot his quarry, that it would be toward dusk. He looked at his watch.

He managed to avoid the use of the lobby men's room the rest of the day, save for two times, then quickly. More than once, he wandered outside, but kept a sharp eye on the entrance and the guests who came and went. Three times, he gave the "high sign" to James as the young man went about his job.

It was close to sundown on his fourth foray to the front of the hotel, when he was rewarded. He watched as some fifty feet away, a dark-colored, U.S.-made SUV that pulled up alongside the covered curb. Jerry Madsen issued from the driver's side and handed the vehicle over to the curbside attendant. His heart rate rose significantly with the triumph he felt. He turned away so Madsen would not recognize him.

Madsen, dressed as expected for a man who had been in the wilds, entered the hotel lobby and headed for the front desk. Webber sprang into action behind him, but held back to within earshot. He heard Madsen ask for the key to his room, and heard the number. He then moved away, but kept an eye on Madsen as he headed for the elevator rank.

Webber, excited and energized, found the stairs and raced up as fast as he could. At the floor where Madsen's room was, he opened the door carefully, and peered into the hallway. He saw no one, entered cautiously and found a corner behind which he could hide. When he realized that Madsen was already in his room, he made for it. He pressed his ear to the door and listened. He heard a toilet flush, then whistling.

He checked the hall, found it devoid of people, and rapped on the door.

He heard the whistling stop, then moved aside so Madsen could not see his face through the security peep hole. There was a twenty second delay.

"Who is it?" It was Madsen's voice beyond the door.

Webber raised his voice an octave. "Room service."

A three second pause ensued. "Room—I didn't order anything."

"Complimentary, sir." Webber altered his voice again.

There was another pause, then the door opened half way. Madsen required two full seconds to realize who he was facing, then his face turned to a deep frown and his mouth cracked open. "What the—!"

"Hello, Jerry. May I come in?" Webber peered at Madsen, his face lowered.

"How the hell, Webber?! How'd you find me?! And what the hell are you doing here?!"

Webber waited no longer and pushed into the room, then made sure the door was closed and latched. He turned to face the startled Madsen. "You were hard to find," he said.

Madsen shook his head, speechless.

Webber walked farther into the room. He spoke without turning. "Why the hell are you here under an assumed name, Jer? That's kinda' ex-pat game."

Madsen hesitated as he collected his thoughts, then, "And why the hell are *you* here, Webber? What the fuck!" He kept his voice low.

Webber lowered his head and turned. He maintained a low, controlled voice. "I was looking for you, Jerry. Obviously. I came to see you."

Madsen shook his head broadly as he crossed the room, entered the bathroom and grabbed a towel. He spoke as he use the cloth on his face and neck. "And so, because you want to see me, you travel two thousand miles? What the goddamn hell is so important?!" He paused, then remarked, almost under his breath, "Damn Janie couldn't keep her mouth shut!"

Webber went to the big, glass sliding door and looked out. "What I can't get past, Jerry, is why you're here under an assumed name. What's wrong with using your own?" He paused. "And who did you meet?"

Madsen, finished with the towel, threw it back into the bathroom as he came into the room. It landed on the tile floor. "No, Webber, no. This is bullshit! You tell me now why you're here! I know how you found me!"

Webber calmed as he turned to face Madsen again. "Hey, let's be pals again, okay, Jerry?" He thought for a moment. "The reason I was looking for you is that I wanted to know how it was going with your guys in the FBI. That's all." He held out both palms, then sat in one of the over-stuffed chairs next to a small table.

Madsen squinted as he stood in the middle of the room. "Whoa. You're telling me you wanted to ask me a bullshit question like that, and had to come all the way out here to ask it?" He shook his head. "No. There's something else going on. Give."

Webber cocked his head to one side. "Okay, Jerry, here it is. Several reasons. First, you take off all quiet-like, on a fishing trip. Little or no notification. You leave Janie behind. Really unusual. I've known you too long. Then you show up here, but you're not here. Then I find out you've been meeting some-one—here—and the someone is in and out pronto." He paused. "That means something's up. The dart gun, right?"

Madsen looked hard at Webber. "How'd you know that?! That I met someone?!"

Webber smirked and sat back. He looked at his fingernails. "Quite a talk-ative young Indian lad."

Madsen took time to look around the room as he ruminated. He shook his head. "Incredible." He compressed his lips, then, "You know full well, Stan, that we do stuff like this all the time. It's our job."

"Mm, no, Jerry, it's my job, not yours. You're a desk jockey. I'm a field guy. I'm the one who has clandestine meetings with the bad guys. Even when I'm not supposed to. You're not. Now, out of the blue, you're running a net? Interesting." He looked up with a smug expression. "And in home territory. Naughty, naughty."

Madsen shook his head in a rapid motion, eyes shut. "It's not what you think."

"What is it I think, Jerry? What was this all about?" His voice raised an octave in sincerity. "You can trust me. I'm your buddy. Remember? You came to me with the weird killing tool. And, hey, I produced." He leaned forward earnestly.

"Yeah, okay. Point. Okay. But listen, we need to keep this thing tight, man. If anybody in the agency, FBI, CID, NSA—all of 'em—find out what I know, we'd be in the soup. You too." Madsen jabbed his finger in Webber's direction then marched away in his frustration.

"Got it. I get it." He clapped his hands once.

Madsen paced away. "I traveled incognito—" He shook his head again. "I should have lied to Janie. That's how you found me, right?"

Webber nodded somberly.

"Anyway, I wanted it quiet because this thing could blow up. And I mean big." He paused and wiped his face with his palms. "I met with my FBI guy. Had to. He rushed out of here because after he heard what I had, he had to stop what they're doing down in New Mexico. It could blow this up. Sky high." He nodded and looked away.

"Interesting." Webber stood and went to the sliding glass door. "So, what now?" His eyes moved rapidly as his thoughts swirled.

"I'm pretty sure, based on what I found, there's someone else involved. Inside the company."

"Really, Jerry. What did you find?" Webber contained his frustration.

Madsen paced around the room, then stopped. "I found out who Nantes was."

Webber froze as he tried to fathom what he heard. "You found out who Nantes was." It was a statement, low in register. He continued his ignorance act. "The guy who got shot with the dart gun, right?"

"Yes."

"How?" Webber continued to stare out through the glass at nothing.

Madsen went to a chair, sat and swiped his chin. "Can't say. Far too risky."

"Mm. And you think there's someone else?"

"It makes sense, Stan. Dots. Connect 'em."

Webber waited, then, "Who was he?"

Madsen looked up at Webber's back. He shook his head. "I'm not going to say, Stan."

"I see." Webber lowered his head as his heart rate rose.

"Too risky, Stan. This has to stay buried. This I will not say. Sorry."

"What about the other? Or others? Your dots."

"I don't know. Nothing yet. Working on it." He wasn't, nor did he know what his next move would be.

"Who you working with? Inside." Webber tried to appear light-hearted, the opposite of what he truly felt.

Madsen's voice was close to a growl. "Goddamnit, Stan, I told you! You know better than that!"

"Mm. Right. Right. I do know better than that." He turned to face into the room, then walked slowly across to the bathroom. "Be right out. Gotta' tap a kidney."

Madsen didn't react as he moved to a chair and sat slumped, then he heard the sound of Webber relieving himself and the subsequent flush. After that was the sound of water running in the lavatory.

Webber came back into the room as he wiped his hands with a white hand towel. He walked across the room to the chair where Madsen sat, then behind it. There, he held the towel out by its opposite end points, whirled it around until it was knotted into a rope-like shape, then dropped it over Madsen's face and onto his throat. It took Madsen a second to realize what was happening, and he reacted by raising his arms and tried to pull the towel away. Webber pulled with all his might as Madsen's legs came up, kicked and floundered as he struggled against the pressure on his throat. Webber heard a bone in Madsen's throat crack, but the victim did not. Madsen's face turned red, then purple, then grey, as he was denied air, helpless. After another twenty seconds, the struggle was over, and Webber relaxed the towel.

He stood back and studied the room. He then returned the towel to the bathroom and hung it carefully on its appointed rack. He looked at his watch, then opened the medicine cabinet and as quickly closed it. Back in the main room, he went to the dead CIA operative and rolled him out of the chair and onto the floor. He stood back, looked around again, then rifled through the dead man's effects. He pocketed his wallet, some paper money and change from a bedside table, then removed Madsen's watch from his limp wrist. He thought for a moment, then retrieved the murderous towel, took it back into the room and dropped it near the body. He then toppled the lamp on the reading table, pulled the covers on the bed until they hung down to the floor, and tossed a magazine onto the floor near the chair Madsen had been in. That he turned onto its side.

He went to the glass door and looked out. It was totally dark, save for a faint fan of light from the hotel exterior safety lamps.

He closed the curtains across the expanse of glass, then checked the room again and headed for the door. He stopped, reflected on something, returned to the bathroom, took the handkerchief from his pants pocket and wiped the toilet flush handle. At the hall door again, he carefully wiped the latch mechanism, then opened the door with slow deliberation. He peered out into the hall, and satisfied it was clear, stepped out and pulled the door closed such that the loudest sound was the click of the bolt entering the striker plate.

He moved along the hall to the stairs at a normal pace without looking in any direction but face forward. He moved into the stair well, stopped to look and listen, then made his way to the bottom and the rear, outside door. He checked to see if there were an alarm, and satisfied there was not, left the building.

He stopped at the first service station he saw in the rental car, pulled in and parked, then got out and headed for the outside phone booth. He dropped several coins into the slot, keyed a number and waited.

In the Pennsylvania farm house, Jack picked up the phone on the fifth ring. "Hello?"

"Is Joshua there?

Jack hesitated, then collected his thoughts. "Uh, I think you got the wrong number. We have a neighbor by that name, but not here."

"Oh, okay. Sorry."

"No problem." Jack hung up the phone, stared at nothing for several seconds, then turned his head to look into the other room. "Hey, Ruth!"

Webber returned to his car and continued the drive to Denver.

# 26

*W*hen Jason arrived at the Akela Trading Post, his watch read 1128. As he slowed his pickup into the vast, open area between the fuel canopy and the main buildings, he scoured the lot where he could park the truck such that it would be relatively unnoticed. There were few vehicles, so he drove around to the back, where he found a place close to the building and out of sight of the highway. He shut the engine down, then peered through the rearview mirrors, inside and out, then the windows, this with his dark glasses affixed. There were three vehicles beside his; an older pickup truck, a well-used car and a pearl-gray Harley-Davidson motorcycle of an earlier vintage.

He checked the time, put his Western hat on, exited the truck and locked it, but not before ensuring that the weapon beneath the driver's seat was safely out of sight. He stood for a moment, then made for the entrance around the front of the huge edifice.

With his hat and dark glasses still in place, he looked around the interior. He reckoned there to be no more than fifteen or twenty people. Several sat at tables, eating, while an older couple got up to leave, and three more meandered through the curio aisles.

He noticed one of the waitresses, whom he figured was from Mexico by her appearance and her accent as she tended to a couple at a table. He didn't see another wait person. He returned to the front door and the outside, then to the east end of the building. From his position, he watched as light traffic moved along the highway. Two passenger cars and a stake body truck arrived. The people in the cars went inside, while the truck stopped at one of the fuel pumps.

His wrist watch read thirteen minutes past noon when he spotted Vera Tyler's pickup leave the Interstate and arc into the big parking lot. He watched, without moving, as she settled the vehicle into a position against a designated parking barrier. He waited ten seconds until he flexed his muscles to move, when he saw another pickup truck slowly enter the gravel-covered area. He saw Vera get out of her truck and move for the building. He watched as she swung her head around to study the other cars and trucks parked on either side. She hesitated, then entered the building.

Frozen in place at first, Jason watched the other pickup. He saw no motion, so he moved to the rear of a nearby car, where he was able to see the old vehicle and its occupants. He saw someone on the passenger side who appeared to be a woman. He watched as she moved her head to look to her left, then to her right as though to look at the entrance. He checked his surroundings to see if anyone was eyeing him. He saw no one.

His gaze fixed on the newly-arrived pickup, he watched as the occupants emerged. A women, who appeared to be well past middle-age, got out of the passenger side, while a man of the same vintage left the driver's side. The woman didn't look at the man, nor did she wait for him, rather she moved directly for the entrance. He watched her move, then glanced at the gravel-dressed dirt at his feet as he searched his memory for comparisons. What was it? Something about her bothered him. He looked up. Yes. She strode as though much younger than her overall appearance, and she seemed more erect, more energetic than her clothes, hair and facial appearance would dictate.

Rather than following directly behind the woman as she walked toward the entrance, the man, who also belied his age appearance, stood apart from their vehicle and scanned the lot. He then donned an old baseball cap, rounded the back of the pickup, and moved toward the shop opening.

Jason turned away and walked several feet away from the vehicle he had been behind as he pondered his next move. He stopped, looked down, then went to the entrance. Inside, he looked for Vera, and spotted her at a table next to the outer wall near the one they had occupied during their visit. He ducked his head, fearful she would see him, and began to wander through the merchandise area, pretending to look at curios. When he came to a display of cards that advertized the area specifically and New Mexico in general, he stopped. He picked out a post card, then went to the cashier station at the main counter, where he found a cup bristling with ball-point pens. He took one, then wrote on the blank address side.

When the Mexican waitress came to the counter, he looked down at her. "Excuse me, could I ask a favor?"

She looked up. "Yes, sir?"

"Uh, there's a woman. She's seated over there near the windows by herself. I'm a friend, and I'd like to surprise her. It's her birthday."

"Oh, that's nice."

"Yes, thank you. Uh, could you please deliver this card to her in a menu? You know, folded inside?"

The girl looked in Vera's direction, where she sat, a glass of water in front of her, hands folded on the table. "She has a menu, sir."

"Well, yes, but could you make an excuse? Oh, and ask her to look at the inside right away? It's important. Okay?"

The girl frowned, then smiled. "Okay."

"Oh, and please don't let her know I'm here. It would ruin the surprise." He reached into his shirt pocket, pulled out a five dollar bill and gave it to her.

"That's not necessary, sir." She appeared pained as she held the piece of paper money tentatively.

"It is to me. Please take it." He smiled and nodded.

"Okay. Thank you."

Jason gave her the card, which she put inside a menu and walked away. He then moved back to one of the merchandise aisles where he could observe the action he had precipitated.

Vera looked up as the girl approached.

"I have a better menu for you," the girl said as she held it out.

Vera hesitated, but with her eyes on the waitress, took the replacement. "Okay. Sure."

The girl reached out and took the other menu. "You should look at the inside. Right away."

"I'm waiting for a friend."

"I know. I'd like you to look inside right now." She pursed her lips.

Vera feigned a frown. "Oh, alright." She chuckled, opened the book-like menu, then looked at the pages. "I—" She looked up again, then made a sweep of the store with her eyes, then read the message on the card as the waitress moved off.

*Don't look around. Close the menu, put it down. Wait 30 seconds, get up and walk slowly to the back of the store past the curios. Act naturally. -J*

She froze for an instant, then did as the message demanded.

As Vera got up, Jason moved for the rear as well. He stood in the shadows between two tall shelves. When she came close, he hissed at her. She looked at him with total surprise as he beckoned her to come into the aisle with him.

"Ja—"

"Shh." He whispered, "The old couple you see—over there—" He gestured with his eyes and a tilt of his head. "They're watching you. I'll tell you later. Listen. Walk slowly toward the front door. Tell the waitress you won't wait any longer. Say it in a normal voice. Go outside, then move as fast as you can for the rear. Go left. That direction." He pointed. "My truck is there. It's locked. Here are the keys. Get in on the passenger side and duck down. Go." He patted her shoulder.

After Vera followed his mandate and left, he watched the older couple look at each other as they tried to figure out their next move. The woman got up and made unhurriedly for the door, while the man went to the counter to pay their bill.

Jason stepped out of the maze of shelving onto the main floor, then made a beeline for the door as well. When he came close to it, he slowed as the woman was no more than ten feet away, then stopped and cocked his head toward the floor and mumbled as though he had forgotten something. He turned as he continued to block the exit, and looked directly at the woman. He behaved as though surprised, smiled, and mumbled an apology. He realized at that moment that he was correct in his earlier assessment of her age. Close up, he saw that she was made up to appear older.

He stepped aside, allowed her to pass, waited, then followed. Outside, he walked toward the far eastern corner of the building while the woman, at the same time pretending to behave normally, had become frantic over her inability to spot Vera, and stalled half-way to her vehicle.

When he reached the corner, he looked in the direction of the female agent. She stood near the pickup truck she and the man had arrived in, looking around. It was then he saw the man, her partner, emerge from the building as well. The man halted, looked at the woman, then at Vera's pickup, then back. They both shook their heads minimally. The man then walked slowly toward the woman and their vehicle, his head down in contemplation. He stopped, raised his head, then pointed in Jason's direction, then at her and gestured toward her end of the building.

Jason hurried to his truck and got in. He looked down at Vera, crouched on the floorboard on the passenger side, then out through the windshield as he started the engine with the ignition key Vera had thoughtfully put there. "Stay down. They're looking for you. I think both are—yeah. There's the guy, he's headed this way. Walking, not running."

He put the truck in reverse and backed out slowly as he checked his mirrors and craned his neck to peer through the rear window. The truck in forward, he inched it toward the corner of the building. As he did, he looked directly at the man and waved. The man waved back with a tentative motion. Jason saw the creases in his worried forehead.

"Stay down until I tell you, okay? Are you okay?"

"Yes." Vera's voice betrayed the cramped position of her body. "What's going on, Jason?!"

"Gimme a minute until we get on the highway and you can sit up."

Jason drove off the Akela property, toward and onto the Interstate. When he was satisfied they were out of sight of the trading post, he told Vera she could get up.

She wriggled her way onto the seat, panting and smoothing her clothes. She looked at him, desperation in her eyes. "Jason, what *is* going on?!"

He extend his hand to her. She took it and caressed it.

"I'm sorry. Those two people, the man and woman? They were not who they were pretending to be. They were in disguise to try to fool you. They were watching you. Tailing you." He glanced at her, but maintained his eyes on the highway and stayed at the speed limit.

She shook her head. "But—but why, Jason?! Who—who were they?!"

He paused. "FBI. I'm quite sure. If they were bad guys, they would have acted differently."

"Why would the FBI tail me, as you say?"

"Because, dear lady, they think I'm alive and that you know where I am." He pursed his lips.

"Oh, god, Jason!" She brushed at her tangled hair as she looked out the windshield, then back. "How did you know?"

"Well, it makes sense. I've thought a lot about what happened in Truchas and after. They're not stupid. They put two and two together and came up with four. If I'm alive, where do I go and why? Am I guilty of espionage, or an innocent victim? That's a question I'd be asking." He paused as he collected his thoughts. "They're sure to have gone to the house. Albuquerque. So, where could I hide? What better place than a remote ranch?"

Vera frowned and tilted her head in a question. "But why not come out in the open about it? With me?"

He ruminated, then, "Mm, probably a couple of reasons. One, maybe they couldn't get a warrant, two, they figured it would alert me and make me go deeper underground."

"God." She thought for a moment. "You know they spied on me. From the mesa."

He looked at her. "They did? How?"

She explained what happened and how she challenged them and chased them away.

"Then I'm right." He peered ahead, seriousness written on his face.

"What now?"

"Not sure. I need to think. This has to come to an end, but there has to be someone else out there. Interested in me." He paused to reflect. "And I can't let them get to you."

"Jason, where were you? I couldn't get through." There was pleading in her voice.

As they approached Las Cruces, he related everything he had done since the last time they were together and the results. She listened, rapt.

As they entered the town, he spoke. "I don't know about you, but I missed lunch. How about we stop and eat?"

They ate at a small locally-owned restaurant. Jason told her more about his long trip, and that he was ensconced in a rented "mobile home" in Pecos. He said they would think of a way to get her back to her vehicle.

Marty and grace had met at the rear of the building. There, they searched what they could, including the other pickup and the passenger car. Aware that if caught, regardless of their status, they could possibly be detained by local or state authorities, they returned to their truck and sat.

They both stared forward.

Grace spoke first. "She's on to us."

Marty shook his head. "Not sure. How?"

Grace shook her head in frustration. "Hey, if Albuquerque is right, and she knows something, she might be on the lookout. We blew it."

"Maybe."

"No maybe. She knows and we blew it. We gotta call it in."

"Wait."

"Wait?"

"Wait. The old guy in the Toyota pickup. He pulled out—from the rear—just as I came around."

"So? You think he had something to do with her?"

"Could be. She coulda' been hiding in the truck."

Grace pondered. "Did you get the plate?"

"No, but I don't think it was New Mexico."

"Well, that sure helps." She made a face and looked out her side window.

"Sarcasm is not called for."

"Sorry." She wasn't.

"Let's hold off. She's got to come back for her truck. That's another reason I think she left with someone."

"Might be right. Could be. So we wait?"

He tilted his head. "Not like this. If she spotted us, she probably has help and got away, and when she comes back, she'd see us."

"Unless we're positioned so she can't."

"Ye-es." Marty dragged the word out.

"Right. We hang here until she—or someone, comes to get her truck." Grace ripped the wig off her head in disgust. "This sucks."

"I didn't get to have lunch. Whatta' ya' say?"

"Might as well. Let me put this goddamn hairpiece back on. Then I'll call it in."

Grayson was crossing the I-40 overpass bridge, north-bound on Louisiana, when his cell chirped. He turned control of the steering wheel over to his left hand and deftly pulled the small device out of his jacket pocket with his right. He flipped it open and held it against his ear. He hoped he wouldn't be noticed by an active-duty member of the APD. "Grayson." He listened. "Yeah, Jan. Headed home." There was a delay while he listened. "Detective Sergeant Wakulinski? Where? Teton County? Wha—Listen, I'll pull over and get his number."

Marty moved their vehicle to a position where they could still observe the front lot, then he and Grace ate lunch, then snacked for dinner, at the Akela Trading Post. One or both kept watch over the empty pickup truck in which Vera Tyler had arrived, either from one of the store windows or from their vehicle. More than once, a store clerk asked if anything was wrong, or if they needed help because of their longevity. The story they invented was that they were waiting for a friend who had experienced car trouble, and had promised to wait for as long as it took.

Marty was in the truck, his driver's side seat in the full back position, napping, while Grace spelled him and watched Vera's truck and the parking lot from inside the store. She nursed a cup of cold coffee and nibbled on a candy bar.

It was close to nine forty-five that evening when a regional bus pulled into the trading post lot and came to a dust-raising halt. Grace heard the hiss of the brakes, then watched as the passenger door opened. A few seconds later, one person, a woman, stepped out. She stood away as the door closed and the bus, its big diesel engine roaring, angled out of the lot and back toward the Interstate. The FBI field agent watched as the woman walked toward the pickup truck she and her partner had been following.

It took Grace a full five seconds to realize who the woman was and where she was bound. She leapt out of her chair, rushed to the entrance, and raced to the federal vehicle. She ignored her disguise and questions that might be raised in the minds of observers. There, she banged into the modified pickup, reached across to Marty and shook him awake. "She's back!"

"Wha—?!" Marty stared at nothing for a moment, then looked at Grace, his eyes glazed.

"Goddamnit, Marty, she's back!"

"Shit! Really? How'd she—?" He stopped as he sensed the answer in his partner's face.

Grace slumped into her seat. She looked out as Vera backed up, and drove away. "Bus."

"Bus?!"

Grace looked over at him as she removed her wig. "She came back on the bus, Marty. The goddamn bus!" She sighed heavily and shook her head.

"Shit."

"She made us. We've been had. It's over."

Marty reflected for a moment. "She made us, or someone else did."

She looked at him. "Guy in the pickup around back?"

"Best guess." He tapped the steering wheel, his face distorted, as he chewed on the inside of his mouth.

"Our guy?" She brushed imaginary dust from her pant legs.

Marty nodded somberly. "Our guy. No dummy."

"Nobody said he was."

Marty started the engine, set the transmission into reverse, checked his mirrors, and backed away from the parking barrier. He looked over his shoulder as he arced the truck back. "Nobody said he was."

At that moment, Jason Thompson was fifty-four miles north of Las Cruces.

# 27

*S*am Buckley, Grayson and Lucero sat at the big conference table in the Albuquerque FBI Regional Office. Centered was a conference speaker phone.

They listened as Grace and Marty related the facts on the ground as they had experienced them. All three men stared at the speaker phone as they listened.

"Do we stick it out?" Grace asked.

Grayson shook his head and leaned back. "What's the point? She's been talking to someone, and she was able to elude a stakeout, most likely with some-one who knew."

"Or spotted you. And that someone has to be Thompson," Lucero added.

Buckley sighed. "I have to admit, you guys called it."

"Well, if you look at all the evidence—" Grayson commented. He looked at the electronic device. "Might as well wrap it up, Grace. Marty. Thanks. Good job. We know more now than we did. She's in collusion."

"Good job, guys," Buckley said, See you tomorrow."

The incoming line went dead and the connection was terminated.

"Can we force her now that we know that?" Lucero asked. He looked from Grayson, to Buckley and back.

Grayson ruminated, then shook his head as he looked at Buckley then at Lucero. "And do what? Use a rubber hose or electrodes on her?" He was silent for a moment, then, "We don't know it's Thompson. She could be having an affair with a married man, for all we know. Hiding from a suspicious wife or a private eye."

"Yeah," Lucero said, "But not likely. Something else to consider." He glanced at both his table partners.

"What?" Buckley asked.

Lucero continued, "One, assume Thompson's alive and well. Two, if so, is he clean or dirty? If he's dirty, why would he be messing around with a widow lady on a remote ranch? Just to hide? We didn't spot him there. If he's clean, why is he still out there in the cold? One possibility in that scenario is he's afraid of being tracked down by one or more bad guys. Nantes had to be working with someone upstairs, and Thompson's a loose cannon. If that's true, he might stay away from the Tyler woman for mutual safety reasons. If he knows we were on her, we've driven him down deeper."

Grayson and Buckley both nodded in silence.

"And," Lucero continued, " what if *we're* being watched?"

Grayson jerked his head back in response. "What?!"

"Hear me out." Lucero tapped the table with his finger. "Bad guys watching us in hopes we'll find their loose end. Thompson. I mean, have we been watching *our* backs? Look at it this way." Lucero turned in his chair and extended his index finger. "If Thompson is alive and corrupted, maybe he'd want to be in contact with Nantes allies. Maybe he doesn't know who or how, so he's circling. On the other hand, if he's on our side, he may be afraid they'll find him. Or he could be trying to ID 'em for his own purposes."

"If he's a good guy, why not come on in?" Buckley asked.

Lucero looked at Grayson.

"You've got the floor," Grayson said.

Lucero licked his lips. "Maybe he feels because we accused him, he's got to prove himself first." He threw his hands out in a shrug. "We never charged him."

Grayson and Buckley shook their heads.

Buckley looked at Grayson. "What the hell is going on in Wyoming?" He frowned.

Grayson studied the wood grain of the table top for several seconds. He then rotated his head to study Lucero's face with his lips compressed. He sat back and sighed. "If we have what I think we have in Wyoming, we have a deceased company man, and what that means is that someone sure as hell followed him. Question is, if so, why, and what did they find, if anything?"

"Agency jet's waiting. Better get cracking." Buckley said. He rapped his knuckles on the hard wooden table and stood.

"Right. I'd like Marc along. Sheriff's holding the investigation."

Although weary, Jason Thompson had driven from Las Cruces to Albuquerque after kissing Vera Tyler goodbye at the bus station. He checked into a motel along the Interstate shortly after midnight.

Their discussions over lunch and dinner had centered around highlights of Jason's foray to the east coast and Canada. They also touched on events she had experienced on the ranch with hiding his old pickup, the appearance of the FBI watch team and her reaction to it. She wanted to know what he would do next, and he told her that he felt his problems would be resolved soon. In reality, he did not.

In the morning, he drove by the house. The car that belonged to his son, Justin, was parked in the driveway. As he drove slowly around the block twice, he noticed a large van parked along the curb. It was painted in a neutral color, and its sides were decorated with advertisements for a cleaning company. He looked for evidence of communication gear on the vehicle, but saw none. He saw no overt evidence of local law enforcement.

He was back at the trailer house in East Pecos by midday, where he ate a light lunch and dozed off, his mind reeling with what he had to do.

Peter Grayson and Marcus Lucero stood on either side of the body pallet that had been rolled out of the Teton County Morgue's deceased body cold locker. Detective Sergeant Wakulinski of the Teton County Sheriff's Office, another uniformed officer, and a woman in a white smock, were at a respectful distance behind them.

Grayson studied Jerry Madsen's cold, grey face, then looked up at Lucero, who watched his wracked expression. He sighed, "Jerry Madsen."

Lucero nodded in silence.

Grayson looked at the people surrounding him. He asked, "Do we know how he died?"

The woman in white took a step toward him, hesitated, then stood next to the pallet. She gestured at the body. "We'll know more after the autopsy, but you may notice the ligature marks on the neck." She pointed with her surgical gloved hand.

"What was used? Can you tell?" Grayson asked.

She touched Madsen's dead neck lightly with her expert finger. "The marks indicate something blunt was used. Not sharp, or thin. Like a cord of some sort." She stepped back and folded her hands across mer middle.

Lucero made a face and turned his head sideways in reflection. "He was in his hotel room?"

Detective Wakulinski answered. "Yes. He was found on the floor in the living area." He looked at the technician. "A hand towel was found near the body."

Grayson turned to Wakulinski. "Can we take a look at the scene?

"So you did know him?"

Grayson nodded. "Yes. Jerry Madsen. Agent of the government. Old friend."

Wakulinski peered at Grayson. "And you're FBI?"

"Yes."

"And I suppose you can't tell me why you were here."

"Quite right. Confidential. Sorry."

"Hm," the sergeant murmured. "Do you have any idea why someone would want him dead?"

Grayson shook his head. "I thought you said he was robbed. No wallet. That's why I'm here."

"We have to ask the question." He smiled and glanced at the others. "Why am I telling you?" He looked at Grayson again. "You know the drill."

Grayson smiled, looked at the floor, then up at Wakulinski. "Of course. I agree. I think he was targeted. But I can't tell you why."

Wakulinski nodded. "If we're through here, we can go to the hotel. He turned toward the door, then stopped, looked at the technician, and said, "Thanks."

"There's someone there I want to talk to," Grayson said.

Grayson, Lucero and James sat in a rough circle in the room where Madsen's body had been discovered by a maid. Wakulinski stood, his arms folded. Outside, in the hall, a uniformed sheriff's deputy stood guard.

Grayson spoke. "James, you say this man waited all day for my friend to return?"

"Yessir." James, pale, sat tensely on the edge of the bed. His eyes darted between all three law men.

"Did he ever mention a name you can recall?"

Before James could answer, Lucero cut in. "How did he seem to you, James? I mean, what sort of a man did you take him for? A professional, or a man who say, worked at manual labor, you know; like that?"

James shook his head somberly. "Am I in trouble?" He looked at each of the men again, his eyes questioning.

Grayson leaned forward suddenly, "Hell, no, James! God no! No way." He shook his head adamantly.

Lucero shook his head in a slow arc. "No, man. You're helping us solve a problem. We're glad you spoke with 'im."

The sergeant nodded his head with emphasis.

James came up with a wan smile. "Good. I thought—"

Grayson continued to shake his head. "No, James. You're not under suspicion for anything."

"Okay," James said. He lowered his head, then raised it, calmed.

"So," Grayson continued, "Did he mention a name? His name?"

James searched his memory. "No—" He dragged the word out. "No, I don't remember him sayin'." He shook his head.

"Okay," Grayson said. He looked up at Wakulinski. "Let's take a peek at the hotel security tapes."

The three lawmen stood in the cramped hotel manager's office as they watched a series of short, black and white, out-of-focus scenes from four video tapes. There was one of the lobby area, one shot of the elevator entrance, and two of the front entrance. In each case, the man they suspected wore a baseball cap, and never looked up.

"He knew he was under a surveillance camera," Lucero remarked.

Grayson and the Teton County detective both nodded.

Grayson reached out and stopped the tape. "This is getting us nowhere. The guy doesn't check in, he tells no one who he is, and according to James, he was fixated on Jerry." He gestured at the video playback machine. "There's James talking to him. He's the guy."

Wakulinski said, "You don't target someone if you're gonna rob 'em."

"Something else," Lucero said. "Why take his wallet and watch? If this guy is a pro, he knows damned well we're gonna respond and ask the questions. It's a dumb-ass thing to do. Unprofessional."

Grayson turned in a tight circle, his hand to his chin. "Desperation."

"Desperation?" Wakulinski asked.

"Yes," Grayson said. "He tracks Jerry here. How does he know Jerry's here? Who told 'im? Why does he track him? What does Jerry know that this guy wants him out of the way?" He peered hard at Lucero. "He freaked. He knew something—knows something—figures Jerry knows something. Wants him quiet. Out of the way."

Lucero was silent as he pondered Grayson's analysis.

Grayson looked at Detective Sergeant Wakulinski. "This is your turf, detective. We'll do our part and keep you in the loop." He hesitated. "One request, though, that you bury the fact that the deceased is—was—government."

Wakulinski nodded. "Got it. No problem." He paused. "The body?"

Grayson was silent, looked away, then back. "Yes. Hm. Here under an assumed name, ID gone. Who knows this?"

Wakulinski made a face and shrugged. "Mm, no one, really. Hotel people think he's the name on the register. Just us." He shrugged again.

"Okay," Grayson said, "Hold off on releasing a name. You know, standard stuff about notification, blah, blah—and that's actually the case, because I'm sure the widow doesn't know." He looked at Lucero.

Lucero nodded. "Need to talk to her."

Grayson lowered his head and pointed at his partner.


Jason Thompson got up, sat on the edge of the bed, looked at his watch, then stood and ambled into the scantily-furnished living room. He looked about until he located an old, dusty Santa Fé phone directory. When he found what he was looking for, he drank a quarter glass of water from the kitchen tap, grabbed his jacket and his ivy cap, picked up the laptop computer, and left.

A little more than a half hour later, he found a parking place in the crowded lot a quarter block away from the Santa Fé Baking Company. As he approached with continued caution, and observed the patrons, he realized he would be welcome, given his attire and facial hair. He carried his laptop, and noticed that he would be a part of that club as well.

Inside the crowded place, he found an unattended table in a corner of the lower portion of the big room. He placed his laptop on the table, opened it, and lay his cap next to it. He looked around. At the next table were a pair of young women, one somewhat overweight, eating and chatting. At another nearby table an older man studied the local paper, an empty, used plate at his elbow. Others were scattered about, and he looked at each one as he moved to the order counter.

It had been several days since he had opened the device that rested on the table in front of him, so he did so with some trepidation. He screwed up his courage, got up and went to a young woman who sat at another table and appeared to be deep into a study of her laptop screen.

"Pardon me, miss."

She looked up. "Yes."

"I wonder, could you show me how to get connected. To the Internet. Not too familiar, you know."

"Sure." She got up and followed him.

After a minute of instruction and key-tapping on her part, his computer was connected, and the girl returned to her seat. He thanked her and sat, at which time his food was delivered. As he took his first bite, he reached into his shirt pocket, pulled out a slip of paper and laid it on the table. He laid his fork down, read the notation, then pressed the first key.

Webber arrived home after dark.

After grabbing a bite and a beer, he went to his basement lair where he powered up his computer, and found that an alert had been logged in. He read the message, wrote it on a piece of paper, deleted and "washed" the delete, then shut the computer down. He then decrypted the line, after which he sat back and looked at nothing as he absorbed the information. His thoughts collected, he checked the time, left the room, re-locked the door, then changed his clothes to casual before leaving.

An hour an twenty minutes later, he turned onto a lonely farm road off of Highway 15, drove another half mile, made a U-turn, and stopped behind an old Dodge pickup truck. With the engine running, he flashed his lights three times and waited. The lights on the truck responded in kind, and as two people got out of the truck, he shut his car engine off and waited while they walked toward him in the dark.

His passenger door opened and a man slid in at the same time the rear passenger side door opened and a woman got in.

Webber looked at the man. "Jack." He turned his head half-way toward the back seat. "Ruth."

Both murmured responses in kind.

"What's up?" Jack asked.

"I need you both to saddle up," Webber replied.

# 28

$\mathcal{J}$anie Madsen, dressed in her robe and slippers at nine-thirty in the morning, sat at the breakfast table when the front doorbell rang. She looked up from her perusal of the *Washington Post* to check the wall clock, took a sip of her cooling coffee, and went to the door. She peered through the peephole lens, and saw the distorted figure of a slight young woman who stood back several feet as she appeared to be surveying the neighborhood, a practiced smile on her face.

Janie opened the door half way. She spoke through the screen door with the vertical black steel safety bars. "Yes? May I help you?"

"Oh, good morning. Mrs. Madsen? Mrs. Jane Madsen?" Ruth bent forward slightly as she spoke, a wide, innocent smile on her face. She carried a clipboard. A large, black leather bag hung from her shoulder. A dark red beret covered her head.

"Uh, yes . . . Who—?"

"Oh, I know this must be an inconvenient time. I see you're not—"

Her voice pleasant, but with a trace of annoyance, Janie interrupted, "No, young lady, it's alright. What can I do for you?" Janie looked past the visitor into the street, then back.

"I'm Ruth Verdugo, Mrs. Madsen, and we're conducting a survey of the area residents for the bond issue." She nodded with emphasis.

Janie winced and frowned. "What bond issue?" She tilted her head.

"Oh, perhaps you hadn't heard. It has to do with the sewer lines." She pointed vaguely. "They may have to tear them up in this area. Age, leaks, you know."

"No, I didn't know."

"Yes. Leaks, you know. Well, I need to ask you a few questions. About the household. I won't be long. Usage survey. May I?"

"Well—"

Her voice half-pleading, and her facial expression the same, Ruth asked, "Please? Couple of minutes. I have to turn this in. They pay me—"

"Yes, okay, but please be brief." Janie opened the door and let Ruth in, then closed it. "In here. The kitchen. I was having coffee. And reading the paper."

"Oh, I like that. I'm a kitchen person," Ruth said in her most pleasant voice. "Can your husband attend?"

Ruth followed Janie into the kitchen, where Janie turned and gestured to a chair at the breakfast table.

"He's not here right now. You'll have to do with just me."

"Oh, that's okay. Maybe others in the household? That's important."

"Nope. No one."

"Well, okay then." Ruth took a chair and sat on the edge.

"Coffee?" Janie asked.

"Oh, no thank you. I know you're busy and I don't want to keep you, and I've had too much this morning already."

"Well, I'm going to heat mine up. Cold."

"Of course."

Janie took her cup to the counter, poured more coffee, then returned to the table. She sat. "Now, tell me what's going on. They're going to tear up the sewer lines?"

"Yes—you know, I hate to do this, but the coffee I had earlier is coming through. You know. Could I bother you?" Ruth tilted her head apologetically.

"No. Yes, of course." Janie got half-way out of her chair. "It's through there. Second door." She pointed.

"Thank you. I'm such a bother." Ruth stood and walked away, the clipboard still in hand. Her large purse remained at her side at the end of a shoulder strap.

Janie sat again. "No bother. Not at all." She made a wan smile to herself as the woman disappeared along the hall, sipped her newly warmed dark brew, then picked the newspaper up.

Ruth closed the door to the bathroom, turned the light on, then hastily set her big purse and the clipboard on the lavatory counter. She opened the bag, reached for a pair of thin, white gloves and pulled them on. She then removed her semi-auto pistol and put it on the surface, then pulled out a long, thin, cardboard box and laid it there as well. She removed two small medical vials. From the opened box she removed the first of two syringes. She studied the label on one of the vials, then the other, removed the protective covering from a syringe, punctured the vial seal with it, turned it upside down, then filled the syringe. She pointed the syringe at the ceiling, pushed plunger in and flicked the syringe to remove the air. She then performed the same ritual with the second syringe and vial. She returned the vials, empty box, pistol and clipboard to the bag, flushed the toilet with a piece of toilet paper, turned the light out and opened the door with a second piece of toilet paper, which she let fall to the floor.

As she came slowly down the hall with her bag shouldered and a syringe in each hand held along each thigh at the ready, she watched the woman at the table carefully.

Janie laid the paper down and started to turn as Ruth came up behind her with little sound. With deft, studied moves, using both hands, Ruth plunged both needles into the back of Janie's neck and pushed the plungers down all the way. Janie reacted by starting to raise both arms, then stopped, shuddered with a guttural gasp, and slumped forward until her head flopped onto to the table with a sickening thud. Her chair scraped back at the same time.

Ruth checked her surroundings, then leaned over and pressed two fingers against Janie's throat to feel her pulse. She detected none. She then verified her possessions, made her way to the front door and opened it. She looked up and down the street, then, confident no one observed her, calmly closed both doors, and walked away. In fifteen minutes, she was on a city bus. Half an hour later, with the beret in a trash bin along with the clipboard, syringes and vials, she sat in a darkened movie theater and watched a movie she ignored as her mind swam with her concerns.

Jack, in order to maintain a low profile and the ability to move his hand gun across the country in relative secrecy and security, struck out in a ten-year-old GMC pickup truck shortly before sunup. He was, in reality, unable to see the sun or its direct light, since the overcast was thick, and rain came in alternating waves. He looked forward to being in a part of the country where this atmospheric condition was a rarity. His attire was that of the farmer-orchardist, with shirt, pants, jacket, footwear and seasoned cap to match.

He drove the Interstates the entire distance until he reached Amarillo, with an overnight stay in St. Louis and the Texas Panhandle town. From there, he angled down across West Texas into Eastern New Mexico on secondary highways to I-25, thence to Las Cruces, where he checked into a motel. His driver's license, should he have been required to show it, was false. That night, shortly after midnight, he went to his truck, took a screwdriver from his emergency tool kit, and struck out on foot from the motel. Two blocks away, on a side street, he found what he sought, an older, slightly battered New Mexico license plate. It was attached to a much older car.

He looked around with a keen eye, then took a small pin-point flashlight from his shirt pocket, knelt down, and with the light in his teeth, removed the plate.

At the motel, assured no one was about, he removed both Maryland plates from his pickup, and installed the newly-acquired stolen plate onto the rear of the vehicle. The two legitimate plates he stuffed down behind the driver's seat.

Early the next morning, after breakfast at a Denny's, he headed west on Interstate 10 in the GMC. The pistol was locked in the glove compartment. His personal belongings were in an overnight bag on the passenger side floor.


Grayson and Lucero stood alongside a black Reston PD detective lieutenant as they looked through the viewing window of the County Morgue. Next to them was a man in a white smock who held a small clipboard at his side.

Grayson stared through the glass, but not at the woman who lay on the slab covered entirely by a sheet save her head, rather at the wall beyond. "Heart attack?" Both his hands were in his pants pockets in a gesture of resignation.

The woman nodded. "We think so. But we believe induced."

Grayson nodded, his head still frozen. "Induced. I see."

"The toxicology's not available, but in our cursory inspection, we found two places on the back of the neck that appear to be hypo puncture marks." The technician gestured toward the policeman.

The lieutenant said, "Right. The daughter found her slumped over on a table. Kitchen. Cold coffee. Newspaper. Morning ritual. M.E. on the scene spotted the marks." He paused. "We got photos of the scene."

Lucero looked at him, while Grayson continued to stare, transfixed.

The officer scratched the back of his neck. "Says she had no history. The daughter says. Heart. Of heart problems."

"Two marks?" Grayson asked. He looked down.

"Yes. Probably a cocktail. One to sedate, the second to stop the heart. We'll know more after we cut her open. And toxicology." This from the morgue technician.

Grayson broke his reverie, freed his hands, turned and paced away slowly.

"The scene was clean?" Lucero asked.

The lieutenant angled his head a in a gesture of frustration. "As a whistle. Nothing."

"Neighbors?" Grayson asked.

The officer shook his head. "We've talked to as many people as possible along the street. So far, no one saw anything or anybody."

Grayson turned, dipped his head and peered at Lucero from under his eyebrows as he clenched his teeth. Then he straightened, held out his hand to the detective, then the technician, as he thanked them.

He removed a card from his inner jack pocket and held it out to the technician. "Can you get me a report?"

He took the card. "As soon as we have it."

Outside, on the sidewalk, both men stopped.

Lucero looked at Grayson. "Someone wants the trail erased." His voice was low and somber.

"Pro. Real pro." Grayson looked up at at the sky and sighed. "Not amateur night." He paused. "Let's get back and talk to Dancer."

Jack was not sure of the turn-off, so he drove past it at half the speed limit. When he approached the old service station a mile and a half farther along on the right, he remembered the landmark and realized he had gone too far. He was tempted to stop and ask directions, but dismissed the thought based upon his training and experience.

He drove another several hundred feet, stopped alongside the highway, and pictured the number of side roads he had passed in the last twenty miles. He recalled three. He scanned the mid-morning sun-bright surroundings. Part of his problem was that the foray that he, Ruth and the Mexican had made was at night and into the pre-dawn.

He turned the truck around and headed back, east. As he approached the first road, he decided it must be the one he sought, and turned into it. He had driven a quarter mile north at less than 25 MPH, when he spotted something that triggered his memory. Along side the road, on his right, a few feet away from the flat portion and up a gentle slope, was a deer skull with antlers. He recalled that Ruth had remarked about it, and the Mexican had said something in Spanish regarding it. Neither he nor Ruth understood, but refrained from asking him what he had said. It had been in a gentle, almost reverential tone.

Jack was now certain he was on the right track, and continued at the same speed.

When he rounded the last bend in the road and was able to see the buildings in the distance, he slowed to ten miles per hour and scoured the area in all directions. He spotted two horses in the pasture to his left, a roan and a pinto. Both, used to vehicular traffic, ignored his approach. He was within 50 feet of the house porch when he saw someone exit the next building north, beyond the house. He reckoned the person to be a woman. He hastily tried to recall what he had seen that dark, moonless night.

He stopped, reached down and killed the ignition, but kept his eyes on the woman who stood 75 feet away, with what appeared to be a pitchfork in her gloved hand. She wore a floppy, wide-brimmed straw hat, long pants and a blue work shirt. Her eyes were otherwise unshaded. She moved toward the pickup at a slow walk. Before he opened his door, he thought of the pistol in the glove compartment, then decided to leave it. The timing was wrong, and he didn't know who else might be near and watching. He stepped out and closed the door. He adjusted his billed cap as he did.

He looked around, then at the woman who had stopped some ten feet away. "Hi," he said.

"Howdy. What can I do for you?" Vera looked at him with calm, sober suspicion.

"Well, I thought this was the Wilson ranch, but I guess not." He smiled and took a step toward her. "There'd be some kids."

"No, sir, it ain't. Never heard of a Wilson ranch, in fact." She awarded him a tolerant smile. "Might be one, but not to my knowledge. Not around here."

He ignored her answer, swivelled on his rough-out boots, looked around, then at her. "Nice place. Cattle?"

Vera scratched the dirt with a boot, looked down, then up. "Yonder. Up on the mesa. Most'er sold off this time 'o year, 'cept a bull and a couple'a mama cows." She made a small gesture with her chin to point the vague direction. She looked at him hard. "I need to ask. Why'er you lookin' for the Wilsons?" She knew there was no such place.

"Well, ha!" Jack looked down and away, thinking fast. "Lookin' for work." His eyes met hers. He had also decided to contract the word with the gerund to appear more folksy. "Guess I got it wrong."

"Okay," she said.

"You got any? Need a hand?" He tilted his head.

"Nope. Sorry. I don't."

"Well," He said, then, "Say, could I trouble you for some water. Dry, you know. Salty breakfast."

"Sure. I can accommodate."

"The house. Old?" He moved slowly in that direction.

Vera started toward the house. "Uh, close to a hundred, I'd say." Her mind was reeling. "C'on in. Get you a drink."

"Thank you, ma'am. I appreciate it." He lowered his head as he walked.

He followed her into the kitchen, where she got a clean glass from an upper cabinet, filled it from the noisy tap, then held it out. "Take a load off. Be right back. Gotta' settle with the horses. Had some feed ready."

He sat, turned to look at her, and sipped the water. "Yes, ma'am. Thank you. I will sit'n wait. Take your time."

Vera made a bee-line for the barn, went to a dusty wooden shelf that protruded from the old, dried board-and-batten wall, and retrieved the 9mm Beretta Nano pistol Jason had had her purchase and insisted that she keep handy. Her heart rate up, she pulled it from the holster, checked it for operation, took it off "safety," then pushed it down between the small of her back and her belt line, and pulled that portion of her shirt out and let it drape over the weapon. She counted to ten, then headed back to the house. On her way, she threw two portions of green baled hay over the pasture fence, in case the stranger was watching.

The man who had asked for water sat where she had left him. He was faced away from her, but turned his head half way when he heard her enter.

Vera walked around the table, sat and looked at him, then the glass, which was half full. "Not as thirsty as you thought?"

Jack looked down at the table top, then up at her. He wore an ironic smirk. "Where is he?"

Vera felt that her heart, still pounding, would burst from her chest. Her mouth went dry, and she tried to control her voice. She wasn't sure of what she heard in her sudden state of shock. "Where is who?" Her voice cracked.

Jack looked away, back at her, and swung his head back and forth in a sarcastic, impatient negative motion. "You know, we can make this pleasant or unpleasant. It's all up to you." His voice was low and menacing.

"I don't know what you mean. Who are you?!"

Jack licked his lips, drew in his breath, then let it out with a sigh. He drummed his fingers on the table. "Where is he? You know who I'm talking about." His voice dropped further. He spoke slowly, deliberately, and with menace.

Vera shook her head. "I don't—"

Jack rose abruptly from his chair and picked the table up as he moved, raising it six inches above the floor. His chair, in turn, tumbled back and clattered to the floor. The heavy table dropped with a thud. He shouted, "Yes, you do, goddamn it! Now cough it up or things will go very bad for you!"

Vera stared at him, her eyes wide as her mouth dropped open. She grabbed the arms of her chair, then leaned forward as she reached for the pistol at her rear belt line with her right hand.

Jack stood straight up and started around the table for her, fury blazing in his blood-shot eyes as he watched her. "You fucking—!"

Vera, still seated, raised the Beretta and pointed it at the interloper. Her hand shook such that the gun wobbled an inch either way at the muzzle end. "Don't come any closer! I'll shoot!" Then she remembered one more thing, and cocked the hammer with her thumb.

Jack stopped cold and stared wide-eyed at Vera. He froze for a moment, his mouth in the shape of the letter "O," turned as though to back off, then lunged toward her in an attempt to wrest the pistol from her. Vera pulled the trigger twice in rapid succession. The first slug entered jack's chest two inches short of his right upper arm joint. The second bored a hole two inches lower and three inches to the left, close to the center of his chest. He staggered, tried to reach the searing hot pain in the upper right of his torso, sprung to his right, looked down in amazement at nothing, then crumpled onto the old plank floor with a loud thump and a yelp. His breath came in gasps and gurgles, since the second slug had penetrated his lung.

Vera rose from her chair a few inches to look beyond the table. The gun remained at the end of her extended right arm. Then she pushed her chair aside, leaped to her left, stopped and stared down at the man on the floor. His chest was covered in blood, and he writhed and moaned, a sight she had only witnessed in an injured animal.

She laid the Beretta on the table and knelt beside him. "I'll get something—to bandage you!" She stood, looked around frantically, then rushed off to the bathroom. She stopped, sprinted back to the table, retrieved the gun, then set out again.

Jack rolled over on his back. He licked his lips as his face curled into a grotesque grimace.

Vera was back with gauze, tape and a towel. She folded the towel and put it under his head, then went about cutting strips of gauze. She tore his shirt open to expose the ragged, bloody wounds and winced. "Stay calm. I'm trying to help." Her voice was little above a whisper.

Jack, his eyes glazed and staring at the ceiling, murmured something she didn't understand.

"Shh. Be calm. I'll tape this over. Stop the bleeding. Gotta' go for help." She covered the wounds with gauze and taped them down.

Jack uttered something else unintelligible, then closed his eyes and arched his head back against the substitute pillow. His mouth took on both the look of a smile and a cry.

She stood, severely rattled. "I'll be back. I'll hurry." With that, she was out the door.

With presence of mind, she took the pistol, grabbed the keys to her truck, and made dirt fly as she raced away along the rutted dirt road, often at speeds close sixty miles per hour in straight stretches. A column of dust formed behind her.

A little more than an hour later, she returned, again at high speed, trailing a swirling dust cloud. She was followed by the sheriff, red and blue lights blinking through the brown haze. Behind them was the county's excuse for an EMT vehicle, a modified, long-bed, extended cab pickup truck.

Vera brought her tired vehicle to within a few feet of the porch at a crazy angle, killed the engine, jumped out and ran to the front door. As she opened the screen, she stopped and looked down. Jack, despite his painful wounds, had managed to crawl to within three feet of the opening, where he lay, his contorted face at an angle against the old wood floor. He had left a long trail of dark, red, coagulating blood, smeared along the way by his palms and leaking chest.

Although the female EMT verified it less than 60 seconds later, Vera knew when she saw him, that he was dead.

# 29

*S*heriff Tenorio was the first to stand by Vera Tyler in the doorway. The female EMT came up behind them and asked them kindly to stand away so she could do her job. As she knelt by the stranger's body to check his evaporated vital signs, her emergency kit by her side, Vera turned and went to the nearest porch support post. There, she grabbed the old, round, weathered, de-barked tree trunk, and came close to collapsing.

Tenorio took his eyes off of the death scene and looked in Vera's direction, then went to her. He put his hand on her shoulder. "You alright, Vera? You're shaking."

"Oh, god, Henry! I've never seen anything like this! Or done anything—I killed a man!" She stared at the dirt beyond the porch.

Tenorio's voice was soothing. "Who was he? What did he want?"

She shook her head. "I don't know!" She went silent, then, in a lower, moderated voice, "I don't know." She came close to hyperventilating. Jason's image came to mind, then that of the two abrasive FBI agents. She knew what the dead man wanted, but was loathe to say.

The sheriff nodded as he let his hand drop. "Okay. Better sit."

Vera turned slowly, went to one of the chairs up against the outer wall and sat. She stared straight ahead, her eyes wide and unblinking. Her thoughts were on her talk with Jason later. She leaned forward, dropped her folded hands down between her legs and let her head flop down nearly to her lap.

Tenorio remained standing and looked down at her. "We'll get to the bottom of this. State police team will be here. Where's your gun?"

She unfolded her hands, lifted her arm and pointed at her truck.

Tenorio went to her pickup as the EMT came out onto the porch.

"Nuthin' I can do now," she said. "Hafta' wait for the crime scene folks. Can't move the body. I hafta' stick around." She leaned forward, hands on her knees, and peered closely at Vera. "You alright?"

Vera looked up, her eyes red and teary, and nodded.

"I think I oughta' give you somethin'. A sedative." She started to reach into her kit.

Vera shook her head. "No. No, I'm okay. Thanks. I'm okay."

"Sure?"

"Yes."

"How 'bout some water?"

"I'm okay. Really." Vera smiled up at her. She pointed to the other chair. "Why don't you sit?"

"Think I will. I'm Kristie."

Vera looked at her. "Vera." She turned her gaze to the horses in the field.

Sheriff Tenorio came back from Vera's truck. He held her pistol with a pen through the trigger guard. He put one booted foot onto the porch floor. "I need to keep this for now. I'll get it back to you after the investigation." He stood at the edge of the porch and pushed his cap back. "Do you feel okay about telling me what happened? State guys'll ask."

Vera left shortly before sundown.

State Police crime scene investigators had been at the ranch most of the day. They had scoured Jack's truck and belongings, had taken half a hundred photographs, and attempted, without success, to find him in the national criminal database based on his phony license, using their radio-link from a patrol vehicle. The senior investigator had spent nearly an hour with Vera, peppering her with questions. With Sheriff Tenorio's backing, they were solidly convinced she was telling the truth. Not one among them thought to call in the FBI.

Vera did, but did not offer.

When she asked permission to leave, Tenorio asked her if she was alright. He also told her she must return soon and "stay handy." She assured him she would follow his mandate.

She came close to not finding a voice when Jason answered.

"Hello," he said.

She nearly broke down, but pulled in deep psychological reserves. "Hello." Her tone was flat, but wavering.

Jason knew instantly something was different; wrong.

"What—what's happened?" He reminded himself to stay guarded.

"We—I—we need to talk." She started to break again, then recovered.

"Okay. Okay. What—? Listen, I'll be there."

"Please."

"You know where."

"Yes."

"I'll start. Five hours. Around midnight."

"Thank you."

"Bye."

"Bye."


When she returned to the ranch, one State Police car and Sheriff Tenorio's were parked where she had seen them when she left. A State Police flatbed truck had come and taken the intruder's truck. Jack's body had been removed, but the thin, broad, meandering river of dark, red, drying blood remained. To an observer, at certain angles of the light, its crystalline surface glistened.

The sheriff and the state cop sat in the chairs on the porch, in the dark. Tenorio had gone inside to turn on a lamp, causing a shaft of dim, yellowish light to emanate from the two, deep-set windows in the porch wall as well as through the screen door.

Tenorio rose and stood behind Vera as she stopped in the front door frame.

"I'll get someone in here to clean this up." He stared past her at the grizzly scene.

She shook her head. "No need. Thanks anyway. I can handle it."

He frowned at her. "You sure? That's a real mess."

"I'll do best I can with mop and pail, then I'll sand it all down. Rug's gone, of course."

Stanley Webber, alias Tanner, met Ruth in a small coffee shop in the town of Herndon, Virginia. They both parked far apart from each other, and waited several minutes before each made their way to the eatery; first one, then the other.

They sat across from each other in a booth in the back. Webber faced the door, and looked toward the front every few seconds. They both ordered a sandwich and iced tea.

Webber played with his glass. "How'd it go?"

"Got the job done." She looked away.

"Good." He slid an envelope across the table to her.

She looked behind herself, then slipped it into her purse.

"Heard from him?" He looked at her.

"No. You?"

Webber licked his lips and shook his head. "He should have checked in by now."

"Did he give you a time?"

Webber angled back, sipped his tea, then sighed. "He should have been on the ranch by now and out. In and out."

"Shit." Ruth looked down at her drying sandwich. "What do we do?"

"If he's been made or worse, the feds are going to get involved. Go to the safe house."

She nodded.

"I'll go poke around the farm."

"Okay. Can I go back for my things?"

He shook his head. "No, Ruth." His voice of annoyance was barely above a whisper. "Can't risk it. Stay away." He looked at her. "Use some of that and buy what you need."

Her face clouded up. "This is not good." She looked at him hard. "What about you? At the farm?"

"I'll manage."

"Not good.' She looked down.

"I have to go to New Mexico. Signal from Nantes' contact. At least I think it's him. Used the right ID code."

She perked up and peered at him. "Really." She turned her head to look into the room, then back. "When?"

"Within the last twenty-four."

She pondered. "Will you go to the ranch? If Jack doesn't check in?"

He looked hard at her as he pursed his lips. "Not likely. If the feds get involved, regardless of what Jack did or didn't do, they'd be all over the place."

Later, when State Police investigators, in Sheriff Henry Tenorio's presence, scoured Jack's truck and found Maryland plates, their inquiries led them to the fact that the New Mexico plate had been stolen. That, combined with the discovery of a vehicle registration for the truck in the name of one Cecil Harding, of Jackson, Mississippi, led them to the conclusion that the federal government, in the guise of the Federal Bureau of Investigation, should join the case.

It was subsequent to that decision that Agent Grayson was interrupted at his desk by Jan, who handed him a message sheet which had originated with the State Police.

Grayson, in a near state of shock, picked up the phone and hit a button. He listened, then said, "Jan, get me through to the state cops on the case down south. Thanks."

Five minutes passed before Grayson was on the line with a State Police Captain. He verified that the woman who had shot and killed a male intruder was, indeed, Vera Tyler, and that the as yet unidentified man was apparently from out of state. Grayson asked that the Tyler woman be held for questioning by the FBI. When the request to detain Vera came to the ranch, the cop on watch informed his captain that she had left an hour earlier.

It was a half hour after midnight when Vera and Jason sat in his pickup on a poorly-lit side street in Las Cruces. Her vehicle was parked across the street. Neither had eaten.

Vera leaned against his shoulder, her right arm across his lap. His arm was around her as he stared through the windshield at nothing. His mind reeled.

He spoke in a low tone. "They're desperate. They know I'm alive, and would like to change that." He paused. "Or at best, find me to find out what I know."

"Oh, God, Jason, who?" she whispered.

"Nantes' people."

"Why?"

"They want to clean everything up. Afraid of where it might lead if I'm alive." He pondered, then, "What did the police—the sheriff—state police—ask you?" He looked to his left.

"Nothing—just did I know him."

"What did he say—the man?"

She sat up, drew in a deep breath and released it. "Just that he—he said, 'Where is he'?"

"How did he approach you? What did—how did he start out, introduce himself?"

She blew more air out and shook her head, trying to recollect. "He—he just drove up—he drove up, got out, and—yes—he wanted to know if it was the Wilson place. Never said a name."

"And?"

"There is no Wilson place. That I know of. But it didn't mean anything then. He said he was thirsty, and we went inside. That's where he got violent."

"Was he armed? A gun?"

"No. But I got suspicious and remembered what you said. I went back to the barn to get the gun." She dropped her head. "Oh, God. Never, never killed anyone . . ."

He touched her shoulder. "I'm sorry. You did the right thing. What you could." He was silent, then, "The sheriff—you say, Tenorio? Did he or the state people say anything about how—?"

She shook her head. "No. They just looked around, said I was lucky, you know." She looked at him above tear-streaked cheeks.

He sighed. "You can't go back."

She sat up and stared at him. "What?!"

He dipped his head, then looked at her. "You can't go back."

She frowned. "Jason—!"

He angled his torso toward her. "Vera, listen. Before you left, did they find anything about him? The man? Anything you can remember?"

She let her mouth go slack as she shook her head slowly and searched her memory. "No. No. No; nothing." She frowned at him. "They took him away. And his truck."

"Do you remember the plates on the truck? Try to think."

She thought, then, "Yes. When I came back after going for the sheriff. They were New Mexico plates."

"Mm." He thought for a moment. "Doesn't mean anything, except it could've been a rental or a stolen plate." He paused. "Problem is, Vera, the FBI will be brought in, and they'll figure a way to push you. Maybe even hold you. It won't be safe." He thought for a moment. "They could get a warrant. Probable cause. Threaten you with arrest."

"But—"

"Look, Vera, there's a dead man in your house. You shot and killed him. Then you leave. If they find a reason to call in the FBI, it'll be a sure sign to them you've gone to meet someone, and that someone is me. They tailed you before. Whether you go back or not, it doesn't look good."

"Oh, God." She looked away, then back. Her face was wracked in pain. She turned her body toward him. "Jason—the animals, my things, I—" She threw her hands up.

He took her hand. "Vera, is there anyone who can do that? Take care of the place for now?"

She dipped her head in thought. "There's Tomás."

"Tomás?"

"He comes up when I need 'im. He's done fence, round-up, maintenance around the place."

"You trust im?"

"Yes."

"Can you get hold of 'im?"

"I guess. Sure."

"How old is he?"

"God, I think in his fifties or so. Why?"

"And you trust him."

"I do. Known him and his family a long time. Good man. Knew his mama. His dad. Killed in a rail accident. Two boys in the army. Good people."

"Good. Let's find him. Can you call?"

"I don't have his number."

"Let's find 'im, Vera. We'll—I'll pay him a month in advance. Think he'll do it?"

"I don't know. Depends."

"Would he talk? To the cops?"

"He knows sheriff Tenorio. They're about the same age. I don't know. If we ask him. What would he say?"

"Simple, Vera, we tell him little. You tell him little. Something like you've got a family situation."

"He'll find out when he gets there."

"By that time, you won't be. We have to do it." He lowered his head and shook it as he looked her in the eye.

"Jason, I don't have any clothes." She tilted her head.

"We'll get new. Vera, it's not a problem. We have to do this. Please."

"Sure. I understand. I love you." She paused. "But the house."

"I love you, too." He squeezed her hand. "What about it?"

"The floor. Blood. It's a mess."

He stared at her in contemplation, looked away, then back. "Does he have to go in?"

"I don't know, Jason. When I left, the police and sheriff were there.

"Okay." Frustrated, he sighed and moved his hand across his mouth and chin hard. "Okay." He looked at the sky. "Tell him the truth. Ask him to trust you. Ask him to trust you and keep mum. Can you do that?"

Her mouth dropped open. "I guess so, Jason."

"Tell him you need his promise. If he balks, walk away."

She was silent, then nodded slowly.

Jason followed Vera in her vehicle to the Crespín place. He stopped 100 yards back, in the dark, his lights off.

He got out of his vehicle and walked halfway along the dirt road until he was able to see the modest house in the distance. He watched as a man came out to greet Vera, then what appeared to be a conversation, and then her hand him a thousand dollars that came from Jason to oversee her place for two months.

After Vera shook hands with the man and returned to her truck, Jason went to his. A mile later, they rendezvoused, where Vera told him Tomás had agreed to her proposition, and that he would feign innocence. He had been shocked, she said, at the amount.

They returned to Las Cruces, where they stopped at a motel. Jason got out of his truck and walked over to Vera's, where she remained in the driver's seat. She rolled her window down.

He looked around, then at her. "I don't like this. Are you good for another hour or so? It's nearly light."

"I guess. What's the matter?"

"There's been enough time for FBI to be involved. If they are, they'll get here fast. If they assume you're with me, they'll be looking for me, too. We need to be far away. Or in a larger mix."

"Where to?"

He thought for a moment. "I don't like even being on the Interstate, but we don't have much choice." He waited, looked down and away, then back. "El Paso. We'll go there. In the morning we'll get you some things, then take a different route back. Off the Interstate."

"Where are we going?" She frowned.

"Pecos."

Agents Grayson and Lucero landed at the El Paso airport in the Agency jet a few minutes past midnight. They were accompanied by two other field agents, a man and a woman, and were met by a member of the New Mexico State Police. They all piled into a black SUV with State Police insignia on the sides, and sped off to the Tyler ranch, the state cop at the wheel. Sheriff Tenorio had retired, leaving two State Police officers on duty at the ranch.

Grayson, after interviewing the lone state officer who had been on the case from the start, decided he needed to talk with the sheriff, and the sooner the better. Thus, a call went out to the county headquarters, and Tenorio was awakened from a deep sleep.

# 30

*J*ason and Vera checked into the El Paso Inn off of Montana Street in El Paso after Jason paid cash to an irritable East Indian desk clerk who wanted in the worst way to know why they had decided to go to sleep at such an un-godly hour. He had his theories, but kept them close.

Grayson, Lucero, the two extra field agents and four State Police officers conferred with a sleepy, irritated, Sheriff Tenorio shortly after three in the morning on the Tyler ranch. They all milled around one of the official vehicles with the aid of State Police SUV headlamps. Some leaned against a car, others paced in small circles, and all yawned from time to time in a valiant effort to stay awake in the early morning chill.

"What the hell is this all about?" Tenorio wanted to know. This he directed at Grayson, who had assumed control of the ad-hoc meeting. He rubbed his sleepy arms and glared at the other people who stood watching and listening.

Grayson, who was three paces away from, and facing Tenorio, lowered his head in the stark, moody half-light of the headlamps. His arms were folded across his chest against the dry cold, even with his dark blue official windbreaker on. "How long have you known Mrs. Tyler?"

Tenorio frowned. "A long time. I repeat—"

"Here's the thing," Grayson interrupted, "we believe Mrs. Tyler is hiding information vital to an FBI investigation. The fact that—"

"What's that got to do with me?!" Tenorio pushed away from the State Police car against which he had been leaning, took three steps, turned and faced Grayson.

Grayson tilted his head and shook it. "Look, I'm sorry we got you up—"

Tenorio ignored Grayson's insincere apology. "I said, what's that got to do with me?!" He leaned in toward Grayson as he jabbed his own chest with his finger.

"Please calm down. Please." Grayson held up both hands, palms out.

Tenorio lowered his voice and slowed his speech for emphasis. "What has it got to do with *me*?!"

Grayson looked at Lucero, who stood in the shadows as the other FBI agents and state policemen, all astonished, watched from a rough circle around the two conflicted men.

"Sheriff, you say you know the woman, Mrs. Tyler. You have for many years. Based on that, can you tell me—us—why she might leave and where she might go? Did she say anything to you? It's all I'm asking, sir."

Tenorio looked at the ground, then up at the FBI Special Agent and pinched his nose. "And I'm telling you that I do not know why she might leave and where she might go, *pendejo*! She didn't say *anything* to me! You get me out of bed in the middle of the night to ask me an asshole question?! You can go to hell! I am going back to bed. I don't give a rotten shit who you are!" Tenorio started away, then turned to face Grayson again. "If I should find the answer to your questions, I will pretend I didn't hear them! Go fuck yourself!"

Grayson and the rest were aghast and silent as Tenorio walked back to his car.

Grayson shouted after him, "Thank you, sheriff!"

Tenorio, without turning, threw up his arm, extended his middle finger, then disappeared into the dark.

Grayson looked at Lucero, whose mind seemed to be elsewhere. He looked at his audience, then at the two State Policemen who had been assigned to remain in scene. "Did either of you hear or see anything at all that would give you a notion as to where the Tyler woman went? What she might do? Anything?"

Both men shook their respective heads slowly and somberly.

Grayson sighed, then said, "Okay." He took a step forward. "We're wasting our time here." He turned to the two FBI agents who had accompanied him and Lucero from Albuquerque. "I'm sorry we dragged you into this. I hoped we'd get something real here." He looked around again. "Okay, well, let's go get some breakfast or shut-eye, whichever is most appealing."

The male agent stepped in closer. "Should we have a look around?"

Grayson scanned the scene and kept his voice low. "If we were alone, I might risk it, but we have official witnesses and no warrant. We have to pull back. We'll meet later. Let's get some rest." He pondered. "We'll get some shut-eye, then have a look at the car and the body."

As the group moved toward their respective vehicles in preparation for leaving, Lucero came over to Grayson. He moved in close and spoke so no one else would hear. "One thing we do know now."

"What's that?" Grayson asked.

"He's alive."

"Oh, yeah." Grayson nodded with emphasis. "Oh, yeah!" He paused. "Alive and out there."

"And he and the woman know we know. He's no dummie," Lucero said.

"That's right, Marcus."

"MVD?"

"Trace the woman?

"Yes."

"Find her, find him."

Lucero made the "thumbs up" sign in the shadows.

Two State policemen remained. Grayson and the other three FBI agents retired to a Las Cruces motel. Later that day, Grayson conferred with Buckley. It was decided they would issue a BOLO with Vera's name, vehicle description and license, with the caption, "Wanted for Questioning, Do not Apprehend; Notify the Federal Bureau of Investigation." A contact number was included.

At the same time, with the FBI in the lead, research began on Jack, all of whose identifications lead nowhere for the time being.

Jason and Vera slept until ten, checked out, got take-out breakfast at a McDonald's, then headed north on U.S. Highway 54, Jason in the lead. Vera followed in her pickup. Both ate as they drove. They had both agreed they would purchase Vera's needs later.

They took a motel room in Carrizozo, ate, and slept until late afternoon. To draw as little attention to them as possible, Jason timed their trip such that they drove north past Lamy to the Interstate after dark. It was close to midnight when they moved through the village of Pecos and crossed the river to the east side and Jason's rented mobile home near the highway that led to the valley of Cow Creek and the wilderness beyond.

Jason ushered Vera into the sparsely-furnished dwelling, showed her the bathroom and bedroom, then returned to her truck and moved it into a heavily-treed area away from the house. He parked it such that anyone looking in that direction from the highway, assuming they could see the vehicle through the thicket, would not see a license plate, which he planned to remove.

There was little in the way of victuals in the house beyond coffee and a half container of orange juice, so, in the morning, Jason went to the local market and bought enough food for breakfast. Mid-morning, in his vehicle, they went to Las Vegas for personal items for Vera, the first of which was a bandanna to wear over her head and a pair of dark glasses to cover her eyes.

They ate lunch at the "Spic 'n Span" restaurant, then stocked up on groceries, enough for two weeks of three meals per day. From there, they headed back to Pecos.

Tomás Crespín had arrived at the Tyler ranch an hour after sunup to find two New Mexico State Policemen in attendance. It was not a surprise to him, since Vera had forewarned him. One was pacing around, trying to stay warm and awake; the other was asleep, prone on the back seat of their patrol car.

Taken by surprise by Crespín's arrival, the wakeful cop stopped and stared at the on-coming old Dodge stake-body truck, then moved toward it as it came to a halt. He held up his hand as though the vehicle were going to run him over.

Crespín brought the vehicle to a halt, got out and slammed the door shut. He adjusted his worn, dirty, broad-brimmed straw hat. "Mornin'," he said.

"Who are you?" the patrolman asked.

"Tomás."

"Why are you here?" The cop frowned.

In the patrol car, the other policeman awoke at the sound of voices.

Crespín looked around briefly, then pointed at the horses in the pasture. "To take care of the horses." He awarded the cop an honest, open face.

"Why?" the officer asked.

"Why? Because horses want to eat."

The officer looked at the ground, away, then at Crespín. "Why are *you* here to feed the horses?" His voice carried menace.

"Because Mrs. Tyler asked me too." He shrugged.

"Your ID. Let me see your ID." The policeman held out his hand.

Crespín hesitated, then said, "Why?"

"Because I'm telling you." The cop pinched up his face.

"I don't have to show you nothin'." Crespín stood his ground and bored his eyes into the cop's.

"I'm ordering you to." His voice was a growl.

"If you want to know who I am, then get Tenorio." He jutted his chin out.

"Look, man, this is a crime scene, and we have the right to ask. Now cough it up!"

Crespín paused, then said, "Why didn't you say so? I didn't know about no crime." With that, he pulled his wallet out and showed it to the officer.

"Thank you, Mr.—"

"Crespín."

"Crespín." He handed the wallet back. " When—when did she ask you?" The cop tilted his head and frowned.

"Yesterday, last night—I don' know." He shrugged again.

The other policeman, ragged from too little sleep, emerged from the black patrol car and joined his partner. "What's going on?" He looked at each of the men in turn.

"Mr. Crespín, here, says the Tyler woman asked him to come and take care of the animals." He hadn't taken his eyes off of the newcomer.

"Really." The sleepy cop, late of the patrol car, wiped his face in an attempt to awaken.

"Yeah, really." The first cop, frustrated, turned and took a step away.

The sleepy cop looked at his partner, then Crespín. "Well, better get to it." He waved Crespín off.

Crespín shook his head and made for the barn. The half-awake patrolman returned to the car and made a radio call to report Crespín's arrival.

"He's got this all planned out. He's in charge." Grayson looked at Buckley across the big conference table.

Buckley nodded. "What about our mysterious friend, 'Dancer'?"

Grayson glanced at Lucero, who sat two chairs away, then at Buckley. "We're working on a meeting site. Waiting for him or her to get back to us."

"You don't know which? We don't know where this person is, or who?" Buckley asked.

"According to Jan, Dancer's using a burner cell. Untraceable. GPS is off. Whoever it is, they know what they're doing."

"Soon?" Buckley asked.

Grayson motioned with his head. "Sure hope so."

"What's the offer?"

"We don't know. Says there's information should interest us. Won't say what or why." Grayson shot another glance at Lucero, who remained passive.

"Trap?" Buckley raised his eyebrows.

"Could be. We'll be cautious. Have a team on it. We'll insist on a defensible venue." Grayson said.

"Could be? Why?" Buckley asked.

"We still don't know who offed Jerry Madsen." He paused. "Although, we're pretty sure it was a man."

Buckley sighed. "Mm. Any ideas where our target went?"

Grayson exhaled heavily. "No, sir, I don't—we don't. But I—we—suspect he's staying close. Within the state. He's going to know better where to hide. Big state, lots of hiding places." He paused. "But he's sure to know we're on to 'im, and we'll be looking for the woman. So, he's got to hide them both." He took a breath. "But he can't stay out in the cold forever. Especially with the Tyler woman with him."

"She hired someone to watch her place?" Buckley eyed both field agents.

"Feed the horses and the chickens." This from Lucero. "Check on her cattle up on the mesa."

"State cops said he's a bit feisty," Grayson commented. "Old guy."

Lucero looked down and smiled, and Buckley nodded with his eyebrows raised.

"He didn't know anything?" Buckley asked. "Checked 'im out?"

"If he did, he wasn't letting on." Grayson shot a glance at the amused Lucero. "Lot like the sheriff. Tenorio. Very protective of the lady. We'll check 'im out."

"Okay, well," Buckley cut in, "keep me posted." He slapped the table and rose to leave.

As Jason and Vera finished their first meal together in a long time, and that in a private place under their control, Jason became silent and pensive.

He looked down at his empty plate, then up at Vera, and took her hand across the small dining table. "I need a favor." He stopped, grinned ruefully, then began again. "Another favor."

She looked at him with sad eyes. "Anything within my power."

"I've been running, Vera, and it needs to stop. But there's one more thing I have to do before I stop."

"Yes?"

"I have to meet someone." He paused. "This someone is probably dangerous. So, dangerous, I might not survive the meeting."

She squeezed his hand as she leaned toward him, eyes wide. "Jason—!"

He squeezed her hand in turn and shook his head. He lowered his voice. "I have to do this. It has to be done. It will allow me to clear my name. Not so much for me, but for my kids. Charles, Flo, Justin. They—the world—the world that knows me thinks I was a traitor. A spy. Dead or alive, a spy and traitor."

"Jason—"

He shook his head again. "No, listen. My kids, even extended family— friends—are tainted by what they believe. Dead or alive, that must not go unanswered."

"But, Jason, who—what good will it do—how can you—?"

He nodded. "It sounds knuckle-headed, I know. But I have a plan. Will it work? I don't know. I have to do it." He stopped and looked closely at her. "I have an envelope I want you to have. It explains everything. Absolutely everything. If I don't make it back, I want you to go to the FBI with it. It names the agent it should go to."

She started to weep, and he squeezed her hand harder, then got up and went around the table to put his arm around her as she dropped her head.

She shook her head and spoke past her pain. "Now you come along. After all these years. Why? God, why?!"

He pulled in a deep breath and released it as he massaged her shoulder. "I know. I know. I'm sorry." He released her gently, straightened and moved away, then stopped. "Don't give up yet, Vera. This may work, and I may survive. If I do, I'll be back, and we can be open."

She nodded and lifted her head as she wiped her face with her napkin. "When?"

"When? The meeting? I don't know yet. Soon."

"Gotta' clean up here."

He looked at her as she got up and began to clear the dishes. "You're incredible, Vera."

"Yeah, right." She sniffed.

He moved toward her, then helped to move the rest of the dinner remains from the table. "The envelope will contain letters I'd like you to mail. There's money for you."

"I don't want anything." She was busy over the sink, and he hardly heard her words.

He came up behind her and wrapped his arms around her slim waist. "Well, then, you'll just have to give it away, won't you?"

She smiled at the wall over the sink. "Yep. I will at that." She turned and faced him. Her voice broke. "I love you, you old son-of-a-bitch! I want you to come back to me, damn it! I don't want or need money. I need you! Us!"

They kissed.

The instructions Grayson received via Jan and the burner cell from Dancer were succinct. He was to come alone and dress in a certain way. He was to follow initial instructions and all that followed to a "T" or there would be no meeting; ever. The most important and revealing, was that a security surveillance team was virtually out of the question. He was to be unarmed and without a cell phone or recording device.

Two days later, on a Saturday, Peter Grayson entered the last car of the first north-bound run of the Rail Runner at the downtown Albuquerque station. He took a seat on the upper deck, and following instructions, faced north. By the time the train began to roll out of the station, there were eleven people scattered about the compartment. Among them were two noisy children, thrilled to be taking their first ride, an old, poorly-dressed man, two older women speaking Spanish, and a couple from Texas on their way to the shops in Santa Fé. The last to board was a woman who wore a plain baseball cap, white running shoes, blue jeans, tan shirt and a black windbreaker. Over her eyes were a pair of very dark, aviator-style sunglasses. She found a seat across the aisle and behind Grayson.

He assumed he was being watched, but, per his instructions, refrained from looking about the car.

True to his mandate, he got off the train as quickly as possible, given the crowd. Without looking back, and avoiding observing fellow passengers, he made his way quickly out of the Santa Fé Rail Yard, along the sidewalks to the La Fonda Hotel. There, he went up to the desk and asked where he might find a Mr. Templeton.

"I'm sorry, sir," the young male clerk said, "I don't know of a Mr. Templeton."

A young woman clerk peering at a computer screen looked up at Grayson. "Did you say Templeton, sir?"

"Yes."

She turned to the message boxes behind her, retrieved a small envelope, and came back to the desk interior. "What is your name, sir?" She looked at the name on the envelope.

"Collins."

She handed the envelope to him.

"Thank you," he said, and left the hotel.

On the street, he opened the envelope, read the brief message on the card, put it back into the envelope, and that into his inside jacket pocket. He then found a taxi and told the driver his destination.

An hour later, Grayson sat at a nickle slot machine in the Santa Claran

Hotel Casino in Española. Again, he avoided looking at people, but did spy at his watch from time to time.

He had been there fifteen minutes when a casino employee, a young Santa Clara Pueblo Indian woman approached him. "Collins? Mr. Collins?"

Grayson turned to her. "Yes. Collins."

"Here." She thrust a piece of paper at him.

He took it. "Thank you."

He read it, spent another minute playing the slot, then got up casually and walked across the casino floor to an area of high-stake slots and sat at one of them along a wall. He was the sole player along the rank of machines.

Again without looking about, he began to insert coins into the machine, when the woman who wore the black jacket, cap, dark glasses and white shoes, who had boarded the train in Albuquerque, took a seat at the machine immediately to his right. Her cap still on, she did not removed her dark glasses.

As she began putting coins into the slot, without looking at him, she said, "Losing proposition, no?"

"That's for sure," Grayson said. He didn't look her way. His heart rate rose.

"Tried the burritos here?" She asked.

"No. Are they good?"

"A little too salty for me."

"I like a little salt."

"I prefer the chile more."

"Who are you?" He asked.

"You know better than that. But you can call me Dancer," She said.

"You *are* a woman."

"I hate to sound flippant, but the last time I checked. We don't have a whole lot of time, Pete, so skip the macho bullshit."

Grayson started to react, but thought better of it. "What do you have for me?"

"Remove your jacket, turn the pockets out and put it over there." She pointed, then watched him from the corner of her eye.

He did as he told and came back to his chair.

"Open your shirt."

"What?!"

She was silent, waiting.

"Yeah, okay." He opened his shirt, looked around the empty space, spun once slowly as she watched, then re-mounted his chair and buttoned his shirt.

"Show me your ID."

"Shit."

"Just do it."

Without further protest, Grayson pulled out his ID folder and laid it on the small shelf in front of her slot machine.

She looked at it without picking it up. "Put it away."

"What do you go by? At least give me that." He spoke as he folded his ID and returned it to his jacket pocket.

"I just told you. Dancer."

"This is getting old," he said.

"You want help, or not?"

Neither of them had looked at the other directly.

Grayson almost choked on his words. "Yes. Yes, damn it! What do you have?"

"Calm down, agent Grayson. Listen carefully. You will get word of a meeting. There will be instructions. Follow them precisely. You will get your help and your answers. Stay here ten more minutes before you walk out; same cover drill. I'm gone." She started to leave.

"Wait!" He growled.

She had left her chair and stood a foot away from him, turned away. "What?!"

"Why all this? Here. The mystery. It's bullshit!" He glared at the slot screen.

"You know why. I had to see you. ID you. This is dangerous. I'm vulnerable. I have to stay deep. Now, do as I say!"

With that, she was gone.

Grayson waited the required ten minutes, then re-traced his steps, faithful to Dancer's instructions. He did not see her on his return to Albuquerque.

# *31*

*J*ason sat at a table in a far corner of the Santa Fé Baking Company, faced toward the door, his laptop open in front of him. At his side was a half cup of cold coffee and a drying sandwich.

In another part of the eatery Vera sat, facing him but not looking at him. She wore her bandanna over her head and sunglasses over her eyes. She tried to remain composed as she pecked at a cubed chicken and crumbled bleu cheese salad with a fork.

Finished with his task, Jason took two bites of his lunch fare, set it aside, looked in Vera's direction and tilted his head. She wiped her mouth with her napkin, stood up, picked up her handbag and left the building.

Jason returned to his truck parked in the lot, and drove out onto southbound Luisa Street. He moved along slowly until he spotted Vera walking at the same rate along the sidewalk in his direction. As he came alongside, he slowed further, then to a stop, reached across the passenger seat and opened the door. Vera stepped off the curb, climbed in and shut her door as Jason accelerated away.

She looked at him. "Get it done?"

"I think so."

"How soon will you know?"

"Within twenty-four hours." He negotiated a right turn onto Alta Vista, sped up and checked his mirrors.

That night, as he and Vera retired, Jason changed the power switch on his cell phone to the "on" position, and set it close to the edge of his side of the bed on the small night table. It awakened him from a shallow sleep at 3:34 the following morning. He picked it up and answered with a "Yes." He listened for five seconds, shut it off and tried to go back to sleep.

Vera murmured something in her slumber, but did not awaken.

A courier, dressed in racing leathers and a blacked-out visor helmet, who arrived at FBI headquarters in Albuquerque on a dirt bike at 9 o'clock that morning, handed a sealed envelope to one of the security guards, then sped away. That, in turn, was placed in Jan's hands ten minutes later, who then took it immediately to the addressee, Special Agent Peter Grayson.

Grayson went to Lucero's cubicle. He held the paper out to him and tapped it with a finger. Lucero took it, still seated, and read it. He handed the document back to Grayson without a word.

"I'll have Jan do a shred and burn," Grayson said.

Lucero looked up at Grayson. "Planning room?"

"Let's assemble the troops."

Half an hour later, the Strike Force Team, five men and three women, plus Grayson and Lucero, were assembled in the Planning Room. All were seated scatter-shot about the cramped room, save Grayson, whom they faced, and who stood at the front of the assemblage. He spent fifteen minutes briefing them on the background of the case, what they could expect, and what the hoped-for outcome might be. He also advised them that he had arranged a meeting for later that day with the Santa Fé Police Department, and that he and Lucero would work out the details of their part.

He then focused a slide of the venue, described the area and used a laser pointer to isolate the salient features.

Melanie Velasquez, a team member, raised her hand and spoke without waiting for an acknowledgment. "Why Santa Fé and why there? I know the place. We got civilians there. How we gonna' take care of that? I mean, if lead starts to fly—?"

Grayson nodded. "Good question, and you have a valid point. First, it's the agreement we've made with our contact. Second, we've had a cursory look and feel it works for our purposes, and we've checked with SFPD. They've used that venue before for take-downs." He paused and studied the room. "It's defensible based on agency rules. Santa Fé's good because it's more confined. After we get the skinny from SFPD, we'll rendezvous up north." He paused. "Any more questions?" He looked around. "Okay, let's assemble the gear. We got two days."

Grayson and Lucero traveled to the Cerrillos Road post of the Santa Fé Police Department. There, they met with a half-dozen officers chosen to work with the FBI under special tactical joint-force assignment to plan the up-coming federal-city collaborative operation to take place in less than 24 hours. Tactics, policies, jurisdictional questions, equipment, notification to other city departments, were all laid out and documented within the confines of a need-to-know basis.

Both agencies worked around the clock, given the urgency presented them by the situation at hand.

The following day, at 1133, a candy-apple red Ford SUV was stopped alongside the curb on Alto street, close to the Senior Citizen's Center at the Centennial Park grounds in Santa Fé. Behind it, at a crazy angle, its red and blue lights flashing, was an SFPD patrol car. Two uniformed officers, a man and a woman, were in the process of detaining a man in his early thirties and his female companion, she in her late twenties. They, in turn, were seated on the curb, their legs crossed under orders, while the officers used their radios and wrote a report.

On West Alameda, which ran parallel to Alto, the City of Santa Fé Water Department had the street blocked off from Solana to Camino Alire to investigate an alleged water main problem. Four men, all with safety helmets on and wearing special reflective yellow jackets, prepared their tools from a truck with flashing orange lights aglow.

At three minutes past noon, a large, black van moved slowly into the Centennial parking lot and into a slot marked, "No Parking Special Event." The vehicle featured big, blacked-out sliding glass windows. No one exited the vehicle.

Two more cars arrived with couples dressed and equipped for tennis. They left their vehicles and moved slowly for the courts, some two hundred feet distant from the tarmac lot.

Seated at one of the rounded concrete picnic tables, were two more people, a man and a woman. They were accompanied by large sports bags from which expensive tennis rackets protruded. In each bag was a police-band radio, cell phone, a 9 mm Glock pistol, a badge and handcuffs. They were members of the Santa Fé Police Department.

Dancer stood near the entrance to the Senior Citizen's Center, watching. She wore the same baseball cap and dark glasses worn on her rendezvous with Grayson in Española. After standing for three minutes, she crossed the parking lot for the sport pavilion, entered, and used the women's restroom. She waited five minutes, then walked out slowly to resume her vantage across the lot. No one paid any attention to her.

Stanley Webber, alias Tanner, walked at a normal pace along West Alameda, on the north side sidewalk, in a westerly direction, having been delivered by taxi to the Gonzales Elementary School parking lot after disembarking from the Rail Runner. Although he maintained a forward-facing gaze, he was alert to anything and anybody who might present a threat. Normally not a nervous person in confrontational situations, he was this day, although not abnormally so, but his basic reasoning led him to be more incautious because of the fruit he was certain this meeting would bear. He spotted the city emergency crew from the city a block ahead, preparing a jack-hammer to cut through the pavement. What he did not know, and did not sense, was that these men were, in reality, members of the SFPD and the Albuquerque-based FBI Strike Force.

He crossed the street, and headed for the pedestrian bridge that spanned the trickle-adorned Santa Fé River, then joined the paved path on the south side. He carried a large DeLorme map of the state of New Mexico, and wore a fedora and dark glasses.

At the same time, Ruth, wearing a white baseball cap with the red New Mexico "zia" flag symbol emblazoned over the rim, dark glasses, and carrying a tote with her bathing suit, towel, and pistol, walked along the Western terminus of Alto Street, then across the lot to the sports facility. Inside, she went to the women's dressing room, changed into her bathing suit, put the tote into a locker sans the pistol, which she wrapped in a towel, and made for the swimming pool. The cap and dark glasses remained in place.

Jason had changed his mind regarding Vera's role in what he was about to do, primarily at her insistence. That, together with his realization that she would be far less anxiety-ridden by going with him rather than remaining behind in East Pecos. With her babushka in place over her head and her unfamiliar sun glasses in place, she took the wheel of the Texas-registered Toyota pickup and parked it on Don Juan Street, a short block away from Alto.

Jason looked at his watch, sighed, then leaned over to kiss her tear-wet face before getting out of the passenger side without a word.

She whispered, "I love you" as she watched him open his door and exit the truck. He acknowledged her sentiment with a simple nod, shut the door and walked away without looking back. In the driver's seat, she dropped her head to the steering wheel and began to cry in earnest.

When Dancer saw the man with the big map cross the grassy area between the tennis courts and the swimming pool, she stepped away from her station at the Senior Citizen's Center and sauntered over to the circular picnic table and bench set nearest the parking lot.

It was then that the female uniformed officer at the Alto curb went to the Center and placed it in lock-down, while the male officer did likewise with the sports center. The two detainees, in reality undercover police, uncrossed their legs, stood, and turned their attention to the activity on the greensward, then took up pre-assigned positions at different points in the lot. They both produced hand weapons but kept them low and close. The four tennis players on the courts nearest the lawn area, although continuing to play, kept an eye on the man with the map and the woman who were closing on each other. Their FBI-equipped tennis totes rested on the court floors next to the open entrance gates.

As instructed, Webber sat on one of the concrete benches, laid the map on the table, and turned to watch the tennis matches a hundred feet distant.

Dancer strolled up to the picnic arrangement and sat, her legs out, her back to Webber, elbows on the table for support. She faced the black van. "Like tennis?" she asked.

He dipped his head . "Yes. I'm not good at it."

"Where do you play?"

"When and where I can."

"Gonna' play here?"

"Too high and dry."

"Did you follow my instructions?"

"I'm unarmed."

"Good."

"What do you have?" He asked.

"This is a bad place," she said. "But I want to introduce you to someone."

Webber hesitated, while his body language betrayed minor shock. "Who? When?"

"Right now, actually."

Jason was ten feet away and closing when she said, "He's here."

Webber turned toward her, then looked up at Jason as he stopped within a few feet of the seated pair. Webber started to rise as Dancer turned.

"I wouldn't do that," she said. "Keep your seat."

Webber was half-way up when he froze and sat down on the edge of the bench. "What?! What do you mean?! What is this, goddamn it?! You didn't say anything about anyone else! What the hell—?!"

Dancer raised her hand, the doors of the nearby van opened, and three men and a woman stepped out. Each wore a dark blue windbreaker emblazoned with "FBI" in large, yellow letters on the backside. They all held semi-automatic weapons at the ready. Grayson and Lucero were in the lead as the team surrounded the three people at the table. Almost in unison, they shouted "On your knees! On your knees!"

Behind them, a shot rang out in the swimming pool area which had been cleared of bathers due to the lock-down. Ruth had escaped and had run back to the pool brandishing her weapon. Her plan had been to cover Webber from that vantage point through the chain link fence that surrounded the pool area. Ordered to drop her pistol, and partly in a state of shock and confusion, she had swung around and pointed it at an officer who fired at her in response.

The four FBI tennis-players dropped their rackets, retrieved their weapons from their totes, raced from the courts, and assumed a peripheral defense stance. The two police officers who had sat with their tennis totes did the same after draping their badges around their necks and signaling to their fellow officers to do the same. The "city workers" on West Alameda also abandoned their unneeded tools and took up defensive positions.

The female FBI Agent and the other male agent from the van frisked Jason, Dancer and Webber, then cuffed the men as they kneeled on the grass-covered ground.

Grayson stood two feet from Dancer. "Stand up. What's the drill?"

Dancer struggled up and brushed her pants. "Know the number for CIA Reston?"

Grayson hesitated, then turned to Lucero. "Marc?"

Marcus Lucero put his cell phone to his ear after hitting a key. "Jan? Yeah. Good. It's over. Clean op. Hey, get me the number for CIA. Yeah, right. Reston. I'll hold." He looked at Grayson and the others in the awkward circle, then at the ground as he waited.

After Jason and Webber were cuffed, they were allowed to stand and were helped up, then told to sit on the picnic benches.

Grayson stood in front of Jason and looked hard at him. "You're Thompson, right?"

Dancer cut in. "Just wait, Grayson. Stay cool." She eyed him with a glare.

Grayson looked at her in silence, then allowed his eyes to move between her and Jason.

Lucero spoke. "Got the number." He closed his cell phone, wrote it on his hand, then held it up.

"I want to say something to you, Grayson," Dancer said. "Get the number from him." She pointed to Lucero.

Grayson, curious at her request, looked from Lucero to her and back, then did as she bid. She then beckoned him to follow her ten feet away and isolated from the others. He frowned and made a face as he stood close to her.

She leaned in close. "I want you to call the CIA. Don't ask why. Do it out of earshot. When they answer, ask for this extension. When you get an answer, read this." She reached into her blouse pocket for a piece of paper and handed it to him. "Keep your voice low. Read that to them."

Grayson read the markings, then looked at her.

"Stay here and I'll go back to the group." She turned and walked away.

When she returned, Webber snarled, "I don't know what's going on here—"

Dancer turned to him. "Shut up, asshole! You're dead meat."

Jason said, "In my shirt pocket. Pill." He leaned to one side.

Dancer said, "Get his pill damn it! He's got a heart problem!"

The female FBI agent reached into the pocket Jason indicated with his chin and put it on his tongue.

He swallowed. "Thank you," he said. He looked at Dancer, took a moment to reflect, then, in a loud whisper, he declared, "Jesus! You're Ang—!"

Dancer shook her head in rapid, short movements, and he stopped, his mouth open in stark surprise.

Grayson came back to the group. "She's legit."

Dancer looked at Webber, then Jason. "This is Jason Thompson. He has come in from the cold. As you can see, he's not dead, and he's one of us. This I can prove, but not here and now. This man, whose real name I don't know, is rogue company. This I can also prove. I suggest you free Mr. Thompson, but keep our new friend here restrained." She held out her hand to Grayson for the paper she had given him.

"Shit," Webber said under his breath. He dropped his head to his chest in anguish.

As Jason trudged back to the Tacoma pickup, Vera watched, unbelieving, from her driver's side seat. She opened her door, jumped out, and left it wide open to rush to him.

"Jason! Oh, my God! What happened?! You're okay! You're back!"

He took her in his arms in the middle of the street. They hugged and kissed as a teen-age boy arrived in a souped-up low rider, his audio system blaring "rap." He leaned on the horn in anger as they blocked his path. The two older people, too happy to care, moved aside and let him through. In the car, the kid shouted "*Pendejos!*" and awarded them the international one-finger salute as he sped away.

As they sat in the idling truck, Jason at the wheel, he explained that he would have to meet with the FBI soon, but that they were free to move about and he could re-join his children openly. They then agreed it would be appropriate to have some food at Horseman's Haven, since he yearned for *carne adovada*.

The female Public Relations officer of the Santa Fe Police Department, at a hastily-assembled news conference, explained to the *Santa Fé New Mexican* reporter and representatives of local television stations, that a joint federal-state-city task force had taken down elements of a Mexican drug cartel. She said, further, that a large haul of cocaine was seized as a result.

Webber was taken to Albuquerque and placed in incognito solitary confinement.

Ruth Verdugo died of a single gunshot wound at Christus St. Vincent hospital.

# 32

*W*hen FBI Special Agent Peter Grayson arrived at Dulles International, he went to the taxi rank and hired a cab. He instructed the driver to deliver him to the Potomac Mills mall. There, he headed for the hardware department of the Costco store, specifically the area featuring lawn mowers. He had been there for three minutes when a slender black man he reckoned to be in his mid-thirties entered the area and began to look at mowers. The man was dressed in blue jeans and a plaid shirt. His footwear were worn work boots. His eyes were covered with inexpensive dark glasses. His head supported a generic baseball cap.

He moved close to Grayson. "Gonna' buy one?" He asked.

Grayson glanced at him, then continued to focus on one of the machines. "Not sure. Mine has about had it."

"Yeah? What brand?"

"Sears."

"How long you had it?"

"Three years."

"Know what's wrong with it?"

"I think it may be the choke."

"What's your name?"

"Grayson. Yours?"

"Follow. Keep me in sight."

Grayson did as he was instructed. In the crowded parking lot, the man entered the back seat of a ten-year-old Chevrolet sedan whose body paint had long ago begun to fade in places. He followed him in, sat, and pulled the door closed. He saw a white man in the front seat at the wheel. The man made no reaction, and didn't turn to look.

"Your cell phone." The black man next to him held out his hand.

The man took the phone from Grayson, powered it off, opened it, removed the battery, and placed the separate pieces in a cloth pouch, which he then zipped closed. "Open your jacket and your shirt."

Grayson opened his jacket and the man frisked him, he then looked his chest over and felt his back through his undershirt.

"Button up. You'll get the phone back."

With a wry smile, Grayson said, "I trust."

The Special Agent was given a black elastic blindfold and told to put it over his eyes. The man beside him then placed a pair of ear muffs over his head and told Grayson to adjust them to cover his ears. He was then told to lean over onto the seat, pull his legs up into the fetal position and fold his arms over his chest. His captor placed a small pillow under his head. The driver started the engine and pulled out of the parking lot onto the main thoroughfare.

The old farmhouse sat on a rise, one hundred feet above the valley floor, where a tributary of the Potomac ran alongside a secondary highway. It was a well-kept, two-story shiplap, with a full basement. A pasture swept down in front of the house. The fields on both sides featured principally corn, but shared the soil with other seasonal crops. Behind the house was a barn in the typical colors of the region, dark red with white trim. A two-car garage blistered out from one side of the house. It was into this structure that the car pulled in. The car was brought to a halt and the remotely-controlled door closed behind it.

Grayson was led into the house, the blindfold in place; the ear muffs absent. He was led through two rooms to a door which opened to a stair which led to the basement. At the bottom of the stair, his eye cover was removed. He blinked, looked around, and found himself in a narrow hallway with bare concrete walls and ceiling. It was somber with low lighting.

"There're some eye drops if you need 'em," his guide said.

Grayson shook his head and smiled weakly. "Thanks. I'm okay. Need a minute to get used to the light."

"Sure. Over here." The man moved off and beckoned.

The black man handed Grayson a clipboard. Fastened to it was a fine print document, the bottom of which had a line for his signature.

Grayson looked at the man.

"Title Eighteen. I know, you're vetted, FBI and all that, but this is different. You could end up dead or rendered if anything you see or hear here ever leaves your head for someone else's. I trust you understand clearly and in no uncertain terms." He raised his eyebrows and awarded his guest a severe look.

Grayson nodded. "I do." He took the proffered pen and signed.

He was asked to stand against a portion of the wall with a blue background, a camera appeared, and his photograph was taken.

From there, they moved to a blank, steel door, where another man took Grayson's jacket and patted him down. The guard then turned to a keypad and entered a code, which resulted in a loud click from the door frame. He pushed it open.

Grayson was led into a windowless room, which he judged to be about twenty by thirty feet, smaller, he imagined, than the footprint of the structure above it. The room was dark, due to the lack of light from the few fixtures which adorned the raw concrete ceiling. Spots of light illuminated two large desks and a series of six consoles along the far concrete wall. These were equipped with computer screens, keyboards, and manned by four women and two men all of whom wore pencil mike headsets. In the center of the room was a large table with a map of the globe over which a special lamp glowed. Tiny, various colored lights, blinked at various spots on its surface.

A woman in her early fifties approached, stopped, looked at Grayson directly, then at the black attendant. "Thank you, staff. Standby."

The man merely nodded and left the room.

She turned her attention to Grayson. "You will not know my name, or the names of anyone here." She paused and surveyed the room briefly, then looked at the FBI agent. "You are in the Third Directorate, or Directorate Three. No matter. What we do here is beyond confidential. Beyond secret. We are few, but we are effective. You are here, agent Grayson, because you need to understand something very important." She stopped, turned her head to peer into a dark corner, then said, "I think you know this gentleman." She nodded her head in that direction.

Grayson watched as a figure rose from a chair in the dark and came toward him into the cone of light where he and the woman stood. Grayson was startled as he recognized Jason Thompson.

The woman looked from man to man. "I believe you know each other, and that no introduction is required."

Jason held out his hand. "Grayson. Good to see you."

Grayson nodded with a smile. "Mr. Thompson. It's been awhile. We thought we lost track of you."

They shook hands.

"Gentlemen, let us sit," the woman said. She held out her hand to indicate a small conference table at one end of the map table.

It was then that a low-hanging lamp over the table came on to reveal a man already seated there. He was well into his seventh decade, with flowing white hair over a narrow, relatively unlined face. He wore a white dress shirt, open at the neck, no tie, and pair of metal-frame glasses. He sat quietly with his hands folded on the table, and looked up without expression at both visitors as they approached.

The woman took her place next to the older man, while Jason and Grayson sat across the table facing them. For nearly a minute, the man next to the woman scoured the faces of Jason and the FBI agent with a sober, penetrating gaze.

The woman said, "I assume you explained to Buckley that you're here to speak with CIA."

Grayson and Jason answered simultaneously, "Yes."

The man began, "You two are here to learn something. I hope you're both wise enough to understand it. Understand it and realize what it means. The document you both signed is serious. Very serious. The Sword of Damocles hangs over your heads. We hold that sword. If either of you should ever reveal anything of what you see or hear here in any way, shape or form, and we learn of it, you will simply disappear off the face of the earth. Rest assured. Period." He lifted a glass of water slowly to his lips and sipped, then set it down as though it were expensive crystal containing a rare vintage wine. "From this day forward, however, you will be members of this elite troop. You may, each of you, from time to time, be asked to perform some duty on our behalf." He tilted his head and looked at both men to gauge their reaction. "You may refuse, of course, and of course, that day may never come."

Jason and Grayson paid each other short, corner of the eye side-glances. Both nodded.

The man went on to explain the reason for the existence of the Third Directorate; that although the Central Intelligence Agency was formed to handle external, extra-national espionage and counter-intelligence, over time, frustrations had built up in the minds of many within the bureau that perceived performance on the part of the FBI and other internal counter-intelligence agencies was severely lacking, especially under the leadership of J. Edgar Hoover and subsequent leaders who had become politicized. That, in turn, had lead to the formation of a purely internal counter-intelligence organization within the CIA to bolster, and at times, even supplant other, weaker efforts. That was justified as well, due to the fact that the CIA possessed data and information derived from their foreign networks which led them to believe, and to prove in some cases, that the connections were either being ignored, compromised, or severed completely, leading to what they perceived as affecting national security negatively.

The woman cut in. "We're not strictly legal."

The man looked down at his hands. "True in a sense, yes, in that we exist outside the framework of the CIA charter as set out by Congress. We are, one might say, 'black ops' within our borders. But we are principally watchers. We pass information upstairs and keep watch over our national interests. We leak as much of what we learn to other agencies, especially the FBI. It is true that on occasion, we need to—and do—perform 'wet ops.' Regrettable, but true. Are we perfect? If we were, much of what happened to our friend, Mr. Jason Thompson, here, might not have happened."

"May I ask a question?" Jason asked.

The man and woman across the table looked at him and waited.

"My secretary at the Labs. Angie."

"Yes?" the woman said.

Grayson looked at Jason beside him. "She's Dancer?"

Jason nodded in affirmation. "Yes. I didn't know." He looked up at the two across the table. He said nothing but held his palms out and open on the table in a question.

The woman spoke. "We knew of the set-up between you, Nantes and Melvin Vaslovic. How you were controlling him and feeding him altered data to pass to foreign interests. At some point we discovered Nantes, who was your control and became Mel's conduit, had gone rogue and formed his own network. We estimate he was corrupted by his clientele. Money, of course. We were able to insert Angie into the mix by placing her close to you."

"You doubted me?"

"We didn't know," the man said.

"We do now," the woman remarked.

"How was Dancer able to find Webber?" Grayson asked.

"Nantes was D3. Third Directorate," the man said. "He was given Mr. Thompson here—Jason—to run, then went into business for himself. He used D3 trade craft to hide trails and build false ones. We had NSA watch his financial traffic and it became clear he'd gone rogue. Dancer—Angie—Jason's secretary— was inserted to watch from the source end." The woman studied Jason's face, glanced at Grayson, then her partner. "We discovered the connection from Nantes to Webber with NSA assistance. Mind you, they did not know who or why. Only we did." He nodded somberly.

"How—how was Angie able to watch me? I never—"

"That will remain with us," the man said quietly. "Suffice it to say that we knew then, and we know now." He looked at Grayson.

Grayson lowered his head and nodded with emphasis. He looked up and asked, "How did Angie get the name 'Dancer'?"

Jason said, "Probably because she was a member of a square dance group."

The others exhibited muted smiles.

"Did you know Nantes had faked my death?" Jason asked.

Both the man and the woman shook their heads.

She answered, "No. We learned later that Nantes had lost control. He lost you. Until you made that call to him. We still didn't know what happened to you, and at the time, we came to the conclusion that Dancer was wrong, and that you had escaped because you feared prosecution. What did happen?" She cocked her head at him.

Jason told them about Cuzco and the woman, his trip to the east coast and Canada, his meeting with Andrei, the revelations about his late wife, Sarah, her involvement, and their help in sneaking him back into the United States.

Grayson mumbled, "Incredible."

Jason looked at him. "But true."

The woman continued. "Answers many questions." She paused, then, "We sent Dancer assets. They watched and analyzed everyone's movements. FBI, state police, BOLO calls, and figured—correctly—that you were not dead. You were good at staying gone, but they were able to find you. When we saw the traffic had dried up and that you had not reached out to Nantes' crew, we felt the odds were great that Dancer was correct about you and we had to find you, bring you in and close down Nantes' crew. We can only assume Webber wanted you gone as well. He thought Dancer was your replacement." She paused and sipped her water. "We decided the best way was to have Dancer dupe Webber—who we then knew as Tanner—to contact you without letting him know who you were. He was planning to revive the network with what he thought were assets within the labs."

Jason ruminated for several seconds while he absorbed her information, then he asked, "How did you track me down? When?"

The woman smiled. "Again, that remains with us."

Jason pursed his lips. He and Grayson glanced at each other.

"Now," the man said, "as to Tanner—Webber. We want him."

Grayson leaned forward. "You—you 'want him'?! He's in FBI custody." He frowned.

The man said, "We want to remove him. Disappear him. After we've squeezed him dry. This is critical. He will be outside the United States, and never return." She paused. "He'd be a loose cannon. His appearance in court would ripple up the chain in a very destructive way. He'd lawyer up and have deals up his sleeve, and the courts would listen. We can't leave him to the justice system. Do you understand?" She bored in on Grayson's eyes.

Grayson looked up at the bare, dark ceiling of concrete, then down as he shook his head, then nodded. He looked at her. "And Mr. Thompson here. What do we do with him? Officially, publicly, he's deceased. How does he re-appear? Do you have an answer for that?"

The woman looked at the man beside her, who lowered his head in reflection.

The man looked at Jason and spoke slowly and deliberately. "You stay dead. You assume a new name. You'll have to stay away from your old neighborhood. You will be off the grid, so to speak. No Social Security card. You have funds now, and you will be well-compensated. As to your family, you will re-join them, but they must be part of the secret. We'd like to send you out of the country to have your appearance altered. Not in a major way, mind you, but enough so that you will no longer be recognizable as Jason Thompson."

Jason bit his lip, but remained silent. He sighed.

"What do I say to Buckley and my people in Albuquerque," Grayson asked. "Washington?"

"You tell them the CIA is taking responsibility. Tell Buckley, given what happened to Madsen and the problems that would be created by any further digging, all concerned have to bury this." She paused. "We will send a rendering team to get Webber, and you close your files. If Buckley gives you a bad time, you let us know." This from the woman. "You will receive instructions."

The man said, "He won't. If he does, we will make his life, and life within the FBI, hell. We'll drop stories to the press that will make you guys look like the Keystone cops." He hesitated. "Has to be buried. *Will* be buried."

"One more question," Jason said.

Both the man and the woman chimed in at the same time. "Yes?"

"About Vera Tyler."

Both hosts smiled, and the woman spoke. "She may be brought into the deception with the same provisos. In fact, we believe her place is the best place for you. You will have enough where-with-all to compensate for any monetary offset. Including over time. This is a national security issue." She nodded and glanced at the man. "In this case, money is the least of our worries."

The man gestured in the affirmative.

Jason and Grayson returned to New Mexico by different routes at different times. Jason was provided with enough temporary appearance-altering aids that not even his closest allies, save his children or Vera, would recognize him in passing.

Grayson met with Buckley and Lucero at an off-site venue, where Grayson, without revealing where he had actually been or with whom he had actually met, informed Buckley of the tactics and machinations they would be required to adopt. Lucero and Buckley both listened quietly. Buckley and Lucero, both with knowing eyes, raised their beer glasses in salute. The three drank, and the meeting agenda shifted to the subjects of family, fishing and hunting.

# 33

*T*he FBI invited the three Thompson children and their offspring to take a ride in an agency jet. They were not told where they were going, even when they landed in El Paso, Texas. From there, their two agency escorts, male and female special agents, who accompanied them in a huge, black SUV, were followed by two more agents in a second vehicle, and they convoyed to the Tyler ranch.

The blood trace left by Jack had been totally obliterated, and the interior of the house made neat and tidy by a local crew recommended by Sheriff Tenorio.

The family arrived around midday, and were seated in the living room, where extra chairs had been placed. Two of the agents stood outside, while two more, the man and the woman who had come in the SUV, stood quietly aside in the living area, their hands across their midriffs, with the seated and curious family. Shortly after everyone was settled, Grayson and Lucero entered from the porch. Both men went around the room and shook the hands and exchanged pleasantries with all present, including the grandchildren.

With tensions rising, and questions asked, such as "Why bring us to the place where our father and grandfather died?", Lucero went to a door that lead to the main bedroom, opened it, and nodded his head.

Vera entered. She found it difficult to hide her emotions as she attempted to block an ear-to-ear grin. She stood while Grayson introduced her as the woman who took Jason in on the night he crashed on the mesa to the west. Soft, even murmured conversation undulated about the room, the gist of which was congratulatory remarks, appreciative nods and 'thank yous.'

Silence ensued until Lucero again nodded through the open door. Five seconds passed with the family circle in baffled silence until Jason walked into the room. Shock and pandemonium broke out, and Vera wept openly as Jason was surrounded and nearly knocked off his feet by his happy and loving family.

When the joy calmed and refreshments appeared, Grayson held a meeting with everyone, while outside, the other agents stood guard against any possible intrusion, which included agents on horseback along the periphery of the ranch. He explained as much as he could, and swore the family to secrecy, against which failure to comply might jeopardize Jason's very existence and their family's cohesiveness and safety. He also told them how they would be able to see their family patriarch in future, and the ways in which their assets and finances could be managed given Jason's official demise.

Vera was welcomed into the family, and plans, short- and long range, were discussed into the night and subsequent days and weeks.

The long-time Thompson residence in Albuquerque was put up for sale.


Stanley Webber, alias Tanner, somehow escaped FBI custody while being transported, but was re-captured immediately by a team of unidentified armed men, and spirited out of the country to parts unknown. He never set foot on U.S. soil the remainder of his life, whose longevity, as speculated in some quarters, was in doubt. A story concocted by D3 and fed via the FBI to explain his disappearance was accepted, under quiet duress, by his wife, family and associates. It is not known whether the authorities were ever able to trace the murders he committed back to him or not. This was, in part, because of a universal cavalier attitude toward those who lost their lives in the relevant cases.


Jack's and Ruth's identities, along with parts of their back stories, were eventually uncovered through an extensive DNA, fingerprint and personal history search. This information was, in turn, although of minimal general concern, nonetheless stanched and sanitized for public consumption by extant authorities.


Angie, known only to a few as Dancer, accepted a new position within the Rio Grande Laboratories organization. She remained an active deep cover agent of the Third Directorate until her retirement.

The dark blue overnight bag that belonged to Tao Wang and forgotten by Webber in a Kansas City rental car, languished on the rental agency Lost and Found shelf, where it gathered dust and was ignored by all amidst many lost items. Wang's suspicious and untimely demise, as with the others, became a "cold case" and remains unsolved.

www.ingramcontent.com/pod-product-compliance
Lightning Source LLC
Chambersburg PA
CBHW020433030726
47495CB00006B/1785